HOLLOW SPACES

HOLLOW SPACES

A NOVEL

VICTOR SUTHAMMANONT

COUNTERPOINT

CALIFORNIA

HOLLOW SPACES

This is a work of fiction. All of the characters, organizations, and events portrayed in this novel are either products of the author's imagination or are used fictitiously.

Copyright © 2025 by Victor Suthammanont

All rights reserved under domestic and international copyright. Outside of fair use (such as quoting within a book review), no part of this publication may be reproduced, stored in a retrieval system, or transmitted in any form or by any means, electronic, mechanical, photocopying, recording, or otherwise, without the written permission of the publisher. For permissions, please contact the publisher.

First Counterpoint edition: 2025

Library of Congress Cataloging-in-Publication Data
Names: Suthammanont, Victor, author.
Title: Hollow spaces : a novel / Victor Suthammanont.
Description: First Counterpoint edition. | California : Counterpoint, 2025.
Identifiers: LCCN 2025005733 | ISBN 9781640097117 (hardcover) | ISBN 9781640097124 (ebook)
Subjects: LCGFT: Thrillers (Fiction) | Legal fiction (Literature) | Novels.
Classification: LCC PS3619.U877 H65 2025 | DDC 813/.6—dc23/eng/20250210
LC record available at https://lccn.loc.gov/2025005733

Jacket design by Robin Bilardello
Jacket images of match © Wendy Stevenson / Arcangel Images,
New York City skyline © aimintang / iStock
Book design by Laura Berry

COUNTERPOINT
Los Angeles and San Francisco, CA
www.counterpointpress.com

Printed in the United States of America

1 3 5 7 9 10 8 6 4 2

To my parents, Chai and Rose, for all they gave me

HOLLOW SPACES

ONE

Then

FOR THE FIRST TIME SINCE HIS TRIAL STARTED, JOHN STUDIED the forewoman of the jury. She wore a floral-patterned blouse and glasses that framed half her face. Her permed brown hair was teased up in the front, her lipstick fresh and glossy. John suspected she had reapplied before the jury entered the courtroom. This was the jury's moment—hers by proxy. Maybe nobody had looked at her this closely in years. She clenched the verdict form—thirty minutes prior, an incomplete form on a plain sheet of paper—like a talisman.

Given the past year, John thought that he would be used to waiting, being a spectator floating in his own shoes, watching a doppelgänger walk through his life. But he still reached out to touch the table in front of him to confirm that he was in fact inside of his body. As a child, he once lay in a drift in a park after a winter storm, hood up over his head, and the weightlessness, the whisper of his breath, the icy tickle of snow landing on his face, and the echo of his thudding heart pressed him so deep inside of his body that his mind stilled, and he looked at the bare branches of the trees above him with the knowledge that this was what dying was like—not an abandonment of his body, but a retreat into the hollows within it. He wanted to return to that moment, to stop staring at the forewoman, waiting for her to answer the judge's question: "Does the jury have a verdict?"

The ritual required the question. Nobody would be in the courtroom at that moment unless the jury had reached a verdict in *The People of the State of New York v. Chong Lo*, but it had to be asked and answered. The forewoman was taking entirely too long to answer it. Although John understood that only a second or two passed, his mind accelerated to a near-incomprehensible speed. John worried again that he was no longer tethered to his body and instead, some pilot occupied it, leading it down tightening corridors until he was here, wedged into a chasm waiting for the final slip.

The forewoman finally spoke. "Yes, Your Honor." Her voice was slightly raspy, but the words were clear.

The jury had deliberated for two days. John's lawyer, Harris Isaacs, thought that the long deliberation was a good sign. The verdict had to be unanimous. Maybe a holdout or two for acquittal was delaying a guilty verdict. A hung jury was essentially a win for the defense; it wasn't a conviction. But Harris also allowed himself to dream that the holdout was on the other side—a lone juror who wanted to convict—and that the others were arguing for reasonable doubt. He didn't mention that dream to John, but John saw Harris's hope in the way he paced the conference room where they waited for word from the jury, the way he spoke to the paralegal, even in the way he doodled on his legal pad. It was Harris's first murder trial.

John heard his wife take a breath behind him, anticipating the next words in the colloquy. Jane had sat through the entire trial, every day, behind him in the gallery, even though he had been sleeping on the couch for months. John wondered if she'd be there but for the kids. Her mind was closed to him; he couldn't tell what she was thinking. He could smell her perfume, faintly, lingering around his clothes or in his hair or maybe his memory. She hugged him before he went in for the verdict—their first physical contact since the day the cops came to take him in for questioning.

#

John thought it would be a day or two before the cops came for him, but as it turned out, the detectives knocked on his apartment door right after he got home from work. Jane chased the children around while still wearing her stockings and work clothes, high heels lying in the middle of the living room floor. As John slid out into the hall to speak to the detectives, Jane looked up from tickling Hunter—no concern, merely curiosity. Brennan was trying to push her mom over to save her little brother, to no avail.

The jowly detective, Bauman, said, "You left some things out when you spoke to us at your office this afternoon."

John said nothing. He knew that most white people had trouble discerning what he was thinking. But the younger detective, McCann, wasn't even looking at him. He stared over John's head at the apartment door. "You want to come down to the station and answer our questions there? Or here with your wife and kids?"

"Let me get my jacket."

John left the cops in the hall. Jane still wrestled with the kids on the floor. She regarded him with a glance, then turned back to her children.

"The police have some questions about Jessica. They think I can help."

Jane had a giggling Brennan pinned with one hand. "I thought they spoke to everyone at the office."

"Yeah, but you know how they are. They want to go back over some things. Less disruptive now than earlier at the office."

"Okay. But why don't you just talk to them here? I can make coffee."

"No. We'll have to get the kids to bed soon."

She let Brennan up and absently held a hand up to stop Hunter from diving on top of her.

"Everything okay?"

"Yeah." John walked over and kissed the kids. "It should take an hour or two."

"Okay."

"Can you call Harris, though? Ask him to meet me at the Twenty-Fourth Precinct."

"Why do you need Harris?"

"Jane, you know that the main things we learned in law school were not to represent ourselves and not to talk to the cops without a lawyer. Can you please just call him?"

She nodded, but her eyes fixed on his. She held herself still—like a doe in the woods.

When John returned from the precinct four hours later, the children were asleep. Jane sat at the kitchen table, still in her work clothes, smoking a pack of cigarettes with a scotch in hand. She jumped up and hugged him, nearly burning him with her cigarette, then hit him with two palms to the chest, heedless of the flakes of ash drifting to the floor.

"What the fuck, John?"

"Sit down," he said as he walked to the cabinet to get a glass. He hoped he wouldn't drop it as he poured the scotch to the brim.

"What did they want? Why did they need to take you to the precinct?"

He sat down across the table from her. He usually didn't smoke, but he took a cigarette from the pack. His hand shook as he lit it. He focused on the matches so he wouldn't have to meet her eyes.

"Are the kids asleep?"

"You know they're asleep. John," she said. Then, a command: "Tell me."

Despite the imperative, there was vulnerability in her eyes again, something he hadn't seen in years. He knew it was the last time he would see it.

"I had an affair," he said.

She stood up and strode out of the room, leaving him at the table, wreathed in smoke.

#

In the courtroom, Jane sat behind John as he stood, and the judge said, "On the sole charge of the indictment, murder in the second degree, how does the jury find?"

John questioned whether it even mattered. The cops believed that he was guilty. So did Jessica's family. They said so, as often as possible, to the *New York Post* and the *Daily News* and ABC *Eyewitness News* and to anyone who would listen. The reporters thought he was guilty. The headlines had been unrestrained. "Devil" was one *New York Post* headline, laid over a picture of his face like an old propaganda poster from World War II. The jury couldn't change any of that. They couldn't find him "innocent." The best they could do was "not guilty." John didn't know if Jane thought him guilty, but he supposed that she wouldn't let him live in their apartment with the kids if she believed he was a murderer in addition to an adulterer.

The kids. No matter how the jury voted, his children were lost to him. They would never look at him again the way children should look at a father at their age. At any age.

The forewoman stared at the verdict form, like she had forgotten the unanimous decision that she and eleven other jurors reached less than an hour prior.

#

Two days after the cops came to the house, when John realized the stories were going to run in the papers and that he was eventually going to be arrested for Jessica's murder, he took out a blank sheet of paper—there were no forms for the words he had to write.

The home office was a mess. The cops executed their search warrant right after the kids left for school. The doorman called John at the office, John called Harris, and the two of them rushed to the apartment to watch Bauman, McCann, and some patrolmen ransack it. The cops took very little—all of John's shoes, some clothes, a couple of kitchen knives, a note from Jessica they found in a desk drawer. They didn't pick up after themselves, but they were gentler with the kids' room. They marched their plunder past the tabloid photographers and reporters they had tipped to the warrant execution, who were disappointed that it hadn't ended with a perp walk.

John understood that he was going to be led out in cuffs eventually. But the first humiliation was going to be the stories in the newspapers the next morning. John knew the formula as well as any other New Yorker. The papers would report the search of his apartment, and unnamed sources would indicate that he and the victim had been having an affair. The second humiliation would be dealing with the firm. As a partner, he couldn't simply be fired. If he were a white rainmaker, they might negotiate a leave of absence or sabbatical until more information was available. As the only Asian American partner with a middling book of business, he was certain he faced whatever the process was to terminate his partnership.

John sat in the ruins of his home, peering at the future degradations—the neighbors staring at his wife and kids, the co-op board trying to force his family out, close friends suddenly lacking time for cocktails or dinners, and his children learning secondhand about parties that they used to be invited to. All of that would occur before—regardless of—any verdict.

The decision to kill himself was one way the formula played out. The kids were young—seven and five. If he went to trial, they'd be another year or two older when it finished—old enough to hear the ugly things about him and fear the outcome of the trial. If John did it soon, with the right kind of note, maybe it would spare his family some of the pain that his living would cause. They could slip away forgotten, extras in a made-for-TV movie. If he could explain things to Jane and his children, maybe they could eventually lead normal lives and not think that he was a monster.

John scribbled out a suicide note trying to explain things, but nothing in it seemed like the truth. It was worse than saying nothing. He burned the letter in his sink, then went back, took another sheet of paper, and wrote out what he would tell the children. He had to organize his thoughts or they would collapse upon each other until the weight of them stifled him, and then all his kids would see was his impassive face and all the love he had for them would be lost inside him—because who had the words for what he had to say? But writing his script, he knew he'd never have the courage to face them or the wisdom to utter words to them that would make any kind of difference in the world they would grow up in because of him. So he burned that paper, too, and took another sheet and started a letter to the woman and man he hoped his daughter and son would become, but that thought was beyond him. What kind of people could they become after what they were going to face? He wrote nothing on that sheet of paper. John stared at it until he heard the nanny bring the kids in from school.

Even tired and whining for a snack, they were perfect. He would never tell them that; who praised children for simply existing? Sometimes, when the children slept and John went in to kiss them goodnight, he stared at the flawless skin of their cheeks, their earnest dream faces, their utter quiet, and wondered how he could have made anything so perfect—much less two of them. But they were there, tangible evidence that he had done something good in this world. That Jane had loved him once. On these nights, John had to restrain himself from scooping them in his arms, settling instead for the briefest brush of his lips across their foreheads.

The nanny went to the kitchen to make them peanut butter and jelly sandwiches. The children threw their backpacks on the living room floor and grabbed some G.I. Joe figures from the table, beginning some game only they understood. They shouted rules at each other without regard for consistency or logic. John sat down in one of the two chairs by a reading lamp, purchased when he and Jane thought that they would have time to sit by the lamp near the window and spend weekends reading books and sipping coffee, then scotch, then fooling around on the carpet. John couldn't remember the last time he sat in his chair. Jane's was piled high with books and clothes the kids had outgrown.

"Kids," John said. They ignored him. He spoke again. "Brennan, Hunter, come here."

Naming the kids had been surprisingly easy. The names came from Jane's family. John saw no point in giving the children Chinese names. He had abandoned his early. His parents were gone and would have wanted white names for the children anyway. For the same reason, John didn't bother trying to teach them the little Teochew he remembered.

The children were unexpectedly compliant. They never paid attention well, but now they walked over to stand in front of him. He still had no idea what to say or where to start.

"Kids," he said, and the words hung in the air. "You're too small to understand, but that doesn't mean that people aren't going to say things to you. So I need you to pay attention."

They were already paying attention; now they were confused.

"Your dad"—he corrected himself—"I. I made a terrible mistake. Your mother is very angry with me."

"You're getting divorced?" Brennan asked.

"I don't know. I don't think so. I hope not. But whatever happens with me and Mommy, things are going to get very bad. We will try to protect you from it, but you're going to have to grow up a lot faster than you should have to."

He knew they didn't understand and regretted not writing something down to help him through the moment.

"People are going to say your father made a mistake and did some bad things."

"But you don't make mistakes," Brennan said.

"Everyone makes mistakes," Hunter interjected. His sister pushed him.

"Stop," John said, and they fell silent. "He's right. Everyone makes mistakes. Sometimes they're big. We take responsibility for our mistakes. Do you understand?"

Both children nodded.

"And one of the bad things that they're going to say I did, it's a really bad thing. And we won't be able to hide it from you. So you're going to have to be strong. And when you think you can't be stronger, you'll have to be, okay? Because you have to be strong for Mommy, too. Do you understand?"

They didn't, but nodded because they thought that it was the right thing to do, and that was close enough for John. He pulled them close in for a hug, and for once, they didn't completely squirm away, but stood firm and wrapped him in their strongest embraces.

#

The visceral memory of his children's embraces brought John back to his body, standing next to Harris and in front of Jane, staring at the forewoman as she said, "Not guilty."

TWO

Then

JOHN'S SHOULDERS SLUMPED EVEN AS HARRIS TURNED TO hug him. There were a few murmurs in the courtroom, but no gasps, no outraged cries. Only the hollow *whump* of the door as Jessica's father stormed out. The judge thanked and dismissed the jury. Then came the business of justice, the rote incantations of procedure and due process slathered over the utter horror of the acquittal: either a man had been tried for a crime he didn't commit, or a killer had gotten away with murder.

After a tap of his gavel, the judge departed. The assistant district attorneys collected their papers with lowered heads, then shook hands with Harris before leaving the room. They didn't acknowledge John's presence. John turned, but Jane was gone.

When he turned back, Harris smiled. "You're a free man."

"I'll never be free of this."

Harris's smile evaporated. "There will be press on the stairs. Do you want to make a statement?"

"You make it. Whatever the normal statements are for something like this."

They found Jane in the hallway outside the courtroom, sitting on a bench. She looked shaken.

"Everything okay?" Harris asked.

She took a deep breath and nodded. Harris extended a hand to help her up.

"We need to walk out together. It will project the right image. Make it easier for the two of you to reclaim your lives. My paralegal has a driver waiting outside. Ready?"

After the dim halls of the courthouse, the bright spring afternoon surprised John. Waiting reporters swarmed them. The entire trial, they had walked purposefully through throngs of press without stopping. Now, though, Harris halted near the foot of the courthouse stairs, two steps from the sidewalk. News cameras, both television and print, would capture the impromptu press conference and magnify it, as if everything in sight was focused on the reporters' questions, Harris's sound bites, and John's face. But John was taken by how small the cluster was in context of Centre Street, the massive building behind them, and the passersby who barely glanced at the street theater coalescing before them.

Harris raised his voice over the babel of shouted questions. "First, my client, his family, and I would like to thank the jury for their service and for reaching a just verdict. As I said from the beginning, this is a case that the district attorney's office should have never brought. Right now, my client wants to get back to his family and try to restart his life."

"What about Jessica DeSalvo's life?" a female local news reporter shouted.

"It would be a terrible tragedy if the police and DA's office let this case go. As we showed at trial, they should have considered other suspects instead of buying the media narrative. Just because headlines sell a tabloid doesn't make the story true. Right now, Jessica's killer is out there. They should look for him."

"What if it's your client?"

Harris rolled his eyes and said, "Next."

"What are Mr. Lo's plans?"

"He's going to spend some time healing with his family."

"Mrs. DeSalvo's parents made a statement after the trial," a paunchy reporter called, then read from his notepad. "'We think the jury got it wrong. John Lo killed our daughter. He is a monster. He will have to live the rest of his life with the knowledge that he took our daughter from us and from her husband. He may find forgiveness from his wife or his children, but he will never have any from us.' Any reaction to that?"

Harris responded like a good lawyer: "We extend our sympathies to Jessica's family. We can only imagine what they must be going through. My client is innocent—"

John placed his hand on Harris's shoulder and stepped forward to speak. Although Harris subtly tried to push him back with his right arm, below the sight line of the reporters, their cameras captured his eyes widening with surprise and fear. John kept his grip on Harris and spoke the first words the press heard him utter, surprised to hear himself speaking.

"I cared deeply about Jessica, as a colleague and a friend. I want to apologize to her family and say I'm terribly sorry about the way things turned out—"

He was nearly knocked to the pavement as Jane looped her arm into his and plunged them through the scrum of reporters and into the waiting car. Harris followed, shouting, "No more questions! Thank you!" As he slammed the car door shut, a final question reached John: "Did you kill Jessica DeSalvo?"

#

Harris never asked him if he killed Jessica.

"I am going to operate from the assumption that you did not kill Jessica," Harris said back at his office after the night Bauman and McCann brought John to the precinct. Harris hadn't let John answer any of their questions and walked him out of the precinct after fifteen minutes of posturing. "But as you know, in order to mount the best defense for you that I am able, I am going to need to know everything that they might have or can use against you. Whatever you say to me is privileged. But I cannot suborn perjury, as you know. If you tell me something today that's the truth, I will not let you take the stand to say something different. Understand?"

"You're not going to let me take the stand either way."

"Almost certainly not. But it depends on how your defense shapes up and what the DA's theory is." Harris pulled out a legal pad. "What do you think their theory will be?"

John thought it was a clever question. If John had killed Jessica, he would know what evidence might exist, why he had done it, and how the best case against him would be presented. Even if he were innocent, given the circumstances, he was best positioned to speculate why the police were interested in him. If he laid it out like it might be the prosecution's theory, well then, technically, he wasn't admitting to anything, was he?

"We were having an affair. They'll probably find good evidence of that."

John and Jane had been close with Harris since law school—he was an usher at their wedding—but he took the news of John's betrayal with nothing other than a nod that conveyed neither approval nor disgust. It was like depositing a coin into a vending machine.

"They'll start there," John continued. "With the affair. They may theorize that she wanted to leave her husband. That she thought she was pregnant. That she arranged to meet me at her friend Cathy's apartment. Maybe she wanted me to join her and threatened to tell my wife in order to make that happen. Or tell the partners at the firm in order to blackmail me. They'll try to convince the jury that I killed her to keep her quiet."

Harris took his time to consider John's statements. John knew that he was trying to decide how much more information he wanted to elicit. Harris picked his next words very carefully.

"Can they place you in Cathy's apartment?"

"Probably. I'd been there before. We met there sometimes."

"That night?"

John shrugged. "I took a car from the firm. Not to the building, but two blocks away. I know of at least two affairs because they took a car to the same place, and the dispatchers"—the firm provided cars for attorneys who worked late—"and drivers gossip about it."

"Where were you going?"

John looked at the corner of Harris's desk. "There's a bar I go to sometimes if I work late. O'Malley's."

He used those precise words with the cops during the first interview in his office, when they asked him where he was that night. Let them draw their own conclusions.

"Will the bartender remember you?"

"I don't know what he'll remember."

"How long were you there? Did you go right home after you left? When did you get home?"

"I don't remember and I walked for about an hour before I went home."

"Is there anything you know that can help you?"

John knew a lot but didn't see how any of it helped him. He looked away. Harris's office was half the size of John's in a building not nearly as nice. It was crammed full of shelves overflowing with files and papers. Harris's chair—a comfy leather executive piece—was the only item John might have found at his firm. John sat in a fraying green fabric chair that looked like it was pulled from a dumpster.

"John? Anything that can help you?"

"Before we jump to conclusions, let's see where they go with this, Harris. I'm the likeliest guy next to her husband, right? It's either the desperate lover or the cuckolded husband. The papers this morning said he was working late. The cops found out about our relationship and brought me in. They're looking for a quick bust."

"But can we give them one? You were sleeping with this woman. Do you know anything?"

John shook his head. He wouldn't ruin anyone else's life just to help himself. Harris turned to the grimy window beside his desk. He stared at the brick wall of the air shaft for many moments before asking, "Were you there that night, John?"

He didn't turn to hear John's answer, and John gave him none. When Harris finally turned back to John, he looked down at his legal pad, devoid of notes except the date. He finally forced his eyes up to John's.

"How's Jane handling this?"

#

Jane's rage seeped through the moment the car door closed, darkening her face like a smoldering sheet of paper, charring at the edges before flaring fully into bright flame. The muffled shouts of the reporters followed them as the car pulled away. Jane fixed her gaze straight ahead. On the other side of Jane, Harris stared out the passenger-side window. Out of sight of the jury and the press, his face was full of worry. It was a short ride to Harris's office, and none of them spoke except to curtly thank the driver when they exited the car. The silence shrouded them on the elevator ride, but Jane carried her anger like a torch into the conference room Harris had commandeered for the trial.

As John sank into one of the mismatched chairs surrounding the table holding Harris's files, Jane finally turned to look at him.

"What the fuck were you thinking?"

John stared into the conflagration until he thought her rage might blind him.

"I don't know," he said.

"You sounded like you were guilty!"

"They think I did it anyway!" John shouted back. "What does it matter?"

"It fucking matters, John! Christ! We have to live with this!"

"Jane," Harris cut in, "it's not as bad as you think. You managed to cut him off before it got too bad."

"They think he did it, Harris. If he didn't say anything, didn't give them anything to feed on, maybe they could doubt. Maybe, over time, they would give him the benefit of that doubt. But now? It sounded like he was apologizing for her murder. They will have no doubt, and if they do, they'll remember that apology."

"What about you?" John asked. "Do you think I did it?"

Harris raised his hands and stepped between them. "Don't do this, guys. We won."

The chair John had been sitting in hit the wall behind him before he realized he was standing, and he swept a box of files off the table to the floor. For the first time in months, he felt like he inhabited his body, ecstatic with rage. Jane and Harris, on the other side of the table, stepped back. John gathered himself and caught the edge of the table like a swooning drunk. He imagined flipping it toward them but leaned heavily on it instead. As suddenly as it came to him, the anger retreated, replaced by regret.

"There was no winning this, Harris, except for you," John said before turning to Jane. "Do you think I did it, Jane? Do you?"

"What does it matter what I think?"

"You're my wife."

"I'm the mother of your children."

"That's not an answer."

"It's the only answer. I don't have the luxury of deciding what I think because I have to think about the kids, which is something you should've done before you fucked that—" Jane closed her eyes and inhaled deeply. "That trial was about giving Brennan and Hunter a reason to doubt. And you fucking ruined it."

She shoved past Harris to the door and slammed it shut behind her. Harris followed her but paused before leaving the conference room. John looked up from the files he had scattered across the floor to Harris with an apology. Harris held up his hand.

"Save it, buddy. This is your mess now."

THREE

Then

JANE WAS LONG GONE. EVEN HARRIS LEFT TO CELEBRATE the victory somewhere, abandoning John to clean the case file he had swept off the table. Most of the papers were copies of vouchers the cops had used to show the pattern of him and Jess taking cars to the same places at the same times. How could he have been so stupid? But no pattern anymore. They were hopelessly out of order. John stuffed them back into the box, then sank into a cheap chair. Another folder contained copies of correspondence between him and Jessica. Love letters, confessions, simple notes, and even inter-office memos. Harris's receptionist sat at the desk, filing her nails, taking messages from reporters looking for comment. Eventually she knocked on the door and asked John if he was leaving. She had dinner plans. John nodded, took the folder, slid it into the case file box, and left.

The last of the sunlight chased the late rush-hour stragglers streaming up Chambers Street. The perfect weather invited him to walk farther, but he descended into the first subway entrance that would get him home. He had to buy a token—he hadn't taken the subway in months. Both the platform and the train were crowded. John worried briefly what he would do if he were recognized. His face had been splayed across the pages of the *Daily News* and *New York Post* at least five times in the past year, including at the start of his trial three weeks before. He could only imagine what the evening news had done with his statement on the courthouse steps. Jane was right; speaking had been a mistake. But no one gave him a second look. He might have been the most famous Asian American in the city—unless George Takei, Pat Morita, or that kid who played Short Round were in New York that day—but he went unrecognized.

When he got off the subway, he purposefully wandered for blocks, waiting for someone to recognize him. No one did. Not because they didn't look at him; people did. They paid the same regard to him as they did to a yellow cab—part of their physical reality and completely indistinguishable from any other taxi. When a woman veered from one side of the sidewalk toward him to avoid walking too close to a Black man in a suit, he wanted to tap the woman on the shoulder and say, "You know that I was just on trial for murder?"

The woman turned to him, surprising him. He had reached out to touch her shoulder before realizing he had moved. She regarded him without recognition, trepidation, or warmth. He could have been a tree whose branch had brushed her shoulder.

"I'm sorry," John said. "I thought I knew you."

She said nothing, instead turning away to look for the Black man in the suit. When she saw that he was nearly parallel to them, she shifted her purse to her arm closest to John and away from the man. As the man in the suit passed them, his eyes flickered toward the woman, leaving no doubt that he had noted her fear, rolling his eyes in disgust. He disregarded John entirely.

After the past year, his anonymity encouraged him. By the time he approached his building, John even began to wonder whether he might be able to rebuild some kind of life. Maybe it was possible that he could get a new job, use a new name, and everyone would forget about the trial and everything that led to it. Perhaps Jane would forgive him eventually, and they could salvage something from the horror he brought upon them.

Calvin, the doorman, saw him approaching. Despite Calvin being one of the chattiest doormen on the staff, he had steadfastly avoided holding the door for John since the arrest. As John approached, Calvin reached out and swung the door open for him. As he walked past, John nodded. Maybe the acquittal changed things.

"So, you got away with it, huh?" Calvin said.

John looked back, and Calvin met his stare.

The elevator door behind John opened, and an older couple got off, gawking at John as they walked past. John put his head down and stepped into the elevator before the doors closed.

The sound of the door to the apartment shutting brought Brennan running to the foyer. John dropped to his knees and let her envelop him, skinny arms squeezing with every ounce of strength—so hard he thought she'd burst his heart. His face was in her hair, eyes shut against tears, until he thought he could safely open them. When he did, he saw Hunter standing at the door to the kids' room.

#

He passed the closed door to the kids' room when he got home after making bail. Jane sat at the kitchen table wrapped in a haze of smoky air, even with the window open for ventilation. John walked in, opened a beer, and reached for the pack of cigarettes on the table.

Jane turned her seat so that she faced the opposite wall. John threw the pack of cigarettes down and stormed out of the kitchen. He opened the door to the kids' room.

They were in their beds. The dim lamp that served as a night-light cast a warm glow across their faces. Their eyes popped open when he opened the door.

"Daddy!" Brennan said, holding her arms out to him.

He leaned over her bed and kissed her cheek as she threw her arms around his neck. He turned to Hunter's bed, but Hunter pulled his covers to his chin and shrank toward the corner where his bed met the wall. John sat on the edge of Brennan's bed.

"Were you arrested today?" Hunter asked.

John nodded.

"They said you . . ."

"You didn't, right?" Brennan asked, cutting her brother off before he could utter the words.

"We shouldn't talk about it, kids. It's grown-up stuff."

"The cops think you did it," Hunter said. "That's why they arrested you."

"But you explained everything, right, Daddy? They'll leave you alone now?" Brennan asked.

John couldn't look at her. "No. Not yet."

The three of them sat in silence.

"Will people say anything at school?" Hunter asked.

"No," said Brennan.

"Do they know?" Hunter asked.

John shrugged.

"With everything that is going to happen," John said, "it's important for you guys to remember that you're your own people. You're not just our children."

"You might go to jail," Hunter said. It was a flat accusation. An invitation for John to lie.

Brennan twisted her sheets in her hands.

"It's possible," John said.

Brennan began to cry. John pulled her close while Hunter glared at him.

"Listen, listen," John repeated until Brennan's sobbing eased. "A lot of stuff has to happen before they take me away, if they take me away."

Brennan looked up at him with big eyes, face aglow with tears. John almost fled the room, but he needed to prepare them.

"Do you know what they said I did?"

"They said—" Hunter began.

"*Shut up!*" Brennan shouted.

"No," John said, taking Brennan's hand and squeezing it. "Let him say it."

"They said that you killed a lady."

Brennan shook next to him like a loosely latched door in a storm. Hunter was still, eyes fixed on John's.

"If people tell you that, what are you going to say?"

"*No! No, he didn't!*" Brennan screamed at her brother, as if he had hurled the accusation himself.

Hunter looked at his father, confused, but said, "I'll tell them to leave me alone."

John nodded. "What do I teach you is the most important thing?"

"Family." The children said this together.

"You two need to be there for each other. Always, but especially now."

He waited a moment for them to absorb the message, and then he settled Brennan down and tucked her back in. He sat on the edge of her bed wondering how he was going to get them to sleep, but they dropped off a few short minutes later. When he left their room, Jane was waiting for him in the living room.

"How could you do that?" she asked.

"Do what?"

"Talk to them. About that?"

"They need to know. First, they need to be prepared for people—for kids—to say something to them. On the playground. In the classroom. Hiding it was not—we can't hide it from them."

Jane scoffed and said, "Nobody just—none of their teachers would dare say—and their friends—what kid would bring it up to them?"

John's experience of children was not only that they were thoughtless about anything other than themselves, but outright meaner than adults in ways that adults somehow forgot after they grew up. Adults weren't the ones who pulled the ends of their eyes up to slant them at

John. Adults weren't the ones who asked him if his name was "Ching Chong Wong" or if his parents named him by throwing pots and pans down a staircase.

"Jane, we've had this discussion." It hadn't been a discussion. It had been one of the worst fights of their marriage.

"I know what you're thinking, John," she said, as if explaining something to one of the children. "Kids can be mean, but it's different now."

"You have no idea."

"I don't? I'm married to you, John."

"Can you even say my real name? Like it's supposed to be said? The way my parents pronounced it?"

"What does that even mean? It's Chong."

"Chong."

"That's what I said!"

John shook his head. She could never master the nuance in the inflection.

"What do you want me to do, John? Fake a Chinese accent? Start shouting at you like some waiter in Chinatown? Did you fuck her because she could say your name right? Okay then!" She chanted his name, each time sinking deeper into a caricature, the vocal equivalent of an illustration of a slant-eyed yellow man with a Fu Manchu and bamboo hat.

"You can stop now," he said.

"You don't get to tell me what to do and when to stop and what I think."

John raised his hands in surrender. "They need to know. They need to know that I might go to prison. The first time they think about losing me can't be the day they lose me."

She shook her head. "If that's what had to happen for us to be good parents for another six months or a year or whatever until this fucking trial, then, goddamnit, we should do it! Our job is to protect them. Not throw them to the wolves and say, 'We did it for them!' so we can feel better about abandoning them! And you had no business making that decision without talking to me!"

"Talking to you? When? You haven't—for Christ's sake, Jane, you haven't talked to me in weeks. I just tried to talk to you, and you turned away!"

"You were having an affair! You're fucking accused of—"

"I know what I'm accused of."

They fell abruptly silent. John walked over and cracked the kids' room door open, but they still slept. He turned back to see the door to their bedroom shutting against him.

#

Brennan pulled away from him, her face radiant with tears, and said, "It's over? You won? They're not going to take you away, right, Daddy?"

"No," John said. "No. I'm going to get to stay with you."

Behind Brennan, Hunter shut the door to their room.

FOUR

Now

HUNTER ROLLED OVER. HIS PHONE RANG WITH A TREBLE bell tone that was supposed to be reminiscent of a classic phone but sounded too digital to be convincing. He grunted. The screen said it was his sister.

"Hey," Hunter answered. Brennan sighed as if she'd been hoping he wouldn't. "Everything okay?"

"You're still sleeping? It's like 9:00 a.m."

"It's a Sunday. But no, I was up. Kinda."

The line was silent, but Hunter felt Brennan shaking her head in annoyance.

"You seen Mom since you got back? She told me to call you so we could have brunch with her."

"There's what? Six inches of snow on the ground?"

"Eight."

Hunter rolled his eyes. "Fine."

"Can you be ready in twenty minutes? We can split a cab over." She told him where to meet.

"Fine."

Brennan hung up on him. Curious, Hunter checked his call log. It was the first time Brennan had called him since he got the phone over a year ago.

Over his shoulder, the girl—whatever her name was—shimmied into her tight jeans. Light from the window fell on her just right.

"You sleep okay?" he asked, smiling.

"Yeah. You?"

"Sure." He hadn't slept. Instead, he spent the night lying next to her, fading between degrees of consciousness, trying to remember her name, watching snow fall through the window, and wondering how he could politely get her to leave in the morning.

"I've never done the walk of shame in the snow before."

"You have nothing to be ashamed about."

"It's nice that you think so. I mean, I literally just met you last night." She balanced on one leg to pull on a sock, still topless. "I don't do this very often. You're just really hot."

"I'm sure you don't, and"—he shot her a roguish smile—"so are you."

She finished pulling her sock onto her foot, climbed back onto the bed, and crawled toward him. She kissed him, heedless of their morning breath. Even though he would have preferred to fuck again, Hunter pulled away.

"Sorry," he said. "My sister and I are supposed to take our mom to brunch."

"That's sweet," she said, somehow already off the bed and picking her bra up from the floor. Hunter stood, ran his hands across his face, and surveyed the room for something clean to wear. By the time he had underwear and jeans on, she was dressed, standing in the bedroom doorway, watching him.

"Let me walk you out before I wash up."

They didn't fill the silence of the ten seconds that it took for her to grab her coat and purse. Maybe she expected him to ask for her number, but Hunter had abandoned the practice of asking for numbers he knew he'd never dial.

"You know, this is embarrassing," she said, turning at his door, "but I can't remember your name."

"Happy to tell you, in exchange for yours."

She looked down, playing coy, then pressed into him, kissing him. She broke the kiss, opened the door, and left.

Ten minutes later, Hunter stood on the corner of Amsterdam and Ninety-Sixth Street, next to an old bank building that had been converted into a pharmacy. Snow piled near the curb like a berm, and rock salt crunched between his boot soles and the pavement. A bright, clear sky shone overhead. Hunter figured that most of the snow would be gone by nightfall. He hadn't made up his mind yet whether he had made a mistake in not getting the girl's name and number.

Brennan arrived looking as she did two years ago or whenever he'd last seen her. Still slender. Her hair was shorter, shoulder-length now. Same skin tone and facial features that led to confusion their whole lives. *What are you? You Asian? Hispanic? Latino? Hawaiian?*

Hunter handed her the coffee he had procured for her. "Cream, no sugar, right?"

"Close enough," Brennan said. "Thanks."

"What did you bring?"

"Bagels and lox."

"What about eggs?"

"She'll have eggs if you want them."

They crossed the street and hailed an eastbound cab with threadbare tires. Without thinking, they sat on the same sides as when they were children—Hunter behind the driver, Brennan on the passenger side.

"Eightieth and York," Brennan said.

The driver didn't respond except to pull away. The siblings peered out of opposite windows as they rode.

"How long have you been back?" Brennan asked as they stopped at a light on Central Park West. Covered with snow in the morning light, the park was too bright to look at.

"A week."

"How was it?"

"You read the news?"

"Of course. Even some of the stuff you wrote."

"Then you know maybe a quarter of how bad it is over there. It's a fucking disaster. I don't want to talk about it."

"Fine." Brennan glanced at him. "So why haven't you seen Mom yet?"

"I've been working up to it. You know, jet lag. Also, God knows if I picked up some sort of bug from traveling. Don't want to expose her to it."

Brennan shook her head but didn't say anything else. When they reached Fifth Avenue, a family crossed in front of the cab, wearing expensive parkas, snow pants, and boots like they were embarking on an Antarctic expedition instead of strolling through a park no more than ten minutes from an espresso in any direction.

"I'm sorry I missed the wedding," Hunter said.

She dismissed his apology with a wave. "It was four years ago."

"Yeah. But I haven't had a chance to tell you."

"You were covering our endless wars." The tone of Brennan's voice was clear—there was nothing to forgive, not because she was past it, but because she'd never cared in the first place if he showed.

"How's Paul?" Hunter's heart rate spiked for a moment as he worried that he had forgotten his brother-in-law's name. Hunter had spoken to Paul twice. The first time was during a phone call from Afghanistan after the wedding to congratulate them. The second time was two years later, a Christmas dinner at their mother's. Hunter's flight had been delayed and Brennan had some court brief due, so they'd only overlapped for fifteen minutes—a handshake while Hunter microwaved the cold ham and mashed potatoes and passed his hastily wrapped presents over.

"I don't know. We split up about six months ago."

Hunter finally looked over to her. "You're divorced?"

"Separated. But heading that way." Brennan continued to watch the city out of her side of the cab.

"I . . . what? Mom didn't say anything."

"She's pretending it didn't happen."

"Why?"

"It wasn't working out. I don't want to talk about it."

Hunter looked back out of the window as they crossed the Upper East Side.

"How long you in town for?" Brennan asked as they passed Third Avenue.

"Indefinitely. I told the paper I had to be here for Mom. They were understanding about it. At least for now. To be honest . . ." He stopped speaking with a shake of his head.

"What?"

"I don't want to talk about it. It's stupid."

Their mother's building was halfway between York and East End Avenue. She'd downsized to a two-bedroom apartment there after the siblings moved away for college. The cab pulled to a stop on the corner. They walked the rest of the way without speaking. They stood in front of the building for a moment. Wind blew off the East River a few hundred yards away, and their eyes watered.

"When's the last time that you saw her?" Brennan asked.

"In person? Last year. You?"

"Yesterday. You should know, she looks different. You ready for this?"

Hunter nodded. They headed into the building and up to the tenth floor. They rang the bell at Apartment D and waited patiently. Eventually, the door chain rattled, the deadbolt turned over, and then their mother opened the door, backlit by sunlight streaming through the large windows in the living room.

"Oh," she said, as if she were surprised, "it's you two clowns."

Brennan hugged her first, perfunctory with familiarity. She stepped aside as Hunter embraced her. Even though he planned for a simple squeeze, Hunter found himself holding her, spinning for a moment in memories.

"Alright, alright," Jane said, breaking out of his arms. She brushed past them like a curtain, shuffled back to the living room, and sank into the couch. Hunter and Brennan immediately began removing their coats and boots—the apartment sweltered. Despite the heat, their mother wore a thick cable-knit sweater and jeans—all bones and clothes.

Brennan carried the food to the small dining room tucked adjacent to the living room and kitchen. Hunter quickly inspected the living room. Two blankets lay crumpled on the couch next to his mother, a stack of books rested on the coffee table, and three empty cups cluttered the side table. A credenza stood covered with old pictures of him and Brennan, including a black-and-white photo of the three of them Hunter had taken before Brennan left for college.

As always, the only picture of his father in the apartment drew his eye. The two children, three and five in the photo, sat on John's lap on a bench in Central Park, everyone smiling. Hunter remembered nothing about the day or what they had to be so happy about.

"Mom," Brennan said from the other room, "can I make you some tea or coffee?"

"No," she said. "Water is fine."

Hunter sat down in a wingback chair across from the couch. His mother inspected him like she did every time he returned home from one of his absences. She looked like she had aged twenty years since he last saw her. Her thick blond hair had thinned into a dry mousegray frazzle. Liver spots peppered her skin, slack over wasted muscle. He barely recognized the woman who raised him. The sound of Brennan grinding coffee in the kitchen carried into the room.

"Why is she making coffee?" Jane asked. "You showed up with cups in your hand."

"They're almost empty," Hunter said. "How are you feeling?"

"Tired. Everything hurts. What do you want me to tell you?"

"Whatever you like."

"The damn doctors, they're worse than lawyers." She directed the last part to Brennan as she entered the room. "They never give you a straight answer."

"What's going on?" Brennan asked.

"You mean, aside from the cancer?"

"I mean, anything specific that's bothering you about the doctors today as opposed to generally?"

"No. I just hate the hedging. The hemming and hawing. The consideration. The consultations."

"You know that there aren't any solid answers."

"Don't tell me what I know. It doesn't mean I have to like it." She turned to Hunter. "See? That's what you get for asking me how I'm feeling. Next time leave it for my doctors or my shrink. You tell me about you. What's your story?"

"No story. I just got back to town."

"A week ago. You couldn't make your way over here to see your mother?"

"Sorry. You know, jet lag, and catching up on stuff I couldn't get done overseas. I wanted to clear stuff off my plate before I saw you. So I could focus on being here."

His mother looked at him like his bullshit had not improved with age, which it hadn't. Hunter shrugged, sank back in his chair, and wished he had slept better the night before.

"What about you?" She turned on Brennan. "Did you tell your brother you won that case?"

"No." Brennan joined her mother on the couch. "We didn't talk about that."

"You used to brag about your wins."

Brennan shrugged. "I didn't brag about them."

"What case?" Hunter asked.

"Nothing," Brennan said. "We won a trial last week."

"What about?"

"I don't want to talk about it."

Their mom cut in like she did when they all lived together and the kids drove her crazy with their bickering. "Brennan, what's the news with Paul?"

Brennan rolled her eyes and sank back in her chair. "Stop, Mom. It's over. Can we move on to something else?"

Their mother turned back to Hunter. "When do you go back to Syria or whatever country you're covering next?"

"No plans right now."

"I hope that's not on account of me."

"It was time for me to come back anyway. I'll just stay a little longer, make sure you're okay," Hunter said.

"Don't put your life on hold for me. I don't want to be a burden."

In the kitchen, the teapot whistled. Hunter and Brennan stood at the same time.

"Wait here, Mom," Brennan said. "We'll get everything set."

The siblings went to the kitchen. Hunter turned off the burner, and the kettle's whistle stopped.

"There's fresh ground coffee in that cabinet," Brennan said. "I keep a supply here. For the late nights."

As Hunter scooped coffee and poured the hot water into a French press, Brennan opened the oven and loaded warmed bagels onto a tray.

"She's feisty today," Brennan said. "It's the pain."

"She was always like this."

"Is the sugar on the table?"

"Yeah, I see it out there."

Hunter arranged the food while Brennan set the table. They sat as they had growing up: Jane at the head of the table, Brennan to her right, Hunter to her left. Their mother took a bagel, sawing at it slowly with an unsteady hand.

"Mom, can I help you with that?" Brennan asked.

"I can do it," Jane said.

Hunter and Brennan exchanged glances and assembled bagels with lox and cream cheese. Jane spread butter over hers.

"Sometimes," she said, "I feel like this. Pushed around, pulled thin. Pulled and pushed. Scraped year after year, thinner and thinner. Melting. Until you're not there anymore. You're just a film of grease on someone else's life."

Hunter reached for her hand. It disappeared in his like a child's hand would. Brennan moved behind her, kissed the top of her head, then leaned forward to nestle against her cheek. Jane embraced Brennan with her free hand, then nudged her back to her seat and pulled away from Hunter.

"It's okay, kids. I'm okay. I'm sorry."

"There's nothing to apologize about, Mom," Hunter said.

"I'm tired. I'm going to lie down now. You guys can stay if you like, but let me say goodbye now, in case you leave before I wake."

She came to them, one at a time like bedtime when they were kids—Brennan first, then Hunter—hugs and kisses, then shuffled off to her bedroom. Her bagel sat uneaten on her plate.

FIVE

Now

BRENNAN RUBBED HER EYES AS HER STOMACH GROWLED. She'd barely eaten anything since "brunch" with her mother and brother. She was two and three-quarters inches through her review of a three-inch binder of documents, the paper embodiment of about one hundred fifty emails and attachments relating to an asset-purchase agreement that her client allegedly breached by failing to make a contingent payment. A team of junior associates had culled about twenty-five thousand emails down to these one hundred fifty. The good news was that the contingency that required the payment had not been met. The bad news was that the emails indicated that her client may have massaged its reported earnings to ensure that it would not meet the contingency.

She picked her highlighter back up and marked some troubling text. The clock on her computer screen told her that it was 8:30 p.m. She was in her ninth hour of work on a Sunday. Her desk phone rang with a quiet, electronic beep. The caller's name appeared on the display. Although she would usually hit the speaker button, particularly on a Sunday in the office, she picked up the receiver.

"How'd you know I was in?" she asked.

"It's you," he said. "When's the last time you weren't here crushing it on a Sunday night?"

Even Brennan didn't know the answer to that question.

"What do you need?"

"Do you have time to swing by my office?"

"Just wrapping something up. Will you be around in twenty minutes?"

"See you then." He hung up the phone.

Brennan sped through the last quarter inch of documents in about ten minutes and made a note to reread them in the morning. She stood up, her hamstrings tight from sitting so long, and yawned. She scanned her office, stacking papers she would need the next day and tossing the remainder into two different stacks: shredding and regular trash. By the time she was done, her desk was almost clear except for her to-do list, the three-inch binder, and a small stack of assorted papers. She made it a point not to leave the office cluttered. As far as offices went, it was an ascetic's cell. She hung no pictures on the wall; no personal books or clippings or much of anything decorated the space. There was a drawer with an extra pair of shoes and stockings, as well as various toiletries. A spare suit and sweater hung from a hook on the back of her door.

She stopped in the restroom on the way to Sean's office on the thirty-third floor, which was two floors above hers. She had seen some people around the office earlier—silent apparitions down a hallway or moving past her door—but the place was empty now. She wore leggings and an old sweater. Comfortable, but shabby. Fine enough for Sean. She gave a quick knock on his open door as she walked in.

He stood behind his desk with his back to the door, arranging a set of files on the credenza in front of his window. Past Sean's reflection in the window, Manhattan stretched out to the north, draped in lights underneath a cloudy, purple night. He wore expensive jeans and a zip-up hoodie that probably cost five hundred dollars in an effort to look like it cost ten. Brennan couldn't see his feet but knew that he was wearing three-hundred-dollar sneakers. He was forty-four but could pass for thirty-five. He took his daily personal training sessions and nightly moisturizing very seriously.

Sean glanced at her reflection in the window and without turning said, "Take a seat. Gimme one sec to finish this."

Brennan leaned against one of the two leather chairs facing his desk but didn't sit. The office was unchanged since her last visit. A sleek, modern desk—picked by a decorator—paired with an ergonomic designer chair dominated the space. A leather couch sat against the right-hand wall. Four photos of Sean's wife and daughters hung in a two-by-two block over the couch. Sean's smile dazzled like a searchlight, sweeping across the room as he turned to her.

"Aren't you going to take a seat?"

"How long is this going to take? I was planning on heading home," she said.

"Oh." The smile switched off, replaced by his serious face, equally handsome but like a warm, dark barroom—full of shadows, significance, and comfort. "First, what do you think about donating to McCarthy's campaign?"

Tim McCarthy was a former assistant district attorney running for the big job—Manhattan DA—on a law-and-order platform.

"Isn't there a firm policy on hitting employees up for donations?"

Sean rolled his eyes and smiled again. "Come on, Bren. You and me are past those formalities. You're basically already a partner."

"I'll think about it." She knew she wouldn't donate. McCarthy was a self-righteous blowhard. "What was the second thing?"

"I just got a new matter. I could use someone like you on it."

"I don't think that's a good idea," she said.

"Why not?" His eyes flickered from her face to the open door behind her.

"Do you want me to get the door?"

Sean shrugged, but then nodded twice. Brennan closed the door and turned back to Sean. "You know why this is a bad idea."

"You're overreacting. We make a great team." Sean had brought Brennan onto the Reliant Tires case because of her trial experience. She accepted the assignment—she was up for partner—even though she hated the case and the client. "We kicked ass in that trial."

"We got lucky. You don't think it's odd that nobody told the CEO they were going to redesign those tires in a way that decreased costs by five percent but increased the chance of failure by two hundred percent?"

"It was a routine design refinement, and you're talking about a failure rate that was already well below one percent."

"But it still put more people at risk."

"Which may have factored into Reliant's decision if anyone had known about it, particularly the CEO. Which is what the jury believed, because we're a great team."

He spoke with absolute conviction, but Brennan didn't think he believed anything he was saying. Or maybe it was her own doubts she was projecting onto him.

"We're not a good team. First," Brennan said, "I don't do mass torts. Not interested in them. And it's the only thing you do."

"It's not the only thing I do."

"What's your case about?"

"We represent Shingen Autos. Apparently, there may have been control issues with the manufacturing of their hybrid-engine batteries."

"What issues?" she asked.

"Under certain conditions, the battery—which is actually a bank of smaller batteries—can overheat, causing battery acid leakage and fires."

"What conditions does it take for this to happen?"

"In the affected units? The car has to be running. You know, like turned on."

"Oh, is that all?" The question was rhetorical, but her follow-up wasn't. "How many affected units?"

"Roughly three hundred thousand. It's a great-selling car."

"This is going to be a shit show."

"That's why I need your help."

"No way. It's a mass-tort case."

"You sounded interested." Sean hit her with his smile again, and she caught herself beginning to smile back.

"I'm not." She crossed her arms, but not before brushing a strand of hair behind her ear. "Even if I was, we can't work together."

"Yes, we can. We get along great."

"Don't be an idiot. You know that's not the issue. I gotta get up to speed on that other case for Thomas Rabinowitz."

"Okay. Fair enough. I just thought that it would be fun to keep working together."

"No," she said, gently.

He sighed and nodded.

"Anyway, I should get going," she said.

"Okay," he said. "You heading home?"

"Yeah. I'm exhausted. Tough morning."

Neither of them moved.

"What is it?" he asked.

"Nothing." Brennan knew she should go but waited for him to come around his desk anyway. Before he got halfway, she walked over and embraced him.

"I'm sorry," she said.

"It's okay," he said and kissed the top of her head. "I don't know what you're apologizing for."

She craned her neck to look at him with his arms still wrapped around her. He wore his serious face. He leaned down and kissed her. He started to press himself against her but then pulled away.

"Unless you're planning to take me with you," he said, "we should stop. I'm getting excited."

"Not tonight, Sean."

Sean cocked an eyebrow and walked back behind his desk to look out the window again. She could see his face in the reflection. For a moment, and only in reflection, he was completely open, bare, searching for something. Or maybe she was imagining things.

"Well, don't let me keep you," he said.

Brennan walked out without looking back. Before she reached the elevator, she felt her phone vibrating in her purse. She expected it to be Sean calling to try to convince her to meet him somewhere, but it was Hunter.

"Everything okay?" she said, answering the call.

"Yeah. Mom called me and asked me to come over. She didn't sound too hot."

"Can you make it?"

"Yeah, I'm on my way there now. Don't get pissy with me."

She reflexively apologized, then thought better of it. "While you've been gone, I've had to deal with her—"

"I understand," he said. "That's not why I called."

Fuck him for cutting her off. He didn't understand the pressure she'd been under and the sacrifices she'd made while he disappeared halfway across the world. But she waited for him to get to the point. She was practiced in dealing with people who aggravated her.

"It's about our father. She called me because she said she wanted to talk about him."

"She hasn't . . . I mean, she doesn't talk about him."

"I know."

"I'll meet—

\#

—you there," Brennan said before Hunter's phone went dead.

He shoved it back into his pocket and walked into his mother's building. The doorman remembered him and waved him through. At his mother's door, he knocked. When she didn't answer, he tried the knob. It was unlocked.

The heat hit him as soon as he was through the door, and he quickly shed his coat. A lamp in the living room cast the only light in the apartment.

"Mom?" he called out. He didn't want to wake her if she was sleeping, but it was better than scaring her to death, which was a legitimate fear considering her condition. No answer, so he called out again. A deep seed of worry began to form well beneath his stomach—like his stomach was hanging out of his body and halfway to the floor. His heart pounded as he remembered the clinic in a sunbaked hamlet on the other side of the world and the smell of blood and bodies and good God, if he found his mother's body—

"In the bedroom," he heard, her low voice muffled further by her closed door.

He pushed the door open, chest heaving as he brought his breathing under control. His mother sat propped up in her bed underneath a thick comforter. Pill bottles, empty glasses, some medical gear, and a can of diet root beer covered the nightstand. Half buried under all the junk, a do-not-resuscitate order was taped to it. An episode of *Seinfeld* played on the small TV on top of a dresser. An empty chair for the home nurse who came for a few hours each day sat next to the bed.

The bedroom was warmer than the rest of the apartment. Sweat dampened his shirt.

"How's it going, Mom?"

"Fine," she said.

"You said on the phone you weren't feeling well."

"I'm not. But when someone asks, 'How's it going, Mom?' I answer, 'Fine.' Don't you?"

"You're impossible."

"I'm sorry I fell asleep on you earlier."

Hunter shook his head at the abrupt conciliation. She had always been like this, constantly switching moods, tacking heedlessly. The thought enraged him, but he swallowed the resentment like thick mucus and said, "You're sick. I understand."

She muted the TV with a remote, then sighed and sank into her pillows.

"I'm worried that the time is short, Hunter."

"You're going to beat this, Mom."

"I meant lucidity, tonight, you ass. I took a pretty heavy painkiller while I was waiting for you. As soon as it kicks in, I'm going night night." She looked down at herself, nearly lost in the bedding, then back at Hunter. Nothing about her illness diminished her eyes, alive with calculation, yet unreachable—like a party seen through a window. Hunter would have more luck reaching through the television screen and touching the face of Julia Louis-Dreyfus than comprehending whatever occurred behind his mother's eyes.

"I've realized some things, lying here all day. Nothing but books and television shows I keep falling asleep to. I can't finish anything. I just catch snippets of conversations, these little fragments of things. They're in and out of my head. It's like trying to catch a particular spot in the ocean, where the light is, and hold it in place."

"I thought you said that you were lucid."

"I'm trying to describe to you the feeling. So you understand what I'm telling you, where it comes from, and why it's important. Sit down, for Christ's sake."

Hunter sat in the small chair.

"I feel like I missed something. Something important. About your father," she added after a pause. "Whether he did that thing they accused him of."

She looked at him, same as she always had. Full of certainty.

"You and I both know that he did."

"I don't know," she whispered.

"He never denied it," Hunter said, gripping the arms of the chair. "You told me that."

"Yes, I told you he never denied it. That's true." Even in her state, Hunter marveled at her lawyer's ability to parse her words. "But I don't know."

"Mom, it was thirty years ago."

She shook her head like she was trying to shake some strands of hair from her face. He touched her forehead. It was hot and dry, like a shirt fresh from a dryer. He had a film of sweat on his forehead.

"Let me take your temperature."

She grabbed his hand as he reached for the thermometer. "Stop it. When I'm done talking, you can do what you want. I'm coming to you. With this."

Hunter pulled his hand back and nodded.

"When I think back to that time," she said, "I feel like there's so many things I barely remember. I don't know if it's the drugs or time or what. But so much is hazy or gone, like imprints in the carpet from furniture that's been moved. Something was there, but I don't remember what."

The heat and his concern for his mother made it difficult to follow what she was trying to say.

"I think I remember your dad worked at a restaurant?"

"Yeah. When he was a kid."

"No. I know that," she said, impatiently. "But I feel like later, too."

"I don't remember that."

"See? That's what I'm talking about. I don't even know if I remember that."

"But that's not even important. It doesn't change what he did."

"I don't know what's important, though. I feel like maybe I told myself a story to make sense of everything that happened, or so that I could live with myself, with you two."

"Mom, what are you saying? Are you saying you lied to us?" He wanted to believe it was the heat of the room searing his lungs, but his sweat turned cold. His heart hammered against his constricting chest.

"No! I would have never lied to you. Not about that." She reached for his hand and missed. Hunter left her hand hanging from the side of the bed. "I let you and your sister make up your own minds. Maybe it's the drugs, maybe it's just coming to the end of things, but now I feel like I should have done something different. I don't know what. Because I didn't know. Because there was no way to know one way or the other. But I think I did a disservice to you both by letting you be so certain. I don't know what I'm saying. I can't think straight enough to work it out."

Hunter placed her hand back on her bed and gave it a squeeze. He couldn't help but think of a corpse's hand and couldn't help but love it anyway.

"Mom," he said. "You need to rest."

She nodded and turned away. The reflected light from the television flickered in her eyes as she stared at the curtained window. Hunter waited until she fell asleep, then turned the television off.

SIX

Now

TEN MINUTES LATER, BRENNAN WALKED THROUGH THE DOOR as Hunter brewed a pot of coffee in the same French press they had used that morning.

"Jesus, it's boiling in here." She shed her coat and was already pulling off her sweater.

"Do you remember how to turn the heat down out here?"

"Yeah."

"Then turn it down. I'm going to look in on her."

Hunter turned down the thermostat and cracked a window. Brennan came out of the bedroom, closing the door behind her. They poured cups of coffee and leaned against the kitchen counter.

"What did you guys talk about?" Brennan asked.

"Some stuff."

"Want to be more specific?"

"She doesn't . . . I didn't understand what she was saying. She was rambling about how she didn't know."

"Didn't know what?"

"I don't know exactly. It was hot in the room and she was all over the place and, Jesus, how long has she been like that?"

Brennan's grip on her coffee mug tightened. "Come on, Hunter. She was sick when you saw her . . . what? Last year?"

"She wasn't like this."

"You knew this is where she was going to end up. You left anyway."

"I had a job to do."

"So did I. And a marriage I was trying to save." The lie slid easily off her tongue because she wanted it to be true.

"For Christ's sake, don't fucking put that on me."

"You put her on me, Hunter. Do you have any idea what my life has been like?"

"Are we going to do this, Bren? Now?"

Brennan forced herself to relax her grip and to take a breath. She had to treat her brother like a difficult witness. "Let's try again. What didn't she know?"

"Whether he did it."

Brennan turned to directly face her brother. "Wait. She thinks he did it now?"

"No. I think she thinks he didn't do it now."

"She always thought that he didn't do it."

They stared at each other.

"Did she ever say that to you?" Hunter asked.

"Yes. No. She didn't have to say it. I just knew . . . She ever tell you that he did it?"

"In those words?"

"Any words."

Hunter tried to hold her gaze, to say she absolutely told him that his father had done it, but he couldn't think of when she did.

"I need to sit down," Brennan said. Hunter followed her to the kitchen table. For a moment, they both enjoyed the frigid air pouring in from the open window.

"When she's gone, it's just us," Brennan said.

Hunter sipped his coffee, looking over the lip of the cup at his sister. He never thought that they looked alike. Hunter resembled his father like one street in Midtown might look like any other, although each had completely different buildings. He could never identify a specific feature that matched the pictures of their dad. Brennan resembled their mother overall, yet certain of her features were strikingly reminiscent of their father: the color and texture of her hair, the set of her eyes, her smile. Sitting at the table, though, they mirrored each other, in the way they held their cups, brought them to their lips, and sipped, and the way they each retreated into their thoughts until the two feet between them may as well have been the distance between Battery Park and the Spuyten Duyvil.

"We both drink coffee like him," Brennan said. She remembered her dad, when they were kids, sitting at a table like they were, lost somewhere inside himself.

"I need something harder than coffee."

Hunter disappeared into the living room. A minute later, he returned with a bottle of Oban and two rocks glasses. He placed one in front of Brennan. They drank the first glass of scotch in silence.

"So," Brennan said, after the first sip of her second glass, "is the conclusion that she led us each to believe that she agreed with us?"

Hunter nodded. "Whenever we fought about it, she refused to take sides. I thought she just couldn't say it because of you."

"Me, too." Brennan swirled her scotch. "Why would she do that?"

"And was she saying tonight that she didn't remember what she actually believed anymore? Is that even possible? About something like that?"

"People can fool themselves into believing some crazy things. I prosecuted guys who came to believe their own lies. At least the foundational ones—like they were good guys or that they had no other options. I suppose that the opposite could be true, right? Convince yourself that you're uncertain about something."

Hunter took a substantial swig of the remaining scotch in his glass. "You still believe that he didn't do it?"

"Absolutely."

Hunter rolled his eyes. Brennan shook her head. "No. No, you don't get to do that to me."

"The only reason you believed that is because she told you he didn't do it."

"We just established that she never told either of us anything, so don't start this fight again. It drove us apart. It's kept us apart."

"That's your fault. You hated the fact that I didn't believe in the fairy tale you held on to."

"No. This is on you. You couldn't get past your anger and resented the fact that I could see the best in him."

"This was a mistake," he said, standing up.

"That's right. Run away. It's like we're kids again. You can't win a fight, so you run."

Hunter stared down at his sister, cheeks flushed from the heat or the scotch or his anger. Or all of them. He always hated how smug she was. And she could be really fucking smug. She had him trapped. If he stormed off, she'd know she was right. That he was a runner. And even though he was, and he knew he was, he was not going to give her the satisfaction.

"Fuck you. You're not any better than me."

Brennan raised her eyebrows. She fully expected him to storm off in a huff like the overgrown brat he had always been, yet he was sitting back down. But it was the last sentence that struck her.

"I never thought I was better than you."

Hunter shook his head but poured a splash more into their glasses.

"You had the luxury of faith," he said. "When people threw Dad in your face, you could just say, 'He didn't do it,' and hold your head up because you knew that he didn't do it. What could I do? I knew different. There's no comeback for 'Your dad's a murderer' when you think he did it. What can you say to that when he got away with it?"

"He didn't get away with it, Hunter. He got charged with someone else's crime."

"He never denied it."

"Are we really going to relitigate this now?"

"No," Hunter said, holding up a hand to placate her. "But did you ever investigate it, Bren? Try to prove yourself right?"

"When I was a prosecutor? No. Setting aside all of the other issues, it would have been a conflict of interest."

"Even on your own time? Like in law school or college?"

"No. Why would I? The jury acquitted him. Did you ever look to find evidence that would have convicted him?"

"He never denied it."

"Except for his not-guilty plea."

The minute hand moved a few ticks on the wall clock before Hunter broke the silence.

"He didn't deserve your faith in him."

"He did. And he deserved yours, too."

"If you really think he was innocent, you should have done something. Doesn't the victim—do you even remember her name?" He asked the question like a challenge. He remembered. Did she?

"Don't be an asshole. Jessica DeSalvo." She couldn't remember the first time she'd heard it. When she was a kid, every other Jessica brought her to mind until, over time, the commonness of the name desensitized her to it except for odd moments, like the time two months ago when a barista called the name at a Starbucks and Brennan thought, *Jessica was killed, and they blamed my father.* "I think about her. She never got justice. Someone went free because they accused our father of that crime."

"Then you should find the killer." Hunter said it flippantly. It had once been a sure way to make her storm off when she was a teenager, to sulk in her room at her impotence. Life wasn't a Nancy Drew book—teenage girls did not solve real-life murder mysteries. But Brennan wasn't a kid anymore.

"You should help."

They stared at each other across the table, waiting for the other to blink, to back down. Brennan broke the standoff by pouring more scotch—a conciliation, not a surrender.

"If you're serious, Hunter, then so am I. Don't we deserve to know the truth? Finally? Maybe it can give Mom some peace. More importantly, don't we owe it to Jessica DeSalvo?"

Hunter knew that truth was a currency the dead couldn't spend. People got killed. What did it matter to them if it was a lover or neighbor or the insurgents or the government or international forces? Hunter looked down at his glass, but there were no answers for his apostasy there.

"If I'm right," he said, "it means you were wrong your whole life. You going to be able to deal with that?"

"I don't know. But what about you?"

Hunter shrugged. Facing the thought that he may have been wrong about something so foundational was like trying to imagine being wrong about gravity.

"If I'm right," Brennan continued, "someone got away with her murder. You said it yourself, we should try."

Hunter shook his head. "This is a bad idea on so many levels. First, you and me do not work. We never worked. We work best when we're on different continents. Second, you'll have an agenda. You can't go into something like this thinking you know the answer. You'll bend the facts to fit your theory."

"I won't. But even if I did, you'll be there keeping me honest, right? Bending the facts to fit the story you want to write?"

"I don't bend facts."

"Neither do I when I investigate things." She was precise without thinking about it. A careful listener would have realized she was vulnerable to cross-examination on the specificity of her answer. *Well, when do you bend the facts? Other than with your family?* She thought of the last trial with Sean. She'd bent no facts; she'd made arguments. She hated that she made those distinctions.

"It wouldn't be ethical—in either of our professions—to cover our own dad's case. So what's the point?"

"The truth is the point. Isn't that why we both grew up to do what we did? Because we believed that the truth was something that deserved to be found?"

She spoke of truth like it was a religion, as if her faith in it excused her hypocrisy. Brennan was Catholic in that way—she believed in truth, but didn't practice it very well personally.

"That belief drove us apart, too. You think it's going to be different now?"

Brennan didn't respond.

"And what if you're right, Bren, and we find the murderer?"

"Turn 'em in? Who knows what we'll find?"

"And if I'm right, then what?"

"For a start, I'll go to Jessica's grave to lay some flowers and apologize. Take time and figure out if there's a way to make up for what he did." He supposed she meant it, but it came off like she was telling him she'd pay him a trillion dollars if he flapped his arms and flew himself to Europe. She didn't believe it was possible.

Hunter took a long sip from his glass. "Do you even have time for this?"

"I'll find it," she said. "And I know you have time."

Hunter snapped his mouth shut. He'd been about to say "I'm busy" without thinking. He'd always taken the opposite position from his sister, because if she was wrong about this one thing, then she was wrong about everything. But that approach hadn't left him anywhere that was ever the right place. "Fine. I just don't see what there is for us to do. The police. The DA's office. Everyone at the time thought it was him."

Brennan almost said that their mother didn't think that he did it, but she was no longer certain. She said, "People make mistakes."

"If we're going to do this, Bren, you have to promise me you'll come to it with an open mind."

"If you do, too."

Hunter nodded.

"Great. Where do we start?"

SEVEN

Now

AFTER HUNTER LEFT, BRENNAN PEEKED IN ON HER MOM. IT may as well have been a photograph of any other night from the past few years. Brennan never knew if she was breathing; the covers were so thick, they didn't stir. But she didn't check. Was it because she didn't want to wake her or because she'd rather find that her mother had passed with sunlight streaming through the narrow sliver she left in the curtains? Why even undertake the exercise of going to her mom's place if she didn't check? More questions Brennan couldn't answer.

Like Hunter's: "Where do we start?"

"I don't know," she had said. Then, like a good lawyer, "Let me think about it."

He said he'd give it some thought, too, but she knew she'd have to make the plans.

Brennan crept into the second bedroom her mother used as an office before she'd given up—before her illness kept her from working. She pulled a set of pajamas from the drawer she'd taken over and tossed her clothes into a laundry basket tucked into the corner. She had trouble keeping the location of her clothes straight, so much had gotten split between her place and her mom's.

Where to start investigating? Thirty years later, three drinks into the night—no, four drinks, she'd poured herself another after Hunter left—the question was overwhelming. They'd taunted each other for decades with the same arguments. She didn't expect anything to be different tonight. Except it had been. Brennan told herself to start with the basics: Who, what, when, where, why?

Brennan pulled a pillow out of the closet along with the spare set of sheets and blanket. Her mother didn't have a bed for guests. Why hadn't Brennan just purchased an inflatable mattress or cot for the office? Why pretend that her mother would magically recover and need her office again for work?

She remembered a day her parents took her to the park. They'd gone with their neighbors and their son. Brennan didn't remember their names. Hunter must have been there, too, but she didn't remember him, only the neighbor boy. The boy challenged her to a race—some tree in the distance and back. She kept pace most of the way, but he was a year older and she was in sandals, and when he passed her laughing on his return leg after touching the tree, she stopped running.

She walked back to where her parents stood. Her father waited for her apart from the others. Her face burned with frustration. She held her arms out to him—she'd never wanted anyone to pick her up so badly—but he stopped her with a hand on her shoulder and met her eyes.

"It wasn't fair," she started.

"Life's not fair."

"He's bigger. I couldn't beat him."

"Doesn't matter. Stop talking and listen." He waited until she wiped a hand across her eyes, then continued. "Maybe you couldn't win. But you will lose every single race you stop running. Do you understand me?"

She nodded.

"You're the big sister. You need to set an example for your brother. I don't want to see you quit ever again."

Her embarrassment metastasized to shame.

Her father stood up and walked back to the other adults, the mass of his disappointment generating a gravity that pulled her along after him.

Brennan settled onto her mother's couch, the weight of the memory and whiskey pressing down on her chest. She reached up to switch the lamp off, telling herself the heat in her cheeks was the alcohol and not the flush from his rebuke decades before.

Why that memory? And why now? Her father had been full of hugs and kisses, Brennan recalled. So many, she couldn't remember any one in particular, just the comfort of all of them at once. Even the last kiss he'd given her was indistinct. All she knew for certain was he'd whispered something to her like "I'll see you again" while he held her. Maybe. The memory was so ephemeral, she worried that she'd dreamed it as a child, that it never occurred. But the hug she lost that day in the park, down to the feel of the plastic sandals on her feet, was as real to her as the blanket she lay under.

After he was gone, Brennan would lie in bed wondering whether, if she had just held him longer or harder or said some magic words, she could have kept him there. She made mystical bargains with herself all through school. *If I get an A on this test, I'll see him again. If I just finish this last mile, he'll be waiting for me.* His failure to return hadn't dissuaded her. *One more hour on this essay, that's what will do it.*

"Why, though?" Hunter had shouted at her one day when they were teens. He stood in the doorway of her room—her father's old office. She stood on a chair, hanging a photo she'd found of her father, probably taken while he was in law school. She climbed off the chair and shut the door in his face. She didn't have an answer for him other than that, when she looked at the picture, she remembered that he loved her the best that he could, which was more than she could say about her brother or her mom, who somehow rode her all the time even though she was always at work. And the only thing he'd asked of her was that she not fucking quit trying to accomplish whatever task she started.

Even now, tucked into her mother's couch, she understood that she'd devoted years of her adulthood, her entire career, trying to accomplish the same spells she'd attempted as a little girl. *If I can win this case, help do this little bit of justice, he'll see that I didn't quit and I'll see him again.* And now, tonight, with Hunter. *If I can prove he was innocent, Hunter can love him again, and he'll come back.* The fact that it wasn't possible didn't stop her from striking the bargain with whatever devil might be listening in the dark of her heart moments before sleep took her.

#

The woman had a devil tattooed on one shoulder, an angel on the other. The devil—a voluptuous red figure—curled herself around a pitchfork, one leg raised suggestively. The angel sat, hands bound before him, gag tied into his mouth, wings pulled around his shoulders like a blanket.

"Which one do you listen to?" Hunter asked.

The woman pulled her black hair behind an ear as she cocked her head to look at him. They were the only two people left in the bar, except for the bartender, a twentysomething so generic looking he probably couldn't pick himself out of a lineup.

"Sorry," she said. "I'll never tell."

Hunter nodded. Another mystery he'd never know the answer to. He hated not knowing things. Who murdered the Notorious B.I.G.? What was the explanation for spooky action at a distance? Where was D. B. Cooper, who hijacked a plane in the 1970s before parachuting out over Washington state with two hundred thousand dollars in cash? When would the Knicks win a championship? Why had he agreed to help his sister investigate a murder when he already knew who did it?

By the time Hunter returned from his mother's place, the streets looked like some ice monster had puked a rancid mix of dirty water, slush, and dog-piss snow all over the city. But when he opened the door to his apartment, the emptiness was worse. So he turned around and made his way to the first bar he could find and stayed until last call. He didn't want to clear his head as much as flood it with enough stimuli that it would suffocate everything he didn't want to think about.

Another failure, though. The bartender collected the signed bill and slid his credit card back to him. Hunter stood and fought his way into his coat. On the trek back to his apartment, doing his best to avoid slipping into filthy puddles, he remembered the aftermath of a snowstorm, walking with his family to Central Park.

The sidewalks had been mostly cleared, and snow piled on the curbside against the doors of the parked cars as high as the windows. Hunter was small enough that they were taller than him. At the time, it felt like he was in the Arctic.

The path they were on crossed over another running perpendicular. Snow covered the rails of the overpass in a long crest five inches high. Brennan scooped up two fistfuls of snow in her mittens, molded them into a snowball, and was about to throw it when their father grabbed her arm and shook his head. Brennan frowned and dropped the snowball. Their parents walked farther down the path, off the overpass, before stopping, backs turned. Their mom pointed to something in the distance until their father stopped to look at it.

Brennan trudged after for a few steps before returning to the railing. She glanced over to their parents and then shoved the piled snow off the railing. A loud "What the fuck?" boomed from below, amplified by the tunnel under the overpass. Brennan jumped back from the rail before their parents turned. Their father strode toward them, an approaching avalanche.

Brennan turned to Hunter. "Tell him the wind blew it down."

Their father bore down on them. "What did you do?"

Brennan was silent.

Hunter said, "I think it was the wind."

Their father looked around, then turned to Brennan. "Go wait with your mother."

Brennan ran.

When she was gone, his father bent at the waist and tilted Hunter's chin up, so he had to look him in the eyes. It was the last place Hunter wanted to look.

"That is a dumb fucking lie, Hunter. Look at the railing. No other snow is gone except where your sister was. She asked you to lie for her, didn't she?"

Hunter would have nodded, except his father's hand was lifting his chin, so instead he said, "Yes," in a voice with no breath behind it.

"I want you to listen to me. We do not lie in this family. We don't lie to each other. We don't lie for each other. We are not liars."

His father increased the pressure under his chin. "You're a boy now, right?"

Again, Hunter said, "Yes."

"And you want to be a man, right?"

"Yes."

"Good men do not lie. Do you understand me?"

"Yes."

"And you're my son. My son is not a fucking liar."

"I won't lie again."

"You're fucking right. If you do, and I catch you, I'll throw you off this fucking bridge, do you understand me?"

Hunter desperately blinked. He didn't want his father to see him cry. If he spoke, he'd bawl. But he couldn't nod with his head tilted so far back the top of his coat zipper dug into his throat. The cold seeping through his wet gloves and boots ran into his veins, and his tears froze in his eyes, and he said, "Yes."

His father took his hand away. Something in his face changed. The anger and disappointment directed at Hunter was gone. No, actually, it was still there. Hunter felt it inside his father—it was just muted, a door closed on a burning room.

Entering his lobby decades later, the cold air chased Hunter in like a ghost. This was the man Brennan was trying to redeem? As he waited for the elevator, Hunter decided to leave her to her delusions. He didn't owe his father anything. Or her. Or his mother. What comfort would certainty bring her in the time she had left?

He fumbled with his keys through the locks on his apartment door, distracted by the thought that Brennan wouldn't let him live it down if he backed out. They'd probably go years without speaking, until on his deathbed, she'd bring the whole thing up again. She had him by the chin, same as their dad did. When the devil on his shoulder spoke, it was with his father's voice. *We don't lie to each other. We don't lie for each other.* How could he not blame Brennan for lying to herself for her father? If he could prove his father did it, he could finally show her the fucking truth. It wasn't his fault—it was hers. It was a mean, savage thought, but imagining the moment was euphoric. His heart thundered in his chest.

He waited for the angel's counterpoint. When she spoke, it was his mother's voice from earlier, muffled and weak, but they were words from his childhood. She'd pulled him aside as a teenager one night when he'd gotten home after leaving the apartment in a rage because Brennan hung a picture of their father in her room and slammed the door in his face when he'd asked why. "It's not her fault she loves him." The night his mother said those words to him, he'd retreated to his room without responding, turning off his lights and ignoring the tapping at his door until his mother gave up. He would not accept that it wasn't Brennan's fault for loving him—otherwise, wasn't it his fault for not loving him? But even now, even drunk, there was nowhere to run from their mother's voice in his head—"It's not her fault she loves him"—so he lay, too warm under his covers, hoping sleep would claim him before she spoke again.

EIGHT

Then

JOHN STEADIED HIS HANDS AS HE READ THE TERM SHEET. HE expected the outcome when Walter told him that they preferred to meet him outside the office. But the terms of the firm's offer were insulting. He placed the paper on the table in front of him.

"No," John said.

Geoff, the firm's managing partner, blinked once behind his thick glasses. His bushy eyebrows furrowed. His mouth, a permanent frown, didn't move.

Walter leaned forward. "John, think about the good of the firm. You know you can't come back."

John didn't take his eyes off Geoff. "This is insulting. My share of the firm is worth three to four times this amount."

"John," Geoff cut in. He spoke slowly, with great authority. "You slept with an associate. Who was murdered. We could force you out. But that won't be the end of it. We can sue you for damages. Take everything you have."

John didn't look away. There had been a time for John when the only acceptable thing for him to say to Geoff was "Yes, Mr. Moore," and later, after he made partner, "Yes, Geoff."

Geoff was the age John's father would have been if he hadn't died while John was in law school. There were two times in John's life he remembered his father expressing satisfaction—pride was an overstatement—with him: the day he graduated college and the day he got into law school. John knew that was because it meant that his life would be better than his father's. That he wouldn't have to work in some restaurant kitchen, live in a shitty apartment, deal with the indignity of being a human water pipe—something everyone needed and nobody ever paid attention to. Things they buried in the walls and in the ground.

That's what he'd been at the firm, toiling away in his office, trotted out to clients to render an opinion on an obscure Treasury regulation. John dreamed of the day when he might be a peer of the firm's elite, the rainmakers, when they would bring him onto deals or refer matters to him. When he wouldn't be subject to the whims of an opaque compensation committee that paid Walter more even though he billed fewer hours at a lower rate than John. When he didn't have to chuckle with a small bow of his head when Geoff quipped, "Got in late, huh? Was there a sale on dog meat?" or with Alan every time he asked him to "whip up some chow mein" when they worked past dinner. Even in those fantasies, John hadn't imagined being in a position where defiance was an option.

Even now, at this shitty wooden table in the room that Walter arranged through the bar association so that John wouldn't be seen walking into the firm's offices or dining with them at the Down Town Association or the Harvard Club, the inculcated hierarchy pressed at the back of John's head, telling him that the emasculation was a gift—because the scraps of the firm's bounty were better than the alternative. John had no doubt that these men—and the lone woman—who had been his partners would be willing to do what Geoff threatened, whether for the good of the firm or to keep Geoff from turning on them.

"Geoff, there is nothing you can do or threaten that would be worse than what I've already gone through." John hurled each word out—not in anger, but in the way a man bails out a sinking boat. "More to the point, you didn't make me partner because I'm an idiot or because I roll over. How many associates and secretaries have you fucked and fired or paid off? I know of at least three women in my years at the firm. How many before then? I'm not a trial lawyer, but I can't imagine a jury is going to like that."

An eyebrow rose on Geoff's otherwise-stone face. John felt lighter, reckless. He wanted to crumple the term sheet up and throw it at Geoff, but then the deal would never get done. Instead, he slid the paper across the table.

"I won't ever sign something like this."

"You won't get this deal again," Geoff said.

"You're right. It will be higher."

John stood to walk out of the room. As he did, blood rushed to his head in a wave, forcing his consciousness up and out of his body. He banished every other thought to get out of the room without collapsing. The sensation was like being carried on the swell of a wave. In the hallway, after the conference room door closed behind him, he braced himself with a hand against a marble column.

He was halfway down the block before he realized he didn't know where he was going. Then Walter appeared with a light tap on his arm. John turned slowly. Walter was slightly winded.

"You didn't run after me, did you?" John had a hard time imagining Walter running and possibly scuffing his shoes.

"I walked very quickly."

"Where's Geoff?"

"In a car headed back to the office."

"You guys had it wait? Thought it would be an in-and-out meeting? That I'd kneel that fast?"

Walter sighed. "It wasn't like that."

John started walking again. Walter followed.

"I'm trying to get you a fair deal, John."

"So, what happened, Walt? Between that fair deal and what you just handed me?"

Walter huffed but stayed even with John. They passed an Irish pub.

"How about a drink?" Walter asked.

It was 11:00 a.m., but John followed Walter inside anyway.

Cigarette smoke diffused the daylight streaming in from the windows. The bartender was a heavy white-haired guy with rolled-up sleeves, a faded dagger tattoo stark against the pale skin of his forearm. John and Walter sat in beaten wooden stools and ordered martinis.

"You going to be able to work after this?" John asked.

"I'm drunk half the day now, anyway. This is just taking the edge off."

"So what do you want, Walt?"

"I want to know how you're doing. We haven't talked."

"We're not going to talk. If you wanted to get me drunk, have me make admissions or whatever you think you're going to get out of this conversation, you should have tried before you gave me terms."

"I didn't give you terms. Those were the firm's terms."

"You just carried them."

"I came so you would have a friendly face in the room."

Walter did not have a friendly face on his best days. But he and John had met their first day at the firm. John stood out as the sole minority in a room of twenty new lawyers. Walter looked like a guy who picked his nose. They weren't ignored as much as politely shunted to one side by the others.

"I'm telling you this as your friend, John. Geoff and the executive committee want your blood. The firm took a hit."

"Profits were up this year. Fifth consecutive year."

"I'm not talking about money. They had to apologize for you. To the clients. To the associates. To their spouses when they went home to questions like, 'How many of your partners are having affairs? Are you having an affair?'"

"You're boring me, Walt. What's the point? I don't give a shit about Geoff's fucked-up marriage or what he told Manhattan Trust. And the associates all know you'd drink their blood if it made you a buck. Geoff, the firm, you—you all fucking hung me out there."

"You were accused of murder."

"Before, Walt. Before that."

Walter turned away, looking through the window to the street. "I don't know what you're talking about."

"You're sticking with that?"

"Why did you have to sleep with her, John? Couldn't you have just, I don't know, found one of those Asian places?"

"Was it that we were having an affair or that she was white?"

Walter rolled his eyes. "Jesus, John. You're not Black."

"You think Geoff sees any shades past Greek?"

"He's not going to move off that offer."

"I want my fair share. That's all. This money means a lot more to me than it means to the firm, so the firm loses more than it gains by lowballing me and pissing me off. And whatever Geoff thinks he can take away from me, remember how much more you all stand to lose."

"Geoff doesn't lose."

"Anything else?" John asked, standing up.

"Remember I'm your friend," Walter said. "I'm trying to get you to a good place here. You're making a mistake."

On the street, John fully pulled off his tie and let it dangle, both the fat and skinny ends on equal footing for once.

NINE

Then

JOHN SAT ON THE BENCH IN CENTRAL PARK, FIGURING HE was close enough to an exit that he wouldn't get mugged. The daylight and foot traffic helped with that, too. In any event, the only thing he had on him was the newspaper he pretended to read so he wouldn't look homeless. He hadn't shaved in a week, and his hair was a greasy mess. He wore jeans and a T-shirt, forgotten since his law school days.

Locals and tourists strolled past him, enjoying the pleasant weather. Jane had more or less demanded that he "take a walk." He hadn't left the apartment in a week. There was a burst of productivity the first weekend after receiving the firm's insulting offer. John made a list of things to do while he figured out his next steps. He tightened loose knobs, cleaned behind and underneath furniture, rummaged through the kids' clothes to set aside stuff that no longer fit and socks without mates. Jane didn't notice that the pull on the bathroom cabinet didn't jiggle and that there wasn't any dust underneath the couch—or, if she did, she didn't comment on it. The kids were oblivious to the sudden spaciousness in their drawers. And the principal on the mortgage was exactly the same. The next day, John crumpled his to-do list into a ball, threw it in a corner, turned on the TV, and watched the morning game shows. After *The Price Is Right*, the soaps started running, and he tried those, too, but after the first hour on the second day, he turned them off and didn't go back. Each day seemed endless.

At first, Brennan tried to engage with him when she got home after school. She asked him to read with her. She cuddled up to him as he lay on the couch staring at the rerun of some show with the sound turned off. She pulled out old board games and set them up, putting pieces out for John. Each time, he said, "Not today."

Hunter occupied himself in whatever room John wasn't in.

Jane was barely home. If she managed to make it home from the office before the kids were in bed, she read to them until she fell asleep mid-story in whichever child's bed she was visiting. Sometime in the night, she would wake and pass John—sleeping on the couch—on her way to the bedroom. If she was too late to catch the kids awake, she would take whatever work she carried home with her to the bedroom, set it out on the side of the bed where John used to sleep, and work until she passed out. After five days without a word passed between them, John wondered if it was some kind of game they were playing. Whatever it was, he knew that he had lost the same way a chess master knew five moves ahead how the game would ultimately resolve itself. But he needed to play it through, so he didn't say anything.

As the weekend approached, John grew anxious. With no school or work, it would be the four of them, with no apparent agenda or plans. But Jane left with the kids Saturday morning while John was sleeping. He woke to find a note on the kitchen table scrawled on yellow legal paper: *Took the kids to my mom's for the weekend. Back Sunday night.*

He managed to make it through the weekend eating the remaining Cheerios (good for four bowls), some boxed mac and cheese, and a mealy apple. He drank the last of the scotch. There were some eggs in the fridge he could have cooked, but he didn't have the appetite. On Sunday evening, he heard the elevator door slide open and Jane and the kids chatting and laughing as they stepped into the hall, their noise growing fainter as they approached. They opened the door in silence. Only Brennan came to greet him, a silent hug before she brushed her teeth and crawled into bed. He didn't see Hunter at all, only heard him go through his pre-bed routine from the couch.

When Jane walked to their bedroom after the kids were asleep, John was awake on the couch watching the local news.

She stopped in the doorway of their bedroom.

"You need to take a walk tomorrow. You can't just sit here all day. And clean yourself up. You look like shit. You're scaring the kids."

She shut the bedroom door behind her.

Sitting in daylight the next day, unread newspaper rolled in his hand, John supposed that he should feel ashamed or angry—or something. Something other than like he was an archaeologist studying himself from some other time, reconstructing whatever lost society the ruins of his life reflected. Jessica's murder, his arrest, and the trial were thousands of years of dust, wind, and rain erasing what had come before; his memories of those times were ocher pictographs drawn on cave walls.

An old man sat at the opposite end of the bench from him, resting his lacquered cane between his legs. He was dressed in black rubber-soled shoes, earth-colored pants, a dark blue windbreaker despite the heat, and a herringbone flat cap. There were four other benches within ten feet the old man could have taken.

"You reading that paper?" the old man asked.

John wordlessly passed the man his paper.

"I read it every day, you know." The old man flipped through the pages. "All of the local papers. Don't even have to pay for them mostly. Just wander through the park. People leave them out. In the winter, it's too cold. So I go to the diner. People leave them there. For other people."

John nodded, waiting for a break so he could walk away without offending the man.

"Let me ask you something." The old man turned fully to John. "Was she worth it?"

"What?" John asked before he registered that he understood very well what the old man was asking.

"Was she worth it?"

"I don't know what you mean."

"I know who you are. From the papers."

John said nothing and looked the other way, hoping the old man would leave him be.

"I mean, the way the papers tell it, you had everything a guy could want. Pretty wife. Two kids. Big job. Was it—

#

—worth it?" Jessica asked, after their first kiss and again, later. But before that, they had been at the firm Christmas party.

"That memo was short." She wore a red gown, carrying a sidecar in one hand, a small black clutch in the other. He had provided advice over the course of two months regarding a tax issue in a case on which she was the senior associate, culminating in a memorandum he circulated to her the day before.

"I don't get paid by the word," John said. He was standing in line at the bar, waiting to order another scotch. The stiff collar of his tuxedo shirt chafed his neck.

"Yeah, but we get paid by the hour."

"It takes more time to make them short."

"But it was shorter than Michelle's skirt," she said, looking around for Michelle.

John pointed to a far corner where Michelle was wedged between Geoff and another senior partner, Alan. She was packed into a little black dress and sipping from a cocktail glass. She took a small step and stumbled slightly. Geoff's arm came up to steady her, then slid down to the small of her back.

"Does she even know how she looks?" Jessica asked.

"In that dress?"

"In that dress. In those heels. Stumbling around with Geoff's hand on her ass."

"It's not on her ass."

"It's damned close."

"Do you want me to go over there?"

"And what? Tell your boss to stop playing grab-ass with a girl who I'm sure actually cornered him?"

"He's my partner. Not my boss."

She laughed at him, so even though he was the next in line for a drink, he abandoned his spot and walked over to where Geoff's hand now casually rested on the upper curve of Michelle's ass. The two partners were talking across her as if they didn't notice her, except that both kept taking long looks down the front of her dress. Neither turned to regard John as he approached.

"Merry Christmas, Geoff," John said, reaching out. Geoff took his hand off Michelle's ass to shake John's hand.

"I didn't know the Chinese celebrated Christmas," Alan said.

"Haven't you received my cards? I send them every year."

"Yes. Of course. I just thought you were extending a courtesy. Or your wife sent them. How is she?"

"She's well. I'll tell her you said hello, Alan. Speaking of which, how's Barbara, Geoff?"

Geoff stared long at John before turning to Michelle and saying, "She's with her parents in Florida for the holidays."

Michelle took a sip of her martini.

"Oh, look! Michelle, you're almost out," John said. "And me, too. Want to take a walk and get another? Maybe a glass of water?"

"No," she said. "I'm sure Geoff can get someone to bring me one when I want another."

"Sure thing." John wished them a merry Christmas as he turned to go. He was two steps away when Geoff called out to him. John turned.

"John, when you get your drink, bring us back a round of martinis, will you?"

John stalked back to the bar. Jessica was gone. He didn't see her again until he left the party after bringing Geoff, Michelle, and Alan their drinks. She stood outside, close to a wall to light a cigarette. She glanced at the glass in his hand.

"You can't just leave with that."

"Nobody's stopping me. You have another one of those?"

She fished a cigarette out of the pack in her clutch and handed it over to him.

"That was a really stupid thing you did there," she said, after lighting his cigarette.

John shrugged. He undid his bow tie and unbuttoned his collar. "Fuck him. What's he going to do to me?"

"I don't know. Mess with your career?"

They finished their cigarettes in silence while John sipped his scotch.

"Are you headed home?" she asked.

"Back to the office. I left my briefcase there."

"Me, too. Walk together?"

They walked the fifteen blocks back to the office, stopping once for John to toss his empty glass into a bin and to light new cigarettes. When they reached the office, Jessica rode the elevator to his floor and followed him to his office.

"Isn't your office on twenty?" John asked.

"I wanted to see yours." She walked around the office as he shoved papers into his briefcase. She picked up a framed picture from his desk. "Are these your kids?"

"I hope so." He laughed and took the picture from her hands. Brennan and Hunter, in front of a blue backdrop at some photo studio that Jane had taken them to, sitting back-to-back, heads turned to grin at the camera. Hunter's grin was full of missing and half-grown teeth. John's heart swelled with boozy sentiment.

Jessica picked up another picture, a black-and-white print. "Your wife?"

"Yeah," he said. "I took this when we were in law school."

"She's beautiful."

"She's amazing."

"She's still a lawyer, too? She's not home with the kids?"

"You know a lot about me."

Jessica laughed. "Walter told me earlier, at the Christmas party. I thought it was impressive—that she kept working."

"What about you? Are you quitting when you have a kid?"

"I don't know. I can't imagine ever being a mom." She sat in one of the chairs facing his desk.

"Why not?"

"I don't want to stop drinking or smoking." She pulled out her pack of cigarettes. "Another?"

"Sure. Just close the door so people don't complain." He turned to open his window. John's view was only the building across the street. The good offices—with open views of the harbor—were on the other side of the building, but it didn't matter at night. With the dark outside, the window reflected his office. He turned a knob, opening a pane outward at head height, which allowed enough clearance for a good breeze to enter, but not enough for a man to throw himself out. John set an ashtray out.

Jessica closed the door, then came to stand next to him. As they smoked, winter air gusted through the window. John loved the cold on the heated flush in his cheeks. As he extinguished his cigarette in the ashtray, Jessica shivered next to him.

"Are you okay?"

"Yes," she said, crushing her cigarette out in the ashtray, next to John's.

"Why did you take your coat off if you were going to be cold?"

She reached up and pulled John's face down to hers. John was surprised but didn't hesitate. She pressed her body into his. She kept one hand on his head, holding it to hers; the other slid down to his chest. He pulled her closer. Euphoria beyond any alcohol or drug he had sampled filled him like helium, and he floated, swaying in the breeze from the window. When the kiss broke, Jessica left her hands where they were. John found his right hand on her hip and the left covering her hand on his chest. Her engagement ring stabbed into his palm; she wore a slim gold wedding band next to it.

She looked at his wedding band, then up into his eyes. "Is this worth it?"

He bent down to kiss her again. The sensation of floating returned. A beautiful emptiness—a return to something primal, beyond any rationality—enveloped him. Jessica pulled her hand out from under his and thrust it into his pants. He crashed back into his body, the beginning of an avalanche throwing them both down. She undid his pants as they kissed. She turned around to face their reflections in the window as John raised the skirt of her gown and pulled her underwear down. He entered her with a relief full of regret, a momentary fear, nearly blind with despair. A suicide. Jessica guided him to a place where he couldn't resist anymore. They made eye contact in the window before coming, one after the other. When John finally withdrew, it was like leaving a river after a baptism. Refreshed. Reborn.

After, as she leaned against his desk to pull her underwear back on, she smiled at him.

#

The memory of that night evaporated from John like a sheen of sweat. Jessica was gone. *Dead*, he corrected.

The old man waited for him to answer. John's lip curled, a half sneer. He stood and walked away without looking back, as directly into the park as he could manage, without regard for direction. He came upon the bridle path and followed it south. Rough gray clay crunched underneath his feet. No one else was on the path, although he could see people walking on the footpath to his right and jogging along the reservoir berm above him to the left.

He stopped walking, looked around at the path as if it would trigger a memory of where he was headed, but he knew that there was no point to it. The path didn't lead anywhere.

TEN

Now

HUNTER LET THE DOOR SWING SHUT BEHIND HIM WITHOUT checking to see if anyone noticed he'd been dragged into the restroom by the woman he'd met sitting at the bar two hours ago. He stopped to latch the door, fumbling briefly with his left hand. She tugged on his right, pulling him toward the wall opposite the door. Her hands slipped off his, and she stumbled backward with a giggle. Amy. That was her name. He told himself to remember it.

He brushed her curls out of her face before kissing her. Amy worked with kids. Not a teacher, an occupational therapist. She'd had to explain to him what her job entailed. She thought he was lying to her about being a reporter. "War correspondent sounds like a fake job," she had said.

"I'm not lying to you," he said into her mouth. He couldn't be sure if he was pressing her into the wall or she was trying to pull him through it.

"Huh?" Her lips slid to the ridge of his jaw, hung there like a drop of water, before running down the slope of his neck.

"About being a reporter." He needed her to understand. There was no one else to talk to about it.

She guided his hand to her breast and raised her mouth back to his. She reached down and grabbed his cock. He'd been about to say something *(I go where I'm told, to do work I don't believe in anymore. But I'm on a leave of absence. Whatever that means.)* but she *(Amy. Not a teacher.)* moaned into his mouth.

He shoved her shirt up so that the rough lace of her bra was directly underhand. She unbuttoned her jeans.

"I never do this," she said. "You can't tell my friends."

He tried to remember if she'd been at the bar alone or broken off from a group to talk to him. He'd been drinking alone, the Knicks game his only company before she'd bumped shoulders with him at the bar.

"You can tell whoever you want," he said before dipping his head to her chest. "I have no friends."

"How do you have no friends?" she asked absently as she worked on his belt with one hand.

He raised his head. It was like swimming underwater in fast-forward; the temporal and spatial disconnect nearly sent him reeling backward. Only the tether created by her hand reaching down his pants kept him on his feet.

"I have colleagues. Acquaintances. Sources. Bosses. But there's no one close."

Amy pressed a finger against his lips, then ran her hands to his hips and pushed his pants down far enough for gravity to complete the job.

She brought her mouth to his ear, draping his face with her curls. Her lower lip caressed the lobe, warm breath spilling across it, and she said, "For the next few minutes, let me get close."

#

Brennan and Sean lay in his bed, facing each other, nude and slightly sweaty. The room was dark, illuminated only by ambient light sneaking through the curtained window. Sean idly caressed her shoulder, her hip, her arm, in a lazy, looping tour of her body.

"Stay," he said. "My wife and kids are at our place in Vermont until next weekend. We have the whole place to ourselves."

"I can't."

"You don't have anyone to go home to."

"No."

"Then stay."

Brennan turned onto one elbow. The movement disrupted Sean's wandering hand. She looked down at him, and the familiar wave of regret came over her. After they had sex, everything about him became too much. His smile was grotesque in its exaggerated warmth. His hair, askew, revealed a slightly thinning hairline. She noticed the sharp scent of his perspiration and the faint odor of onions from dinner on his breath.

"I have a meeting at nine tomorrow." She wasn't meeting Hunter until eleven. But the lie was easier than telling him that she didn't want to wake up with him. "I can't stay here, then run home to shower and change."

He rolled onto his back and pouted. It wasn't a good look for him. Not for the first time, she imagined the petulant monster he must have been growing up as an only child in Westchester. Still, she fell for it, feeling like she was throwing a dollar on the worst bet at the craps table. Small stupidities in the face of bad odds. She put her hand on his shoulder, then ran it down the length of his torso.

"Just because I can't stay, doesn't mean I have to leave right away."

He shook his head. "If you have to go, then go."

"Come on, Sean. You don't have to be like that about it."

"Like what?"

"Like a spoiled kid."

"If I wanted someone to call me spoiled, I'd be in Vermont with my wife."

"If I wanted a clingy little boy, I'd let Paul come home."

Sean pushed himself up into a sitting position. He held his anger in his jaw and lips, like the entire bottom half of his face was compressing.

The glossy, processed magazine-spread version of Sean was gone. It was the driver's license version now, all unflattering angles and bad lighting. This part of him was hers, something secret that only his wife knew—maybe. From the way Sean talked about it, she had stopped seeing him years earlier as anything other than a to-do list. So now it was Brennan's alone, the first real emotion Sean had experienced all day.

"Look, I'm sorry. I'm going through some things with my mom. And my brother." Brennan paused before she went on, noting that her husband no longer made the list of things that merited mention as something that was on her mind. "It's been a long couple of days."

"You have a brother?"

"I told you that."

"You've never mentioned him. Seriously."

"He's never around."

"What's going on?"

"My mother is dying. It's close now."

"Why didn't you say something? How long has she been sick?"

She rolled onto her back so she could stare at the ceiling instead of looking him in the face. "She's been sick as long as I've known you. It's not your problem."

He placed his hand on her shoulder.

"Bren," he said, "whatever we're doing, whatever this is, I care about you. You can talk to me."

"I don't know what there is to say. She's dying. My brother came back to town to be here for it."

"You guys aren't close?"

"It's complicated."

"That's my specialty."

She rolled her eyes and swung her legs over the edge of the bed, letting them pull her up to a sitting position.

"Honestly, you don't have to pretend to be interested. And I don't want to dwell on it."

"Okay, whatever. I'm not going to tell you your business. But I'm here."

She collected her clothing, one article at a time, and dressed. He watched her, covered partially by a gathered sheet. A thin black sweater was the last thing she slipped on, standing by the foot of the bed. She pulled her hair free of the neck of the sweater. They waited, separated by the length of the bed, for the other to speak first.

Brennan wondered if Sean's wife dressed like this, up early to take the kids to school, while he sat in his bed, typing away on his phone answering work emails. Did his wife pause, at the foot of the bed, to share some secret before leaving him there, before he put his work mask on? Was it something true—her fear that her daughter wasn't going to be as smart as they were, the crush she was developing on one of the dads from school, her anxiety that their whole life together was a massive mistake? Or was their only intimacy the clipping of fingernails, scummy hair in the drain, the smell of each other's shit? Regardless, all of that started with talking and listening.

"I gotta go, Sean."

"Like I said, I'm here if you want to talk. You look like you want to talk."

"I don't. I want to go home."

He nodded and reached for his phone. Brennan let herself out.

#

Brennan let herself into her apartment. The ambient streetlight from the windows, electronic clocks on the cable boxes and appliances, and pinpoint power indicators on various devices scattered about the apartment ensured it never got truly dark. And the muted hum of the city and whisper of the refrigerator—broken occasionally by a car horn or the ice maker dumping cubes into the freezer tub—constituted the best silence she could achieve without noise-canceling headphones.

Paul used to be there when she got home, set up at his desk working, on the couch playing video games, or asleep in their bed, blankets thrown askew as if he weren't the stillest sleeper Brennan had ever known. The conversations, assuming he was awake, were always the same.

"What's up?" he would ask.

"Nothing," she would say, whether she was dragging herself in from an eighteen-hour day of trial preparation or from getting trashed at whatever bar she found herself in or if she had just fucked Sean or any of the other guys from the affairs she had before him. They might go days without more conversation. She didn't mind.

She pulled her boots off without turning the lights on. She knew where everything was, even in the dark. It had been her apartment before Paul moved in. It remained her apartment after they separated. Even when they had lived together, she always felt that he was a guest who had overstayed his welcome, an intruder, a mouse scurrying underfoot.

She threw her coat over the easy chair in the living room as she walked past to the bathroom. It finally felt clean again, clear of Paul's beard clippings, pomades, toothbrush, and floss.

"Do you miss everything in here on purpose?" she had asked one morning after Paul got out of the shower.

"What?"

She answered by pointing to the Q-tip lying on the floor next to the garbage can.

"Oh my God." He gave an overly dramatic eye roll that she used to think was cute, but that now reeked of femininity.

"Yesterday, it was your floss."

"Seriously? This is what we're doing?"

"There's piss on the floor next to the toilet where you fucking dripped. Can't you wipe it up?" She pointed to the marks on the floor, spatters barely visible on the gray tile.

"You're kidding, right? How do you know it was me?"

"I don't stand when I pee." Leaving the bathroom, she added, "Clean it."

Another year passed before he left. Even gone for six months now, he hung around like a stale cigarette odor. It wasn't only the random shit of his that turned up—like a pair of his socks buried in a drawer. His absence was a phantom limb. She felt it in the way she crept through her apartment in the dark, like he was sleeping. She forced herself to leave the bathroom door open as she brushed her teeth, the buzz of her electric toothbrush a mosquito in her ear.

Finished with her bedtime routine, she climbed into bed and checked her phone. It was early enough that, if she fell asleep, she might actually get a fair amount of rest. She shut her eyes, spreading her arms and legs out in the bed, stretching across the expanse unimpeded by Paul or Sean or anybody else. The night Paul left, she relished occupying his side of the bed. Every night since, she stretched out across it, a flat plane of space-time without gravity, the sheets cool without the warmth of his body.

Her phone was still in her hand. She wanted it to vibrate with a message. She didn't care whether it was a text from Sean or a work email or an Amber Alert. But it was still, and she didn't sleep, but lay there in the solitude of her bed, an astronomer studying the constellations of her worries.

#

Hunter waited until his thighs hit the edge of his mattress before collapsing onto it, inching forward across the covers until his face found his pillow. He pushed himself onto his back and reconsidered putting the girl into a cab at the bar. Annie, the schoolteacher. He was confident of those details. After she'd dropped his pants, she asked him if he had a condom. He didn't, so he got her off with his fingers as she whispered instructions into his ear between kisses with her hand wrapped around his cock. Between concentrating on her and how drunk he was, he knew he wouldn't come from a hand job—although there was a moment during her orgasm when Annie's head was thrown back into a nest of her curls, teeth clamped on the base of her thumb, eyes squeezed shut, when he could have invested himself in starting that climb. Instead, he let her return from whatever oblivion she'd visited and, when he was sure she'd be able to stand, let her go so he could pull up his pants.

Remembering Annie's orgasm excited him. His erection pushed against his jeans—he'd failed to undress before diving into his bed. He kicked his pants off and took his cock in his hand.

"Let me finish you," Annie had offered while he threaded his belt through the buckle.

"It's okay. In my condition, it might take a while."

"So let me come home with you. We can take a while."

He checked himself in the mirror. "I have a meeting in the morning."

"Working on a story?" she asked, adjusting her bra and shirt.

"Editors killed it."

The thought of his editors, the assignments, and the headlines and word counts that dulled the truth of what he saw obliterated whatever desire remained—to do his job or find the orgasm that eluded him earlier.

Hunter abandoned his effort, barely pulling his underwear up before he passed out.

ELEVEN

Now

HUNTER DIDN'T KNOW WHAT HE EXPECTED FROM HARRIS'S office, but it wasn't a brightly lit reception area with sleek, modern chairs and a couch set around a coffee table. A sturdy old receptionist sat at a slim desk to the side. Behind her, awards and press clippings decorated the wall. Sunlight poured in through a conference room with a frosted-glass wall. Brennan chatted with the receptionist, whom she seemed to know well. Hunter surveyed the magazines on the coffee table—a curious mixture of *Time*, *The Economist*, *The New Yorker*, and *New York Law Journal* with stray copies of *People*, *Us Weekly*, and *Bon Appétit*. He looked up and spotted Harris walking toward him.

The last time Hunter had seen him was a Thanksgiving more than ten years before. He didn't look any older. Maybe more salt in his hair and a couple of lines around his eyes. Hunter reached out to shake hands, but Harris knocked it aside and wrapped him in a sincere hug.

"I missed you, kid," Harris said. "It's good to see you both. Together."

Brennan cut in. It was hard to imagine that Harris felt the depth of emotion that he had just displayed given how much had passed since they last saw each other, but Brennan was getting the same treatment.

"Good to see you, too, Uncle Harris," she said.

"I told you to cut it with that."

"I know you like it. And I like when you tell me to cut it out."

Harris rolled his eyes and waved for the two to follow him down a hallway lined with offices.

"How's Uncle Andre?" Brennan asked.

"Good. On my last nerve as usual. He keeps asking me when you're going to come join me here."

Brennan smirked. "Seems like all your offices are full."

"We'd make room for you."

"I'm making my own way."

Harris nodded as he stepped aside at the door to his office, waving them into it. The office was on a corner of the building. Hunter could see the Battery Park City high-rises dwarfed by One World Trade Center, the Hudson River, and New Jersey to the west. The rest of Manhattan stretched away to the north. Harris closed the door and walked to his desk.

"How do you get any work done with this view?" Hunter asked.

"It rains sometimes," Harris said as he sat behind a massive desk. The center was clear except for a sleek laptop, but stacked piles of paper surrounded the edges of the desk like a wall. Brennan and Hunter sat in dark leather guest chairs facing the desk.

"How's your mother? It's been weeks since I last saw her. I was hoping to get up there this weekend if she's up to it."

"She's hanging in there," Brennan said. Harris stared at her waiting for her to add detail, but she didn't. There were moments of silent communication, pain and sympathy.

"I'll make sure I get there this weekend, if not sooner," Harris said. "She's a tough woman, your mom. Don't give up hope."

Brennan nodded and looked down at her hands. Harris turned to Hunter.

"I'm glad you're home, kid. But I guess after the things you've seen, I shouldn't call you 'kid' anymore, right? I have to say, I was worried about you over there. But proud of you. We need people to tell those stories."

Hunter shrugged. He hadn't expected the time warp to thirty years ago when he was a kid.

"How long are you back in town for?"

"I don't know. Indefinitely, I suppose. This situation with Mom . . ."

Harris nodded, then looked at Brennan. She looked at Hunter, and the two engaged in a silent negotiation to see who would put the issue on the table. Harris beat them to it.

"I thought you two would have come earlier," Harris said. "Honestly, I was surprised that you didn't come as teenagers, the way it went with you two."

"What do you mean?" Hunter asked.

"It seemed like such a waste to me and Andre. Your mom, you know her. She keeps her thoughts to herself. It wasn't my place to step in. And you, Hunter, didn't need me telling you anything. Don't look at me like that. You're not here for pleasantries or to catch up with an old man. You're here for business. I respect that. So let's be direct, no?"

Hunter nodded.

"Like I was saying, I had hoped you two would have gotten here sooner. She needed you, Hunter."

Heat rose in Hunter's face, but Harris's inherent authority kept him in his chair as he said, "My mother did fine. She supported my decisions—"

"Not talking about your mother, even if she needed you, too. I meant your sister."

"Excuse me?" Brennan snapped, surprised.

"It's hard growing up feeling like it's just you in the world. She was like the last kid who believed in Santa Claus. Everyone else thought your dad did it."

"He did do it," Hunter said.

"The jury didn't think so."

"The jury thought that there was reasonable doubt."

"The point is"—Harris leaned forward in his chair—"you were the only person who could understand what it was like for Brennan. Dad gone. Mother in pain. Carrying the accusation like a brand."

"I carried it, too," Hunter said.

"Exactly. Alone."

"Because she believed in fairy tales."

Brennan turned on Hunter. "Fuck you."

"Neither of you had to do it alone," Harris said. "But you ran off, changed your name, and hoped people forgot about you."

Hunter glared at Harris. He remembered his father sitting in the same pose with a hard look, but his father had carried the promise of violence in his stillness. Harris apologized to the plants in his garden when he picked vegetables.

"I'm not going to say that you're wrong, Harris," Brennan said, looking between Harris and Hunter, trying to get one of them to look at her, "but we're not here to argue."

Harris leaned back in his chair. "You're right. I was out of line."

Tension poured from Hunter as if from an overflow spillway. He jumped to his feet and paced behind the guest chairs. "We'd like to see your files. We're looking into what happened."

"He was acquitted," Harris said. "There's nothing in those files going to say otherwise. I can't show you, anyway. You know that," he said to Brennan. "It's all privileged."

"He's dead," Hunter said. "He doesn't care."

"I care. He can't waive. Who's gonna tell their lawyer anything if they think we'll blab the minute they're in the ground? Both of you should know better."

Hunter and Brennan shared a look. They did know better but had hoped that, given the circumstances, Harris would bend the rules.

"Maybe you can show us the nonprivileged stuff," Brennan offered. "And talk to us. You must have had theories. We need a place to start."

Harris sighed. "What's the use of looking back at stuff that will just bring you pain?"

"Because if I'm right," Brennan said, "they never found that woman's killer."

"That's not your problem."

"Isn't it? If someone got away with it at my father's expense?"

"You're not a prosecutor anymore."

"I could never have looked into this as a prosecutor."

"So you two want me to give you the resources to tear yourselves—and your mother—apart again?"

Hunter said, "Yes."

"What does your mother think about this?"

"She's not all there," Hunter said. "The painkillers have her all muddled. She can't remember now what she thought. For Christ's sake, she thinks he worked at some restaurant."

"I think he did," Harris said. "After the trial. In the Village."

Hunter threw his hands up. "Whatever. The point is that we need to do this. Not for her. For us. She's not even going to know."

Harris shook his head gently. Brennan sighed and stood up.

"We understand," she said. Hunter turned to look out the window.

"The two of you are too old for me to tell you what to do," Harris said. "But I'm going to tell you anyway. Don't do this to yourselves. All you'll find are more things to drive you two apart. I knew that case as well as anyone, and I couldn't tell you who did it." He addressed Hunter, "But I'm telling you it wasn't your dad."

Harris then looked Brennan in the eye. "You pursue this, you're going to learn things about him. You'll risk all your memories of him, of what kind of man he was, and for what? More doubt? You'll never know for sure what happened."

#

"Was he always such a dick?" Hunter asked out on the street. The frigid air whipped around them as they walked toward Brennan's office.

Brennan rolled her eyes. "Just because he says things that you don't want to hear doesn't make him a dick. You didn't help us by pushing back so hard."

"I wasn't going to let him talk to me like I'm some kid."

"I'm just saying that you have to remember it's not about how much someone's pissing you off. We're trying to accomplish something here."

Hunter shook his head, but said, "Fine."

After they parted at Chambers Street, Hunter walked a few blocks south. The Badger was still there, dark tinted windows underneath a weather-beaten shit-brown sign. It wasn't the worst bar in Manhattan, but it was close. Two or three old drunks hunched over the bar, tumors growing on the filthy wood. A stout Latino man with salt-and-pepper hair perched at the far end of the bar, sitting on a stool closest to the television mounted above the premium liquors. He was halfway through a burger dripping grease onto the limp lettuce that constituted the house salad.

"Still alive eating that shit every day?" Hunter asked. "I thought you'd be dead, Vega."

Vega turned, his eyes lighting up with surprise.

"Oh! This guy," he said, a Brooklyn accent laid over a gravelly voice. "I thought you skipped town."

"I'm back."

"Good for you." Vega shoved more burger into his mouth.

Hunter gestured at the screen. "City looks like they're doing well." The team was up by two goals. Hunter signaled the bartender for another round.

"You trying to send me back to work drunk?" Vega asked.

"It's just two. You'll be fine, especially with that burger in you."

Vega rolled his eyes, but downed the remnants of his first pint as the bartender brought the second.

"So, what do you need?"

"What? I can't visit a friend?"

Vega shook his head. "Don't bullshit a bullshitter."

More than five years had passed since he'd been in the bar, but they were going through the routine like Hunter was still covering the local beat.

"This one is personal," Hunter said. "It's on a piece I'm thinking about doing on an old murder."

Vega turned to him. "I thought you were covering international. Wars and shit."

"I needed a break."

"Murder ain't much of a break."

Hunter shrugged. Vega looked back at the television.

"So what are you looking for?"

"Police files. It's a case from like thirty years ago. A woman was murdered. Jessica DeSalvo."

"That's old. Before my time. It may take me a while to find those files, if they even still exist."

"I understand."

"A homicide may be a lot of files."

"I know. But I need access to all of them."

"Did you do a FOIL request?" Vega asked.

"I'm hoping that this could be expedited. I'm trying to move fast."

"What's the rush?"

Hunter smiled. "I'm only as good as my last story. And my last story sucked."

"This one a good one?"

"Shouldn't be anything that's going to blow back on you."

Vega nodded. "If you were any other guy, I'd say no. But I liked that you kept me on your Christmas card list, even after you changed beats."

"I liked our lunches and hoped that we'd pick up when I came back."

Vega laughed. "The last thing you said before you left was that you didn't want to ever see this bar again."

Vega stood, slid his suit jacket on, and left. Hunter paid the bill, his beer untouched.

TWELVE

Now

THE LATE NEWS WAS ON BY THE TIME BRENNAN GOT TO Jane's apartment. Hunter was on the couch scrolling through his phone, cheap beer in hand.

"Is she awake?" Brennan asked.

"Took her meds and nodded off an hour ago."

"Thanks for staying with her." Brennan sloughed her purse and her workbag off her shoulder and onto one of the wingback chairs facing the couch before flopping into the other one. She still wore her coat despite the heat in the apartment.

"Long day?" Hunter asked as Brennan rubbed her temples.

"Yeah. Not over. Probably have another hour of work to do when I get home."

"You should have just gone home."

"I wanted to look in on Mom."

"You can take a night off."

"Because you're finally here?"

"Don't start. Better late than never, right?"

I'll see you again, she remembered her father saying before never returning. Brennan said, "Sometimes late is as good as never."

Hunter's mouth creased—an expression he'd picked up from their mother when she wanted them to know she was pissed but was also going to demonstrate restraint. Brennan wanted to throw something at him. Instead, she pulled out a file folder stuffed with paper from her workbag.

"I had to give you these," she said.

"What is this?"

"I printed out all of the stories I could find on the investigation and trial. Most of it is the *News* and *Post*, but a couple of pieces in there from the *Times*."

He flipped through the stack of paper. "You had this lying around?"

"No. I pulled it off of Lexis today."

"Did you read them?"

"Today? Yes."

"You ever read them before?"

"No. Not really. You?"

"I looked up some articles when I first started in the newsroom. Didn't read all of them."

Hunter began to flip through the articles. Brennan got up, took off her coat, and grabbed a beer from the fridge.

"I shouldn't drink this. It's just going to make me more tired," she said. She brought the bottle to her mouth and drank half in one draw. "When you get to it, you may recognize the name of the prosecutor. Timothy McCarthy."

"Who?"

"He's running for district attorney."

Hunter looked up from his reading. "Other than that bit of trivia, did you get anything else from these?"

Brennan shrugged. "The trial ones are informative. They're mostly reporting evidence and testimony. But they didn't cover every day of the trial, at least not that I saw. And the details mainly focus on the sensational stuff."

"It's the stuff readers are interested in. We can't print the entire trial transcript."

"I'm just saying we can't rely on it as a complete record."

"I wasn't expecting to do that. I know the limits of reporting, the same as you know the limits of what gets presented at trial. We're all doing our best to get at the truth."

"The reporting on the investigation is infuriating. The press convicted him early."

"Because he was the guy."

"I thought we were approaching this like good investigators? That means open minds."

Hunter raised his hands in surrender. "Fair enough."

"If you're not going to take this seriously, then why are we doing it?"

"Back off. I am taking it seriously. It doesn't mean I can't have opinions."

Brennan shook her head but let it go. "In the end, these stories are mostly useless."

"Then why did you bring them?"

"To identify the players. People we should interview." Brennan held up a sheet of paper. "I made a list."

"So, give it to me."

"Make your own list. Then we can compare."

Hunter didn't like it, but he nodded. "I'm working an angle on the files."

"The trial files?"

"The police files."

Hunter went back to the stack of stories. Brennan finished her beer, watching him read like he was a stranger on the train. She knew more about her assistant at the firm than she knew about her brother at this point. She tried to feel badly about it but found it was like doing a seventh shot—she didn't feel any different.

She stood, put her coat on, and heaved her bags onto her shoulders.

"Meet here tomorrow?" she asked.

"Yeah." Hunter didn't look up.

"I'll text you when I think I'll be done with work."

As she walked to the door, Hunter said, "You're still really fucking bossy, you know."

She gave him the finger as she left.

#

Brennan had arranged the stories in chronological order, then by paper. *Daily News* then *New York Post* then *The New York Times*. Hunter didn't think she'd have her assistant do it; Brennan must have done it herself. So she was still a big fucking nerd.

None of the stories contained the photographs that ran with them, just the captions describing the photo. "Police leading John Lo from his building."

Hunter closed his eyes and tried to imagine the photo. He had never seen it, but all perp walk photos were essentially the same: some grainy black-and-white shot of a suspect, walking out of a building, hands behind their back, a cop on each arm. The difference was that in this case it was the building he grew up in, and the perp was his father. But Hunter couldn't picture his father's face. Did he try to shield it from the camera? Pull his shirt up or his jacket over his head? Or did he walk from the door full of bravado and indignation? Did one or the other indicate guilt or innocence? The uncertainty reminded Hunter how little he knew his father—how much he had been cheated and spared.

Hunter couldn't remember what subject it had been, only his classmates' stares as his mother walked into the room and beckoned him over. She didn't even look at the teacher, whom she had interrupted giving some instruction to the class. It was a shocking incongruity—his mother in the classroom in the middle of the day. The vibrating, urgent tension radiating from her and into the herd of children, a primal force; all the children were suddenly ready to bolt and scatter. His sister held the door ajar in her school jumper—unwilling to enter the classroom yet refusing to let their mother out of her sight. Hunter stood numbly and went to his mother. She held their hands, and they walked from the building into a waiting car. He remembered being worried that he had left his backpack behind.

In the car, he finally asked his mother—who had yet to speak a word—what had happened.

"You'll need to ask your father."

Close to their building, their mother pulled raincoats from her bag.

"Put these on. When we stop in front of the building, pull the hoods over your heads. Cover your faces, like you're playing peekaboo. Can you do that?"

They dashed from curb to door—the raincoat's hood magnifying the rustle of fabric against his hair, the heavy breathing, the smell of sweat and breath in his hands, cupped over his face, slivers of light through his fingers. This armor of flesh and nylon strangely muffled the click of cameras and shouted questions of reporters. His mother's hand grasped his arm nearly underneath his armpit, her rings digging into his back unrelentingly. The doorman shouted for the reporters to "back—the—fuck—up!" The hallway came in sudden coolness and dim light, but Hunter kept his hands on his face until, in the elevator, his mother knelt down and peeled them—wet with tears—away. The flush in her cheeks fluoresced through a sheen of her own tears. She kissed his head and said, "You're home now."

None of that was in the news stories he was reading now. They mentioned his dad's "wife and two children," and sometimes even noted that they were a girl and a boy of certain ages. But they were objects in the stories, unnamed living victims juxtaposed against Jessica, as in: "Mr. Lo, married with two young children, is rumored to have had an affair with Ms. DeSalvo."

Hunter had no idea what Jessica looked like. The captions read simply "Jessica DeSalvo"—probably some headshot or wedding picture—or "Ms. DeSalvo with husband, Mark, in Central Park." He was sure that he had seen her photo in some paper when he was a kid but couldn't remember. Now she was only text on a page.

The early reporting suffered, as it nearly always did, from speculation, incomplete information, and the agenda of the leaker. Underneath, though, like a geological feature, was a common landscape. Jessica was murdered in an apartment in the blurry border between the Upper East Side and East Harlem. Her friend, Cathy, lived in the apartment. Cathy found her body when she returned from a movie. The *News* reported Jessica's husband, Mark, worked late before going home. In the first stories, immediately following the murder, police sources speculated about a home invasion. Death appeared to be from stabbing; the murder weapon was not found. A day later, after the initial rush, the *Post* and the *News* ran victim profiles. Her résumé—varsity tennis player at her Greenwich high school, college at Penn, law school at Columbia. The anguish of her parents radiated from their quotes, even all these years later. From her mother: "Please find the monster that killed my baby girl!" Cathy told a reporter about how life was never going to be the same without her. The reporters noted that her husband was too grief-stricken to comment.

On the fourth day after the murder, the stories turned. A police source revealed that Jessica had been having an affair. Cathy let Jessica use the apartment so that she could see her lover but did not know who he was. In the *Post*, an unnamed detective said, "Maybe Jessica shouldn't have put herself in that position." The *Times* broke the story that her lover was a partner at the law firm where she worked. *Interesting*, Hunter thought. Who was their source? The *News* and the *Post* clearly had good police sources, but the *Times* hadn't stayed with the story. The law firm angle, however, not only brought them back—they broke the news. Hunter bit his lip and continued reading.

The sixth day, they ran stories about the search of the apartment. His father's name, in print: "Police searched the home of John Lo, a Chinese American partner at Taylor Wood & West, the Wall Street firm." The next line: "Sources close to Ms. DeSalvo claim she was having an affair with a partner at the firm." No source to connect the two facts, yet allowing the obvious inference to be drawn. Hunter tried to remember the day of the search, but it was unremarkable. The next day, a classmate (*Was his name Jeremy? That kid sucked.*) said to him, "Your daddy was in the paper today. And I know why." Hunter wasn't able to learn why his father made the news. He didn't ask his parents. He just hoped that it would go away. It never did. But over time, the whole thing faded, a patina over which he lived his life, thicker here in New York, thinner elsewhere.

More stories. The police leaked a note from Jessica found in his father's desk that confirmed the affair. No mention of an alibi. Over the next five days, shorter articles as new facts and angles dried up. Hunter presumed that the cops were doing the boring part of the investigation—eliminating other suspects, trying to find the murder weapon, tying off loose ends. Two days before the arrest was reported—the day before the arrest—a columnist for the *Post* castigated the cops for slow-walking the investigation. The columnist reinterviewed Jessica's mother. "I don't know what they're waiting for," she said. "Jessica was a good girl. I'm sure that monster forced her into the situation so she could keep her job. They're letting my daughter's killer walk the streets, a menace, and for what? Nice girls like Jessica already have so much to worry about in Manhattan. They shouldn't have to worry about that peril."

After the arrest, the papers breathlessly published stories with previously reported facts. The *Post* ran the "Devil" headline. Her husband finally gave a statement: "No matter what differences Jessica and I had, I loved Jessica. I miss her." Harris made his first appearances with the same quote running in the three papers: "Whatever my client's relationship with Ms. DeSalvo, there is no evidence connecting him to the crime. The police have rushed to judgment. My client looks forward to the truth coming out at trial." The DA's office opposed bail on the theory that "Mr. Lo could flee to China." None of the stories mentioned that he was born in the United States and had never been to China. The judge granted bail pending trial despite that argument. The bond required was significant, but his father posted it and surrendered his passport. The columnists excoriated the judge the next day for letting his father not only walk the streets, but presumably return to the home he shared with his wife and two children.

Hunter tried to remember what those days had been like for him, what he experienced in school, what it had been like in the house, but all he had were memories of having memories of those things. He finally understood what his mother had been raving about the other night. He managed to recall standing in Brennan's room years later, his freshman year of high school. Brennan had eventually moved into their father's old office. They'd just arrived home wearing their different schools' uniforms.

He had come to her room to see if he could borrow her dictionary, but before he could, she said, "It's not any better, is it?"

"What?" he asked.

"I thought when I got to a different school, it would be behind me. I don't know if it's because Viv and Kelly came to Dalton, too, or because girls are just mean, but people know. About Dad."

His sister hadn't spoken to him about their father in years. Hunter didn't ever bring their dad up with her—her pain was a warehouse fire, no place for a child and best left to burn itself out. For Hunter, he carried the memories of their father like a shaken soda can, something to put away for someone else to deal with. Mostly, they took their cues from their mother, who focused relentlessly on the present and never mentioned him, until the topic of their father was like a stain that couldn't be cleaned. Eventually, they just ignored its constant presence.

"What happened?" he asked.

"It doesn't matter. They're wrong. He didn't hurt that lady." Hunter remembered feeling like he was standing on a dock while water surged past him—a strange, still vertigo. He had assumed in their communal silence about their father that she had grown out of her childish belief in his innocence, that her realization that he'd been guilty was the root of her pain.

"But he did," Hunter said casually, certain Brennan knew how he felt.

Brennan's hand went to her chest in a fist, a wounded gesture she picked up from their mother. But whereas their mother did it for show, Brennan's movement was strikingly vulnerable, raw, injured, and alone. Forever after, even in war zones reporting among dying men, the desperate and grievously stricken casualties crawling for aid or comfort brought to mind his sister in that moment. But at least those soldiers had others they could count on.

"I thought we were on the same side," Brennan said. Her skin was flushed and suddenly sweaty, as though she were embarrassed. Hunter expected blood to seep from underneath her clenched fist.

He remembered wanting to say something like *I am on your side*, but what came out of his mouth instead was, "You're a fucking idiot if you think he didn't do it."

Brennan threw the dictionary from her desk with enough force that it cut the upper part of his forehead where the corner of the book hit him. He couldn't remember if she had screamed at him, too. But she slammed the door—he recalled the specific squeak from the hinges. After, he sat on his bed, feverish with anger, watching blood drip from his brow to the wood floor of his room. That night, after his mother got home from work, she brought a warm rag into his room and wiped the blood from his hairline and off his face, like he was four instead of fourteen.

"Do you want to talk about the fight you had with your sister?" she asked.

"What's there to talk about?"

"Do you think that maybe you could have handled the situation differently?"

"She's wrong."

"Does that matter? She's your sister."

"And she's wrong. The truth matters. She can't really believe that he didn't do it. Everybody knows he did it."

"Your sister believes that he didn't."

"Then she's an idiot. Or a liar. Like him."

His mother looked at his closed door, like maybe his sister was out there, listening in. Or perhaps there was something in his eyes that she couldn't face at that moment.

"Your father did a terrible thing, Hunter. None of us can change that. But I told you before, it's not your sister's fault that she's his daughter and loves him. It's okay for children to love their parents, even if they're not perfect."

Hunter didn't say anything, stunned that his mother agreed with him, full of the vicious elation of the righteous.

As a man, reflecting back, Hunter remembered the rush of certainty mainly for its present absence. He had heard what he wanted to hear in his mother's carefully chosen words. He looked over at her bedroom door. What had she meant when she said his dad did a "terrible thing"? That he killed a woman? Or that he had an affair? Or both? Or neither?

Hunter looked back at the stack of papers in his hand, keenly aware that his eyes were dry and bleary. His cell phone buzzed on the table.

"Hey, Vega," Hunter said. "Please tell me you're up late because you found those files already."

"Yeah, about that." Vega's voice was barely audible against a background of street noise. "Two things. You ever hear of Bobby Bauman?"

"No."

"He was the lead on this case. Dude's a legend in homicide. Retired as chief of detectives about a decade ago. Gotta kid on the force, too. I don't know him, but he's got lots of connections."

"Uh huh," Hunter said. "What was the second thing?"

"Do you know who the prosecutor on the case was?"

"I just learned that."

"You gotta tell me that this isn't some kind of campaign thing. Nothing like that."

Hunter stood so he could pace as he spoke. "No. Not at all. Has nothing to do with that guy."

"You've been gone for a while. McCarthy has juice. Guys here love him, you know? He's always had our backs."

"I'm not going to hang you out there, man. You know me. We go way back. I won't screw you over."

Vega laughed. "I can cover my own ass, man. I'm trying to help you. People are invested in this guy winning. They find you're doing a story around this or whatever, it may be trouble for you."

"How would they find out?"

"That's what I'm trying to tell you. Between Bauman and his kid and McCarthy, I pull this file, someone may hear about it. You sure you want to dig in this dirt?"

Vega had never waved him off a story before, which made Hunter hesitate for a moment before he said, "Yeah. It's fine. I'll be fine."

"Okay, then. I'll see what I can do."

After Vega disconnected the call, Hunter dialed Brennan.

"Is she okay?" she answered.

"Mom? Yeah. She's sleeping."

"I was heading to bed. But thanks for the scare. What's up?"

He told her about the call with Vega.

"That it?" she asked.

"One thing I learned overseas is not to underestimate dangerous situations."

"We'll be careful," she said. "What about the stories? What are your thoughts there?"

He didn't like how quickly she slid over his warning, but he decided to move on. "What do we really know about Dad? And what do we know about Jessica? Maybe we start with someone from his firm? Who knew him. Maybe knew them both?"

"My list started with Cathy," she said. "With Dad, *we* knew him."

"Are we going to have to start arguing about this already?"

"Don't be difficult," Brennan said. "We can work it from both sides. There's a guy. He was friends with Mom and Dad. I've crossed paths with him a few times over the years. Can't remember his name right now. I'll get it tomorrow. Whoever we can line up first. Then the other."

"Good idea," he said. "See? Maybe we'll do this without fighting the whole time."

THIRTEEN

Then

GETTING HUNTER OUT OF THE HOUSE WAS DIFFICULT. HE didn't talk or listen to John. Brennan had to intervene, bringing socks and shoes to her brother, whispering in his ear—promises, threats, entreaties—before he finally huffed and started to dress. John stood at the door to their room, hand wound tightly on the neck of the doorknob until Brennan came over and took his hand and led him to the front door.

"I'll bring him, Dad," she said.

He stood at the door for a while, waiting. He barely breathed; the concentration required to stand still negated all other thought, reflex, mental function. If Hunter didn't turn the corner to the hallway in the next five seconds, either John's heart would stop beating or he would rampage through the apartment until he found him and dragged him by the arm to the door, blind to his son's tears and deaf to his screaming until, in the elevator, he would squat down level with Hunter, stare into his eyes, and insist that he be silent or "else," all the while, Brennan silently standing off to the side, until after a moment, she would insert herself between them and place her hands on each of them and John would tremble like a pile of rubble on the edge of collapse.

It didn't come to that. Three seconds later, Brennan turned the corner, dragging her brother by the hand. The two of them stood before John, but Hunter wouldn't look at him.

"Ready, kids?" John asked.

"Yes," Brennan said.

Hunter kept his eyes on his sneakers. "I don't want to go."

The urge to slap Hunter pressed at John's throat like vomit. If he could swing the door open, get into the elevator, the nausea of rage would pass. He opened the door, slamming it into the wall. The kids started and backed away.

"Let's go," John said, waving the kids past him.

Hunter was the first out the door.

The three of them stood in silence on the elevator ride down. Calvin, the doorman, was in the lobby.

"We're going to the park," Brennan said to him. Hunter waved.

"Have fun, kids!" Calvin said. He and John did not acknowledge each other.

Once outside, the kids raced ahead toward Central Park. John trudged behind them. The humid air was a wet towel pressing on him, lightened occasionally by an intermittent breeze. It was the first time he'd been alone with the kids since the end of his trial a month earlier.

The day before, Jane had opened the door to the office. She didn't enter. John stared at a blank pad he had taken out with the aim of listing contacts to begin calling about finding work.

"I have to work tomorrow," Jane said. "The sitter's at a wedding."

John waited for her to say it.

"Can you watch the kids?"

"Of course. They're my children, too."

There was a brief pause where they each waited for the other to speak further. Jane broke off first, closing the door behind her. John returned to staring at the blank pad.

Hunter refused to hold his hand when they crossed Central Park

West. Brennan grabbed him by the wrist and held it against Hunter's squirming. Once in the park, Brennan and Hunter followed the path from the entrance to the first fork, before looking back at John for direction. He shrugged and waved indeterminately. Hunter looked to Brennan, who took a path leading away from their usual playground. The kids sprinted along the paths, climbed boulders dumped by glaciers during the last ice age, and chased each other through grassy patches. John followed. Brennan did not once turn to see if he was there; she could have wandered for hours, never checking until she needed water or food, at which point she would simply turn around, believing fully that John would be standing behind her ready to find a hot dog cart. But Hunter engaged in a fumbling countersurveillance. He wouldn't make eye contact with John or let his gaze rest on him as he looked around, but he found excuses to stop to fidget with his sneakers or sit on a bench for a moment or even run a circle around a tree in order to be able to ensure John was still following.

Roughly an hour after they entered that park, they found themselves at the Bethesda Fountain, the nearly hundred-foot-wide structure on the south side of the Lake. Brennan and Hunter ran a wide circle around it before they sat on the benches lining the walls of the Terrace and waited for John to catch up.

"Where are we going, Dad?" Brennan asked.

"Wherever you're taking us."

"We're not going anywhere," Brennan said.

John looked around, trying to figure out a place to go. Buildings rose above the canopy of the park in every direction. To the south, stairs rose to Terrace Drive, which passed over a walkway to the Mall. People wandered in and out of the Terrace with no apparent destination.

Still looking around for an idea, John asked, "Where do you want to go?"

"Away," Hunter said. The boy who had spent the last hour—the last month—avoiding any contact with him stared him in the face.

"Where?"

"From here."

"From the park?"

"Yeah."

"You want to go home?"

"No."

"Somewhere else?"

"Yeah."

"I'm not going to guess, Hunter. Just say where you want to go."

The last few words came out in a growl, a vibration like a dam cracking—the imminence of destruction. John didn't raise his voice, but a couple nearby turned to stare. John ignored them. Hunter pushed himself off the bench and walked away. He didn't look back before stepping off the red brick of the Terrace onto the black asphalt path leading to the east side of the park. In a few seconds, he would lose sight of Hunter. Brennan jumped up onto the bench.

"Daddy, he's leaving."

John waited for Hunter to decide how far he was going to take it.

"Daddy?"

Hunter disappeared around the bend. Brennan grabbed John's hand and tried to pull him along to follow, but she couldn't make him move. She let go and ran after Hunter, looking back over her shoulder, trying to keep both in sight. As she crossed onto the asphalt path, she began shouting her brother's name. As she reached the point where the path wound and she would lose sight of him, Brennan looked back to John, eyes dazzled with tears.

"Daddy! Please!" And then she raced out of view.

The nearby couple walked away, eyes on John. The man—an older guy with thick glasses—said, "You're going to lose your kids." His wife pulled him away.

Everyone on the Terrace was moving except John, who remained as still as the statue atop the fountain. Seconds passed. John wanted to believe he was still because he was proving a point, but the truth was he was scared that if he chased Hunter, he would beat him when he caught him.

A minute passed. The children were old enough to know how to return to the fountain, or even find their way home if they needed to. What if he let the kids go? Or if he walked into the Lake and slipped beneath the still green water? Could their lives be any worse off? He had no illusions about the long-term prognosis of his family life. The end of the trial hadn't changed the malignancy festering in their home since even before his affair. If he left, would it sever the transfer to his children of all of his flaws and mistakes he'd made? Would his family be more whole without him? Over time, would they pretend that he'd died, maybe in some tragic accident? He imagined Brennan catching up to Hunter, their fear when they realized that John had not followed them. If he wasn't there when they returned, would they find a policeman or aim for the west side of the park and navigate home from there? John bet on the latter—because Brennan would want to avoid getting John in trouble with the cops.

Five minutes elapsed before the kids came back into view. They stopped at the edge of the Terrace, holding hands. Hunter remained ready to run. The children were tiny mirrors of himself, of Jane, of their marriage. Their mother passed her nature directly to them with her immunities, first in the womb, then by her breast, finally in song and touch and breath. His influence passed into them like radiation—a perverse nourishment of fear and anger, but also resolve and courage. Not that John believed he had those qualities, but because the kids needed to develop them in the face of his faults.

The urge to hold them, to embrace them and crush them to his chest, surged upon him. But he recognized this emotion as a weakness, so instead of smiling and waving Brennan and Hunter over and catching them up in his arms, he nodded to them and tilted his head toward the path they had come down. The kids relaxed slightly, an exhale and separation of hands, and walked in the direction that John indicated.

It didn't take them as much time to walk home because the kids didn't play as much. Brennan first tried to get Hunter to race her across a patch of grass to the top of a boulder, but Hunter shook his head and moped along. Later, somewhere in his introspection, Hunter found inspiration for a game he proposed to Brennan, but she flatly rejected it. They each wanted to complain to him about the other, but when they turned to do so, they'd jerk their heads back in the face of his glares. They settled for casting angry looks at each other. But near the edge of the park, they encountered a college student walking a puppy. They petted it as it ran around their ankles and jumped up to lick their hands. The rest of the way to their building the kids spoke to each other again in rushed sentences about the kinds of dog they wanted and what they would name it.

A few doors down from their building, John spotted Calvin lingering by the door, watching them approach. Two men stood farther up the street on the sidewalk chatting. Calvin glanced their way. Brennan pulled on John's hand until he looked down at her.

"Thank you for taking us to the park today, Daddy."

Why was she thanking him? It had been a shitty trip. But John gave her hand a squeeze.

He looked up again as the two men approached. One produced a camera and snapped pictures of John and the children as they walked to their building. The other held a microphone attached to a portable tape recorder hanging from a shoulder strap.

"Mike Mullens, *New York Post*. Can I ask you a few questions?"

Hunter and Brennan stopped walking, confused. John, his focus on Mullens, bumped into Hunter's back and grabbed his shoulder to keep him from falling. He should have recognized Mullens. His column had repeatedly pushed the theory that John committed the murder.

"Keep walking, kids," John said.

"How are you adjusting to life now that the trial is over?"

The kids were not moving. John pulled Brennan by her hand while pushing Hunter forward by the shoulder.

"Did the jury get it right?"

Twenty feet from the door.

"Is there anything you want to say to her family?"

Ten feet.

"How did your wife handle the news about Jessica DeSalvo?"

He was at the door.

"How did you explain the trial to your children?"

That would have been the last question if Calvin had held the door open for them as John expected. Instead, Calvin had retreated into the building, leaving the heavy door closed behind him. As John fumbled to open the door, Mullens kept shouting questions while the photographer snapped photos.

"What are your plans for the future? Do you think people like you deserve to get their lives back? How did you feel playing with your children in the park today knowing that Jessica DeSalvo is dead?"

John finally wrenched the door open and shoved Hunter through. He still held Brennan's hand, but now it was in front of him, about shoulder height, and she was nearly dangling from his grasp. The last question chased them through the door: "Do your children think you killed Jessica?"

He barely noticed Calvin as they waited for the elevator but heard him slip back outside before the elevator arrived.

In the elevator, Brennan finally spoke. "Daddy, you're hurting me."

John looked down and realized that he was crushing her hand. He let go of her and Hunter.

When they got into their apartment, Hunter stalked off to his room. Brennan collapsed on the couch. John slunk into his office, sank into his desk chair, and lowered his head to his shaking hands. He wanted to claw at his own burning face. He thought of the chef's knife in the kitchen. German steel, sharp enough to cut a ripe tomato into neat slices without squishing the insides all over the cutting board. He decided that he would start in their guts—Calvin, Mullens, the photographer.

If he was fast enough, they wouldn't know what was happening until they were already mortally wounded. The shock would put them on the ground, and then he would cut their throats. He had to go soon, before the reporters left. But if he could waste enough time, staring into the black at the back of his eyelids, maybe the rage would pass, and they all could continue to live. Even as that thought shot through his mind, John knew it was a lie. His life was over—had been for some time. If he hurried, he could take some measure of revenge on his way out. He began compiling a list in his mind—the order of the murders. But first, he had to attend to those downstairs.

Resolved, John opened his eyes. But Hunter stood in the doorway. He regarded John a moment, then stepped into the room and closed the door.

FOURTEEN

Then

JOHN REMEMBERED HOW HUNTER USED TO COME INTO THE office to ask him questions. Hunter never simply poked his head in. Depending on his mood and the nature of the request, he would come skipping or sneaking in, all the way around the desk each time, wrap his tiny arms around John's shoulders, and nearly whisper in his ear. *Can I have a piece of cake? Can we go to the park? What are you doing? Brennan's bothering me. I love you.*

Now, Hunter stopped a few steps into the room, staring at his father, hunched in his chair, head in hands. John sat back carefully and met Hunter's eyes.

"Were those men reporters?"

John nodded.

"Will they ever leave us alone?"

"I don't know. Sooner or later."

"I thought you won the trial. Why are they still following you?"

"It's not like the movies. Some people will always think that I did it."

"Why do they think you did it?"

John looked down to his hands. "It's complicated. It's a grown-up thing."

"Did you have an affair?"

"How do you know what that is?"

Hunter shrugged, diffident for the first time since he entered the room. "I've been around. It's New York City."

John had hoped he would never have to tell Brennan or Hunter directly about cheating. He understood well that they would learn the fact of his infidelity. If they were older, they would already know. As it was, John figured that in a few years they might look back to see what the trial was about or ask a friend or finally piece together scraps of overheard conversations. But he didn't want to see their faces when they learned.

"I'm not talking about this with you. It's not a kid thing."

Hunter stood his ground. "Please. It's so much worse not knowing why."

"I don't know how to explain it, Hunter. People make mistakes. A lot of times, those mistakes hurt other people—even people we love. Sometimes especially people we love."

"Did you cheat on Mommy?"

"Yes."

"Why?"

John looked out the window. John had spent every day since he left the holiday party with Jessica asking himself that same question. There wasn't enough breath in him to speak all the words necessary to give a full answer—each bit of context rested on another. Pieces of understanding circled back on each other, crossing over and under, endlessly—a vast, sprawling rainforest of why. How could he capture the scale and complexity of the underlying phenomena—the individual seconds and memories that constituted the whole and made it real? He could no more point to a single event to explain the reason any more than he could point to a single tree and say, *That is why the rainforest is here.*

Still, Hunter waited for an answer.

#

Jessica waited for him, stripped to her underwear and reading a paperback romance on Cathy's couch. The cheap pink sheet that Jessica used when they borrowed Cathy's apartment covered the couch.

"You know, if I were your wife, this is how I'd be waiting for you every night."

John dropped his briefcase and undressed by the door. "Yeah? No kids?"

"I told you, I don't see myself as a mother." She let one foot drop to the floor and raised the other to rest on the back of the couch. She held the book in her left hand. Her right slid down her stomach to her hip.

By the time John removed his socks, Jessica's hand was rocking inside of her underwear.

"Does your wife do this for you?"

"She used to."

"Do you like it?"

John nodded. "What about your husband? Doesn't he like this?"

"He loves it. But I love doing it for you."

He remained at the door, watching. The other side of the door was the place where the laws of society applied. His children were home in bed. So was Jane, probably, even though it was only ten. His work lay on his desk where he abandoned it before rushing out. On this side of the door, Jessica threw the book to the floor. The hand in her underwear moved faster. Her other hand grabbed impulsively at her breast, then her thigh, back to her neck. Her eyes alternated between rolling up into her head and meeting his.

"If you don't come here, I'm going to finish without you."

"Go ahead. I want to watch."

Her eyes closed, and he wondered how much was performance and how much was authentic. Then she finished, eyes squeezed shut, biting her hand to keep from screaming out, absolutely her truest self. Lightheaded, John walked to the couch, removed her underwear and gently kissed where her hand had been. Jessica shook, enduring the exquisite sensitivity, before lifting his head up to hers to taste herself on his mouth. John kissed her, teasing himself with her wetness. When she was ready, she pulled him inside. He pushed her bra up, and she twisted underneath him so she could unclasp it. He fought against his impending orgasm. It was a door he needed to keep closed, but everything in his body pressed him to open it.

"I can feel how close you are," Jessica said. "Do it. I already came."

John held himself against his orgasm, pressure building until his resolve faltered, and the force of his climax hurled him out of his body into a weightless ecstasy. Then gravity asserted itself. He tried to withdraw, but Jessica pulled him back.

"Just another second," she said, arms pulling his weight onto her.

Later, after they had cleaned themselves up, they squeezed back onto the couch. Jessica's hand rested on his chest.

"Do you think about your family when you're with me?" she asked.

He lay next to her in an unrefined sludge of contentment, guilt, infatuation, and anxiety. "I try not to."

"I think about Mark. I want to feel guilty. But it's like the guilt gets me going, you know? So I think about him before, during, after. It seems kinda fucked up, right?"

"I don't know. Lots of people have affairs. Maybe it's common to feel what you're feeling."

"Sometimes I feel like a monster."

"Because you want to be bad?"

"Everyone wants to be bad sometimes. I don't ever want to be good."

She ground herself into his thigh.

"I have to go soon," John said.

"Isn't she usually asleep by now?"

"What about your husband?"

"He's probably still out."

"What time does Cathy get home?"

"She told me she'll get out of the movie at eleven and call." She glanced past John at a clock on the wall. "It's ten thirty now."

"Think she might want to join? We can wait for her."

Jessica laughed, but leaned forward and whispered in his ear all the things she would do with her friend for him. She spared no details, no matter how depraved. She climbed on top of him. He couldn't believe he was erect again already. She glided upward along the length of him until she caught the tip of his cock just inside her. She adjusted her hips to a comfortable angle and slid back.

Inside her again, John felt no urgency to leave. They fucked slow, in no hurry. Then they came to a place where the pace increased. Jessica bent down to kiss him, then raised herself up again.

"Do you ever think of leaving your family for me?" she asked.

"I don't want to lie to you," he said.

"I'm not your wife. You don't have to lie to me."

"Yes. I think about leaving them for you." Her weight was fully on his hips, her hands occupied with her own pleasure.

"Good. I like that. Why?"

"Because when you fuck me, I don't have to feel anything. I don't have to be anybody. I can just be inside you."

She smiled.

"I won't leave them, though."

"Even if Cathy came back, and we did all the things I told you about?"

"Even then."

Jessica stopped moving and pouted. Then she bit her lower lip and pushed down on him until he was as deep in her as he could go. "What if you got me pregnant?"

"That would be complicated."

"No, it wouldn't. It's the most natural thing in the world. Like what we're doing. What if I wanted your baby? Would you give one to me?"

She began moving again, faster. Something in the game, in the concept, excited her. He felt it in how her hips moved, how alive she felt around him.

"What if I told you I wasn't on the pill? Would you still come inside me?"

"Yes." If it meant he could be inside her, erased, he absolutely would.

"We can throw these lives away," she said. "Start a new one. Give me your seed. Let me grow it for you."

She rode him like she meant every word. She closed her eyes, concentrating, then brought herself to a sharp orgasm. John followed, an aching burst, followed by a drained soreness. Jessica climbed off him immediately. John sat up so she could sit next to him.

"I have to go."

"I know," she said. She patted his knee but looked away through the curtained windows.

Shame and thoughts of Jane, work, and the kids trickled into the fleeting emptiness he had achieved like sewage from a leaky pipe. He gathered his clothes. Jessica disappeared to the bathroom.

She returned, still nude. Seeing John dressed, Jessica came to him and kissed him on the cheek, then ushered him the four feet to the door. Of all of the acts in his infidelity—obfuscating, fucking his not-wife, compartmentalizing, concealing—leaving was the most alien to John. He wanted a smooth exit, but each time felt forced, as if he were lingering too long. But on the other side of the door, he felt as if he had fled a restaurant without paying the bill.

He walked down the stairs from Cathy's apartment to the street, head down, praying he wouldn't pass anyone who might witness the guilt and shame etched into his face.

#

Hunter read the guilt and shame in John's face like a new word from one of his children's books. He scanned his posture, the tightness of his mouth, a slight wrinkle in his brow, and the uncertainty in his eyes the same way he would sound out letters, gleaning meaning from context, adding it to his emotional vocabulary. It was like watching Hunter learn a swear word. John spent years at Jane's insistence guarding his language, trying to keep *piss* and *ass* and *shit* and *fuck* out of his children's mouths, and for what? Their dictionary had been filled with anger, resentment, and self-loathing instead. How could that be any better?

"Why did you cheat on Mommy?" And when John didn't respond, he insisted. "Answer me."

Since the kids were born, people loved telling him and Jane things like this kid looks like you, or your wife, or he has your nose, or she has your eyes. But John didn't need anybody to point it out to know whose fury he was looking at.

"Go away," he said.

Hunter didn't move.

John stood and pointed to the door.

Hunter tensed, tears forming in his eyes. But he didn't leave.

"I want to know," Hunter said, voice quieter now, shaking. John took a step toward Hunter, still pointing at the door. Halfway to his son, Hunter's resolve broke and he tried to turn to run. Before John was conscious of it, he was on his knees, with Hunter pinned to the closed door, facing him.

"What?" John growled. "Now you want to leave?"

Hunter was weeping, but not struggling. John understood that Hunter could feel the rage radiating from his father's hands, passing through his little body like an electric current, preventing any movement, maybe even breath. John felt the child's flesh yield under his fingers and wondered if he could simply squeeze through it to the bones, to grind them in his hands like a fairy-tale giant. Hunter's eyes searched his own, absent of the obstinacy from moments ago, now pleading to be spared. In the violent stillness, John was free for a moment of all thoughts except of his desire to break his son's arms and the thinness of the will that kept him from doing so.

Then John's hands slid down Hunter's arms, leaving red impressions where he had squeezed them, until he held Hunter's hands. John sank back until he sat on his heels like a monk, head bowed, tears running off his cheeks, falling to his lap.

"I'm sorry," John said. "It just happened. These things just happened. It's not how I wanted it to be."

Hunter pulled his hands from his father's.

John knew he ought to say something, to salvage something from the disgrace. But there was no salvaging, only the debris of his failure slowly sliding along the door until Hunter could open it and slip from the room.

FIFTEEN

Now

BRENNAN AND HUNTER HADN'T BEEN TO TAYLOR WOOD & West since they were kids. Neither of them remembered the offices. The receptionist led them to a conference room with dark wood paneling and a massive, polished table. Hunter reclined in one of the chairs, dressed in jeans and a black sweater. Brennan stood at the window in a gray suit. Beyond the window, Manhattan stretched away in ordered, dark buildings and chaotic lights beneath a formless sky.

Walter Roberts opened the door without knocking and strode over to Brennan. Walter was in his late sixties but looked older. The comb-over he attempted did little to conceal his severely receding hairline.

"Brennan!" he said warmly, shaking her hand. "It's good to see you."

Walter stared at Hunter for a moment before reaching out to shake hands. "And you, I haven't seen you since you were a boy."

Walter stepped back and stared at Hunter. "You look exactly like him."

Hunter shrugged, uncomfortable with the comparison.

"Thank you for meeting with us," Brennan said, as they sat around the table. "Friday evening, you must want to get home."

"Anything for John's kids," Walter said. "What did I tell you, Bren? First time I ran into you in that deposition? What were you, a year out of law school?"

Brennan remembered the day, before she became a prosecutor, when she was an associate at another Wall Street firm, sitting at a long table full of lawyers, a court reporter, and some witness she didn't recall. She was nervous that it was her dad's old firm on the other side of the matter. After the deposition, Walter pulled her aside and told her he'd been friends with John.

"You said my dad would be proud I was following in his footsteps," Brennan said. "That I should let you know if I needed anything."

Walter smiled. "The offer still stands. You probably don't need advice or help from an old man anymore, but say the word, and we can grab some drinks and figure out how you can take over the world."

Then his smile fell away, and he said, "I heard about your mother. I know we lost touch over the years, but we knew a lot of the same people. Is she hanging in there? I heard she left her firm."

"She's fighting," Brennan said.

Walter nodded sympathetically and said, "So, how can I help you two?"

"It's not much more than I explained on the phone," Brennan said. "We're just trying to find some information on our father. We didn't ever get to know him really. With our mom sick, it just reminded us of how little we know our parents. Really, how little anyone knows their parents, I guess. So it would be good to hear about him, you know?"

Walter leaned back in his chair. "I understand. I can't imagine how tough it was for you kids. Your dad was my closest friend here. We started together and . . . I think, you know, it was hard for him to fit in here. We're obviously much better about that stuff now, everyone is, but back then, the things people would say."

"You don't have to explain," Brennan said.

Hunter nodded. They'd both heard their share of racist comments.

"Your dad, he was brilliant. They really had no choice but to make him a partner. And he was a little tornado. The old guard, they didn't want to take him seriously, but he didn't let it get him down."

"Did he have other friends here?" Brennan asked.

"I hate to say it, but other than me, not really. He went to office parties. But he was distant with people. He'd chat with you if you were working on a project, but he wasn't inviting guys out for drinks after. You know the type, right?"

Hunter leaned forward. "What about the women?"

Brennan shot her brother a look, then redirected. "Sounds like he was lonely."

Walter glanced between the siblings for a moment before answering Brennan. "I don't remember him that way."

"He must've been friends with Jessica DeSalvo, though," Hunter said.

Walter nodded slowly. "Yeah, I guess so."

"Can you tell us about her?"

Walter shrugged. "Isn't that an awkward question? I mean . . ."

"A little awkward," Hunter said, "but we're adults and you knew both of them, right? We just want to understand him better. Can you tell us what she was like?"

Walter looked down at his hands, hesitating. Brennan slowed her breathing. It felt like Hunter was rushing, and she sensed Walter raising his guard. But Brennan resolved to trust her brother—interviewing people was his job.

"I worked with her sometimes. I can't remember if your father did, but the firm was smaller then. You sort of knew everyone. I mean, it was a different time, too. It's embarrassing to admit, but affairs like that weren't uncommon. I was oblivious to that stuff. Honestly, it didn't even register to me that something might be going on between them."

Brennan leaned forward. "What was she like?"

"Jess was a good litigator. Smart. People gravitated to her. She was very engaging in a conversation. It was tough losing her like we did. The both of them. A really sad chapter for the firm. And me, personally. I was friends with them both. I try not to think about it."

"Do you know how she became involved with my dad?" Brennan followed up.

"No." Walter sat back in the chair and looked between Brennan and Hunter. "She had a lot of friends here. Not to be insulting, but you know, maybe she felt bad for him."

"Why?" Hunter asked.

"Because he was an outsider." Walter finished his water and stood up. "I should get back to work."

As they walked to the door, Brennan asked, "If any of the other partners who knew him are still around, we'd love to get a chance to talk to them, too."

"Most of them have retired. I'm getting close myself, not that you can tell," he said and laughed.

"What about Jess?" Hunter asked. "You said she had lots of friends. Any of them still around?"

Walter crossed his arms and thought for a moment. "I can't think of anybody. It was a long time ago. I mean, it doesn't feel like it. But then I think about how much has happened since. I'm sorry I can't be more helpful."

SIXTEEN

Now

THEY DROVE TO LARCHMONT THE NEXT MORNING. BRENnan hated letting Hunter drive, but she was hungover and didn't want to deal with the hassle.

"Why do you have a car anyway?" Hunter broke the silence as they crossed the Henry Hudson Bridge into the Bronx.

"Paul and I got it last year. Figured if we were going to have a kid, it would be easier to have one to get around. Obviously, that didn't happen. Now we share custody of the car. I get it every other week. At least until our lawyers figure out the asset split."

"You were thinking about having a kid? With *our* parents?"

"I figured I could only do better," she said. "But I'm probably wrong about that."

Traffic was light, and it was too early to knock on a stranger's door when they arrived in Larchmont, so they found a diner to kill time. The place looked like it was suffering from a forty-year hangover, but Brennan didn't care so long as they had eggs and hash browns, which they did.

"Should help with the hangover," Hunter said after they both had coffee in front of them.

"I'm fine." She added cream to her coffee. It steamed from a cheap, narrow acrylic mug. The feel of the mug told her that she was going to hate the coffee. There was no sweetener on the table, so she asked the man sitting alone at the next table if she could grab a packet from his. She'd noticed him when he sat a few minutes after they arrived. He was only about ten years older than her, handsome, with gray hair that was almost white. He was the kind of guy she would have flirted with if she'd run across him the night before, but she just thanked him without smiling when he passed her the sweetener.

The waitress did everything but dump their plates on the table. Brennan's scrambled eggs were overcooked and thin, but the potatoes were fantastic, salty and simultaneously crunchy and soft. She knew it was her imagination, but she could feel them absorbing the leftover whiskey in her stomach. Hunter ate a bagel and stared out the window at passing traffic.

"You got Mom tonight?" he asked. They'd been trading evenings with Jane.

"Yeah. Why? Got a date?"

Hunter shook his head.

"What do you even do when you're not at her place?"

"Same as you, I suspect," he said. "Work. Hang out with friends."

"Those are two lies."

"I have friends."

"Name one."

"They're my friends from the bar. And"—he spoke over what he knew would be a sarcastic response—"I don't think you're in a position to judge."

"I'm sure the bar I stumbled out of last night is a gigantic step up from whatever cave you're hanging out in."

"You're not better than me just because your drinks cost twice what mine cost."

"I'm just giving you shit, Hunter." She forced a swig of coffee down, chased it with water. Both tasted the same. She looked up at her brother. "We need Cathy to talk to us. Without pushing her like you did to Walter. It's why he rushed us out."

"That's not what happened. He would have known if we were beating around the bush. Better to get right to it so he wouldn't think we were playing games. But yeah, he was definitely uncomfortable."

"So maybe we try a different approach with Cathy."

Hunter nodded, unconvincingly.

Brennan prodded at the bags under eyes and checked her reflection in the black screen of her cell phone. "Seriously, do I look like shit?"

"You look fine." The waitress dropped the check without saying a word. Hunter pushed it toward Brennan. "Thanks for breakfast," he said.

After Brennan paid the bill, they drove to the address Hunter had tracked down for Cathy Cooke. She lived away from the water, toward the Thruway, on a tree-lined side street still dusted with crusty snow. The trees were bare, but there were a lot of them. Brennan figured the block must be beautiful and shady in the spring and summer. Pretty houses stood quiet on crowded lots. Cathy's, a modest gray house, was second from the corner, the smallest on the block. Hunter parked in front, and they walked to the door avoiding the iced-over parts of the path.

A woman answered the door half a minute after they rang. Brennan tried to find something remarkable about her but couldn't. Medium hair, medium build, medium height. Her hair was dyed blond, but gray streaks crept in among the darkening roots. She wore a Gap sweatshirt and khaki pants.

"I'm sorry to bother you, but are you Cathy Cooke?" Hunter asked through the plexiglass in the storm door.

"Who's asking?" Her voice was completely at odds with her appearance. Low and gritty, it carried the remnants of an accent from one of the outer boroughs, like grout stains on a white tile wall.

"My name is Hunter Leigh. I'm a reporter. This is Brennan."

Just Brennan, she thought. Clever of him not to mention that Lo was her last name. Give Cathy some interesting information—he's a reporter—so that she was processing that instead of focusing on the omission of her surname.

Cathy gave them a look that said, *So what?*

"Did you know Jessica DeSalvo?" Brennan asked.

Cathy's face moved imperceptibly, a shimmer of sly fear before the plain-lady face returned. But when she spoke, her accent strengthened, almost enough to place. "That was a long time ago. What do you want with that?"

"We had a few questions," Hunter said. "We hoped you could answer them."

"Why should I talk to you?"

"We're looking at this case because it wasn't really resolved," Hunter said, his words carefully chosen.

"No. I guess it wasn't."

Brennan was sure that she was going to close the door in their faces, but instead Cathy opened the storm door and stood back so they could enter. Inside, a small hallway faced a flight of stairs to the second floor. She led them around the stairs, back to the kitchen, and offered them seats at a small dining table.

"Coffee?" she asked as she poured herself a mug.

"Yes, please," Brennan said.

Hunter asked for one as well.

Cathy poured their coffees. "I make a big pot on the weekends. Not because I'm expecting visitors, but because I like to drink it iced in the afternoon. Even when it's cold out. This house stays very warm."

The coffee was perfect—a dark Italian roast—and Brennan had to remind herself to take it slow. It would be harder for Cathy to rush them out if they were still drinking.

Cathy finally sat down. "So you want to do a story about Jess, huh?"

"Can you tell us about her?" Brennan asked, in a sympathetic voice. She could choose her words carefully as well.

"What do you want to know?"

"We want to get a sense of what she was like. How did you become friends? What did you like about her?"

"We met during college. A friend of mine from high school went to college with another girl who interned with Jessica. They put together a beach rental down in Avalon, you know, in Jersey, and I got sucked into it. I ended up hanging out with Jessica a lot that summer. We just clicked, which was funny. She was a super preppy Ivy League girl from Greenwich. And me, Bay Ridge, trying to save enough money for an associate's degree or paralegal school or whatever I was doing."

Cathy took a sip of her coffee. Brennan waited patiently. She'd interviewed enough witnesses to know eventually Cathy would keep talking, if for nothing else than to fill the silence.

"She was so much fun that summer. She wasn't one of those girls who came down, got shit-faced to the point where you were embarrassed for her, or had a different guy in and out of her room each night. But I mean, she wasn't a Goody Two-shoes either. She was funny, but without being mean. And so smart. It was nice being with her."

Hunter pulled a digital recorder from his pocket and pressed record as he placed it on the table.

"Do you mind if I record?" Hunter asked and immediately followed it up with: "So you stayed in touch after that summer?"

Hunter's smoothness in changing focus from the recorder impressed Brennan.

"Yeah. A phone call here, a postcard there. But when she was coming to New York for law school, she asked me if I knew anyone looking for a roommate. I told her we should live together."

Brennan sipped her coffee as Hunter continued the questioning. "How long did you live with her?"

"Three years. Her whole time in law school. I was back at City College. Got my finance degree."

"How was she as a roommate?"

"Perfect. She wasn't the neatest girl, you know. But she was steady, didn't do drugs, and she was just as fun and sweet as she was that summer down the shore. We'd go to a bar on Fridays, flirt with guys. But she was mostly work, work, work."

"Do you have any pictures of her?" Brennan asked.

Cathy looked at the ceiling like she could see through it. "Not out. Maybe in an old album somewhere."

"Was she close to her parents?"

Cathy nodded. "I was jealous of her for that. My mom left us when I was a kid. I barely remember her. She had issues. Drugs, whatever. I wasn't close to my dad. And then he died when I was a teenager. Work accident. He was a contractor and slipped one day. For some reason, he wasn't wearing a safety harness and stepped into an elevator shaft. My older brother got me through high school. After, it was just me, basically. But Jessica's family was always there. Stopping by when they were in the city. Taking us to lunch or dinner. I'd go up to their place for holidays. Nothing had ever gone wrong for them, any of them, in their lives. But you couldn't resent them for that, they were so nice."

"What about her husband?"

"Mark?" Cathy glanced out the window. "You talked to him?"

"Not yet," Hunter said.

"Haven't seen him in a while. What's it been? Maybe fifteen years? Twenty?"

"You stayed in touch after Jess died?" Brennan asked.

"Yeah. We were close. Because of her. But, you know, people lose touch. The more his career took off, the less time he had to keep up with old friends."

Hunter picked up the questions again. "What was he like?"

"Smart. Very handsome. God, Jess was so smitten when she met him. He was all she'd talk about. Then they got married. The three of us would hang out a lot. They were always trying to set me up with guys, but it never stuck."

Cathy took a long sip of her coffee and looked into her mug. Hunter started to speak, but Cathy held up her hand.

"But this isn't what you're here for, is it?"

"We're just trying to better understand," Brennan said. "Looking back at old news stories, you don't get a sense of her. As a person, you know? She couldn't speak for herself or explain things to the press or at trial."

"What's the point? What's your angle? Nobody gives a shit about an old murder."

"Don't you?" Hunter asked. "Don't you want to know what happened?"

"Me?" Her laugh was like vinegar and curdled milk turned to sound. "I know what happened. That guy, John Lo, killed her and got away with it."

Brennan's stomach fell, and her breath hitched. She felt the blood rushing to her face, but hoped her expression of neutral interest hadn't changed. She didn't trust herself to pick up her coffee mug. She avoided glancing at Hunter.

"Tell us how you know," Hunter said.

Cathy leaned back—her simple dinette chair, a throne—and said, "Who else could it have been? That man had everything to lose. His wife and kids, his job. If she told his wife . . ."

Cathy tried to look somber, but Brennan saw a vicious light in her eyes. Cathy pitched forward. "She thought that she was pregnant."

"That was in the papers," Hunter said. "But she wasn't, according to the autopsy. Let's take a step back. You saw her the day that she died?"

"No. She had a key to my place. Like I told the cops, I worked and then saw a movie. I was supposed to call her after, but when I did, there was no answer. I figured that she was . . . you know . . . occupied."

"She used your apartment . . ." Hunter drained the last of his coffee and let the rest of the question hang over the table.

"To have sex? Sometimes."

Hunter looked over to the coffeepot as he asked the next question. "When did that start?"

Cathy retrieved the coffeepot and refreshed their mugs.

"A few months before. Less than a year, more than six months. It wasn't a lot. Just a few times. I went to Vegas with a boyfriend for Labor Day weekend, and she offered to feed my fish while I was gone. When I got back, she told me that she had an affair."

"What did she tell you?" Brennan asked.

"She thought Mark was sleeping around. And work was stressing her out. So she had a fling, something to blow off some steam. It wasn't anything serious. I thought it was hilarious, this preppy, prim-and-proper girl, getting some on the side. I offered her my place if she wanted to use it."

Hunter raised an eyebrow. "You were Mark's friend, too. Were you worried about him?"

"You have to understand," Cathy said. "She was having a terrible time with Mark. She would show up at my door looking for a place to crash if they had a bad fight."

"How bad?" Brennan asked.

"Look," Cathy said, glancing at the recorder on the table, "I'm not friends with Mark anymore, but I don't want to say anything that will get him in trouble."

Hunter reached forward to place one hand near the recorder as if he would take it back if she asked. But Brennan knew that Cathy would talk. Everything about her—the look on her face, her posture—betrayed a desire to gossip. She just wanted an excuse, so Brennan gave her one.

"You don't have to say anything that you're not comfortable sharing," Brennan said. "We're just trying to understand what happened, and your perspective is helpful."

"Jess and Mark were toxic. They didn't put that in the papers back then. I mean, Jess was my friend, but she was . . . volatile as she got older. Especially when she drank. I don't know how to describe it. It was like she didn't care about anything. And Mark, he was like a super macho guy, right? Total Jersey Shore. Wouldn't back down from nothing. No matter how smart he was, or how much he tried to improve himself, that part was always there."

"You mentioned bad fights," Hunter said. He withdrew his hand from beside the recorder.

"I saw them hit each other. He corrected her grammar or something, and she just lost it. We were drinking, of course, smoking a cigarette outside the bar, and she slapped the smoke right out of his mouth. He shoved her to get her off of him, but like into a wall. I had to grab her, or she would've got right back at him."

"Just that once?"

Cathy shrugged. "We drank a lot. I saw them get physical with each other a few other times. And they each told me about times when they got carried away when I wasn't around. It was like they wanted me to, I don't know, kinda work things out between them. Like I was a god-damned marriage counselor or something."

"So, you offered her your apartment," Brennan said.

"Her having sex at my place didn't seem like a big deal. I figured, her meeting someone was a good thing. Maybe she'd fall in love and get the courage to leave him. She would change the sheets and clean up and everything. You couldn't even tell that she had been there. We had shared a bed a bunch of times, so I wasn't . . . I don't know. We were kids."

"Did she tell you who she was sleeping with?" Hunter asked.

"Just that he was married." Cathy rolled her eyes. "Like it was a huge secret. She was so dramatic about it. 'Cathy, it could ruin this guy's life.' Like I was going to tell the *Post* or whatever or that anybody cared."

Brennan asked, "So you didn't know that it was John Lo until you saw the papers?"

"No. I was surprised when I saw his picture. I mean, I figured she worked with the guy, who else did she have time to meet? But I didn't think she'd be into a Chinese guy. When she first told me that she'd cheated, I asked what the guy looked like. She said like an average guy. Chinese guys were not our average."

"How many times was she seeing this guy?" Hunter wanted to steer the conversation away from race. At some point, Cathy might note that he and Brennan were both half Asian and start making connections.

"At work? All the time. At my place, there was that time during Labor Day, then it picked up again after the Christmas before she died. That's when I told her she could use my place."

"Do you think Mark knew? That she was having an affair?" Hunter asked.

Cathy's eyes went to the digital recorder, but she didn't ask Hunter to switch it off. "He called me once. Said that he thought, you know, that she might be sleeping around. I told him that he was crazy, she'd never do anything like that."

"He thought you'd tell him?" Hunter offered.

"Like I said before, after a while, it was like I was his friend as much as hers." Cathy shrugged. "I felt bad about lying."

Brennan asked, "Would he have hurt her if he knew about the affair? If he thought she was pregnant with someone else's baby?"

"It wasn't—" Cathy started, but snapped her mouth shut and thought for a moment. "I mean, who knows? I don't think so. But he wanted a kid bad. Jess didn't. It was one of the things they argued about. If someone else got her pregnant and she wanted that baby? I don't know how he'd take that."

"You were telling us before about the night she was murdered," Brennan said.

Cathy watched steam rise from her coffee. "She told me that she needed a place to meet the guy. She called him that. 'The guy.' She was tired of Mark. She said that he had issues and she wanted to leave him. But she was worried she was pregnant. She didn't know whose kid it was. She said that she was going to tell the guy that the baby was his. I said,

'How can you tell him it's his?' She said that she just knew." Cathy made a face. "I guess she would if, you know."

"What happened after the movie?"

"I tried calling her. When she didn't answer, I walked around for a bit and tried again. No answer. But by that point, I thought she must be finished. So, I went home. The door was unlocked. I remember that. I mean, you did not leave your door unlocked in that neighborhood. So that's when I knew something was really wrong.

"I opened the door. It was a small one bedroom." She gestured at the space. "My whole apartment could have fit into this kitchen. The main room was tiny. The couch was out of place, so I had to walk over and look over the top of it. She was on the floor, in front of the couch. At first, I didn't know what I was seeing. I was like, 'Why is she sleeping on the floor?' But she was so still. Then I noticed the blood underneath her. The carpet was soaking it up. She wasn't breathing."

Cathy shook her head as if it would erase the image, then looked over to Hunter and Brennan. "I'm going to have nightmares tonight."

"I'm sorry," Hunter said. "I know this must be difficult."

Cathy nodded.

"What did you do next?" Brennan asked.

"I banged on my neighbor's door. Called the police."

"Anything else?"

"What do you mean? After they came? I gave a statement. Started thinking about where I was going to live. I didn't think I'd be able to stay at my place even if they let me back in."

"Before the police came, did you go back and check on her? Look around?"

"No. I was so scared. I only went back twice. That night, to get some clothes with the police, and later to move out."

"Where did you end up staying?"

"At the Plaza."

"For the night?"

"For the week it took me to find a new place to live."

Brennan cocked her head. "That must have been expensive."

"My boyfriend paid."

"Why didn't he let you crash with him?" Hunter asked.

Cathy looked down at her hands, then back to the siblings, but didn't speak.

Brennan understood. "He was married, wasn't he?"

Cathy nodded, then stood. "I think it's best if I had some time alone now."

Hunter picked up his recorder as the siblings stood to leave.

Brennan said, "Thank you for talking with us."

Cathy shook her head and said, "It's just a pity that he got away with it."

SEVENTEEN

Now

HUNTER TAPPED AT HIS PHONE AS BRENNAN SIPPED HER beer in a bar around the corner from their mother's place. TVs in each corner of the bar played highlights of sports Brennan didn't follow. The ride back from Cathy's passed without conversation except to argue about the best route back. Brennan was sure that Hunter felt vindicated—nothing Cathy said pointed away from their father and toward another suspect. She tired of waiting for Hunter to gloat, but his attention was still on his phone.

"Making a date for later?"

"It's my friend from the NYPD. He's being kinda cryptic, but I think he found the files from the investigation. I'm going to meet him later on this week. Want to come?"

"If he's worried about McCarthy or other people catching wind of this, you think he wants two of us traipsing into One Police Plaza?"

"If you don't want to come," Hunter said, "it'll be easier that way. I figured you had work or something anyway. I was inviting you as a courtesy."

"And because we're working this thing together."

Hunter picked up a menu listing ten different kinds of burgers. Without looking at her, he said, "I think we did good together, today. The two of us."

"Me, too."

Hunter put down his menu, his face thoughtful. "That last thing about her staying at the Plaza. That feel funny to you?"

"Beyond us making her admit to an old affair?"

"But wouldn't that person have access to the apartment? I mean, that's why Dad and Jess met there."

"Nothing about that in the coverage of the trial," Brennan said, speaking as the implications occurred to her. "From the stories, it seemed like Harris beat the jury over the head with reasonable doubt. They couldn't definitively put Dad in the apartment. Anyone else could have been there. Cathy's boyfriend. Maybe another boyfriend Jess had. But if Harris knew Cathy had a married boyfriend, it may have given him someone else to point the finger at."

Hunter didn't get a chance to respond because the waitress came over for their order. She was a cute young blond and smiled warmly at Hunter.

"Do I know you from somewhere?" the waitress asked.

"I don't think so."

She placed her hand on his shoulder like it was something she wasn't thinking about, except that she was. "I could swear. Do you live around here?"

"Our mom lives around the corner," Hunter said. "We're grabbing some food before we head over."

"Well, let me get you fed then. What can I get you?"

They ordered. Hunter watched the waitress walk away, then turned back to Brennan, who made a face.

"Gross," she said.

"What are you? Eleven? We're adults. People flirt."

Brennan sat back in the booth. "Whatever you say. We may have to go back eventually—to Cathy. When we know more. Same with Walter. He was useless."

"We had to start somewhere."

Hunter went back to tapping at his phone. Brennan pulled hers from her purse and answered work emails until their beers came, followed by the burgers. The waitress found reasons to linger briefly at the table each time.

"She should just sit down," Brennan said.

"She's being friendly."

"Are you interested?"

"She's cute."

"But?"

Hunter shook his head. "I don't think it's the best time to start dating now."

"When was the last serious relationship you had?"

Hunter took a large bite of his burger and made Brennan wait while he chewed. Brennan dipped a fry in ketchup and refused to look away. Hunter finally swallowed and shrugged.

"It depends on what you mean by serious. I was on and off with a colleague for about five years. Whenever we were in the same place. We covered a lot of the same stuff, which is how we met. She married some other guy like three years ago. Had a baby. Said she got tired of waiting for me to commit."

"Why didn't you?"

Hunter shoved more burger into his mouth. Brennan dipped another fry and waited.

"I used to tell myself that I didn't love her," Hunter said. "But I did. She was fearless. A great reporter. She was inspiring, the way she went after stories. Great sense of humor. And smoking hot—don't look at me that way, that matters, too."

"So, what held you back?"

Hunter drained his beer before answering. Brennan took a much smaller sip of hers.

"Other things mattered more to me. I didn't realize that at first, or I wouldn't have let the whole thing carry on for as long as I did. But I loved my job, and she loved hers, and it made it hard to be in the same place. Also, I loved being available to other women. I meet a lot of people. There's a lot of opportunity for new experiences. I wanted that more than I wanted stability or commitment."

Brennan said, "Maybe she would have been open to that?"

"An open relationship? Don't you think we had that conversation?"

"How am I supposed to know? Maybe you communicated with her as well as you do with your family."

Hunter rolled his eyes. "We talked about it, and she was open to it in the beginning. Hard not to be in our situations, but things shifted over time. We'd get randomly jealous of each other. Then, the more she wanted a kid, the more she—and look, I don't want to make it sound like she wanted a kid because she was a woman or anything like that. It could have as easily been me wanting a family and her wanting to live her life or whatever."

"You don't have to say that to me because I'm a woman."

"I'm telling you because I don't want you thinking that I'm some asshole who couldn't get over wanting to fuck around so I left a great woman waiting."

"You literally just said that you wanted to be available to other women."

Hunter took a breath. "It was more than that. I don't want to fall into the same traps Dad fell into. Marriage. Kids. Some bullshit office job. Living life like you're being smothered in everyone else's fucked-up expectations of what your life should be."

Brennan felt like he was speaking about her. "You think he felt that way?"

"How would I know? But how else do you explain what he did?"

"We don't know what he did, right? Isn't that what we're trying to figure out?"

"I mean the affair."

They didn't speak much as they finished up. Hunter paid the bill and slipped a napkin with his name and number into the billholder.

"I saw that," Brennan said as she walked to the door.

Outside, her cell phone rang. It was a blocked number, but she answered anyway, in case it was a client.

"Brennan Lo?" It was a man's voice, muffled in part by the wind and traffic sounds. Brennan pressed a hand to one ear, but the sounds were on his end as well.

"Yes?"

"Leave Cathy alone. Leave Walter alone. Leave everybody alone. I know what you're doing. Stop now before something happens that can't be undone. Understand that I know where you work. Where your brother works. Where you live. You can't find me, but I can find you. Your father killed that girl. So leave it be."

EIGHTEEN

Now

BRENNAN SCREAMED AN OBSCENITY INTO THE PHONE, BUT the caller had already terminated the call.

"Work?" Hunter asked.

Brennan shook her head and told him about the threat. When she finished, the two just looked at each other as the cold wind blustered between them.

"We should tell Mom," Hunter finally said.

"They didn't say anything about her."

"Bren. She needs to—"

"Needs to what? Go into hiding? Buy a gun? She lives in a doorman building, keeps her door locked, and can't get make it from her bed to her front door most days. I don't want her to spend her last days worrying about us."

Hunter gave her an unhappy shake of his head. "Fine. But if this gets serious, we gotta stop."

Brennan wondered what someone could do to their mother that was worse than what her own body was doing to her. Still, she was less certain about the decision than she appeared as they walked toward their mother's building.

"It's gotta be someone from McCarthy's campaign," Hunter said. "He's the only one with something to lose here."

"Unless it's the killer."

"Assuming the killer is even alive, how would he—or she—even know?"

"What I don't like is that he knows who we talked to. I mean, we left Cathy's a few hours ago."

"Maybe Cathy called someone?"

Brennan stopped and looked around.

"What?" Hunter asked. "You think we were followed?"

She shrugged. There were probably fifty people in her line of sight and countless cars parked on the street or driving by.

They found Jane in the living room. She was sitting on the couch, wrapped in a blanket.

"Mom! You're up!" Other than to use the bathroom, it had been a couple of weeks since Brennan saw her mother out of bed.

"I felt better," she said. "I decided to tidy up."

"You don't have to do that."

"I got bored."

Hunter made his way to the kitchen. "Can I get you anything, Mom?"

"Tea. Please."

While he was in the kitchen, Jane gestured to the file of press clippings on the coffee table. "Why are you looking at those?"

"Just curious." Brennan tried to convey nonchalance, but her voice sounded chastened and guilty.

Hunter walked in from the kitchen. "Kettle's on."

His eyes immediately fell upon the papers. Jane noticed.

"What are the two of you doing?" she asked.

Hunter sat in a chair facing his mother. "What do you mean?"

Jane fixed him with a stare. "You know what I mean."

"We're looking into it," Brennan said.

Their mother shook her head as her hands balled around folds in the blanket beneath them. "I finally have the both of you home again. We already lost so much time to that. I can't... I don't want to die listening to you fight about your father."

"It's not like that, Mom," Hunter said.

Brennan started to gather up the papers. "We just wanted some answers."

"Answers to what? It was thirty years ago!" Jane raised her voice as much as she was able. "You think you can come to any conclusion now that you couldn't then? How? Reading these news stories?"

"We're talking to people," Hunter said. "We think we can get the original files and evidence, too."

Their mother's mouth tightened into a line. "Oh? You're talking to people? What people? Am I one of those people? You going to ask me any questions?"

Brennan shook her head and started to speak, but Hunter cut her off. "You started this, Mom. The other night."

"I was out of my mind on painkillers."

"No. Listen. You said our father worked at a restaurant. Neither of us remember that. You know things we don't—"

"I know a lot you don't—"

"So then tell us!" Hunter was suddenly on his feet. "Just the name of the restaurant, even! We don't remember. Don't we get to know anything?"

Jane looked up at him from the couch. "Stop. Please. The two of you tore yourselves apart your whole lives over him. What do you think this will get you? And after? What then? You go back to hating each other over a dead man neither of you really knew?"

"I knew him," they said simultaneously, notes in a minor chord—Brennan's loss and yearning resonating over Hunter's anger and disgust.

"Not like me," she said. "And maybe I didn't know him all that well."

"You were married to him," Hunter said.

"And Brennan, how well did Paul know you?"

Brennan flushed and looked away. Her mother was speaking in generalities, but Brennan couldn't shake the feeling that she knew about her cheating.

"I married him. I was the mother to his children. And I didn't know him well enough to know he was having an affair," Jane said. "I didn't know him well enough to decide one way or the other whether he killed her. I still don't know. And because of that . . . how much time did the two of you lose? How much time did we all lose? What kind of lives are you living?"

She shook her head.

"It was easier, after all I lost, after all I didn't know, to let you guys go ahead and be certain. To let you believe that you knew. Because the doubt, from the night he was arrested, that doubt festered inside me like a cyst. Or a tumor. Because what if I didn't agree with you? What if I lost you, too? But I ruined you. The two of you. Your certainty drove you apart. I did that. Because of my doubt."

Hunter and Brennan glanced at each other. Their mother pulled the blanket tighter around herself.

"One of you is wrong. Is figuring out which of you it is going to suddenly make it all better? Have you even thought about what happens if you do figure it out?"

"The truth matters," Hunter said.

Their mother rolled her eyes. "The truth is you're trying to validate thirty years of mistakes. Leave me out of it. I'd rather die alone than listen to the two of you fight about this like when you were kids."

NINETEEN

Now

"THAT COULD HAVE GONE BETTER." HUNTER PULLED ON black leather gloves as they left their mother's building.

"How did you expect her to react?" Brennan hadn't bothered buttoning her coat yet. After the heat in her mother's apartment, she welcomed the cold air. "You think she wanted to be reminded of . . . all of that?"

"Do you honestly think she needed any reminding? She's the one who started all of this when she called me over."

"Why did you leave the papers out?"

"How could I know she'd go and clean the place?"

Brennan shook her head. Hunter had never been anything but certain that he wasn't at fault.

"Do you think she'll be okay?" Hunter asked. He'd almost told his mother about the threatening phone call, but didn't—mainly because he didn't want Brennan to blame him if his mother panicked.

"She managed to clean," Brennan said as she started to walk away. "I suppose she'll manage her dinner and her pills."

"Where are you going?"

"To find a drink. Coming?"

#

"You're lucky I didn't have any plans tonight." Hunter tapped Brennan's shot glass with his own before dumping it into his mouth.

Brennan took her shot of bourbon. It was their third, each spaced by a pint of beer. Despite the drinks, Brennan's anxiety smoldered like a low-grade fever.

"What's the deal with the restaurant thing?" she asked. "You keep bringing it up."

"I don't know. Maybe it's nothing. Maybe Mom brought it up that night for a reason. I just want all the facts. It's the way I am. I see a question; I want the answer."

"So, how do we chase down some place that probably doesn't exist anymore to see if someone there remembers Dad from thirty years ago?"

"There's social media groups for everything. I'm in a group with kids from my college newspaper. I've found sources that way."

He glanced at his phone, considering whether to pull up an example.

"It's a little early for that waitress to call you," she teased. "Wouldn't want you to think she's easy."

"Her name is Jenna."

"How do you know that?"

"She already texted me to give me her number. So she could toss the napkin."

"Slut." Brennan pulled her phone from her bag.

"That's not very progressive of you."

"Fuck you."

Hunter laughed, but Brennan reached out with two fingers to poke him hard in the arm.

"No! I'm serious!" she shouted over the music. "You don't get to sail back into the city and come to my bar and fucking judge me."

"Your bar?"

"Like that! 'Your bar?'" She did an exaggerated impression of his baritone voice and inflection. "Yeah, my fucking bar. I drink here like I own it."

"Sounds like a problem."

Brennan looked down at her phone and tapped at it briefly. She crinkled her face in a way that guys probably thought was cute when she did it on dates. Hunter used the moment to send a quick message ("drinks soon?") to Jenna.

"Are you done judging me?" Brennan said when he set his phone on the table.

"Fuck you. You judge me all the time."

"All the time? You've been gone for years. While I take her to doctor's appointments, make sure she has all of her medicine, has food in the apartment, has someone to talk to."

"I talked to her. Emails all the time. Calls stupid early or late my time so it wouldn't throw off her schedule. Listening to her voice get raspy and fade on choppy calls before my phone would cut out. Watching the old her, the woman she was, disappear on shitty video calls."

Brennan's anger morphed suddenly into drunken sincerity. "She was so stressed, Hunter. Constantly worried about you. Whether they'd grab you, make a video of you, hood over your head . . ."

Hunter had seen the videos without the pauses or cutaways they used on the news. He'd done stories on how things had gone wrong for the other reporters and the aid workers who'd been grabbed, imprisoned, and executed. They were his sources, acquaintances, friends. He'd reported on furtive searches, bad-faith negotiations, and sometimes-failed rescues, all the while in the same danger.

Brennan leaned forward as if that might bring them closer. "It wore her down."

Hunter snorted. "She'd get on these calls with me, and all I wanted was to just . . . get a touch of home. And I'd ask her how things were going, and she'd unload on me about you. About how she was worried about your job. The guys you prosecuted. How she was worried when you left the government to go back to private practice because you hated it. About how stressed you were with work. How she thought you were too good for the guys you dated."

"Yeah. Must have been a drag to hear about how your sister was doing."

"You were literally just saying the same thing about your brother."

"You always did this, Hunter," she said. "No, no, listen to me. You fucking always did this when we were kids. We'd be having a nice time. Like that time over Christmas break when we were in high school."

"Oh Jesus, this again?"

"It was a great day! All I wanted to do was—

#

—go to the Met."

"Huh?" Hunter asked, one eyebrow raised, crunching on a spoonful of cereal.

"I said I want to go to the Met."

Neither of them had plans that morning. Their mother was working. Usually, they'd sit in their own rooms, reading, watching TV, or playing video games separately. But when he passed her doorway spooning cereal into his mouth, she looked up from *The Two Towers* and said, "Let's go to the Met."

Speaking between chews, he said, "Let me finish my breakfast."

After years of passing each other in the same apartment like office workers from different departments, she was surprised to find that she actually enjoyed spending time with Hunter. He made her laugh, had interesting takes on the art, and asked for her advice about some girl he liked. It grew dark as they walked across the park on the way home.

"We should hang out more," Brennan said.

"Yeah, sure."

They circled around the north side of the Great Lawn. In the dimming light, Hunter's face assumed the same contours of her hazy memories of her father's.

"You look more like him, now, as you get older."

Hunter stopped walking. "Jesus. Why do you always have to bring him up?"

"I miss him. I think about him all the time. He just . . . pops into my head, you know?"

"Get over it. He sucked."

"I have . . . I can't talk about him with anyone else."

"I don't want to talk about him." He stopped walking, cheeks flushed from the cold and anger. "I don't want to be like him. I don't want to remind you—or anyone else—of him. This is why I hate hanging out with you."

Tears welled in her eyes. "This was such a fun day. And you—

\#

—ruined it."

Hunter threw his arms up. "I didn't ruin anything! He fucking ruined it! That day! Every day! Our whole lives, Brennan!"

When he finished, the two of them glared at each other across the landscape of empty glasses.

"I'm not doing this with you when you're like this."

Hunter's head fell back in frustration. "You never wanted to have this conversation, because you know I'm right."

She shook her head, and the room rocked like a boat. She enjoyed the feeling even though she put her chances of vomiting when she got home at greater than even. She focused back on Hunter. "That's not true, Hunter. This is about you. Your absolute glee in tearing down the person I loved."

"He was a terrible man, Bren, even if he didn't kill that woman. He cheated on Mom. He made that choice! He didn't deserve your worship."

"People can be both good and bad. You can love bad people."

"But you can't pretend they're not bad."

"He wasn't a bad man. Nobody is any single thing they do or think!"

"You're a fucking hypocrite. You sent people to prison for single mistakes—"

"Absolutely," Brennan said. "I'm not saying people shouldn't be punished for their crimes. But doesn't there have to be a way back?"

"How? What did he do to earn his way back?"

"I don't know." She couldn't remember well the time after the trial. But she remembered one thing. "He was a good father to me," she said quietly. "That was something."

"Oh come on, Brennan. He was awful to us."

Hunter leaned back in his chair, arms and legs spread like he was the only person in the bar, taking up space in a way Brennan would never do, and rolled his eyes. She resented him and the air he touched.

"Did you ever see a hero, an icon you didn't want to tear down? Don't fucking roll your eyes at me. Since we were kids, every conversation with you, if someone said something nice about someone, you'd pipe in with a 'Yeah, but what about this or that?'"

"Because they're people. And people are shit. We're all . . . Look at us. Look at Dad." Hunter leaned forward. "Name one person. I'll tell you why they suck."

"Jesus Christ," Brennan said in exasperation. It wasn't an answer.

"He rioted in a temple," Hunter said with a smirk.

Brennan took the bait. "He fed the poor. Cured the sick. He forgave."

"And what right did He have to do that?"

Brennan wanted to throw a drink in his face, but all the glasses were empty.

"Go ahead, Hunter. Keep deflecting. Keep running. I know that underneath this whole facade is a little boy trying to make up for a daddy who disappointed him. But we've had thirty years to figure shit out. The fact that we didn't is on us. It's on you and me."

Hunter glanced down to his phone.

"I have a message. We done here?"

"Yeah. Whatever." Brennan grabbed her phone and walked to the bar to pay the tab.

TWENTY

Now

BRENNAN FUMBLED WITH THE DEADBOLT WHILE TRYING NOT to spill the rum and Coke in her hand. She swung the door open to reveal a smiling Sean. She had shed her jeans as soon as she got home after leaving Hunter in the bar, but her sweater was warm, and she didn't want to contort herself to unsnap her bra, so she poured herself her drink and waited bare legged for help to arrive.

"Hey, sexy," she said.

He stepped through the door and kissed her. She leaned into the kiss; it was easier to let him support her weight than try to hold herself up. Sean stumbled back a step, nearly into the hallway again.

"Whoa there," he said, lifting her back upright. The drink sloshed in her glass—or maybe the liquid was still and she was rolling from side to side. Or she and the glass were still as the apartment rocked like a cradle. The physics were complicated.

Sean leaned her against the wall inside her apartment and swung the door shut with his foot. He reached for her glass.

"No," she said. "Make your own. This one's mine."

"Are you okay?"

She shoved him playfully as she made her way to the kitchen. "I'm fine. Wanna drink?"

"Sure."

The bottle of rum waited on the island separating the kitchen from the living area. She resisted the urge to steady herself against the wall as she set her glass down next to it, opened the fridge, and retrieved the can of Diet Coke she had opened when she got home—after checking all of the rooms and behind the shower curtains. The dark apartment spooked her after the call earlier. It was part of the reason she called Sean.

Sean stood at the end of the island. In the absence of his smile, Brennan found she didn't want to look at his face.

"Stop looking at me like that," she said as she filled a glass with ice.

"Like what?"

"Like Paul. He used to look at me like that. Conceeeerrned."

"I'm a little concerned."

"Don't be." She dumped rum into the glass until it was three-quarters full, then abruptly righted the bottle. Stray rum ran down the side. She ran her hand up the length of the bottle collecting the tendrils and then sucked her fingers as he watched. She slid his glass to him.

"You forgot the Coke."

"Come and get it."

She hated the feeling that he was humoring her. She wanted to be handled, but not like this. Why didn't he fucking get it?

Sean hesitated, then approached her, taking the can of soda and pouring some into his glass. There was only room for a splash. When he picked it up, she jabbed her glass at his. The impact sloshed the drinks onto their hands.

"Jesus, Brennan!"

She smiled at him over her glass. "Sorry. Guess you'll need to punish me."

Sean shook his head. "You're trashed."

"So? Usually you like me trashed."

"I'm just . . . I didn't . . . This is not what I was expecting."

Brennan rolled her eyes. She wanted to saunter to the couch, plunge into it, and invite him to sink into her and then go, but her one hip leaned against the counter, and she wasn't sure that she could push herself away without falling.

"Come on, Sean. Lighten up. I thought my texts were pretty explicit about what I was expecting. It's why you left your family at home to come here, right?"

Sean's face darkened like concrete wet with rain. His lust was a string drawn between shame and compassion, vibrating in a deep bass Brennan felt in the pit of her stomach. If she kept plucking, Brennan knew it would break—it always broke the same way.

"You were out with your brother?" Sean asked.

"Oh, for fuck's sake." Brennan shoved herself upright. She wobbled, then stumbled around the island to the couch. When she reached it, she stopped, sure that if she reached down to place her glass on the coffee table, she'd collapse.

"I need help," she said. Sean took her drink and set it down. Brennan sank to the edge of the couch, reached up to hold Sean's hips, and leaned her head forward against him. She wanted to sleep, that feeling of being dragged into unconsciousness, those ephemeral moments when she shut her eyes and felt herself spinning, body heavy on the bed, alone.

"Last chance," Sean said. "Do you want to talk? Tell me why you really asked me to come here tonight?"

She might have been able to, bowed against him, in the darkness of her closed eyes, pressed against the rough fabric of his jeans like the mesh screen in a confessional. She could've admitted that she wanted to orbit Sean like an outlying planet, close enough to be trapped by his gravity, but too distant for his radiance to warm her—for him to be another point of light indistinguishable from countless untouchable others in her sky. She could've whispered to him about the abject loneliness of her certainty, the pain she'd inflicted on the men who loved her, her lifelong betrayals of her father in her moments of doubt or when she elided his existence, the horror that his absence had made her life easier, the preemptive grief that choked her when she visited her dying mother, and the bleak desolation promised by a future without family or friends.

"After she's gone," Brennan whispered, "it will be just me and him."

"I didn't hear you," Sean said.

Brennan raised her head to look up at him, blinked the shimmer from her eyes, and began to unbutton his pants.

"I said I need help getting undressed for bed."

#

"Admit it, you can't wait to get me undressed," Jenna said.

Hunter laughed. "I only said I'd rather go topless than wear a Mets shirt."

"I didn't know I was going to go out after work," Jenna said, then smirked. "But keep talking like that and you may blow it."

"I'd hate to squander a late lead. Although it might remind you of your favorite team. Is that why you invited me out? So I could close better than the Mets?"

"I wanted to unwind after work, but my coworkers are boring. You—apparently a guy with no friends—said you were available."

"I was out with my sister." He wondered if she'd made it home alright.

"So you ditched her to meet me?"

Hunter shrugged, trying to avoid the thought that he should have seen Brennan home. The call she'd received weighed on him the longer the night went on.

"She'd had enough to drink, and I had a cute girl to meet."

Jenna rolled her eyes at the compliment.

Hunter knew he was drunk, but she delighted him. He hadn't laughed this much in a long time. They developed a natural, teasing rapport quickly, their banter sprinkled with biographical details like chocolate chips in ice cream. She hailed from some town he'd never heard of near Albany, studied literature at NYU, then worked at a tech company for a few years until it went under a couple of months before. Since then, she waited tables while she worked on a novel and decided what to do next.

"So, you told me before that you're back in New York between assignments. How long is that?"

Hunter shrugged. "Not to bring the mood down, but my mom is really sick. So, I'm thinking I may stay around until . . . until that situation is resolved."

"I'm sorry." Jenna reached across the table and squeezed his wrist.

"It's okay," Hunter said. "She's been ill for a while."

"But it changes, right? When the end is imminent? My dad, he got cancer when I was at NYU. It never really went into remission as much as slowed down at times, I guess. So we had a lot of time to get right with the way things were going. You'd think that would help at the end, but it didn't."

Hunter set his hand over hers, still on his wrist, and gave it a brief squeeze before withdrawing.

"What about your mom?" he asked.

"Oh, she's kicking around upstate. Works as an administrator at SUNY Albany." Jenna sat back and picked up her beer to take a full sip. "What about your dad?"

Hunter thought about lying. Given the turn in conversation, they were more likely to end up crying on each other's shoulders instead of finding the other comfort he was looking for. "He's gone. I try not to talk about it. But enough about parents. You know about my sister. What about you? Any siblings?"

"Two sisters. They're married. One lives in California now. The other is still upstate. It must be nice having your sister nearby. You must be close."

"No. Not really."

"I hate to ask, but is it your fault or hers? Checking for red flags." Hunter didn't know what his expression looked like, but Jenna's smile faded. "I'm kidding. I was trying to . . . I make jokes to keep things light. Sometimes it goes wrong."

Hunter said, "No, I get that, and I don't mind. Honestly, it's really complicated. She's a good person. Amazing, really. But we see the world differently. Which is a bullshit answer, everyone does, right?"

"Sisters, right? It's fraught, I get it. But"—she dragged the word out as she dredged her mind for the rest of her thought—"I'm picking up something else. Or I'm reading too much into your face. It's hard to tell. I don't know if you know this, but I had a long shift and a couple of drinks. I am, however, really very perceptive."

Jenna sipped her beer and waited for him to respond. Hunter figured she was used to getting answers with that face and her demeanor—a mix of easygoing sympathy and bemusement that invited disclosures.

"She thinks that I act like I'm not accountable," Hunter said. "If you asked her, she'd tell you you're wasting your time. That I ruin things because I can't admit when I'm wrong."

"Are you? Wrong?"

"Of course not." He gave her a rueful smile and dumped the rest of the beer into his mouth.

Jenna studied his face as if his thoughts were broadcasting on a frequency she could find if she could tune him correctly. Hunter considered laying it all out. Even with the boozy teasing, Hunter basked in Jenna's sincere warmth. It salved something raw inside him—the places he avoided letting the other women he met touch.

Jenna got tired of waiting and asked, "What's going on in your head?"

After my mother's gone, my sister is all I'll have left is what he wanted to say. But the instinct to keep those areas hidden died hard. As much as he wanted to show her the broken pieces, he didn't want her to confirm how bad it was.

"Can I be honest with you? My job, the travel, everything about me, my family makes it hard to form real connections. I pretty much only deal with . . . transient relationships. Flings. Whatever you want to call them. There's already so much we all carry with us, but something like that? It's weightless. Just two people being their best selves for each other for an evening. Maybe the next morning."

Jenna crossed her arms. "That's a rehearsed bullshit answer."

Hunter shrugged. "I like to make sure that everyone's clear-eyed."

"It's a little presumptuous."

"Getting the timing right is tough. Too soon, and I sound cocky. Too late, and I'm an asshole who took advantage of you."

"You can be both cocky and an asshole even if your timing was good."

"How was my timing?"

"Honestly, a little early. But I'm not looking for a boyfriend and I'm in a forgiving mood. So let's get out of here."

TWENTY-ONE

Then

JOHN STARED DOWN AT THE CLASSIFIED ADS, STACKED across the broadsheet pages in indecipherable tiles of dense text and abbreviations. Staggered throughout the page were ads outlined in blue ballpoint pen. He didn't circle them like some people did—not that he had looked through a classifieds page in decades. John smirked at the irony: he'd cheat on his wife, but God forbid he stray outside the lines on the classifieds page.

The legal jobs were all paralegal or secretary postings, if they were at a firm of the caliber of Taylor Wood & West, or otherwise associate listings at personal injury defense firms. Nothing approaching the status or income of his old position. If he couldn't have as prestigious a position or make as much money, there was no point in remaining a lawyer, so he expanded outside of the legal listings—construction jobs, restaurant jobs, anything. He dreamed that he would find a new life, a new career buried in the wall of text, but nothing appeared, no stroke of inspiration. Just words and half words in tiny print, entire futures waiting for the right eyes to find them. But not John's. He was selecting ads at random to draw his boxes around, trying to capture the potential in them. It was something better than sitting on the couch waiting for another day to end.

He looked up. Jane stood in the doorway.

"I thought you were at work," he said.

"I was. But we need to talk and not when the kids can overhear us."

"Okay."

"You need to find work."

John waved to the sheets of newspapers open across his desk.

"Come on, John . . ."

"I'm looking."

"You need to actually look. For something realistic."

John glanced down at an entry he didn't remember squaring off. "High-end restaurant seeks waitstaff. Min exp 5 yrs." He didn't remember reading it, much less running his pen around the edges of the ad no less than four times. He was not a competitive candidate for the position.

"I'm trying."

"Seriously? Outlining entries does nothing."

"What do you want me to do?"

"Have you picked up the phone?"

"Nobody's taking my calls."

"I get it, maybe you can't face your friends. But tell me the truth, have you called a single one of those ads?"

He searched the ads for one he had called. "Dental office seeks manager. Bookkeeping exp pref. Min exp 3 years." He had not called that one. Nor any of them.

"We're going to run out of money, John. It's been two months since the trial."

"Me taking just any job isn't going to fix that."

"Call Harris. Maybe he needs help with his practice."

John snatched a page from his desk and began crumpling it.

"You think," he said as he continued to wad it in his hands, "that he wants me around? He wants to send this message to his clients? 'I can get you off, but then you'll end up here with me, getting my coffee, sweeping my floor, organizing my files.'"

"You don't have options."

"When the firm buys me out—"

"You know they're not going to pay what you want."

"I'll get something. It will carry us for a while. Or I can use it to start my own firm."

"Who will your clients be? How many companies are going to hire an accused—"

She stopped speaking.

"Accused what?"

They stood apart, the questions they had never discussed pressing them into opposite sides of the room. Or maybe that force had been there even before Jessica's murder. John remembered how it used to be that he and Jane could not be in a room before they drifted together, attraction like magnetism locking them to each other. But the polarity had reversed, and the eerie, unseen force pushed them in opposite directions.

"The kids can't keep coming home to see you like this. When's the last time you showered?"

It had been two days. "Are you asking me to leave?"

"They need you, John. They need you to try—"

"Because if you're asking me to leave, I will."

"Stop. I didn't come here to fight with you."

"What do *you* need from me, Jane?"

She stood rigidly, a tree coated with ice. "I need . . . They need their father back."

"And us? I'm not just their father. I'm your husband. I—" He stopped himself. His cheeks and ears burned as if he had been drinking. He hated the feeling. He knew what he had been about to say but didn't understand why the words would not issue from his mouth. He looked up, and Jane stood across the room. Her mouth was a thin line of frustration. Her eyes were—

#

—closed. His may as well have been, too. The room was darker than any they had shared in the city. No streetlights glowed through the windows. Only the dimmest moonlight dusted the room with silver. The ceiling fan spun silently, the slight movement of air cooling the sweat on their bodies. Their legs lay entwined.

"Can I tell you something crazy?" Jessica asked.

"Yeah. Sure." He raised himself up to an elbow so he could look down at her.

"I sympathize with her. With Jane."

"What do you mean?" John found it difficult to gauge her mood in the darkness.

"All those things you told me about her. How hard she works. How much she does for your kids. It's gotta be exhausting. I wonder how she does it. Could I?"

"You could."

He felt Jessica take a breath laden with impatience. The tension passed from her legs into his like bass from a speaker.

"Do you think she wants more?"

"Than what?"

"Than being a mother. A wife. A lawyer."

"Huh?" John couldn't decipher Jessica's intent in asking the questions. Her face gave nothing away. In the dark, he could only tell that her eyes weren't open.

"Do you think she wanted to be more? To be something else?" Jessica elaborated.

"We met in law school. She wanted to be a lawyer. She became one. She wanted to get married. So we got married. Then she wanted kids. We had them."

"That's all she wanted?"

"I remember asking her, the first night we went home together, laying in the dark like this, 'What would you do if you could do anything?' She said, 'Be a lawyer.' I said, 'What kind?' She said, 'A working lawyer.'

"When she got hired, I asked her, 'What now? Where do you want to be in five years?' 'Employed,' she said. I laughed and told her she sounded like my immigrant parents. She told me that they were smart."

He saw Jessica's mouth twitch, and she settled into the mattress more deeply.

"Her dreams are increments," John continued. "I can't even call them dreams. They're more a to-do list. One time, I asked her, 'What's your dream vacation?' She said she didn't have one, just places she wanted to visit. She gave me a list 'in no particular order.' Everything is like that. She's on a ladder. She only tells me about the next rung. Maybe there's more. Maybe she knows what's at the top. Maybe she dreams of it. But she never tells me."

He stopped speaking. Jessica reached out to lay her hand atop his arm.

"It's okay," she said.

"But it's not. She's an ocean I can't see the bottom of. When I set out, I thought I understood her. Now I'm adrift, and I don't understand the currents or the winds or anything. Every day, all I can think is that I shouldn't be out there. But I can't find my way back."

He stopped speaking to see if Jessica understood, but it was still dark, and her eyes were still closed. She took her hand off his arm, but John didn't notice. He continued, "I can only understand her in these little things she says she wants. Every day, I know her less."

Jessica shifted, and their legs uncoupled.

"I'm sorry," John said. "This weekend was supposed to be for us."

"I brought her up."

"Still. I didn't need to . . . I mean, this whole thing was meant to be a vacation from our problems, right?"

"Yeah."

He reached out to slide the back of his finger up the length of her arm. The downy hair he never noticed in the light passed underneath. He stopped when he reached the place just below her shoulder where he knew two freckles lay side by side, almost touching, separated by the slightest margin of fair skin. From a distance, they looked joined. Discovering they were separate marks required study of her arm akin to astronomy. He knew where they were, even in the dark, because he mapped her as they lay together and told each other that it meant nothing.

"What was your dream?" John asked.

The pillow shifted next to his elbow as she shook her head. He knew if he moved his finger to the corner of her closed eye, it would be wet.

"I wanted to be a singer."

"I didn't know that."

"I don't talk about it."

"I didn't even know you sang."

"I used to. In school. Choir in high school. But there was this band."

"When?"

"College. I was dating a guy. He played guitar. I'd sing. Covers at first. But then we started writing stuff together. Really it was me. I wrote those songs. We found a drummer, and a guy to play bass. Actually booked a couple of gigs. Then he dumped me. The band broke up. That was it."

"You didn't try again?"

"No. I loved singing. There were things that I was trying to tell people. But doing it for real, I learned that I was only okay. None of the songs I wrote said anything a hundred other songs weren't saying. And our sound wasn't anything different from a hundred bands. I sing fine, but I wasn't going to win *Star Search* or anything. I didn't want to starve trying to do something I was mediocre at. Even if I loved it."

John leaned over and kissed her forehead. He understood mediocrity. He knew from a young age that he was destined to it. No matter how hard he worked, how well he performed, he would not be a leading man, or a Major League baseball player, or president, or a Supreme Court justice, or even a rainmaker partner. Part of it was that his primary talent was relentlessness, not an exceptional legal mind. Yet he'd spent his life watching other mediocrities rise to exceptional heights because of circumstances, connections, and comraderies he could never duplicate because his skin was yellow, his eyes were sloped, and he was a foreigner in the land where he was born. At the end of his life, however grand his ambitions, however he fulfilled the promise of whatever abilities he had, the sum of it would be middling. That was what the American Dream promised for him.

"I don't look at it like I gave up," she said. "I just found a new dream."

He waited for Jessica to share, but she didn't.

"You trying to go to sleep?" he asked.

"No."

"Why do you have your eyes closed?"

"I'm trying to picture this as something real. Just you and me. The quiet. The dark. Nothing else."

The concept was too much for John. His wife and kids were a hundred miles away, but he felt them lingering outside the window. The night had brought them closer. The only time he had been able to push them from his mind had been in the warmth inside her, her moans in his ear, the feel of her stomach, slick with sweat pressing against him when she arched her back so he would fill her the right way, so she could take everything he wanted to give, and it was real for John then. Lying next to her, even closing his eyes, the moment was gone, left inside Jessica, an ache in the empty core of himself.

She slid her leg over, snaking her calf underneath his.

"I love the way you're with me. You make me really happy. I don't know how to describe it, because I know it's not real. But it's like I'm lost inside this book or story, for now at least. When we're together, I feel like maybe, maybe I could write another song, something true. About hope. Even though this is hopeless. Isn't it?"

His answer was to take her hand. She turned her shoulders toward him and pressed her face into his bare chest and kissed it once, then again.

"What was your dream?" she whispered against his chest.

"When I was a kid?"

"After that. When you were an adult."

"I only wanted to make Jane happy," he said.

Jessica tilted her head back; her eyes were—

#

—open wounds. The icy stance shattered as Jane threw her hands up.

"What, John?"

"I—" He tried to compose the next words in his head before speaking them. He had spent years, he realized, formulating this confession as he sat alone in his office, or walked through the park, or held the strap on the subway, or tried to find the bottom of each glass of whiskey. He had written and burned entire manuscripts trying to explain what he was about to say.

John wanted to start in the beginning, when they were leaving their first-year criminal law class. He didn't remember why they began chatting in the hallway; they'd never spoken before. Maybe it was to compare a note or to comment about some other student, but he found his eyes locked with hers. She didn't look away, and he fought to hold her gaze. The idle chitchat streaming from their mouths did not match the intensity in her eyes. Hers were earth colored, speckled with green, gold, amber, a forest floor in miniature. He said something that she found amusing, she laughed, and it was wind blowing through the trees as all the color in her eyes danced with light. He knew he would bend every fiber in his body to see that delight for as long as he could bring it to her.

In the early days, when they made love, she'd wrap her hand behind his head when he was close and lock eyes with his, begging him to fall into her. And even as she held him above her, he would plummet into them—through them—and in the moment of blindness when he came crashing through that canopy, he felt completely inside her. When his sight returned, floating over her again, he saw the pieces of himself strewn across the landscape of her eyes.

After her labors, in the hospital, exhaustion and joy clouded her eyes like smoke, the aftermath of the burning intensity necessary to guide her babies into the world. And in the blind eyes of Brennan and later Hunter, he saw hers.

"I loved the way you used to look at me. In the beginning. All I wanted was for you to keep looking at me like that," he said.

"I don't know what you're talking about."

"I need you to see me the same way. Again. Or tell me it's possible."

"You fucked another woman!"

"I know."

"I can barely look at you now."

"Even before all of this, you stopped looking."

"You're blaming this on me?"

"No. On us. Just the affair. But on us. Yes."

"Fuck you."

"Before I met you, Jane, I didn't know who I was, or what kind of place I could occupy in the world. And when you looked at me—the way you looked at me—I found something there: a man I could be. I thought that if I work hard, if I do what's right, I can be that man. And I got there, didn't I? For a little while? And then you stopped looking at me. Not just the way you used to look at me. You stopped seeing me altogether."

"For fuck's sake, we had babies. I had a job. What did you want? Because I didn't make sexy eyes at you, we're here? That's what you're saying?"

He knew she was baiting him. They'd been married long enough for him to know the pattern. He was supposed to shout, throw his papers or smash his fists into his desk or slam a door so that she could throw a hand up and stalk off to the bedroom to sit in silence without ever hearing what it was he was trying to tell her or without having to see what he wanted her to witness. Thinking of the pattern reinforced the urge to act on it, rip a drawer from the desk to hurl it randomly or punch a hole in the plaster wall. The rage was a solace, a warm bed he could close his eyes in so he wouldn't have to think about all the things that lay beneath it.

But he also knew that when Jane sat on the bed and stared at the closed door, asking herself the same question he asked himself—*Why are we doing this to each other?*—her answers were as hollow as his. Because they promised. Because of the children. Because it was better to stay together with the countless little injuries they visited on each other rather than see the other's eyes on the way out the door. But none of those answers solved anything, provided comfort, or washed away the disappointment etched into their days. So instead of throwing the glass of water he found in his hand, John took a shaky sip and set it down.

"You don't know how much I admire you, how grateful I am that you raised our children, how proud I am of your career. But you left me."

"You fucked someone else."

"You may as well have. You left me. Except you didn't leave. And you didn't let me go, either. And I did the same to you. You want me to pull it together for the kids, but why? What was so great about our old life?"

"We owe it to them."

"We owe them our best. That was not it. If you want me to be who I was, or better, I can't be that man alone, without you."

Her eyes dropped, and she shook her head. When she looked back, he could see in her eyes again those pieces of himself he had left inside her years ago, still scattered there, desolate and abandoned. When he left them there, he imagined they were the foundations of a happy marriage, but now he saw that they were the wreckage of two people who would never be happy.

TWENTY-TWO

Now

"WHEN YOU SAID MEET FOR DINNER AT YOUR OFFICE, I DIDN'T think you literally meant eat in your office," Brennan said to Harris, Chinese takeout menu in hand. "Not that it's not a nice office."

"Any idea when your brother's going to get here?"

"He hasn't been responding to my texts. But he said he'd be here." She slid the menu back across the table to Harris.

"Speak of the devil," Harris said as the receptionist escorted Hunter into the room.

He shrugged apologetically. "Sorry. I couldn't break away."

"You're thirty minutes late," Brennan said. "You could have let us know. We've been sitting here—"

"I said I was sorry. What else do you want me to do?"

"Enough, guys." Harris pushed the menu over to Hunter. "We're all here now. Let's order."

"We're eating here?" Hunter asked.

"You two are eating here."

"I thought you were having dinner with us?" Brennan said.

"No. I invited the two of you for dinner."

The siblings exchanged a glance.

"I had a visit with your mom," Harris started. "She found out about what you two were doing?"

"She wasn't happy about it," Brennan said before Hunter could speak. He was losing patience with Harris and the whole situation. But Harris wouldn't waste their time—or at least she hoped he wouldn't.

"I told you two. Nothing good can come of this."

"Harris, I know I was late, and I'm sorry," Hunter said, casting the apology at his sister like a dirty sock, "but I don't need a lecture. We let things sit for too long. Maybe that was a mistake. But I think it's better that we waited until we had the skills to do this right."

"Okay. Then order your dinner. They'll deliver to the lobby. One of you will have to go down to pick it up." Harris slid two cards across the table. "These are guest passes. They'll get you in and out of the building and the office door."

"I don't understand," Brennan said. "Why are we going to eat here if you're not going to be here?"

Harris turned around and pulled a heavy brown leather-bound volume from a low shelf filled with similar volumes behind him. At first glance they looked like the bound U.S. Code books and case reporters that lined shelves in legal offices and judges' chambers everywhere. Harris lifted the cover, the stiffness of the binding audible in a whispered crackle of bending leather.

"These were pretty expensive for me at the time. A pure vanity item. You'll be able to tell that I've only opened them a couple of times in thirty years. But I wanted to commemorate that win. I thought that, you know, there might be nights sitting in that shitty office I used to have, facing endless defeats and compromises, wondering whether I was good enough, when I'd be able to pull one of these off the shelf and remember that a man placed his life in my hands and I delivered."

For the first time, the siblings saw Harris the way their parents might have—not as a cheerful "uncle," but a man who decided to spend a career immersed in tragedies on the side of the accused. But he gave a wry smile, and his mirth returned. "I guess it says something I pulled them down so little."

He slid the book across the table to Brennan.

"You had the trial transcripts bound," she said.

"Like I said, I'm pretty vain." He stood up and gestured to the shelf behind him. "They're all here. Feel free to pop in whenever you like to read through them. If it's after six, the room is yours. If you want to come during the day, give a call to Cynthia to make sure we're not using it. Or you can take some home and swap them in and out. But I suspect you'll want to work from here for a few days. Stay as late as you want."

He leaned back against the low shelf and idly tapped a stack of banker's boxes set next to it.

"Thank you," Brennan said.

"Yeah. We appreciate it," Hunter said.

Harris grabbed his coat and briefcase off one of the chairs and left them in the conference room. Brennan inspected the boxes. Each had a hand-typed sticker on its side and top, wrinkled and stiff from age. Hunter joined her. Up close, they could see the topmost box's sticker read PEOPLE V. LO: TRIAL.

Hunter reached for the lid, but Brennan placed her hand atop it. "I can't."

"Why not? He left them here and fucking put a spotlight on them."

"I can't assist another lawyer in violating his ethical duties."

"Nobody is going to know."

"I'll know."

Hunter rolled his eyes. "I'm not an attorney. You order dinner, then start on the transcripts."

Brennan hesitated. If she left, as Harris had, she would have deniability, however formalistic. If she stayed, would she be accomplishing indirectly what she could not directly do herself? But it wasn't as if her brother was in her control. In fact, she had told him not to open the boxes. She couldn't restrain him, physically or otherwise. And not all of the contents would be privileged. Some of it was probably merely evidence, copies of police files, various filings with the court. When she realized that she had spent more time thinking about whether to let Hunter open the boxes than she did before cheating on Paul or fucking Sean despite his marriage, she went to collect the takeout menu from the table. Her guilt and apprehension disappeared as quickly as those from her adulteries.

"It's funny," Hunter said behind her. "This is the second set of thirty-year-old boxes I've seen today."

"Is that some kind of sex joke?"

"No. I mean that literally. I'll show you in a minute."

By the time Brennan finished ordering dinner, Hunter had his laptop open on the table and a portable scanner attached to it. He began to flip through documents on his screen. The first few were pages of handwritten notes.

"My source in the NYPD came through. There was a lot of paperwork. I scanned it. Also photographs."

"Of the crime scene?"

"Yeah. I scanned some. I saved those for last because I needed to do them at a higher resolution and it takes longer. I didn't get everything, but I got the ones that seemed important. I just hope we don't end up with any gaps."

Brennan nodded. "I'm sure you got what we need."

He shrugged. "Hard to tell what might end up being important as we learn more."

"Will you be able to get back in there?"

"Maybe? My guy was jumpy because of the whole McCarthy thing. I'd like to avoid it."

"I get that." She had spent the week or so since the threatening call taking random routes to the office and looking for people following her. She felt paranoid, but the feeling that she was being watched hung on her. She wanted to ask Hunter if he felt the same but didn't want him to think she was unnerved.

"Before I—" Hunter stopped before he said *get started on these boxes*. He didn't understand her discomfort, but he could respect it by not mentioning what they were doing. "Let me ask you, you ever see a picture of Jessica?"

"No," Brennan said. She was only a name to her.

As Hunter clicked a few times on his laptop, he said, "I hadn't either until this afternoon. It was, um, tough for me. Probably because the first ones I stumbled across were crime scene photos. But they had this one in their files. I thought it might be easier if you saw this one first."

He turned the screen toward her. Jessica stood in a doorway—her office behind her, as if she'd been stopped on her way out. She smiled wryly at the camera, arms crossed, as if to say, *Really? You want my photo now?* Based on the cocktail dress, Brennan surmised someone took the photo as they were leaving to some firm event. Brennan thought she would have been merely generically attractive, but her eyes—even in the scan of a thirty-year-old photo—were striking. The same thought Brennan had every time she regarded a photo of a dead person passed through her mind. *You were here. And now you're gone.* She remembered the stories Cathy told about her, tried to imagine the woman on Hunter's screen laughing with her friends on some beach, walking down the aisle on her wedding day, waiting in some apartment for her father . . .

"Thanks," Brennan said.

"That's it?"

"What do you want me to say?"

Hunter didn't answer. He turned the laptop back toward him and walked over to pick up a box to carry it to the table.

Brennan pulled a notepad and pen from her bag and opened the cover of the first volume of transcripts like it was a lid on a casket.

#

The can of Pepsi opened with a metallic tearing sound and immediately began to foam over. Hunter almost broke a tooth slamming the can to his mouth to sip it down before it could spill onto one of Harris's bound transcripts. Brennan, reclining in a chair across from him in Harris's conference room with her shoeless feet up on the table, laughed at him. They'd spent the last four evenings there, working through the boxes and the transcripts, taking notes, and in Hunter's case, organizing the files from the police and cross-referencing it with Harris's files. They took turns leaving early to go up to their mother's place, spending an hour with her before she turned in.

Brennan was on the last volume. Hunter, finished with scanning and cataloging the various files, worked his way through them again, trying to ensure he hadn't missed anything before he started with the transcripts. The plan was for Brennan to begin reviewing the files from the boxes when she finished the transcripts, but it was her night to leave early.

"It's interesting," Hunter said, wiping his mouth with the back of his hand.

Brennan didn't look up. "We agreed that we were going to save our thoughts until we both were able to see everything."

They had made the rule the first night as a practical matter—if they kept stopping to talk about the things they saw, it might take them weeks to get through everything. But there were other benefits. They could discuss their views with the same context. And, if they didn't talk, they wouldn't argue. It reminded Hunter of when they were kids, spending hours in the same room doing different things with no need to make conversation or even acknowledge the other's existence. They'd slipped into the dynamic like putting on shoes they hadn't worn in years—a moment of strangeness followed by a comfort so complete it was forgotten.

"I think it's important enough to break our rule."

"Are you sure?"

"I think so."

She kept reading. She had to go see their mother after she finished and had work to do after that trip. She'd mentioned it at least three times since she arrived.

"Bren."

"Jesus, just fucking tell me."

"Anything in the transcripts about a handprint?" He turned his laptop around so she could see the screen. "This handprint. It's in the police files, but not in Harris's. They lifted it off this chair."

Hunter shoved a diagram of the crime scene from Harris's files to the middle of the table and pointed to an overturned chair next to the table near the door. He pulled a photo of the crime scene and placed it next to the diagram. The chair had been knocked over so that its back faced the ceiling.

"The print came off the back of the seat, facing the floor here. Underneath."

"What the fuck? You're sure this isn't in Harris's files?"

"Positive. I checked twice."

"Nothing in the trial transcripts. This is a . . . I mean. This is a fucking massive constitutional violation. Harris's whole defense was reasonable doubt. This print puts someone else in the apartment. It's an acquittal."

"He was acquitted," Hunter said.

"Yeah, but it doesn't matter! They needed to disclose it! What if the . . . When you read the transcripts, you'll understand. This was a close trial."

"Maybe this is why you got that threat?" Hunter said. "McCarthy knew this would fuck up his campaign? The polls are close."

"But why not just have the cops yank this from the file?"

"It's one thing to have someone try to scare you using a burner phone or something. No real evidence of that. But asking some cop to pull the files and destroy the evidence, there's a paper trail. A lot more risk."

"Speaking of risk, what happens if he finds out we got access to this? What's the escalation?"

Hunter shrugged. There was no way to predict.

Brennan said, "That can't be Dad's handprint, or they would have used it."

"Maybe Cathy's boyfriend left it. You know, before that night." The print could have been there for weeks if nobody sat in the chair. But Hunter wasn't convinced that was the case. There were only two chairs, and the print was in too central a place.

"About that," Brennan said. "No mention of Cathy having a boyfriend at the trial, either. Or about Jessica and her husband fighting. Harris would have used that. Anything in his files about that?"

"No."

Brennan glanced out the window as she processed the information. She huffed and looked back to the transcript. "Okay. Whatever. I'll think about it more when I get to the files. But they're leads, right?"

#

Jane lay asleep on the couch in the stifling heat when Brennan arrived. What would she do in spring when the building turned the heat off? Assuming she lived that long. Guilt coursed through Brennan under the sheen of sweat. She dropped her tote bag, laden with work, onto one of the two wingback chairs set across from the couch and set her purse next to it.

Her mother was a child-sized bundle in one corner of the couch. Brennan tried to deduce why she was there instead of in her bed. The TV was off, there were no books next to her—nothing to indicate why she'd chosen to sit there, pull the soft woven throw over herself, and nod off.

Brennan came around the coffee table and sat at her mother's feet, but she didn't stir.

"Mom? What are you doing on the couch?"

Her mother's eyes flickered open in a delicate spasm that reminded Brennan of butterflies taking flight.

"I was waiting for your father to get home from work. I must have . . ." She blinked. "That can't be right."

"It's okay, Mom. Let's get you into bed."

Brennan helped her mother up from the couch. Her mother leaned on Brennan as she led her to the bedroom. She was the weight of a newspaper.

"This temperature good for you?"

"Yes. It's fine."

She got her mother settled into bed, then went to the kitchen to grab a glass of water for her. When she returned to the bedroom, her mother drank deeply.

"Brennan, I think my medicine fucked me up tonight."

"It's okay, Mom."

"I was scared."

"I'm here now. I'll sit with you. I brought some work. I'll be right outside that door."

"Can you leave it open?"

"Of course."

Her mother aimlessly flipped channels until she settled into an old episode of *Law & Order* followed by another episode and still another after that. Brennan reclined on the couch, editing legal memos while the voices of Jerry Orbach and his various partners and Sam Waterston and his fellow prosecutors carried through the open door, until she shut her dry eyes for a moment only to wake up to a window lit with the weak pre-light of dawn the gray of television static.

Brennan brewed herself a coffee and worked through a backlog of emails on the laptop as she debated whether to shower here or run back to her apartment. Her mother's phone rang before she could decide. Brennan picked up the old cordless handset on the table next to the couch, hoping it wasn't her mother's aide calling in sick. It was still too early for a telemarketer.

Even as she said, "Hello?" a deep, muffled voice spoke over her. "I know this number and this address, too. I told you to stop. You won't like it if I have to tell you again."

TWENTY-THREE

Then

THE KITCHEN REEKED OF GARLIC. JOHN'S FINGERS WOULD smell of it for the rest of the day. Brennan, on a step stool to his left, worked on peeling the skin off her second clove, slowed by its sheath and paper sticking to her fingers. Hunter, on a chair to her left, made a show of picking at the tough shell of his clove whenever he thought John was looking at him. John peeled the rest of the head, placing the flat of his knife over each clove and smashing down with his fist to crack the sheath. In smashing the first few cloves, John demonstrated to the kids how to modulate the force, from a press light enough to crack the sheath without compromising the clove, to a blow hard enough to smash the garlic. The kids didn't care.

John remembered his father showing him how to peel garlic in their tiny apartment, thick wooden cutting board larger than the Formica counter on which he worked, hands like a robot at some factory: garlic, knife, smash, clove to one side, sheath and skin to the other, repeat. In that old apartment, the light in the kitchen was dim—the window opened into a shaft. His father didn't give him garlic to peel, maybe to save himself the aggravation that John suffered as Brennan dropped her freshly peeled clove on the floor and Hunter flicked his to spin on the counter. So John only watched until the day he needed to mince a clove of garlic for his own purposes, his own food.

John worked at half the speed of his father despite having nearly four times the space, a granite counter, and better light. The cutting board was the same size. John embraced this failing. It meant he wasn't a kitchen worker like his father, fresh off the boat despite decades in this country. He glanced over at his children, their white features—Jane's features—a badge of citizenship he'd never be able to obtain despite being born ten miles from the kitchen they stood in.

The head peeled, John swept the sheaths and paper into the trash.

"This is how you hold a knife." John demonstrated the grip his father taught him, index finger and thumb on either side of the blade so it wouldn't slip and to give him fine control of the cutting edge.

"When can I hold the knife?" Brennan asked.

"Do you want to hold it now?"

She reached for it.

"No!"

She had reached for the top of the blade, the only open space for her hand. Brennan jerked her hand back, and Hunter started and almost fell from the chair.

"Like this, reach for the handle," John said, flipping the knife in his hand to present Brennan with the handle. "So you don't cut yourself or me."

Brennan took the knife. She placed the tip to the cutting board and adjusted her grip to mimic the one he demonstrated. The blade was longer than her forearm. John resisted every instinct to yank the knife out of her hand.

"Can I cut something?"

John pushed some garlic toward the knife. She positioned the knife and pressed down. The clove split.

"That was easy!" Despite the enthusiasm in her voice, Brennan placed the knife down gingerly and lifted her hand slowly, as if it were a snake that might recoil and strike her.

"Hunter?" John asked.

Hunter looked at the knife.

"Why are we even doing this?" Hunter asked.

"Because you need to learn how to cook."

"We can learn when we're older. When we can't get hurt."

John picked up the knife. "This isn't a debate. Watch."

"We're watching, Daddy," Brennan said. She had taken Hunter's hand.

"I won't be around forever to show you how to do this."

John minced the garlic. He worked fast, but not as fast as his father, and as the pile of minced garlic grew, some of it sticking to the edges of the blade, some of it scattering, none of it matched the memories of the neat piles his father chopped.

"Come here." John turned to the stove. He poured a thick layer of oil into the sauté pan and turned the burner on. Hunter dragged his chair over so he could stand on it. Brennan crowded in between them.

"Do you put the garlic in there?" Brennan asked.

"Not until it's hot enough."

He waited. The kids stood silently.

"What are we making?" Hunter asked.

"Sèungtāo iū." When was the last time he spoke Teochew? He hated that it sounded foreign to him.

"How do you say that?" Hunter asked.

John repeated the words, trying to capture his parents' pronunciation the best he could. "Sèungtāo. Garlic. Iū. Oil."

The children repeated the words. Their attempts amplified the American English that John could not get out of his own voice. As much as John resented people's surprise that he spoke English with no accent ("You talk like an American!"), he hated himself for speaking Teochew like he was raised in America ("You talk like an American!").

As a kid, he was a foreigner when he left his house and when he came home.

"What's it for?" Brennan asked.

"Anything. You put it on food, the same way you would with giạm-chăi or bhātyōng."

He could see that the kids didn't remember what those things were. Why should they? Where had he been before his arrest, trial, acquittal? Working. He didn't have time to cook—especially food that Jane tolerated, at best.

"We're making it so we can put it on noodles later. Mị. Egg noodles."

John scraped the minced garlic into the pan, and the oil sizzled around it. The timing was tricky. The garlic needed to be bronzed when it was done. Turn the heat off too early, it would be pale; too late, it would burn. The kitchen grew slightly smoky.

"It smells bad," Hunter said.

John didn't say anything. Maybe his kids would develop a taste for his food (his parents' food) in time—muē, deudòu, guédiāo, chábẹung, būibūi bhāt, teung—all of it hójiāt. But he knew that they would feel less authentic than him and probably forget the names of the dishes he made for them before the taste left their mouths. After his parents died, John's Teochew degraded over time like herbs left in a cabinet.

John turned the heat off.

"It's still cooking," Brennan said, on her tiptoes so she could look into the pan.

"Yes. Until the oil cools. Then we put it in a jar."

"Is that it?" Hunter asked, ready to break their huddle, jump down from his chair, and leave.

"I'm trying to teach you something here."

"I don't want to learn. I don't like it."

"You haven't even tried it."

"It's gross."

John took the handle of the still-sizzling pan. He needed to—

#

—inhale.

John was in the middle of a two-hundred-page merger agreement trying to spot any tax issues raised by the contemplated structure when Jane got home from work. She kissed him on the forehead as she walked to the bathroom. The couch was on the way to everywhere in their old apartment. He had almost forgotten she was home when he heard the toilet flush, the sink run, and then Jane sat next to the one leg, crooked at the knee, that he had up on the couch. She still wore her work skirt, but her blouse was untucked.

"I have news."

John didn't look up. "Did you get your brief filed?"

"Yeah, but that's not the news."

"Okay?"

"I'm pregnant."

John looked up from the agreement and blinked. It was like he stumbled onto a blank page in the middle of a book, reading a sentence and suddenly a vast emptiness. His lungs, his heart, everything was still.

He needed to breathe, and inhaled so deeply he thought his ribs might crack.

Pregnancy was a possibility. They'd fallen into a laissez-faire approach to birth control. At some point, she stopped taking the pill. They weren't "trying" as much as they weren't trying to stop it. But because they weren't trying, at first they used condoms. One night, in the middle of messing around, John fumbled through the nightstand and came up with an empty box. Jane pulled him inside of her and said, "Just pull out." They never replaced the condoms. A few months later, drunk, he mistimed the exit. The next time after that, as he grew close, Jane said, "Just this once." It wasn't just that once, though. After a few months without conceiving, they stopped thinking about it and finished however the moment dictated.

"That's amazing," he said, because he knew he should say something positive. He leaned forward, and they hugged awkwardly, him folded over his left leg on the couch, her bending sideways to receive the hug. John sat back and waited for Jane to say something else, but she stared at her hands folded in her lap.

"You okay?" he asked.

Jane nodded, inscrutable.

"You didn't tell me you thought—"

"I didn't want to get my hopes up," Jane said. "We've been trying for so long."

John cocked his head but didn't say anything.

"I was only a week late. So I held out another week."

"Are you okay?"

"I don't know that I'm ready. You think, I'm a grown woman, I have a good education, we make good money. Lots of people with less have good kids. I must be ready. But . . ."

She shrugged and looked over at him.

"You're going to be a great mother."

"Thank you," she said, blinking at some tears as she tilted her head back. John laughed.

"What?" she asked.

"It's okay if your mascara runs. You're home."

Jane squeezed his leg just above the ankle. "I'm about to gain a lot of weight and get super hormonal. I don't want you thinking I'm a mess already."

"I love you, babe. You know I don't care if you have runny makeup."

"I'm going to go change."

"I'm going to finish reading this," John said, holding up the stack of paper.

"I'll come out and sit with you."

John turned back to the page. He blinked, but the text had lost all meaning. It was like reading *Romeo and Juliet* his freshman year of high school. He knew what most of the words meant, but they made no sense in their arrangement. He slogged through the next two pages, and when he looked up, Jane was on the other end of the couch.

"I couldn't decide what to read," she said.

"Yeah," he said. "Having trouble here, too."

She shifted so her legs ran the length of the couch, resting right next to his hip. He started to rub them.

"What's up?" she asked.

"I keep thinking of my father," John said.

"What about him?"

"There was a day we had a fight. An argument. I was eleven or twelve. I don't know what we were arguing about. But these things, they had a pattern. When I pissed him off, the angrier he'd get, the more I couldn't understand him. The words. I couldn't keep up with his Chinese. So I'd say, 'Please speak English.' And he, you know, he wanted me to be an American. Even when he was angry. Which was a lot of the time. So he'd try to yell at me in English. But his English was terrible. So I'd just, you know, talk circles around him. I thought I was so fucking smart, just talking circles around him. Which made him angrier. And I was so cocky about it. He wanted me to be American—I was really fucking American then, with this smirk. Like I was so much better than him because his English wasn't very good."

"I've seen that smirk. It cuts two ways. Sometimes it's charming. Sometimes it's infuriating. Sometimes both. You can be a real asshole about it."

John nodded. "I knew what I was doing. He knew it, too. He wasn't stupid. Anyway, the day I'm talking about, we're standing in the kitchen, he was making tea, the kettle was just starting to whistle, and we're arguing about something. So he loses it, slips back into Chinese. And I say, with that fucking smirk, 'I can't understand you.' He grabbed the kettle and threw it."

Jane's eyes widened. "He threw it at you?"

"No. I don't know. I don't know that he threw it at me. It was a small kitchen. If he was aiming for me, I think he would have hit me. Maybe he stopped himself at the last minute, so it missed."

"What did you do?"

"I ducked. Then I yelled, 'What the fuck are you doing?' The first time I ever cursed at him."

"Jesus, John. You never told me this."

"I don't think about it much. He's gone now. Who wants to think about that shit?"

"What happened?"

"He stood there. The look on his face. Like he had just woken up. It was surprise. And then he registered what he did, right? I can't even describe it."

In many ways, seeing the aftermath was worse than having the kettle thrown at him. His father's face—flushed, eyes twitching underneath a nearly imperceptible crease in his brow—immediately wiped blank with a blink. Then his eyes darted about to piece together the kettle, scalding water running from its spout and top onto the floor, the divot in the wall from where it hit, maybe two feet from his son whose arms were cast wide, screaming an obscenity at him.

John realized, sitting on his couch telling Jane the story, that it wasn't the "fuck" that had woken his father, it was the raw urgency of the question. It had not been rhetorical. What the fuck was he doing? His father hadn't known despite the decision to do it. His father's head dipped, but his eyes didn't leave John's. There was no panic or embarrassment or relief in them, but rather a fathomless loss that made John remember an older version of himself, standing at his father's bedside holding his hand watching his chest rise and fall and rise and fall and waiting and then another rise and fall and waiting and waiting and a rise and a fall and then a waiting that never ended.

"I didn't understand, at the time, why he looked like that."

"Like what?"

"Like someone had died."

Jane stretched out over him, coming to rest with her head on his chest.

"You don't have to be like him," she said.

John didn't respond. She was wrong, of course. He was his father. And that afternoon, maybe the way his father looked at him wasn't because John wouldn't be able to look at his father the same way, but because his father knew that John would recognize that he was the same, that his father was the very air in his lungs, and not something that he could just—

#

—exhale. He wanted to swing the pan in his hand, casting a slick of oil that would calm the roiling ocean inside him—even if it burned them, scarred them, ate at their skin. He sucked in air, smoky with singed garlic. Still, the imperative to hammer away at the stove shook his hand enough to rattle the pan on the cooktop.

To his left, Brennan stepped off her stool and backed away, but Hunter stood his ground—an ember waiting for an accelerant.

The impulse to kick the chair out from underneath Hunter dragged at John's foot like a receding wave. The kid thought he was safe up on his wobbly chair next to the scalding pan because it was in his father's hand. But Hunter lived in a wreck perched on a rocky shoal, beset by a rampaging ocean. How could he know that children dwell in whatever frail emotional shelters their parents erect from the salvage left at the end of endless days? Brennan recognized the imminent collapse—she backed away, even reaching out to take her brother's hand to pull him with her. But Hunter didn't want to merely see the structure fall, he wanted to demolish it, so he yanked his hand from hers. The movement triggered John's own hand, and it twitched upward before he arrested the motion.

Hunter stepped backward to avoid his father's arm and off the seat. He grabbed at the back of the chair, bending at the waist to reach, catching it in his fingertips just long enough to stop his fall and bring his foot to the edge of the seat. But the momentum carrying him backward pulled two of the chair's legs off the floor and overbalanced it. There was nothing left for Hunter to grab as the chair tipped over.

John dropped the pan and swung his right arm out to the side, catching Hunter's shirt but punching him in the chest even as the pan, mostly upright, hit the stove with a metallic clap, splashing hot oil over the stove and onto John's left arm. Instead of falling backward onto the tile floor, Hunter's feet slipped off the chair, which snapped down onto its side. Hunter was too heavy for John to hold up, so he swung like a pendulum down and toward John, sweeping the fallen chair into Brennan and John. Hunter's swing ended with the chair on its side pinned between him and his father, the edge of the seat jammed into Hunter's belly. Brennan screamed as she grabbed her right leg. John let go of Hunter, who backed away, viscous tears hanging from his eyes like the beads of oil hanging from the dropped pan. John's left arm burned where the sèungtāo iū had hit it.

Hunter looked up at his father and said, "I hate you."

Brennan shouted, "You apologize, Hunter! He just saved you!"

Hunter looked between his father and sister, then ran from the kitchen.

John stepped over the chair to the sink and began running cold water. Welts rose already on his arm, red splotches like splashed paint, his rage trying to burst from his skin. Brennan waited for him to say something, but he kept his eyes fixed on his arm. She shuffled off as he stretched his arm underneath the faucet. The cold water poured over his burns, bringing a momentary relief, but the pain returned and lingered until he drank himself to sleep.

TWENTY-FOUR

Now

BRENNAN WATCHED THE GARLIC BROWN IN THE OIL BEFORE dumping the chopped broccoli into the pan. She rocked the pan, flipping broccoli to coat all of the pieces with oil. There was a brief flash of flame as water from the crowns vaporized in the oil, aerosolizing and igniting it.

"Look at you," Hunter said from the doorway. "Fire and everything."

Brennan dusted the broccoli with white pepper, then pushed it into a serving bowl with chicken she'd already sautéed and put the pan back onto the flame. She added fresh garlic to the pan.

"It's a nice apartment," Hunter said, returning from his "tour" of her two bedroom. "How long have you lived here?"

"Bought it ten years ago? Something like that."

"I know I'm not in town much, but I can't believe I've never been here." He lived ten blocks away.

"I'm sorry. It never occurred to me that you might want to visit."

"Anyway, glad we're meeting here tonight. And thank you for cooking. I'm so tired of Harris's conference room." They'd spent nearly two weeks of evenings in it, even after the call to their mother's apartment.

The constant scanning for people tailing her was exhausting. Hunter had waited outside Harris's building one evening for thirty minutes before entering to see if anyone was surveilling the entrance but hadn't made anyone out.

Brennan refocused on her cooking before the garlic burned. She tilted a package of lo mein noodles into the pan, then added oyster sauce to the noodles while tossing them.

"You're good at that little flip."

"Thanks."

"Looks tasty."

"Dad's recipe."

"Seriously? You can't possibly remember."

Brennan shrugged.

Hunter looked back over his shoulder. "You have his desk. He leave a recipe in it?"

"No recipe. Mom cleaned it out before she let me use it when we were kids." From the day she started doing real homework, she sat at that desk. When she took her dad's office as her bedroom, the desk stayed—Hunter wanted nothing to do with it. When she was in high school, Brennan told her mother that she wanted it when she graduated college and begged her to hold on to it when Jane moved crosstown into her current, smaller apartment after Hunter left for college. Brennan dragged the desk through her starter apartments—the hulking slab of it occupying as much space as her twin bed in small New York City bedrooms. It was another piece of magic she tried to weave, keeping his desk as if it might one day conjure his return.

"Obviously she left some stuff in it," Brennan said. "Paper clips and whatever. But nothing like his papers or anything. I have his pen. The fancy one he used. That was in there."

Brennan brought her focus back to adding all of the components of the lo mein back to the pan—chicken, broccoli, and fresh scallions—but she sensed Hunter shaking his head behind her. She added more white pepper, tossed the lo mein in the pan, then tipped everything back into the serving bowl. They sat at her table and served themselves.

Brennan watched Hunter's face as he pulled the noodles dangling from his chopsticks into his mouth. He looked at Brennan, his stare an accusation.

"This is exactly—" He took another bite. "How did you do this?"

"I remembered the flavor and texture. I asked Mom what she remembered, which wasn't much. I stalked Chinatown for the right noodles and oyster sauce. Luckily, the packaging was pretty much the same as what I remembered as a kid. The trick was the white pepper. I had to look up recipes to see what other people added and then play with it until I figured it out. With just the oyster sauce, it was close, but not exactly there."

"I have no idea what you're talking about," Hunter said. "I never really cook. You know, being on the road and everything. Also, I'll tell you this, I always felt self-conscious trying to make Chinese food. Like I was faking it or something."

He took another bite. "But this takes me back."

It took Brennan back, too. She remembered how her father smelled when she would rest her head against him as a child. She couldn't describe it—it wasn't fragrant like soap or laundry, or musky like a cologne, or herbal like a mint. It was subtle; she remembered having to be close to him to pick it up. But close up, it filled her head like the scent of warm bread. Nobody she'd ever met smelled like him—except for rare moments over the years, standing near her brother, when she thought she imagined it if the air moved right. But she hadn't given her brother more than a perfunctory hug in more than a decade. Even when he first left to cover fighting in Afghanistan and the Middle East, he'd squeezed her shoulder at arm's length.

"You ever run across anyone that knew him?" Hunter asked.

"Only Walter Roberts. At least, he's the only one who mentioned him to me."

When they finished eating, Brennan cleaned up while Hunter set up his laptop on her table. Brennan returned with two beers.

"Anything in the files or transcript change your mind?" she asked.

"I don't think so. You?"

She shook her head. "What was the biggest gap for you? What do you think is the biggest problem with the theory that he did it?"

"The handprint on the overturned chair. That was the only clear set they couldn't identify. They had prints for Cathy, Jessica, her husband, Mark, and Dad."

"I still can't fucking believe they buried it."

"I did some thinking after we talked about it." Hunter sat forward on his chair and turned to face the back. "If anyone sat in the chair and leaned back, it'd get wiped away, or at least smudged, right? Implies that it was a pretty fresh print."

"Detectives asked her about it indirectly," Brennan said. She'd read Cathy's statements carefully. "She said she hadn't brought anybody to her place in the months before the murder."

"That might be true, I guess. Maybe Cathy only saw her guy at hotels or something?"

"Why pay for a hotel if she has an empty apartment sitting there?"

They sipped their beers while they considered the possibilities.

Hunter broke the silence. "What about you? Biggest issue with the theory he didn't do it?"

"He was there that night," Brennan said. "The car-service voucher shows he took a car from the firm to an intersection a block away. Clever police work, to check those."

"Yeah, I saw that testimony, but explain it to me so I'm sure I understand it right."

"Big law firms, like the one dad worked for, they use car services to drive lawyers home when it's late. Back then, the attorney swings by the dispatch desk, gives them the address they're going to and the client that should be billed, and the dispatcher fills out a voucher. The vouchers used to come in little books with carbon copy backs. The lawyer gets the original to give to the driver and the copy stays in the books."

"I think I saw the original books in the police files. Harris had copies."

"Which you scanned out of order." Brennan had resisted reordering them in order to move through the rest of the evidence.

"Not my fault. That box was a mess."

"In any event, now it's all computerized or they use an app, but even when I got out of law school, they were still using the voucher books."

"Okay. So he took a car somewhere close."

"And his prints on the broken beer bottle."

"They were partial prints. Not a conclusive match," Hunter said. Brennan appreciated his concession and offered her own.

"Yeah, but they're suggestive. Along with the car-service voucher, it puts him in the apartment," she said.

"So you accept he was there, somehow broke the bottle, but didn't kill her?"

"Like I said, it's the biggest problem with the theory that he didn't do it. But how do we know he broke the bottle?"

"So he drank a beer, and someone broke the bottle later?"

"It's possible. Don't forget there were partial matches to Jessica's prints on it, too. Maybe she picked up the bottle to use as a weapon?"

Hunter sighed.

"I know," Brennan said. She wondered how she'd already almost finished her beer. "We can speculate all night."

"If it was Dad, the only people who know what happened in that room are dead. There's no way to be sure."

"The way to conclude it was him is to rule everyone else out. That's what they tried to do at the trial. It's why they had to bury that handprint."

"The husband," Hunter said. "Cathy said he hit Jess."

Brennan picked up the thought. "He found out about the affair, maybe? And maybe she told him that she was pregnant. Cathy said he wanted a kid, and Jessica didn't want one with him. Her having a kid with another guy makes him jealous. They fight and it gets out of hand? Or he stews and decides to follow her and kill her?"

"His alibi was weak, too."

"Not just that, though. Cathy's, too. The whole thing kinda stank. By the end, Harris had the jury believing either of them could have killed her. Not to mention a random stranger."

"Maybe." He didn't sound convinced, but he acknowledged, "I thought the husband's testimony was bad."

"What stood out to you?"

"Said he worked to ten, then walked home. But he told the police he took one route and then gave another at trial."

"Yep. And did you notice the cops' interviews of his coworkers?"

Hunter took a moment to understand. "There was the guy he worked with who said that he left before nine."

"And Mark said he was home by eleven and was there for an hour before he got the call from Cathy that something happened. But the doorman told the police that he thought Mark was in and out, maybe twenty minutes at most."

"Doorman changed that when they reinterviewed him. Said he didn't remember. Maybe it was an hour."

"He said that more than a week later," Brennan said. "After Dad was arrested."

She brought her beer to her lips and discovered it was empty.

Hunter grabbed the empty bottles from the table and walked around the island to her kitchen area. As he searched for a recycling bin, he asked, "What's your issue with Cathy's story? Aside from the fact that she didn't mention her affair or the fighting to the police."

"She knows a lot and she knows nothing. Jess tells her about her lovers, but doesn't give her the names? Weird. She has a married boyfriend who can pay for her to stay at the Plaza for a week but who hadn't been to her apartment in months? She doesn't tell them that Jess and Mark fought? That Mark wanted a kid, but Jess didn't? I guess I can see it if I squint at it. She couldn't believe that Mark did it for some reason and was trying to protect her friends. Did you see that in any of the cops' notes?"

"Nope. Maybe they didn't ask her? Maybe she didn't remember to tell them?" He opened her fridge.

"Doubtful. But my other problem is her story of where she was that night. Movie, alone, then a drink at a bar, alone. Cops asked her which movie and the bar, but did you see any notes that they checked on her alibi?"

Hunter walked back over with fresh beers. "No."

"And going back to the prints. Cathy's make sense. She lives there. But why did they pick up Mark's prints there? There were a couple on the cabinets, right? According to him, he only showed up when Cathy called him about the murder. Said he was there once or twice for dinner with Jess, but not close to that night. Did the cops let him wander around the scene touching things?"

"It's interesting to see you like this. Is this what you're like at work?"

Brennan shrugged one shoulder. "Sometimes."

"You're good at this."

"I did it for a living." It occurred to her that he was complimenting her. "Thank you."

"I wonder if we can get that handprint run." Hunter flipped his laptop open and started to type. "I guess I can ask my guy."

"What else?" Brennan asked. "Anything in the photos of the scene?"

"I was just pulling them up again." He turned his laptop so they both could look at the screen. Brennan couldn't tell if it was a good scan of a bad photo or a bad scan of a mediocre photo. The photographer had tried to get most of the room in frame, but the flash had washed out the foreground while leaving the background in heavy shadows. A narrow band in the middle was properly exposed. In that space, Jessica's bare feet appeared from behind the couch, which obscured the rest of her body.

An end table sat, incongruously, behind the couch, which must have been turned during whatever struggle occurred.

"Next one?" Hunter asked.

They flipped through the photos together, matching the angles to a sketch of the scene one of the detectives had made. The scene was as Cathy described it to them. Small room, the couch and Jessica in the middle, head turned toward the couch, eyes closed. The blood showed in the photographs as a nearly black patch in a dark carpet. The overturned chair—the one with the handprint—was next to the table. The broken beer bottle was scattered against the base of the opposite wall. A foot to the right, it would have shattered the window.

"I don't think we're going to get that much out of these," Brennan said.

"Maybe where the handprint chair is? Someone comes into the apartment, puts his hand on the back of the chair, like this"—Hunter stood to demonstrate—"to lean against it. Leaves his prints. Then flips the chair down, maybe as he attacks her?"

The next photo was an autopsy photo. Hunter closed it. "We don't need to go through those, right? I've seen enough bodies."

"No." Neither of them were doctors. They wouldn't learn anything from the photos that they didn't already know from the medical examiner's report. Jess had been stabbed, once, underneath her ribs. It was probably a kitchen knife, which had never been recovered. Jessica died quickly—the knife had been driven diagonally upward underneath her ribs from her left to right, slicing through one lung and part of her heart.

Perhaps it was the image of the autopsy photo that made Hunter ask, "What about the threats to you? To us? What should we do?"

Brennan shook her head. "I don't know. Keep being careful?"

"What if we leak that they hid the handprint? If the damage is done, there's no point in hurting anyone to keep it a secret."

"Except for revenge," Brennan said. "But more importantly, if it becomes a story, who's going to talk to us? Plus, doesn't it burn your source?"

Hunter nodded. "It just makes me nervous. For you. And Mom."

"Same here. We're being careful. We'll be okay." Brennan hoped her voice conveyed the confidence that she didn't feel. Her phone chimed. "Mom."

"She okay?"

"Yeah. But maybe we should head over. You got anything else going on tonight?"

Hunter smiled, then shook his head as he closed his laptop. Brennan tried to follow along as his face cycled through a series of expressions. He finally noticed she was staring at him.

"What?"

"You didn't answer the question. What's going on?"

"Nothing. I can go with you to Mom's."

"But if you have plans, I got it," Brennan said.

"It's fine." He sighed. "I was going to head over that way anyway. I have plans. They're on that side of town."

"Oh?"

"It's nothing. I'm meeting a friend at a bar over there."

Brennan pulled her coat on. "That bar near Mom's place? The one with the waitress?"

Hunter smiled. "I'm taking the Fifth."

TWENTY-FIVE

Then

THE BAR WAS EMPTY EXCEPT FOR THE CIGARETTE SMOKE hanging in the air from the ceiling to the sawdust-covered floor. The bartender—a heavy, splotchy old guy—ignored John for five minutes before shambling over to take his order. The only other patron was a wrinkled bag of skin collapsed on the bar.

Walter walked in, throwing weak autumn daylight across the room until the door closed behind him. Walter looked down at his shoes on the sawdust floor, then at John.

"You're kidding me, right?" Walter asked as he stood next to John.

The bar was an asshole in the wall at the edge of plausible walking distance from the firm. There were twenty better bars closer to the office, and nobody from the firm would live this close to Chinatown. As far as John could imagine, he and Jessica were the only two people from the firm who knew the place existed.

"I thought you couldn't risk being seen with me. Nobody we know would ever walk into this place."

"My suit is going to smell like piss and cigarettes the rest of the day."

"I'm going to be honest with you, Walter, that's probably an improvement."

Once, Walter may have laughed at that joke. Now he shook his head and pulled out his wallet.

"Let me pay, John, and we can go to a real place."

"Why don't you take a seat?"

"I don't want whatever is on these chairs to get on my pants."

"Fine, then stand. What do you want to drink?"

"Bring me something imported in a bottle," Walter called to the bartender. Then, to John, "Because I can't imagine any glass in this place is clean."

John raised a worn glass filmed with scratches and filled with whiskey to Walter before taking a sip. "It just needs to be clean enough."

They didn't speak again until the bartender dropped a Heineken and walked back down to read a *Post* splayed open at the opposite end of the bar.

"I won't tell you that you have friends in the building, John. But there are guys who are pushing for a fair outcome for you. It's the only reason you haven't been voted out yet. Gerry clerked for Marshall, so he's blabbing on about due process and whatever. Everyone thinks it's bullshit, but he has a vote. The rest of them can see themselves in the same pile of shit you're in. Well, probably not the murder trial, but they've fucked enough secretaries and associates to not want that to be grounds for ouster from the partnership—at least not without a fair payment."

"So they know they're no better than me."

"They weren't accused of killing someone."

"The offer Geoff made, it wasn't a fair offer."

"They're preparing a complaint." Walter sketched a circle on the bar in condensation with the butt of his bottle. "It's almost ready to file."

"It better be ready soon, or it's going to have to be a cross-claim."

"You hired a lawyer? Who? Nobody worth anything would sue the firm."

John looked down at his wrinkled shirt and jeans, then to Walter's suit. John's old leather jacket hung from the back of his chair. "Do I look like I need anybody worth anything? I just need someone who is going to plead all the right salacious details and talk to the *Post* and the *News*."

"Nobody would ever hire you after that."

"They're not exactly lined up right now."

Walter sighed and pulled a pack of Marlboros from his jacket. He took two out and handed one to John. They lit the cigarettes.

"They're going to roll over you, John. No judge is going to be sympathetic to you. You're a stain on the bar. You think you'll get a jury who wants to find for you instead of us?"

"You keep saying 'they,' Walter. You not a part of the firm anymore?"

"I'm your friend, John. I'd pay you. But they don't listen to me."

"You're my friend? What would you do? If you were me?"

"I'd take the money. Buy some property. Collect rent. Something where I didn't have to show my face again."

John shook his head. "That's not for me."

"John—"

"There has to be a way, not for me to come back. But let's say I take the money. There has to be another firm that can use me. I'm one of like ten lawyers with my expertise and experience—"

"Listen to yourself. Any firm takes you or tries to put you on a deal, they may as well shoot themselves in the head. You said it yourself, there are nine other guys who can do what you do. You made partner because you're Chinese and Geoff thought that might help us with the Japs because he doesn't care to distinguish between Orientals. And fuck him, he was right, we got those clients now. And they're not going to jump across the street if you do. I'm telling you as your friend, you got no future as a lawyer. Put it out of your mind and think about something else."

Walter sucked down the rest of his bottle and held it up to the bartender.

The jowly old bartender walked over to Jessica.

"This guy bothering you?"

"No," she said, putting her hand on John's arm. "He's with me. And he wants a whiskey."

The bartender looked at her hand, then at John, then at how well they were dressed. He turned to pour the drink.

"You're late," Jessica said.

"Had to call Jane before I left."

"This isn't the kind of place where a girl like me should wait by herself for very long at this time of night."

John looked around. It wasn't quite eleven yet. The bar was half full of sullen-faced old men, a couple of off-duty cops, and a pudgy woman whose black-and-gray roots contrasted starkly against her blond dye job. The sawdust on the floor clumped in drifts near the corners.

"Then why are we here?" John asked. "We could have met anywhere else."

"This is fun. Nobody will stumble across us here."

"Nobody is going to find our bodies here."

Jessica laughed, then leaned in close. "Come on. Loosen up."

The bartender brought his drink, and John drank half of it in a single sip. Jess slipped an arm inside his jacket and around his waist.

"I missed you," she said.

"You saw me earlier."

"I know. But not like this."

"Like what?"

"Where we can stand this close to each other."

Every place where her body touched his—from the press of her hip, to the firmness of her breast, to her small hand resting just underneath his ribs—smoldered like charcoal under ash.

"I love standing this close to you," he said.

He remembered when he and Jane used to stand like this, for no reason other than they couldn't bear to be in the same room without standing like this. John took another sip of his whiskey and pushed the thought from his mind.

The bartender dropped two more drinks without waiting for them to order, then another two. The third round came as John finished a story about Jane.

"So we're in the park, and she's chasing Brennan, who I think was about three or four. Just in circles. I'm holding Hunter, who was tiny. His skin was so soft. Have you ever smelled a baby's skin? I don't know where it comes from. It's not soap. I miss that scent. It smelled like happiness. Anyway, she's chasing Brennan, and I remember—you know, there were some complications with Brennan. The whole birth and labor was scary. Jane was afraid. But she was also so calm about the whole situation. Maybe it was because she saw how nervous I was. But there she was, this person I thought I knew so well, and there's this whole new piece of her I'd never seen, this calm in a crisis. It reminded me of the beginning, you know? When you're first dating and you find something new every day that you come to love about a person. And then you think you know everything there is to love about a person. And then she surprises you. Or reminds you."

John blinked a few times.

"I'm sorry," he said. His face darkened. "I forget where I was going with this."

"It's wonderful how much you love them." Jessica slipped a hand into his. "I mean it, John. Did you ever wonder why I haven't asked you to leave them for me? I mean, aside from the dirty talking."

"Because you're married, too?"

She began to roll her eyes, but a thought interrupted, and she shrugged instead. "Yes. I guess. When we married, I was so in love with Mark. I knew he was immature, but I figured we would grow up together, then grow old together. He's really smart, you know. And I know he thinks I'm not as smart as he is. He doesn't hide it. At first, maybe he thought it was cute. I guess I looked at it like he was taking care of me. But then I grew up, and it was patronizing. And for him, well, it's not cute anymore when I'm 'wrong.' I know he feels contempt for me. He'd never admit it. But it's laced into every word he says to me. It poisons the way he looks at me. It infects my skin when he touches me. And isn't that where we'd end up, too?"

John looked at her intently but didn't answer.

"Maybe not exactly there," she said, "but in the neighborhood. Because eventually I'll want to hurt you. And you'll want to hurt me."

"You've mentioned . . . Does Mark . . ."

"We hurt each other," she said. "When we drink, sometimes it gets physical. It's not serious. It's like we can't figure out whether to fight or fuck each other. I'm not proud of it."

"It doesn't have to be that way."

"It's usually me who starts it."

"That doesn't matter."

"It does," Jessica said. "To me. I can't touch a man without wanting to hurt him."

"Again, it doesn't have to be that way."

Jess scoffed. "Do you know what I love most about you?"

John's breath caught for a moment, the dread tight in his throat, like he had watched someone step in front of a bus. They had never spoken the rule, but it had become their central tenet. However apparent it was, even during their weekend away, if they didn't admit to it, they wouldn't have to grapple with what love might portend.

Jessica continued as if oblivious to the slip. "You have hope. And it's not only the hope in your kids. You love her so much; you'll stay and try no matter what. I'm so jealous of that. I want to steal it. I just want to be around that kind of hope. Because I don't feel it except for when I'm with you. That maybe I'll have that someday. But if you left them for me? What then? I'd eventually feel the same contempt for you that Mark feels for me."

Jessica ran a finger underneath her eye and blinked.

"Why not find someone else you can feel that with?" John asked.

"If this is what every marriage is, why go through the trouble of trying to find a better one? Nobody is happy, so why not just do what I promised? But a part of me looks at you and thinks, if you can do it, I can do it. I can hope like you. I can be a good person, too."

John didn't recognize the man she described. His mouth was dry.

"But it's not real, right?" Jess said before downing the remains of her drink.

He gulped the rest of his and held the glass up for another drink.

#

John examined his glass in the dull light streaming from the doorway. Maybe Walter had a point. They were hopelessly filthy. When the bartender dropped Walter's second beer, John slid the glass to him.

"Another. In this glass please."

Walter swigged half his beer.

"As a friend," Walter said, "do you want to talk to me about her?"

"Talk about what?"

Walter shrugged. "Have it your way. The trial made it seem like you two were in love."

The bartender tossed some ice in John's glass, grabbed a bottle of bourbon off the shelf, and poured until the ice crowned over the thin surface of the alcohol. John salivated; he wanted to drink so badly.

"I don't think you did it, John," Walter said. "Honestly."

"Thanks, but I don't want to talk about it."

"I'm probably the only person you can talk to about this." John turned to fully regard Walter. Walter's eyes were fixed on the bottles behind the bar. "I'll deny it if you ever say so, but I knew. Maybe you thought you were being careful in the office, but I knew."

"No. Maybe you see it now after the fact, but no way you knew at the time."

Walter turned to him, his face as soft and kind as John had ever seen it. "I saw her leaving your office once. I was dropping by to ask you about that tax issue on that settlement I was structuring. I guess she'd left a file on your guest chair, so I moved it to sit down while I waited for you to get back from the bathroom."

"You looked at it?"

Walter rolled his eyes. "No. A slip of paper fell out."

John already knew—he remembered the slip of paper, placed inside a folder, before the first time they met in Cathy's apartment—but he asked, "What was it?"

"An address. Some place in Spanish Harlem. And a personal note."

John pictured her handwriting, both the address and the unsigned note: *I'm so wet for you.* Walter had known for months before the end. His mind racing with the implications, John didn't notice the bartender return with his refilled glass.

"Once I knew," Walter said, pushing John's glass to him, "the signs were easy to catch. The little things like how she would find excuses to visit your office or the fact that you left exactly five minutes apart on nights you would meet."

"You knew when we left?" John asked without touching his drink.

"Come on, John, it was a mystery. And the two of you were my closest friends there. It was fun to figure it out. To be part of the secret, especially since neither of you knew that I knew. A secret within a secret. Why didn't you say anything to me?"

"Why didn't I say anything to you?" John asked, eyebrows raised.

"I was your partner, your friend, John. This is the kind of thing friends tell each other. A lot of guys would even brag about it, to be honest. The other partners, they don't share stuff like this with me. But you and me? We worked together more than ten years. How many drinks in better bars than this?"

"What else did you know?"

Walter waved the question away. "Just those little breadcrumbs I mentioned. It seemed like you guys were probably already, um, you know, pretty into it before I even noticed anything." John ran a hand over his face, trying to clear his mind.

"Look, we don't have to talk about this if you don't want to." Walter placed a hand softly on John's shoulder. "But I see you suffering, man. And it's not just because of the firm or the trial. I know what it's like to be lonely, too."

Walter paused for a moment to let his words sink in, then squeezed John's shoulder and let his hand drop. "Do you want to talk about how it started? With Jessica?"

"What does it matter?"

"She must have liked you, seen something special in you. Maybe remembering why she chose you would make you feel better now? Or maybe it was just she was unhappy, too. Maybe you had that in common?"

John finally sipped his whiskey. "I should go."

Walter cocked his head at him.

"Fair enough, but if you change your mind, I'm around."

John drained the rest of his glass in a sip. His throat burned and eyes teared. He coughed once.

"Walter," he said and coughed again, "we never talked about the kind of stuff you're asking about. What does it matter to you anyway?"

A wince passed like a squall across Walter's face. He sipped his beer to obscure it. "We were friends, too. I'm sure you know that. And it's just . . ." Walter looked down at the filthy bar. "You're not the only one who misses her."

Walter turned to flag the bartender for another beer.

"Yeah, well, I'm sorry for your loss." John grabbed his jacket and walked out.

TWENTY-SIX

Then

JOHN WALKED TOWARD CHINATOWN, SLIGHTLY DAY DRUNK, reeking of cigarettes and whiskey. Others on the street were bundled against a brisk October wind—he passed two old ladies in quilted jackets with scarfs wrapped around their necks, but his leather jacket was open to welcome the cool air. He hoped Walter was still sitting in the bar, waiting for his beer.

John's cheeks were flushed—partially the cold, some of it the booze—as he turned onto Mott Street past a seafood restaurant, bass and carp swimming in glass tanks in the window above giant, spindly crabs piled atop each other, waiting for their turn in the steamer. He passed the arcade where he had brought Brennan and Hunter to play tic-tac-toe against a chicken in a cage. Stores with imported furniture and trinkets. Coffee shops with Colombian brew and Chinese bean cakes. Farther up the street was the storefront where John bought his noodles and bean sprouts and soy milk. His parents, if they were alive, would be walking the street here, like the other grandparents, in cheap shoes, polyester pants, nylon coats zipped high against the wind, carrying bags of provisions, stopping in stores and negotiating in differing Chinese dialects.

John stopped to take three deep breaths, inhaling the smell of roast duck. He felt like he was being followed, but whether it was by Walter, a memory, guilt, or the implications of Walter's knowledge, John didn't know. He looked back down Mott Street from the corner of Bayard and recognized no one.

Walter had known about him and Jessica. John couldn't believe it. They'd been so careful. They made plans by phone or in person. They rarely put anything in writing, but there were notes and letters despite their better judgment. John would sometimes sit at his desk at home, the family asleep, and write letters. He maybe delivered one in ten that he wrote. The rest were shoved into a hidden drawer in his desk—a novelty when he bought it, designed to hide important documents like a deed or a will. He never used it until he started writing his letters.

He addressed them *Dear J—*, and sometimes he didn't know whether he wrote them to Jess or Jane. Maybe both. For his whole life, until he met Jessica, he approached writing as a purely utilitarian exercise. He had never been moved to write poetry or prose or anything other than to-do lists, school assignments, and legal memoranda. He was a great legal writer—concise, precise, and easy to follow. No metaphors, allusions, alliteration, similes, meter, or rhyme to wrestle with. Just facts, law, and analysis broken down into their simplest component words.

But a day or two after the Christmas party—the beginning of everything—John sat at his desk, door closed against the secretaries, the associates, and his partners, and started to write Jessica a note. He hadn't seen her since that night after she left his office. Two sentences: *Dear J—, I would like to talk. When is a good time?* John never wrote in cursive well, so over the years, he developed a quick, casual block letter style, all caps, but with a flow nearly like script.

John looked down at the slip of paper. The message looked like a summons, brusque and impersonal. John added another line after the question: *I enjoyed sharing that cigarette with you.* He scribbled out that line and wrote instead: *I want you. To see you again.*

Sitting back after writing that, John saw how stupid the sentiment was. First, the blatant confession *I want you*. Was it too forward? Was it even true? He barely knew her. They were both married. Is that why he appended the *To see you again* at the end? To blunt the intensity of the prior sentence? Stepping back, in totality, the note was unlike anything John had ever written. He'd explained law, rendered opinions, transcribed statements, drafted contracts, listed tasks, and summarized facts. But had he ever written the truth? It was a little one, confessed on the scratch pad. But the scribed desire demanded some sort of further attention. Elaboration? Decoration? Form or substance? He tried writing the words again, focusing on the sensation of the pen on a new sheet of paper. Was there a transference of energy into the paper beyond the friction of the ballpoint moving across the sheet? If he gave the note to Jessica, would she feel the tension of his writing it in her fingertips? In copying the words, John added another line to the end, almost a non sequitur: *I want to know why me? And why you?*

Arranged on the page as they were, the words almost looked like poetry. John blushed, embarrassed that he had started jotting a quick note requesting a meeting and it had devolved into something resembling a song lyric.

#

Jessica laughed and pulled the hotel sheet up to her chin. "I wrote a song once with the lyrics 'why me' but threw it out. It sounded whiny."

Warmth spread across John's face. "You know that's not what I meant."

"Relax," she said. "I'm just teasing you." She leaned over and kissed his cheek—he could feel her lips spread into a smile as she did it.

"On the other hand," she continued, as she settled back, "maybe I'm not. I'm a disaster."

John turned so he could face her better. She let the sheet fall when she kissed him, and it lay in her lap. She wore her smile the same way—a careless modesty covering less than it revealed.

John's lip curled into a half grin. "With that kind of attitude, no wonder you wrote a song like that."

Jessica grabbed a pillow and hit him in the head with it. Before he could recover, she sprang on top of him, knocking him onto his back against the headboard, straddling him. She grabbed his wrists and held them against her thighs.

"I didn't get to do this before," she said.

John took a second to record as much of the moment in his mind as he could—her weight on his hips, how her breasts looked, her legs smooth underneath his hands, the cocktail of mirth and melancholy in her eyes. She raised one hand to touch his cheek and then his hair.

"You're going to be bad for me," she said.

"Then why did you come?"

"I got your note."

In the end, after eight drafts of varying lengths—all of which John dumped in a subway trash can on the way home—he left a simple piece of paper on her desk late one night: *J—, I've been thinking of you. Can we have dinner?*

"I liked that you were thinking of me," she said. "I was thinking of you."

They ate at a small, dimly lit Italian place in the West Village. Dinner was a blur of wine and laughter. When he hailed a cab for her, she took his hand and pulled him into it with her. The driver asked them where they were going, and she gave him the name of an old hotel in Midtown. John raised an eyebrow, to which Jessica responded, "I don't have a curfew. Do you?"

She waited at the bar while he booked a room and handed him a scotch when he returned with the room key. He left cash on the bar, and they brought their drinks with them to the room. It was small, mostly the bed. Jessica shut the curtains against the windows across the street while John threw scotch into his suddenly dry mouth. Jessica turned to face him. The bed lay between them, an obstacle and invitation. She tossed her coat across the bed.

"Be a dear and hang that up for me?"

John hung his as well on some hooks near the door. When he turned back, her suit jacket was laid across the foot of the bed, and she was removing her earrings.

John watched, a question across his face.

She placed her earrings on the bedside table and took a sip of her wine as she unbuttoned her blouse with the other hand. "Yes?"

"Why me?" he asked.

"Hold that question for a bit." So John held it while she draped her blouse, and then her skirt, across her jacket. He put the question to the side when she crawled across the bed to him, rising to her knees at the edge closest to him, pulling him close to kiss him, pushing his jacket open and then off his shoulders, loosening and then undoing his tie, never taking her mouth from his until after her hands found his belt and solved the puzzle of the buttons and zipper of his pants. When she took his cock into her mouth, he wondered if he was her only lover, and if so, why she'd chosen him, and if there were others, why him as well. But his lust eradicated the questions—and nearly every other thought. He couldn't wait to taste her anymore and flipped her onto her back. He brought his lips down to her and took his time, measuring out pleasure, creating tension as she stretched her body across the bed, contracted to pull his face to her hips just so, and then expanded again, arms out grabbing at the sheets, until her release, which he felt through the whole of his breath and into his chest like a hum. She pulled him up and onto her and told him that turnabout was fair play, that she wanted to finish him with her mouth. But when he was close, she said she wanted to feel him inside of her, to hold his body to hers, and she wrapped herself about him when he came.

After, they lay in each other's arms until Jessica got up to go to the bathroom. John pulled the hotel sheet over his lap. When Jessica returned, John smiled at her and said, "Okay. I held it. Now, why me?" And she laughed at him and joked about her song, and time was circular in the room, and the question wouldn't leave John as she straddled him, reminding him of his note and saying, "I liked that you were thinking of me. I was thinking of you."

"It's hard for me to imagine why you would think of me."

"Maybe you're lucky? Or cursed? Or maybe I think you're very handsome in your suit? Something about your eyes? Let me keep some of my mystery. You start asking questions like why, and things may become serious. We're agreed, right? This isn't anything special. We're just working through some things?"

John nodded, but the question rampaged through his mind like a song even as she kissed him again and they made the most of the time they were stealing.

#

The question clung to John with the cold air when he entered the coffee shop on Bayard. He sat in a booth toward the back, ordered a cha siu bao and some siu mai. He had sat there once before, with Jane on their third date. They caught the subway down after their last class one day in October. He wouldn't have been surprised if it was the anniversary of that date.

John had ordered nearly every type of dim sum on the menu for Jane so she could sample them all. They arrived before a rush, so it seemed like one minute they had the place to themselves, and the next they were surrounded by a crowd shouting at the staff. Jane's favorites were the cha siu bao and the rolled chow fun. After, he gave her a tour of his usual errand route: the grocers, the butchers, the fishmongers, and the bakers. She held his hand, and he was thrilled even though they had already kissed at the end of their first date.

After eating, they stood together on the 1/9 platform. Jane leaned against one of the painted steel columns, long blond hair falling straight down to her shoulders, her cheeks still slightly flushed from the wind. John wished he had his camera, she looked so beautiful.

"Why are you looking at me like that?" she asked.

"Because you're really pretty."

Jane didn't say anything. Her eyes were open, waiting for him to move closer, and he did. They kissed until Jane giggled and said, "I hope my breath doesn't smell like garlic."

"I can't tell. We ate the same things."

"Thank you for taking me," she said. "I really liked it."

"You're welcome. It's the first time I've taken a girl—a white girl—down here."

"Really?"

"Yeah." He turned his head to look up the tracks to see if a train was coming. Nothing stirred in the dark tunnel. "You know how it is, right? A lot of girls like you, they're not looking for someone like me."

"Are you asking me to help you figure out your girl problems? You're standing awfully close to the tracks to be taking that chance."

"No!" he said, then saw her grin. "I'm sorry. In my experience, you know, Italian girls want to marry an Italian guy, Irish girls want to marry Irish, and on and on. Sometimes I think I have something with a girl, and then she tells me, 'No, I'm sorry, I can only date a Jewish guy.'"

"What do the Chinese girls tell you?"

"They want a Jewish guy, too." He laughed. "But seriously, nothing ever just worked out like that for me with a girl like you."

"And?"

"And when I met you, I thought you'd be the same. You'd tell me you only date the sons of uptight, square-jawed guys who wear fancy sweaters and own sailboats. But here we are."

"Here we are," Jane said. John never imagined someone could smile with their eyes so completely as Jane did.

"So, why me?" The question fell out of his mouth before he knew he asked it. John felt like he was hanging over the edge of the platform, heels in the air, with a train oncoming. This was certainly not the smooth-talking leading man he saw in films and imagined women like Jane wanted.

"If I wanted any of that, I'd have married my college boyfriend." She slid a hand up to hold the lapel of his jacket. "My God, all my friends thought he was perfect. And my mom would have left my dad for him. I tried telling myself, through four years of college, look at this guy! He's tall and handsome, he's going to make a mint, and he'll give me good children. But I imagined sitting through dinner with him for forty years, with all of those empty days—because he didn't want me to work—and I have to tell you, John, I knew I'd only make it to four. He somehow got more boring as college went on. I already knew everything he ever told me. I'd seen everything he wanted to show me."

The air moved in the station, carrying the distant rumble of a train.

"When I first met you," Jane continued, "you promised me something. Something different. Something interesting. It's there in your eyes. So that's why. Now kiss me, fool."

John leaned forward until their lips came together. He pressed his body to hers, holding her against the column as the train rushed into the station, screaming past them like a gale, Jane's hair whipping around their faces. He'd never been so disappointed that a train arrived before.

Ten years later, John sighed at the memory and ate the last of the siu mai. He couldn't remember the last time he ate there, but everything—the food, the staff, the customers—was the same, except for him. John pushed the empty plates away and left a ten on the table—at least five dollars too much. He didn't want to wait for change. As he left, he remembered that the fall before Jessica and the Christmas party, he'd called Jane at work and suggested that they meet at the coffee shop for lunch.

"Why?" she asked.

"We went on a date there. I thought it might be fun to walk up for cha siu bao together."

"Did we? I don't have time to walk up to Chinatown."

"Come on. It's twenty minutes to walk, and it takes five to eat."

"John," she said, "go if you want. You know I don't even like those things. I'll eat something near my office."

She spoke to someone in her office and hung up the phone. He held the receiver to his ear, the hollow echo of the open line reverberating, growing louder in his ear, promising connection but never delivering. It was a lonely sound, a tone humming inside him his whole life. Each time he thought he had drowned it out, it resonated forward through the years, until it was a deafening hiss laid over his waking day.

TWENTY-SEVEN

Now

"I FEEL PRETTY CONSPICUOUS HERE," HUNTER SAID FROM the passenger seat. Theirs was the only car parked on the street, facing a sand berm running horizontal across the far end of the block, obscuring the beach and Atlantic surf that lay beyond. Two-story homes—mostly with light-colored siding, but occasionally red brick—lined the block behind empty, narrow sidewalks and short, bare trees. Brennan thought she could make out in the rearview mirror a lapis strip—Jamaica Bay—underneath an unblemished robin's-egg sky. The house they watched, a narrow box with a brick first story and shingle second story, lay midway between the ocean and the bay on Rockaway.

"Not much we can do about it," Brennan said.

"I know. I just hope McCann's not in Florida for the winter."

They'd both agreed that trying to catch people in person was best.

"We'll give it another hour. If he doesn't turn up, we can try to track him down by phone."

A black SUV turned the corner behind them. Brennan perked up. She caught a flash of the driver, a man with short white hair, when he drove past them without stopping before disappearing around the next corner a moment later.

"What if McCann's the one who's been making the threats?" Hunter asked.

"Then this is probably a bad idea."

They didn't speak again until an old blue Ford Taurus turned onto the street from the far avenue.

"God, let this be him," Brennan whispered. To her relief, the driver turned into McCann's driveway. The trunk popped open the moment the car stopped.

Brennan and Hunter crossed the street against a cold wind blowing in from the Atlantic, just as an old man with thinning white hair and a woman in a knit wool hat climbed out of the Taurus. The woman rooted through her purse as she shuffled toward the door of the house, while the man walked to the trunk. He looked up as the siblings approached, a cop's glare lashing at them from a broad face. Brennan had seen more than a few of them in her career. They were a landscape feature she barely noticed anymore.

"Detective McCann?" Brennan asked.

"Retired. Who's asking?"

"My name is Brennan. This is my brother, Hunter."

McCann cocked his head and narrowed his eyes like he was trying to read some confusing text.

"I feel like I should know what this is about," he said.

"It's about an old case of yours. A murder."

"I had a lot of those." She watched him riffle through old cases in his head. The woman stopped halfway to the door to watch, and the bags of groceries in his trunk waited to be collected.

"It's—" Brennan started, but McCann held up his hand.

Another second passed. He said, "John Lo. You're his kids."

They nodded.

"We'd like to talk to you about the case," Brennan said.

"You should have called."

"We thought you might not speak to us if we called."

"You were right. But you would have saved yourself the trip." McCann reached into his trunk and pulled out two paper bags of groceries to cradle one in each arm. He turned to the woman. "Bonnie, stop standing there and get the door."

"Sir," Hunter said, as McCann walked to his door while Bonnie sifted through God knows what in her purse, "we're sorry for dropping in on you like this, and we don't need to discuss it today. But we wanted you to see our faces, so that you'd know that we . . . that we're not trying to make trouble. We're only looking for answers. Personally. For us."

McCann reached his front door where Bonnie stood, the keys finally in her hand. She spoke to him words neither sibling heard over the wind, then turned to unlock the door. McCann disappeared into the house, but Bonnie turned back to them.

"Do you mind grabbing the last bag in the trunk?" she said, then shuffled through the door, leaving it open behind her.

Brennan retrieved the bag and closed the trunk. Bonnie was waiting for them inside a narrow foyer with a white tile floor. She hung her coat on a row of hooks lining one wall. Hunter closed the door behind them, casting most of the foyer into shadow. A beam of cold light blasted through a small smoked-glass window in the door, illuminating Bonnie like a spotlight.

"Thank you," Brennan said.

"He likes to complain," Bonnie said, "but he's always in a better mood if he gets a chance to chat with people. You can hang your coats next to mine. The groceries go to the kitchen, just through there."

Hunter managed the coats while Brennan followed Bonnie's directions to the kitchen.

"Let me get these unpacked, then we can talk." McCann placed oranges and grapefruit into a bowl on the counter. "You can leave that with me."

Brennan placed the grocery bag on the counter, then joined Hunter and Bonnie in the small dining room off the kitchen. The siblings sat at an oval polished-wood table set beneath a low-hanging chandelier while Bonnie went to boil a kettle of water. McCann entered, draped his coat on the back of one of the chairs, and settled his bulk into another across from Brennan. Bonnie shuttled the accoutrements for tea into the room: teacups, spoons, a creamer, and a sugar bowl.

"I don't want to be a bad host," he said, "but I hope you recognize this is an imposition."

"We do," Brennan said, "and we're grateful for any time you can give us."

McCann grunted, leaned back, and said, "So tell me exactly what you're doing here."

"We wanted to get some color on the investigation," Brennan said. "Things we wouldn't know from reading the news stories or the trial transcript."

"But why? What's the point? The guy—your dad, he's dead, right? I remember seeing that. You want me to tell you he didn't do it?"

"Actually," Hunter said, "I think he did it. But my sister doesn't. You can imagine that it makes family dinners pretty strained."

"What do you do?"

"I'm a reporter."

McCann glanced at Brennan. "You?"

"A lawyer. I was a prosecutor."

McCann's eyes flickered between the two of them. "So the two of you think you can do my job better than me thirty years after the fact?"

Brennan patted at the air as if to calm an angry animal. "It's not about that. There's just so much we don't know. You know how young we were. Our mom never spoke to us about what happened. Dad definitely didn't. Everything we know came from kids taunting us or tidbits people mentioned over the years or references in old files and news stories. We probably won't learn anything more than you knew at the time, but it will be more than we know now."

Bonnie entered with a steaming kettle and poured water into their cups before returning to the kitchen. The siblings let the cups sit to cool a bit. McCann spooned sugar into his with a fist like a toddler.

"And what's the goal here? You going to write a story about this? Or a book?"

"Like we said," Hunter said, "this is for us."

"I imagine if we were to find something new," Brennan said, "we'd turn it over to the authorities. But thirty years later?" She gave an abbreviated shrug to let McCann know that she wasn't optimistic about the prospect.

"If I talk to you, I don't want what I say coming up in some news story or a book," McCann said. "So strictly off-the-record, Mr. Reporter, you got that?"

"Understood," Hunter said.

"And you, counselor. You know how it is. We don't bring cases unless we think it's our guy. So I don't want to sit here and fight you on why you think your daddy didn't do it."

"I only want whatever facts and thoughts you have."

McCann nodded. "Ask away."

"How well do you remember the case?" Brennan asked, taking the lead.

"I remember it pretty good. It was one of my first homicides. I got partnered up with Bobby Bauman so he could break me in. He ended up making chief of detectives down the line. Anyway, he caught the case because he was the best we had at the time. And it was a unique case. Got a lot of media attention. Fancy victim. Your dad's race. At the time, that stood out. He was the only murderer I caught that didn't plead guilty or get convicted of something."

"Why do you think that was?" Hunter asked.

"Jury had reasonable doubt."

"But why?"

McCann grunted. "The whole thing was circumstantial. The defense attorney did a great job. Still, I thought at worst, we'd get a hung jury. The acquittal surprised me. I spent a lot of time after thinking what I could have done better to nail him."

"Let's come back to that in a bit," Brennan said. "Can you tell us how you settled on our dad as the suspect?"

"We ruled out a robbery or home invasion pretty quick. Nothing was stolen. No forced entry to the apartment. When her friend, Cathy, I think it was, told us why Jessica was at her place, Bauman thought it was either the husband or the boyfriend. It's almost always one of those two. The husband . . . what was his name?"

"Mark," Hunter said.

"Yeah. He showed up to the scene. Cathy told us she called him right after she called the cops. We interviewed him. I thought his alibi was weak. Said he left work, walked for a while before getting home, and stayed there until he got the call from Cathy. Parts of that story didn't match exactly with other witnesses, but we couldn't disprove it."

"Did Cathy tell you that they used to fight? Jessica and Mark?"

McCann thought for a moment. "What do you mean 'fight'?"

"They apparently hit each other."

McCann's brow creased. "I'd remember if she told us that."

"If you knew about that, would you have pushed harder on his alibi?" Brennan asked.

"What do you think?"

"So how did you get to my dad?"

"We figured that her boyfriend was probably someone from work. So we interviewed the lawyers there. One of the partners, I forget his name, he gave us a list of people she was friendly with. We interviewed them. One of them was your dad."

McCann finished his tea before resuming. "Your dad told us that they were friends. Honestly, that first conversation, once we saw him, we didn't give much thought to him. Neither of us—me or Bauman—could picture a girl like Jessica having an affair with someone like him. No offense."

Hunter tensed beside her but didn't say anything.

"The next day, we interviewed a bunch of Jessica's friends. They told us that Jessica mentioned that her boss was into her."

"They said she had told them that like, what, nine or ten months before she was murdered?" Brennan asked. She remembered the reference in the scans of the detectives' notes.

"Yeah. That sounds right. I'd have to see my notes to be sure. So we went back to the firm. Talked to all the partners again, including your dad. Same stories. Then we talked to the one partner, the guy from the first day. He explained the way these law firms worked to us."

"Let me guess. He basically said that she may have called any of the partners her boss?" Brennan asked.

"Yep. Something like that. But he also mentioned that your dad and Jessica had been getting coffee a lot the past six months or something."

"Just out of the blue? He explain why he didn't tell you guys that the first day?" Maybe Brennan missed it, but she hadn't seen anything like what McCann was describing in the detectives' notes, only pages recording various partners saying the same thing: Jess was smart, hardworking, and reserved. Had lots of friends in the office.

McCann smiled. "Bauman got it out of him. Made this whole show of closing his notebook and putting it away. Said to him, 'Look sir'"—McCann's voice changed into what Brennan assumed was an imitation of Bauman—"'we know you don't want to get anyone in trouble or embarrass anybody, so this is just between us, okay, but do you got any gossip, anything that might help?'"

"So this partner, he told you then?" Brennan asked.

"Yeah. He also suggested that we check the car-service voucher books." McCann told them that he and Bauman collected the voucher books going back at least a year. "We noticed that your dad had vouchers showing repeated trips to various intersections about a block from Cathy's apartment. In a few instances, he and Jessica took separate cars to the same location within fifteen minutes of each other. The pattern started in January, six months before Jessica's murder."

"That was clever," Brennan said. "The vouchers got you both the affair and our dad in the area the night of the murder."

"If he'd taken a cab," McCann said, "it would have been untraceable. Cash only back then."

"Why did you guys interview this partner first?"

"When we showed up at the firm, we asked who Jessica worked most with. It was that guy, what was his name, Walter something."

"Walter Roberts."

McCann nodded.

"Did you look at him?" Brennan asked. "He'd have been her 'boss,' too, right?"

"We did. Everyone in that firm had an alibi that checked out except your dad."

"Okay, then," Hunter said. "What bothered you about the case, though?"

"What do you mean?" McCann asked.

"I mean, your theory fits, but there were things that didn't fit it, right? Like the handprint."

McCann nodded. "That fucking—"

"Language!" Bonnie called from the kitchen.

"Sorry. The goddamned handprint. Yeah, it was a problem. But didn't match anything else in the place. Nothing to indicate that it was left the night of the murder."

"Except that it was on the overturned chair," Brennan said.

"Yeah. Honestly, it bothered me. My first homicide. I wanted it perfect. But Bauman? Not so much. Between us, he suggested that we lose it. I told him, 'No way.' I mean, Bauman had a great reputation, so I didn't think he was serious. And McCarthy, the ADA, he was a cocky bastard, he wasn't troubled by it."

"He's running for DA now," Brennan said. If McCann was the one making the threatening calls, maybe he would slip.

"Yeah. He's an asshole. Lucky for him I don't vote in Manhattan."

"What did he say about the handprint?"

McCann squinted as he tried to remember. "Told us the jury would never buy that a random guy happened to be in the room and leave only one handprint on a chair but not the door or anything else. I mean, he was right, right? Defense didn't even use it at trial."

"The defense didn't know," Brennan said.

"Wait. What do you mean?"

"I talked to the attorney. It wasn't in the defense files. He didn't know."

McCann shook his head. "I don't believe it. Bauman wouldn't actually do that."

"Did you see them turn it over?"

Another head shake. His shoulders dropped an inch as he considered the information.

"You ever try running those prints again?" Hunter asked.

"Not after the trial."

"It's a big problem," Brennan said, as if she were commiserating. "Risky to go to trial with that hanging out there. You didn't know?"

"I told you I didn't. Bauman took the lead on the trial stuff. I moved on to other cases." McCann watched the steam rise from his tea before speaking again. "There was a lot of evidence that pointed toward your dad. And a lot of pressure on us to bring a charge. You know how it is with the press." He shot a look at Hunter. "I don't know what kind of shit McCarthy was getting, but me and Bauman were drowning in it. Frankly, McCarthy thought that your dad would fold once he indicted him. He didn't expect him to take the risk of trial."

They waited for McCann to speak further, but instead he asked, "You talk to anyone else?"

"The partner, Walter. Cathy Cooke," Brennan said. "Do you know where Bauman is?"

"He died about ten years ago. Right after he retired. His son's a cop. Ran across him a couple of times before I retired. Kinda got fast-tracked because of his dad, know what I mean?" he asked, then looked between the two of them. "No. I guess you don't know what that's like."

He stood up. "Looks like we've finished the tea. Can I get you anything before you go?"

Brennan's cup was still half full.

Hunter extended a hand. "We appreciate you sitting down with us."

McCann shook their hands and walked them back to the front hall.

"One last thing," Brennan said, as she grabbed her coat from the hook. "Cathy mentioned that she was having an affair with someone. The guy paid for her to stay in a hotel until she could move out of the apartment. She say anything about that to you?"

McCann held her gaze for a moment. "She didn't mention anything like that to us."

"Guess you couldn't picture a girl like her doing something like that either." Brennan shrugged, then said, "Thank you for your time."

He opened the door, blasting them all with cold air, even before the siblings had pulled their coats on.

TWENTY-EIGHT

Now

THERE WAS NO HOLD MUSIC, ONLY SILENCE. IF NOT FOR THE timer on his cell phone ticking steadily upward, Hunter would have thought that they'd been disconnected. The timer showed they'd been on hold for close to four minutes. The phone was the only thing on Brennan's table. She made a face at the phone like she could startle a sound from it. It didn't work.

"We should have gone to his office," Brennan said.

"Let's just see—" Hunter said.

"Hello?" a man's voice carried from the phone's speaker. Hunter hit a button on his screen unmuting the microphone.

"Hey, Mark?" Hunter hated it, the unabashed warmth and familiarity he affected, as if he were calling an old college friend. It was a telemarketer's trick to keep people on the line when they heard a stranger's voice. Hunter perfected the technique over years of calling leads and sources on stories, keeping them on the line until he could figure an angle to get them talking—or even giving him nonanswers in ways that were revelatory.

"Yeah?"

"Sorry to call you out of the blue like this. My name is Hunter Leigh. My sister is here with me, and you're on speaker."

"Do I know you?" Only four words, but the Jersey accent came strong through the phone. Hunter imagined Mark, sitting in his office, close to the end of the day, probably thinking about dinner, the ten things he had to do before he left, the twenty things he'd leave for the next day—not about three decades ago.

"We've never met, but we're John Lo's kids."

The silence on the line was so complete Hunter thought they'd been put on hold again until a sound—a creak, maybe Mark sitting upright in his chair—carried from the speaker. Brennan jerked her head at the phone, a cue for Hunter to keep speaking before Mark hung up.

"Please, this will take only a few moments," Hunter said.

"What do you want?"

"We wanted to talk to you about—"

"I didn't know your father."

"—Jessica."

"Why? What could you possibly . . . How could you drag this up?"

"We'd like to meet you. In person. We've been meeting with people who knew her. Like Cathy Cooke."

"She talked to you?" The siblings' eyes met. Brennan had heard it, too. A discordant note beneath the surprise in Mark's voice, a quiver of fear. "What did she say?"

"I can tell you when we meet, if that's okay with you?"

"Why are you meeting with people about Jess? What do you think you're doing? She's been dead for . . . I've been remarried for fifteen years now."

"We know," Hunter said to stop Mark's momentum. If he didn't, Mark would tie himself and them into knots. Hunter's voice shifted, and although he didn't sound that different, he invested his words with an intensity that demanded attention and promised understanding. "We know you lost your wife. We lost our father. We . . . I owe you an apology. For what my father did. You don't owe me anything, but I'd like the opportunity to see you, to hear your story, to understand your loss."

Silence, then Mark said, "I'll think about it."

There was no click or tone, only the screen of his phone scrolling "Call Ended" before cutting to black.

Hunter sat back, but Brennan stood and stomped over to grab her briefcase and purse from the couch. "We should have just showed up."

"He wouldn't have talked to us."

"Get up," she said. "I have to get to Mom's."

"I can cover tonight, if you want."

"Fine." She slung her bags back onto the couch. "Thanks."

Hunter pocketed his phone and pulled his coat off the back of the chair. Brennan's stare bore into his back.

"What?" he asked without turning.

"We don't have to apologize to him," Brennan said. "You shouldn't have said that. Dad didn't do anything wrong."

Hunter spun to face her, his face a showcase of incredulity. "He had an affair with his wife! At best!"

"Fine, but that is not on us," she said, waving a hand wildly back and forth to indicate the two of them. "You made it sound like we wanted to apologize for Jessica's murder. You said you'd keep an open mind—"

"Brennan, it's open, but nothing's changed, and this may be the only chance we have to talk to this guy and I—our family owes him an apology."

"Just go," she said, dismissing him with a slight hand wave. It was their mother's wave—a coup de grâce of passive aggression—employed when she tired of fighting and wanted to suck the joy out of whatever they did that she didn't approve of. *Mom, we're going to Atlantic City after prom.* The wave. *Mom, I want to go to Stanford, not Columbia.* The wave. *Mom, I'm going to take an overseas beat.* The wave. *Mom, I can't stay for the holidays. I gotta be back in Pakistan.* That fucking wave.

But what did it say about him that he took the permission each time, a shield against later recriminations, as he walked out the door, like he did now?

\#

His mother turned her head when he entered her bedroom.

"I thought Brennan was coming tonight."

"She had to work late," Hunter said. "You took your medicine?"

"No. Not yet."

"You're supposed to stay on track."

"God, Hunter, what does it matter if I miss a dose at this point?"

He sat at the chair next to her bed. A commercial for laundry detergent played from the television. "What are you watching?"

"Reruns. I don't want to get invested in any new shows."

"I hate when you talk like that."

"Like what? Like I know what my prognosis is? I know you and your sister want to ignore it, running around on your errands like I don't know what's going on."

"We're not hiding anything, Mom. You know we're talking to people, trying to get some answers. Or at least understand why everything happened the way it did."

She sighed. "Sure. I didn't think you would stop. The two of you are too much alike."

"Who? Me and Dad?"

"You and your sister."

On the screen, the commercials dumped into a promo for the eleven o'clock news, which blinked away, replaced by Rachel and Phoebe sitting on a couch in Central Perk.

"It came to me today," Jane said. Her gaze was fixed on the television. "The name of that restaurant. Frontier. I used to pass it sometimes, down in the Village. He worked there after the trial."

Hunter searched for the restaurant on his phone. It was still there.

"This show is very stupid," his mother said. "Like you. Ignoring my situation."

"I'm not ignoring it! I'm sitting right here. I've been coming here for weeks."

"Okay. Fine."

Hunter's phone buzzed in his hand. It was Jenna. She wanted to meet at 11.

"Hot date?" his mother asked.

"Don't read over my shoulder," he said, typing out *See you then*.

"I wasn't. You get this look on your face. When a girl pays attention to you. Since you were a boy. Like when . . . what was her name? Shannon? When she used to call looking for you in high school."

"Uh huh. What look is that?"

"Like this," she said and tried to imitate a self-satisfied half smile. But her dry, thin lips barely raised next to her sunken cheeks, and no warmth appeared in her pallid skin. There was almost nothing about her that was recognizable compared to the image he would have sketched of her, an ageless amalgamation of her face imprinted in his consciousness from the day his eyes adjusted to the light of the world from the darkness of her womb through the day he left home for college. He tried to impose that memory on the ruined woman lying before him, but the image wouldn't come, only the angry shadow of loss.

"What?" she asked. "You don't like my impression?"

He forced a chuckle from his airless lungs and said, "Loved it. Really captured me."

"Your father used to get that same look when he was pleased with himself."

Hunter couldn't remember a time his father smiled, half or otherwise. "I guess it's genetic. He didn't smile all that much."

His mother muted the television and closed her eyes. Maybe she was trying to remember a time he smiled, too.

"Not in the later years, no," she said. "But when I met him, John smiled all the time. Like he'd just gotten one over on someone. Or he was going to share a secret with you. It was . . . he was handsome when he was serious. You know, when he was concentrating. That smile, though, it would come out of nowhere. And this guy you thought you had figured out, it was like there was this whole other man in there, bright and full of happiness."

Hunter looked down at his hands, clasped in his lap. "Yeah? I didn't know that guy."

"I thought I did. Toward the end, I wondered if he was real or if I made him up."

"Did we . . . was it us?" Hunter asked, hating the sound of his voice, like he'd gone back in time thirty years. "That made him so angry?"

Jane opened her eyes. She slid her hand across the comforter until it fell from the edge. She extended her fingers to reach his arm but missed. Her hand rose again, shaking, and she attempted again, stretching weakly, until her hand fluttered down to rest on his forearm, like a butterfly alighting.

"No, darling," Jane said. "It wasn't you kids. Your father and I, we weren't happy after the first couple of years. To be honest, I didn't even give it much thought at the time. We had a plan. Get our careers off the ground. Make partner. Secure our livelihoods. Have some kids. Raise them right. It was supposed to work. It was working. Happiness was superfluous."

She pulled her hand back to the bed.

"I think he got tired of waiting for me to be happy," she said. "What was I supposed to do about that? I'm not a happy person."

Growing up, he'd assumed his mother's disposition was the norm, that there was no joy in adulthood. His initial experiences of other kids' parents—distant and courteous contacts, like they were shopkeepers offering juice or a snack—did not draw attention to how different his mother was. Only later, when he saw mothers giggling at television shows during sleepovers, or when friends invited him to stay for dinner and he witnessed moms trading jokes with their children, did he begin to sense the void in his mother. Like a swimming pool with no water, she held the memory of happiness, was even built for it, but it wasn't there.

"I thought it was him," Hunter said. "Growing up. I thought it was the things he did that made you sad."

"Well," his mother said, eyes fixed on the drawn curtains obscuring the view of Manhattan that lay beyond, "that didn't help."

"Yeah, but what about us? Me and Brennan?"

She turned her head toward him. Her right hand lurched on the cover like a landed fish. "Go," she said. "Just go."

Hunter got up and walked to the door. He said, "You always blamed me for leaving, but you were always telling me to go."

Her hand rose from the bed, slowly, like a crane was lifting it. She gave a slight wave without looking at him, then let it fall to the bed. Hunter waited another moment for her to tell him to stay before closing the door behind him.

#

"When do you leave again?" Jenna asked. She lay in the crook of his couch, one leg running straight down the length of the seat, the other bent at the knee, resting against the back cushions. While he'd been getting water for them, she'd pulled a throw pillow off the floor to prop her head up. Their clothes lay scattered around the couch. Offerings before an altar.

Hunter handed her a glass as damp as they were. His apartment was heated as if it were the dry cold of February, but it was a clammy night in the endless gray days of March. He stood, hoping that he'd stop sweating, and gulped his water. Jenna ran her glass over her forehead, like she was sitting on a porch in August, waiting for an answer.

"I still don't know. Why?"

"Just curious. I didn't know how long you could go without working."

Hunter shrugged. "A while, I guess. I don't make much, but not many expenses as a single guy on the road a bunch. Managed to save a lot over the years."

Jenna sat up and sipped her water, surveying the room. "Mind if I take the tour? We kinda skipped it when we came in. Not that I minded."

Hunter shrugged and swept a hand across the room. "You're looking at most of it."

"Show me. I'm curious."

He helped her up from the couch and pointed to a closed door. "That's the bathroom. Nothing to see there." He showed her anyway, then his bedroom.

"I see why you stopped me at your couch. You make your bed like you do your hair." His bed was made, but unkempt. Jenna walked to it, sat on the edge, leaned back, and looked about dubiously.

"You actually live here?"

"What's wrong with it?"

"Nothing. It just feels like, I don't know, a hotel. Except hotels have more character. And furniture."

"I finally bring you to my place, and you insult it?" Hunter wasn't offended. He understood that his apartment had the personality of a vacant dorm room. Nevertheless, he felt honor bound to at least protest.

"I mean, kinda. I get you're on the road a lot, but you've been in town months now. You didn't get anything to make it more . . . you?"

"What makes you think this isn't me?"

"I hope this isn't you," she said. "You can't be this. I thought you'd have some framed photos from your travels. Maybe an old movie poster considering you talked my ear off about Kurosawa. Something personal somewhere. Like a place for your clothes."

He sat next to her on the bed. "I didn't want to invest in a place that I'm never at. And there's plenty of space in the closet."

"If you're barely here, why do you keep it? It's not like you're using it to store your things."

Hunter shrugged. "I used to have more stuff. After college, when

I was starting out. I figured I'd sublet it when I started my overseas assignments, so I got rid of stuff. Eventually, places like this, hotel rooms, short-term rentals, they felt more like home than the apartment I used to have that was cluttered with shit I didn't use and didn't look at."

Jenna leaned over and kissed his shoulder. "I'm going to put some clothes on. Give you something to take off later."

Hunter followed her back to the living room, and they scavenged through the discarded clothing on the floor for their underwear. After Jenna pulled her T-shirt over her head, she walked over to a photo hanging on the wall.

"My mother and my sister," Hunter said. He'd taken the photo in high school, the day of Brennan's graduation, near a window to take advantage of the diffuse light. Brennan looked at the camera as she rested her head on their mother's shoulder. His mother's eyes were cast slightly off to one side; she'd been looking out the window. Neither smiled. The photo didn't show that Brennan was sitting on the edge of their father's desk or that she and Hunter had barely spoken in the months before he took the photo. It didn't show the camera that made the image—his dad's old Minolta X-370. Jane made him use it after he got into photography in high school, and he handed it back to her that summer after he made enough money to get a new Nikon.

"They're beautiful," Jenna said.

"My mom has a version of this hanging in her place. It's the three of us, smiling. She wanted it. Us standing there like assholes with stupid fake smiles plastered across our faces waiting for the timer to go off. But I snapped this while setting the camera up. It's probably the truest photo I have of the two of them. Mom's looking off, thinking about something else, like she always was. Brennan looking right at you, like she's daring you to tell her something. Basically her in a nutshell. And they're stuck together."

Jenna searched the faces in the photo, comparing them to Hunter's.

"This is the only picture you have up in your whole place."

"It's the only one I like."

TWENTY-NINE

Now

FRONTIER WAS ONE OF THOSE NEIGHBORHOOD PLACES IN the West Village that were as old as—maybe older than—Hunter was. It must have been trendy once, but now the room felt like an old pair of jeans—worn, but comfortable—down to the place settings. It had just opened, and a couple of early diners were already seated and flipping through menus. Hunter asked a server for the manager and sat at the short bar to wait. Eventually, an old man approached him from the kitchen.

"I'm Claude," the man said, extending his hand. He had a French accent weathered down by time. "I own this place. How can I help you?"

Hunter shook Claude's hand, ignoring the mat of hair that covered the backs of his fingers and hand. Claude slicked his silver-black hair back with gel, but it curled at the ends, tufting behind his ears and at his neck. Bushy eyebrows overhung his eyes like a snow shelf before an avalanche.

Hunter introduced himself. "I'm looking for folks who may have known my father, John Lo. My mom told me he worked here—probably about thirty years ago?"

Claude's face scrunched, the bushy eyebrows nearly touching. "Lots of people worked here."

"He was a Chinese American guy. Accused of murder. Acquitted." Like his news reports, Hunter thought. Reducing incredible tragedies to the fewest possible words. He resisted the urge to leave.

"Oh, yes," Claude said. "That was a long time ago. I mean, I barely remember him other than that he worked here. What was it? A few days? A week? I don't remember."

"So you knew him?"

Claude shook his head. "No. I met him, briefly. Before he quit."

"He quit?"

Claude looked away to watch a waitress carrying bread to a table. "From what I remember."

Hunter wished Brennan was with him. Claude seemed like a guy who would be very eager to tell a woman what she wanted to hear. And, Hunter admitted to himself, Brennan was skillful at getting people to talk. But he hadn't told her about the visit. They'd barely spoken since their recent argument except to confirm who was staying with their mom. He knew dropping by Frontier was a long shot, but there wasn't much else to occupy his days.

"Anyone still around from then?"

"Just me. You know how it is at restaurants. We've had some old-timers, but there's a lot of turnover."

"What do you remember about him?"

Claude thought for a moment. "Not much more than what I've told you. I wanted to give him a chance, you know, to get back on his feet. But he quit. He left a bag. I remember that because he just walked out in the middle of his shift."

Hunter leaned back, watching Claude carefully. His father had never left a job unfinished, but it didn't look like Claude was lying. Again, he wished Brennan were with him. She had a better read of these things than him.

The muscles in Claude's face moved, as if the memory were a crumb he could dislodge, and he said, "One of the waitresses took it to give it back to him."

"Who was that?"

"Nicki. Nicki Berger. She worked here for a while, but she left a long time ago. We lost touch."

\#

The back of Hunter's neck tingled as he stepped into his apartment. Instinctively, he stopped his forward motion, one hand on the doorknob, and scanned the room. None of his limited furniture was out of place, but he had seen something that he barely registered and could no longer see.

"Hello?" Hunter called. Jenna couldn't have returned to his place after she left that morning. She didn't have a key. His mother did; maybe she'd given it to Brennan.

He listened, but there was no sound other than the ambient noise he otherwise never heard. He stepped fully into the apartment, closing the door gently behind him and letting his backpack slide off his shoulder to his hand. If someone was there, it was the best weapon he had at the moment, weighed down as it was with his laptop and some books he kept on hand to read at his mother's.

Someone waiting for him might expect him to creep through the apartment, so Hunter moved quickly. The kitchen was the first room he checked, but it was empty. He grabbed a carving knife from the magnetic rack over his counter.

He strode directly through the living room to his bathroom and yanked the shower curtain back. Nobody. Hunter spun and took the corner into his bedroom. There was no way to be sure the bed was as he left it—his method of bed making was to yank the covers up to the pillows and leave it. He checked his closet, feeling increasingly silly at the knife in his hand.

Since the last threat to Brennan, there had been no others. But they had spent two weeks going through the materials at Harris's office, so to an outside observer, it might look like they had stopped. In the last few days, however, they'd visited McCann and called Mark. Hunter had warned Brennan to be careful; maybe he was spooking himself.

He tossed his backpack on the bed and returned to the kitchen to replace the knife in its rack. He saw it when he passed through the main room and understood why he'd stopped when he'd first entered the apartment. Before they left that morning, Hunter and Jenna had eaten breakfast at his table—egg sandwiches from the local deli. They'd thrown out the wrappers, but he'd left his coffee mug on the table.

Set next to it was a single bullet.

He pulled his phone out to call Brennan, but as he did, it vibrated in his hand. A blocked number. Hunter answered.

"I told your sister to lay off," a muffled voice said.

"She's never listened too well."

"Then you fucking listen. If I have to leave another one of those things with you, it won't be on your table."

THIRTY

Then

BRENNAN TAPPED ON THE DOOR. JOHN KNEW IT WAS HER BEcause of the way she used her fingertips, pinky to index finger, softly, twice. He slid the letter he was writing into the desk drawer.

"Daddy?" Brennan asked through the door.

"Yeah."

She opened the door, slipped around it, gripping the knob as if the building had tipped onto its side and if she let go of it, she would drop the ten feet from the door to the other side of the room. She wore her school uniform even though she had been home for nearly an hour. He hadn't seen her or Hunter since they arrived, but he had heard them arguing through the door, sniping at each other for various perceived offenses.

"Are you working?" she asked.

"Yes." His desk was clear except for his Montblanc pen.

"Can I do my homework in here with you?" She saw the look on his face. "I promise I'll be quiet and won't bother you. Hunter is really annoying me."

John didn't want her in the office with him. But maybe it would be better for the kids if they had some separation.

"Fine. But you have to be quiet."

Brennan darted from the room and returned with her backpack before John could change his mind. She sat on the floor and pulled out some penmanship worksheets and a pencil. She laid across the floor and began to practice cursive letters across the top of the page. It was nonsensical for her to practice writing in that position. She was making it more difficult than it needed to be.

"Brennan."

She snapped her head up, eyebrows raised in concern.

"Do you write like that in school?"

"With a pencil?"

"No. Lying on the floor."

She shook her head.

"Then why practice that way now?"

Brennan shrugged. John huffed and pointed to his desk. With nothing on it, there was plenty of space for her papers. She pulled her father's reading chair to face the desk. When she sat, she was small enough that her feet only grazed the floor. She bent over her paper and began to trace the dotted lines teaching her how to write a cursive *b* before casting herself into the uncharted space where she had to repeat them without the guides. When she completed the first line, she looked over.

"Don't you have work to do, Daddy?"

He shook his head. She knew he didn't have work. Could she even remember a time when he worked? When he would wake, shower, and walk them to school, wearing a suit, a shirt and tie, carrying his briefcase? Could she recall holding hands with him as they crossed the street, the little squeeze he would give before letting her race ahead to the next corner, or how he would lift her up in his arms to kiss her face before she disappeared into her classroom?

He knew nobody would ever look at him the way that she did. When Brennan was small, he used to hold her out in front of him, spinning her through the air in the playground, her laughter delighting him, her eyes teary with joy. When she looked at him with happiness, it dampened the anger always radiating within him. In those moments, he could forget—no, not forget, rather forgive himself however briefly for the way Jane looked at him before she'd slam the door when they argued, or when he would stumble home drunk, or every night he climbed into bed when they still shared a bed. Except when was the last time he had made Brennan smile or laugh or even giggle?

He still could lift her and spin her through the air. But even if her laughter was the same unguarded child melody—a single innocent trumpet ringing pell-mell through its entire range, reckless of structure and key—his guilt roared like a subway train through the concert.

Brennan concentrated on the lined paper in front of her as he studied her, but then glanced at him, eyes wide with concern as if she were a nurse and he a dying patient. Or was it because she was a prisoner and he her warden?

He didn't understand her at all. He thought he would recognize some of himself in her, but she seemed to be entirely composed of the qualities he wished he had but lacked. Whatever DNA of his that she carried had been refined, creating a being unrecognizable as his progeny.

The next day, Brennan came back to work at his desk while John forced himself to read through the classified section of the newspaper yet again. The day after, Brennan completed a sheet that involved counting various animals and adding the totals of different groups together. Cows and chickens. Chickens and horses. Cows and horses. Each day she appeared at his desk after school and toiled away. Hunter did his homework at the kitchen table or at a little desk in the kids' room.

One afternoon, Brennan looked up from another handwriting sheet and said, "Can I tell you a secret, Daddy? If you promise not to get angry."

"Sure." John was looking through bank statements watching the savings he and Jane had carefully built, a breakwater against a disaster, erode further and further. Jane's salary on its own—lucrative as it was—couldn't keep the kids in their private school and the nanny employed and the mortgage and the co-op fees paid and food on the table. Eventually, they'd have to put the kids in public school or maybe let the nanny go—after all, why did they need a nanny when he wasn't working? To make sure he didn't have to show his face at the school, of course, with the teachers and parents looking at him, one of the few Asian faces and the only one who was tried for murder. Better that they not associate him with his kids.

"Dad?"

"Yeah."

"My secret? Can I tell you?"

"You know what they say about secrets, Brennan?"

"What?"

"Two people can keep a secret if one of them is dead."

Brennan cocked her head, trying to decipher what he meant. John regretted saying it. She was old enough to read into the statement, maybe even believe he was trying to send her a message.

"What's your secret, Brennan?" he said before she could put more thought into what he had said.

She smiled and leaned close, so she could whisper to him.

"Before you started working from home, when you still went to your office, I would come in here and sit in your chair to do my homework and pretend I was you."

John knew this. The nanny had told Jane, and Jane had mentioned it to him one night as he climbed into bed with her. But he pretended to be surprised.

"Really?"

Brennan laughed. "Yeah. I want to have a big important job like you one day. And a nice desk like this one."

"Yeah? Well, you can have this desk if you do that."

Brennan's eyebrows rose, and she spread her hands across the surface of the desk like she might try to start scooping it up then. John sat back to imagine her as an adult, sitting in her own place, hunched over the desk, casebooks open around her as she scribbled on a yellow legal pad. He knew that she was doing the same, hopefully better than he was, because the adult daughter he imagined was a stranger. He had no idea who Brennan might grow up to be. Maybe by the time she was an adult, she wouldn't give a shit about his old desk, too big for whatever starter apartment she might live in, too stodgy for her tastes, which would be metal and plastic if television and movies were to be believed.

"You okay, Daddy?"

"Yeah."

A few days later, after the weekend, she crept in while he drafted a letter with a counterproposal to the firm that would let him return on a provisional basis with impossible-to-achieve business generation and billable hour goals. When he looked up from scratching out *3,500 hours* and writing *2,750 hours*, he saw that she was drawing with a box of colored pencils.

"Don't you have homework?" he asked.

"This is my homework. I have to draw someone important."

John's chest constricted when he saw the image, but he walked around his desk to stand behind her so he could see it better. It was a humanoid figure, rendered in her child's hand as a somewhat proportional series of rectangles representing his limbs and torso topped by a circle representing his head.

Brennan used a blue pencil to point as she explained her drawing. "I made your shoulders big, because you're strong. You can lift me over your head. And see this on your hand? That's your wedding ring because you're married to Mommy. And I know you used to have short hair, but I like it longer like you have it now, so I let you keep long hair in my drawing even though I know you'll cut it when you go back to work. And because you're smart, you see I drew all your books here? And your desk, too, because you work so much."

"What am I wearing?"

"Your blue suit. The one you wear to important meetings."

It was the suit he wore the day the verdict came in during his murder trial.

"Do you like it?" she asked, looking up at him from the chair expectantly.

He looked back to the drawing. Brennan saw him in the shapes on the page, a version of him that didn't exist—not because he wasn't rectangles holding up a circle, but because she had not captured his weakness, his faithlessness, his stupidity, his villainy. He turned away, worried the weight of the expectations and illusions on the paper would crush the desk.

How many women had looked at him the way Brennan did now, full of trust and love and faith that he was a good person? His mother died before she could see him for what he was. Jane saw and couldn't bear the sight of him anymore. She endured his presence because Brennan still looked at him like the past two years had never happened. John didn't know if he could bear to see Brennan grow to look at him like Jane did, but he knew he wasn't strong enough for her to keep seeing him like she did now. Jessica had seen, too, in the end.

The night he got back from fucking Jessica for the first time, he brushed his teeth and glanced at himself in the mirror. He expected he wouldn't recognize himself as the man who had betrayed his wife earlier that night. But the same face that looked out at him that morning from the other side of the glass stared back with the same amount of anger and revulsion as it always did, no more and certainly no less. The only additional emotion was the disappointment that not only was he able to look at himself in the mirror without flinching, but the face in the glass was more recognizable than it had ever been.

"It doesn't look like me," he said.

"But . . . but I told you, Daddy. I showed you how—"

"It doesn't look like me. And even if it did, you should draw someone else for school." John stepped back and crossed his arms. "You can't go in with a picture of me. You should draw your mother."

Brennan was blinking against the tears collecting in her eyes. "But other kids are going to draw their dads."

"Draw. Your. Mother." John was barely able to breathe. Brennan's chest was heaving. His rage sucked all of the oxygen from the room.

Brennan grabbed her pencils and ran to the door, where she turned. John waited for her to shout or call him a name or accuse him of being a terrible father or throw her pencils at him or do any of a dozen things he would have done. Instead, she glared at him. He stared back—her anger was a painful relief, like pressure on a bleeding cut. But then Brennan wavered, tears fell down her cheeks in fat drops like the start of a summer shower, and she spun away and through the door, leaving John alone in his office with her drawing.

THIRTY-ONE

Now

BRENNAN'S DOODLES FILLED HER LEGAL PAD. SHE'D INtended to take notes about the deposition transcript on her laptop screen, but her pen started moving on the paper—loops, circles within boxes within circles, then triangles divided into smaller polygons, then slashing lines like meteors from the top of the page driving through the aimless shapes before the deeply drawn furrows met the edge of the pad and spilled into air.

She looked back to the screen. She hadn't focused for the past four pages she'd scrolled through while her pen worked. The answer in the transcript was senseless. She paged back to the last parts she remembered and tore the sheet of doodles from her pad and laid it on the desk.

She turned the page horizontal, the shift in perspective transforming the bolts of ink into cracks across the surface of the paper—as if it were a stone tablet that couldn't bear the weight of the thoughts she left unwritten. They weren't mysteries to her. Her parents. Her brother. Her disastrous personal life. The threats against her and now Hunter. These all exerted bathypelagic pressures on her, but the dark, cold tonnage of them held her together. The cracks, splitting the mindless hieroglyphs she'd scrawled on the page, mirrored the fractures she felt crawling across her skin. She hardly dared to breathe, fearing the slightest movement would finally rupture the hull that had carried her to this depth.

The newest threat to Hunter had shaken her. Hunter called to check on her immediately afterward, and they'd agreed not to go to the police. What was the use? Anyone smart enough to use a burner phone and get into his apartment would have worn gloves. It was clear to them both that whoever was threatening them selected his apartment because, unlike his mother and sister, he had no doorman—therefore, no potential witness standing around at all hours. Like Cathy's old building. They also couldn't be sure the threat wasn't coming from the police. After all, the bullet came on the heels of their meeting with McCann.

The siblings gamed out the threat. Their stalker wanted them to stay quiet, but how much further was he willing to go? Neither of them believed he would do anything that might end up being a story that would trace back to him—or McCarthy, if that's who he was working for. And if it was Jessica's real killer—Hunter still did not believe it was possible—the killer would face the same double bind. Pressure them enough to stop them, but nothing extreme enough to draw attention. Yet the threats still unsettled her. As a prosecutor, the threats were mainly theoretical (someone *might* grow violent) or abstracted (a glare, a smile, a disgusting comment). The same for Hunter's work in war zones. It was dangerous, but nobody was targeting him personally. Still, the siblings agreed that they shouldn't back down as a matter of principle and practicality. The truth—whatever it may be—was the best way to end the threat.

Brennan ran her hand along the edge of her father's desk. She'd owned it far longer than he had. She cherished it as a relic of him, but it told her as much about him as a saint's bone revealed of the beatified. She was a grown woman with a child's faith in a man long gone. She couldn't even remember the reasons she'd believed in his innocence other than that she *knew* him. But what child knows her parents? Even now, her mother lay in a bed dying, and Brennan doubted whether she had ever been happy—or even tried to find happiness.

Brennan glanced up at her laptop screen—more than a hundred pages to read. She'd lost fifteen minutes doodling and staring at the page sitting in front of her. She needed to concentrate. But one particular line stretched across the page uninterrupted—a highway across a vast plain. It demanded an offshoot. Brennan picked up her pen and slashed another crack across the paper two-thirds of the way down. The new line grew a fresh branch as her pen cut another path to the same edge of the page. Then another. Every new pen stroke fragmented the paper into facets. None of the delineations brought any clarity. Her mind became muddier by the moment.

Brennan crumpled the page. The screen of her laptop was dark. She reached forward to wake it, but instead picked up her phone.

Hunter answered. "Yeah?"

"How's Mom?"

"When I left, she was sleeping."

"Anybody follow you? Any more surprises at your place?"

"No. And my door's latched."

"You around? I'm going to get a drink." She choked the words out like a drowning woman.

Silence. If he said no, she might text Sean, but she knew that he was at some Broadway show with his wife. Paul? Never. She could drink alone, find someone else at the bar—

Hunter sighed. He loved to let her know when she was putting him out. Every favor came with a loan statement reminding her that she owed him some incalculable interest that could never be repaid. She didn't have that kind of emotional capital. But she was willing to take on that mortgage tonight.

"Let me throw some clothes on," he said. "Where do you want to meet?"

#

Brennan's hair hung in a cold wet sheet that draped down the side of her cheek as she turned to see Hunter enter the bar. He closed his umbrella, water trickling off the point into a scattered trail running across the dirty wooden floor toward her. He took the stool next to her at the bar.

"You didn't need to have one waiting for me." Hunter reached for one of the two beers in front of Brennan—the full glass, not the one with a quarter pint remaining.

She grabbed his wrist—still slick with rain—and said, "They're both mine."

Hunter withdrew his hand from beneath hers, flagged the bartender, and pointed to her pint.

"You're wet. You didn't bring an umbrella?"

"I didn't realize it was raining." When she reached her lobby, she'd seen rain falling through the cold LED streetlight. It seemed insubstantial, barely more than a mist surprised that it was heavy enough to fall through the March air. Five blocks of fine droplets painting her, beading on her jacket until she shoved the door of the bar open, catching the light as if her jacket were coated in diamonds. Now, she was merely wet.

"They ruined us, Hunter."

"Hold up, Bren. I don't even have my beer yet."

They sat without words until the bartender—a brunette in a faded Fall Out Boy T-shirt—glided past, leaving his beer in her wake like a discarded thought.

Hunter took a heavy swig. "You were saying?"

"I was good friends with this girl in law school, Wendy." Brennan explained that Wendy's dream was to work for the ACLU or the Center for Reproductive Rights or something. They'd gotten drunk after their last spring exam the first year of law school, and the conversation drifted to family. Brennan laid out her father's story as she knew it at the time.

"When I finished, Wendy sat back, arms crossed, face like she'd been slapped. 'You forgave him?' she asked. And I said, 'Forgave him? He didn't do it. He was acquitted.'

"'I'm not talking about the murder, Bren. The affair. She was his subordinate. It was wrong.'

"'From everything I understand,' I said—barely giving any thought to how little I actually understood, 'it was consensual.' But Wendy didn't buy it. She said, 'Brennan, he preyed on her.' I told her she didn't know anything about it, but she just said, 'I don't know how you could defend him.'

"'He was my father,' I told her. 'I love him. How could I not?' And then she said, 'What about this Jessica? She didn't forgive him.' What was I supposed to say to that? All I could say was, 'She died. What was he supposed to do?' But Wendy just said, 'Not have an affair with his subordinate.'

"She was so smug about it. So I got defensive. 'But he did. So now I have to hate a dead man over a mistake he made when I was a child?' And Wendy said, 'It's the principle.' Then she started to go, but before she left, she looked right at me and said, 'I really think less of you that you'd compromise on this.'"

Brennan finished relaying the exchange to Hunter and drained the rest of her first beer.

He shrugged. "You know I'm on her side, right? You telling me this to pick a fight?"

Brennan exhaled. "I don't want to fight with you. I'm not telling you this so that you'll agree with me. Don't you understand? I mean, you ever have a conversation like that? About why you're wrong to love—or even hate—your father? Anyone ever ask you why you never forgave him?"

Hunter glanced over his shoulder at the bartender while he mulled the question.

"After college," he said, "when I got back to the city, I tried going to therapy." He'd ended up seeing an older woman therapist. He didn't need a session to know why he'd picked her. She was the opposite of Jane—short, plump, compassionate. "Toward the end of a session, she asked me why I'd never forgiven Dad.

"I thought it was a pretty straightforward question, so I said, 'What he did was unforgivable.' But you know how therapists are. She looked at me with that friendly smile and asked, 'Was it? Is it for you?'

"'Why should I forgive him?' I asked. And she said, 'Why not?'

"'He's dead,' I said. 'He doesn't care. He didn't care. He hurt everyone around him. He doesn't deserve my forgiveness.' Then she leaned forward—I can still see her kind face, and how much it pissed me off—and said, 'Forgiveness isn't for other people. It's for ourselves, so I think the real issue is, do you believe you deserve forgiveness?'

"I never went back," Hunter said.

Brennan caught the bartender's attention and held up two fingers. She turned back to Hunter. "Why didn't you go back?"

"Ten minutes ago, you said that they ruined us. Why should we forgive them?"

"You're deflecting. I asked you why you didn't go back to therapy."

Hunter finished the last of his beer. "I didn't want to deal with it. He has like zero impact on my day-to-day life. If I forgave him, would it make it like our lives never happened the way they did? Nothing—literally nothing—would change. So why tear myself apart for that? It's a fucking academic exercise."

"Doesn't feel so academic sitting here."

They waited for the bartender to deliver the fresh beers without speaking.

"I never went to therapy," Brennan said.

"Why not?"

Brennan shrugged. "I had it under control. I was checking all the boxes. Career? Good. I had friends. Never had trouble dating. Family was fucked, but everyone has family issues. I never wanted to be happy. Happiness felt like a show my friends would put on for me. 'Oh my God! Dave is sooooo amazing! And he's not afraid to just, you know, cry!' Then a year later, and fucking Betty's like, 'Dave doesn't ever talk to me about anything. I feel like I'm raising this baby on my own. And he never wants sex anymore.' Who needs that shit?"

"Relationships are work."

"Don't mansplain relationships to me."

"I'm not!" Hunter raised a placating hand. "I'm commiserating. I never wanted to do that kind of work either. Why do you think I'm here with you?"

"So we're not working at this?"

"Working at what?"

"At being sister and brother."

Hunter laughed. "We don't have to work at being brother and sister. That's what we are. A *good* brother? A *good* sister? Fuck if I know where to even start with that."

"So then why are you here?"

"You called."

Brennan drained half her beer. Hunter gulped from his glass to chase her progress.

"Do you think you could ever get there? Forgive him?" she asked.

"For murder? It's not our place."

"If he did it, isn't it, though? A little bit? I'm not saying on behalf of Jessica or the people who loved her. That's not for us. But he hurt us, too. Can't I forgive him for that at least?"

Hunter shook his head. "You're a better person than me."

"That's not what I'm saying."

"I'm just saying, you knew how to deal with him as a kid. Make him happy. And after everything went to shit, you believed in him. You don't think I was jealous of that? That I wished I could be like you? But then you'd throw it in my face, and it made me hate you for that." Hunter paused. He traced doodles in the condensation on his glass with the tip of his thumb. "This shit about forgiveness . . . it brings all that up again, and it makes me feel like an asshole. Like I'm not as good as you because

I can't get over it and make peace with him. But how can you forgive him, yet you never forgave me for doubting him?"

"I cheated on Paul."

Hunter stopped, his beer halfway to his mouth. "Why are you telling me this?"

"So you know that I'm not a better person than anybody, even you."

Hunter put his beer down. Brennan leaned back on the barstool and stared at her hands in her lap.

"This is what I've been trying to get at. My friends, they don't want to deal with me anymore. They knew Paul. They didn't understand why I did it. I didn't have an excuse like, 'Oh, I met someone else who was wonderful.' Or, you know, 'Paul's an asshole who pays no attention to me.' Nope. Nothing like that. It was just . . . flings. For no reason they could understand. Just me, fucking my life up. Like Dad."

"Did Paul know?"

Brennan shook her head. "What was the point of telling him? I couldn't explain it. Better to say that I didn't love him, I wasn't ready. That I made a mistake in marrying him. That was true, too."

Hunter didn't say anything for a moment. He touched her shoulder. "I understand. I don't think you're—"

"I'm sleeping with a married partner."

"Jesus Christ, Bren!"

She started laughing. Hunter laughed along with her until her laughter abandoned her, leaving her bowed over her hands, hair forward over her face, shoulders quaking with silent sobbing. He stood between their stools and wrapped his arms around her shoulders. Her head settled into his chest, and as she gasped for air, Brennan caught the ghost of her father in the warm air trapped between them before it disappeared behind the scent of her rain-wet hair.

Hunter let her go as she took a breath, carefully wiping underneath her eyes even though she wasn't wearing any makeup.

"I gotta get back to work," she said.

"You okay?"

"Yeah. No. But what am I going to do? I have work to do."

"I mean about the escalation in the threat," Hunter said. "I know you said you were fine. But if that, if everything else, is too much, you can . . . I don't know. Put the Dad stuff to the side for now. Let you focus more on work. On Mom."

Brennan straightened in her chair. "What about you? If you have to go back to work? Leave the country again? Will we have enough time to see it through when we pick it up again?"

She felt like a failure even considering his offer. She knew that she would never have peace unless she did everything she could to get an answer. If she was right, there was a killer out there. If she wasn't, she deserved the truth.

Hunter nodded at the resolution on her face.

"But we need to be careful," Brennan said.

"I've been thinking about that. Maybe if I come at this from a different angle, it won't get attention. I found the restaurant he worked at. Mom told me." He told her about meeting Claude. "He gave me the name of someone who knew Dad. I've been trying to find her. But it's a common name."

"Why though?" Brennan asked. "Seems like a waste of time."

He threw a noncommittal shrug. "I don't know. A hunch? I got lots of time and not enough friends? Maybe there's something there."

Brennan waited for him to elaborate, and when he didn't, she told the bartender to close her tab.

THIRTY-TWO

Then

JANE LAY SLEEPING BEHIND HIM. HER WEIGHT ON THE MATtress and the nearly imperceptible movement of her breathing radiated across the universe of the empty bed between them—radio waves from some distant galaxy. It registered on his bare back, a whisper of life as he spun through the cosmos, one arm flung over the comforter and the other curled underneath his pillow. He had no trouble falling asleep throughout the day, sometimes at his desk, other times on the couch. But each night dragged, an abyss of time that did not pass until he opened his eyes to daylight as if he had not slept at all.

The day he went with the police, when he told Jane about the affair, he spent the night on the couch. He told himself it would be a week, maybe less. But each night afterward, he brought out a pillow with a spare blanket and lay in the dark, listening to the sound of the refrigerator compressor, the ticking of the clock, the occasional muffled whirring of the elevator through the walls, hoping that the next sound would be the last one so that he could sleep instead of being trapped in a semiconscious limbo trying to avoid thinking about Jessica or Jane or the children but powerless to keep them at bay. In the morning, the children found him, laying there bleary-eyed and harried, as if he had fallen asleep in front of the TV watching a horror movie. Jane never mentioned it—she wasn't speaking to him unless it was absolutely necessary.

After a while, he tried other rooms—his office, the floor in the kids' room—but sleep didn't find him there either, and the couch was the most comfortable place to lay awake, eyes open or closed, wondering if the next whiskey would be the one that knocked him out.

Eventually, months after his acquittal, after Jane and the kids returned from Thanksgiving with Jane's family, Jane came out of the kids' room. John was drinking bourbon on the rocks from a tall glass like it was iced tea. His skin burned with the liquor, and he had to piss, but he wasn't sleepy at all.

"You have to sleep," she said. "You look like shit."

"So?"

"If you're waiting for me to invite you back to the bed, I'm not going to."

"Then what? Are you telling me to get a hotel room?"

"No. I'm saying you take your side of the bed when you're ready. But don't expect an invitation."

A remark like that in the past would have started an hours-long fight, but he didn't feel anything.

Jane turned at the door to their bedroom.

"Just don't touch me."

The next night, he went back to their bed. He thought that returning would remedy the insomnia. Maybe after the first night and the tension of trying not to wake her as he lay beside her or after the second or third nights when she woke and turned her back to him or the fifth night when Jane fell asleep in Brennan's bed reading with the children and he still couldn't sleep. The trial, the acquittal, and months later, slumber faded in and out like an unreliable radio signal.

He would have talked to Jane about it if they still spoke. Sometimes, lying there waiting for unconsciousness, he'd imagine the conversation—

placing it in a specific time, right after their wedding, before Brennan was born, when neither of them knew anything about insomnia, when Jane still listened to him.

"I'm having trouble sleeping," he would say, laying in their old bed, the one Jane brought from her apartment when they moved in together.

"Why?" she'd ask.

"I don't know." He was lying in his imagination. But the lie was safe there, and she didn't pry, so he didn't have to face it.

"Well, is there anything I can do?"

Tonight, he tested some of the truth. "I think I'm having trouble sleeping because I can't see a way out of this mess."

Jane would have reached out to touch his shoulder. In his mind, Jane said what she sometimes said to her future children: "Close your eyes. Tomorrow will be a different day, with fresh ideas, and new opportunities."

But his eyes were closed, and he had lived through hundreds of tomorrows, and he only had old disappointments to show for it. The days weren't any different from each other in any way that mattered. Some days were hotter, others cooler, wet, dry, long, short, windy or not, they were an endless parade of the same regrets and guilt buried in unmitigated boredom.

Some nights, he imagined talking to Jessica. He remembered them walking for coffee on occasion, blue paper cups in hand. They barely spoke about anything when they got coffee—maybe a tricky legal issue, most often office gossip. But it was the most significant time they spent together without sex and fear. He placed them along a deserted street—maybe Pine Street—on a damp March afternoon. It was perpetually gloomy on Pine Street, one of those streets that was so narrow and where the buildings were so tall, more than half of it was cast in shadow even at midday.

"I'm having trouble sleeping," he'd say, filling a quiet moment. The heat of his coffee burned his palm even as the blustery wind chapped the back of his hand.

"For how long?"

"Since you . . ." *Died.* Even in his imagination, he couldn't say it.

Jess would raise an eyebrow, appraising him like a reticent witness.

"Since I, what?"

He'd take a sip of coffee to buy time—it scalded his mouth in his imagination—and search the street for sunlight to stand in, but there was nothing except a pall of mist. He usually gave up here—recycling back to the beginning of the conversation or simply remembering walking with her—but when he was desperate he pressed on.

"Since you." Definitive, but ambiguous.

"Is it guilt? Over what we're doing?"

Guilt was too obvious, too easy to admit, and too hard to reconcile. There was nothing to be done about guilt except make amends—but Jess was dead and Jane was unforgiving.

"You can tell me. I feel guilty, too. If I let myself think about it."

John wondered if this was something she had ever said to him while she was alive—if he was imagining a memory he had forgotten. He couldn't remember, and he waited for the version of Jess that was alive in his imagination to explain. But she sipped her coffee patiently and waited for him to talk.

"We both know this is all we can have," he said.

He knew how she would react. He had said this to her once while she was alive. Even with Jessica gone, he couldn't break the loop.

He stopped imagining Jess and Pine Street and instead rolled onto his back, praying that the change in position would help. It didn't, and he lay there, tracking time by counting Jane's breaths, losing track after several hundred, starting over, repeatedly, until Jane rose to use the bathroom in the night and he wasn't conscious of her returning.

THIRTY-THREE

Then

HARRIS WAS MOSTLY FINISHED WITH HIS BURGER. JOHN HAD managed only three or four bites of his own before starting in on his fries, eating them one by one, savoring the saltiness of the first four before setting the fifth one down half-eaten. John picked up his empty whiskey glass and, turning to catch the eye of the waitress, held it up to her to signal for another—his third. Harris was working through a heavily iced Pepsi. They were among the last of the lunch diners at some Irish pub off Broadway south of City Hall. Christmas music played faintly in the background.

"You going for a record?" Harris asked.

"What else am I doing today?" John picked up a fry and forced himself to eat it.

It was the first time that they had seen each other since the trial ended. John picked the restaurant—it was a place the two of them had occasionally met for lunch before everything went to hell, conveniently located between their two offices. They'd already gotten through the ritual pleasantries.

How's Jane? Fine. Still pissed. *How are the kids?* They're getting big.

How are you holding up? A shrug. *What are you doing?* Trying to figure out what's next.

Then it was John's turn.

How's business? Doing great. Winning your case put me on the map. *You seeing anybody?* There's a couple of guys, but nobody serious. *How are things with your mom?* Still strained, but she's getting used to the fact that I'm not going to marry a nice Jewish girl.

After the waitress dropped John's third drink at the table (was he drunk or did she wink at him when she did so?), Harris pushed his empty plate away and wiped his mouth.

"I'm sorry I haven't come to see you and Jane in a while."

"It's not like we're hosting any dinners."

"No. I guess not. Cigarette?"

John took one.

"You drinking a lot?" Harris asked after he lit his.

"Sometimes."

"You need to get your shit together."

John lit his cigarette and chased the smoke from his mouth with a sip from his drink. "The firm won't take me back, Harris."

Harris nodded and took a drag off his cigarette to think. "Take whatever they're offering and move on with your life."

"Whose side are you on?"

Harris shook his head. "Don't be an asshole."

"It would be easier," John said, "to take their bullshit deal if I had something lined up for after. Right now, they're waiting me out. I can't do any legal work before resigning or I'll violate the partnership agreement, and I'm not getting any distributions. They'll just starve me until I take the deal."

"So why wait?"

"I'm trying to give myself time to think of something, some way to salvage the situation or to get them to raise the offer, or how to move past doing this—I mean, I worked my whole life to get to this point, to do the things I was doing. I'm not even forty years old. I had twenty-five more years in this career. And now, what?"

"Twenty-five years is a long time to find something else and get back on top. You can take the money and hang out your own shingle. Be a generalist. I know it's scary, but clients will come. You're a good lawyer, John. People will forget about . . . about all this."

John gulped the rest of his drink. He turned to look for the waitress with his empty glass raised, but Harris reached over the table and placed his hand over John's and brought it down to the table. John turned back, ignoring the slight vertigo the alcohol caused, and looked down at Harris's hand.

"Are you trying to take advantage of me, Harris? You know I'm not into men."

"You've had enough, John. And fuck you." Harris pulled his hand away.

"Relax. I'm kidding."

"I'm not. You're in a shit place right now, and yeah, life isn't going to be great for a bit. But it won't get any better if you keep drinking and keep avoiding the fact that you need to move on."

"Would you hire me?"

"You don't do criminal law."

"You said yourself, I'm a good lawyer. I'll get competent. Your practice is picking up—thanks to my case. Would you take me on?" John didn't know if he was trying to prove a point or begging for a job.

"I'm not looking for any partners right now."

"As an associate?"

"I can't support another lawyer yet. Not full-time."

John ran his hand over his face and shook his head. They sat in silence as Harris called for the check and paid it. Harris stood, pulling his jacket off the back of his chair.

"Come on, John. Walk me back to the office."

John followed Harris out to the street. "I hope you don't mind if

I don't walk back with you. It's not like I have great memories of your office."

"Yeah. Sure."

"Thanks for lunch." John reached out to shake Harris's hand. Harris stepped forward and embraced John instead.

"I'll let you know if I hear about anyone looking for somebody like you," Harris said.

"Nobody's looking for something like me."

#

Harris held up one hand, nearly displacing the ash from the cigarette, and laughed. "I don't think any nice Jewish girl is looking for someone like me!"

It was the punch line to a story about how a friend of his mother's tried to set up her daughter with "a nice Jewish boy" like Harris. He had been home, along with his boyfriend at the time, to visit his mother. His mother had introduced Chad as "a friend from law school," and Miriam hadn't picked up on the various signals—or maybe she had and ignored them. Even as John laughed, he noted that Jane tracked the end of the cigarette and knew that she'd be up to clean any ash that strayed from it or the ashtray in front of them, despite the three drinks she'd consumed.

It was a good night—the two of them and Harris and Chad sitting around the small dining table in their new apartment down in the Village. It was their first dinner hosting since the wedding. John cooked steamed fish with ginger and scallions, broccoli and garlic, steamed eggs, and rice, of course. Served and eaten from their new wedding china—absurdly formal in context, given the paper napkins on the table, the cardboard boxes they'd yet to unpack scattered throughout the room, and their paint-spattered T-shirts and jeans. Jane poured the Heineken accompanying dinner into the crystal wineglasses they also acquired in the wedding. After dinner, they had moved to scotch.

"Thank you both so much for helping us today," Jane said.

Chad swirled the ice in his glass. "I'm just glad you marked the liquor box so we could find it."

"Only the box with the shitty stuff," John said. "I hid the good stuff from Harris. It's wasted on him."

"So a two bedroom," Harris said. "Anything we should know?"

"We just got hitched," Jane said. "I'm three drinks in. Probably five before you go. So yes, I'm pregnant."

Laughter echoed off the bare surfaces of the apartment—they hadn't laid the carpets yet so they could paint. John's gaze fixed on Jane, the light in her eyes as she laughed, the force of her presence reverberating through him, a resonance in his chest that felt dangerously close to a pulmonary embolism. When he tried to take a sip of his scotch, he slipped and some of it dripped down his chin and onto his shirt.

"God, John, you're such a slob," Harris said. "Jane, you could have done so much better."

They all laughed, even John, even though he knew that Jane's parents and some of her friends told her the same thing at one point or the other, and not in jest. Jane told him about these incidents, upset on his behalf, but John sometimes suspected that Jane worried that she was missing something obvious, that she should have listened to their voices instead of whatever it was that kept her with him.

"You guys are going to need to leave soon," John said, "while I'm still able to try to help Jane fill that second bedroom."

Jane rolled her eyes and punched him in the shoulder. "You're a fucking comedian."

Harris's eyes widened. "She is drunk! I don't know that I've ever heard such language coming from the mouth of a lady!"

"'Cause you've never had a lady, Harris," Chad deadpanned.

Later, after more drinks and many hugs, John closed the door of their home behind Harris and Chad. When he turned back, Jane stood near the table, cluttered with glasses and empty packs of cigarettes and a full ashtray. She glowed in the amber light cast by a lamp in the far corner.

"Glad we had the windows open and that fan on," she said, pushing the ashtray away to the center of the table. A plastic window fan set in the window near the lamp created a balmy cross breeze from the remnants of a warm, muggy day.

"Me, too." He looked at the table. "We going to clean that?"

She pulled her T-shirt over her head. "Later."

She walked to the bedroom, unbuttoning her jeans as she went. John followed. The bedroom was dark, lit only by ambient light from the street and the living room lamp. The bed was pushed into the middle of the room so the freshly painted walls could dry. She slid her jeans and underwear down and stepped out of them. He took her in his arms and kissed her. His hands glided over her thin layer of perspiration, cool in the draft from the window. He brought his mouth from hers, descending to her neck, around to her collarbone, down to one breast—lingering for a moment—down the side of her belly where he knew she was sensitive, until he found her hip bone with his lips. At this point, he was on his knees, hands atop the swell of her hips. He drew a line with the tip of his tongue along the crease of her hip until he felt the first brush of short hair against his cheek. He used one hand to lift her leg to drape his shoulder, conveniently opening space for his mouth to find the piece of Jane that he was looking for. He kissed it like a breeze, and Jane gasped and reached back for the bed to hold herself up as her legs grew weak. He guided her so she could rest her hips on the edge of the bed, and listened to her, each cue and direction, all of them conveyed through a twitch in her legs or roll of her hips or sudden exhale, until her desire arched her back like a drawn bow, until she came with a deep moan and curled forward around herself and his head. She held his face and kissed him, little dabs on his forehead, even as she fought to catch her breath between them.

"I don't think . . . I've ever . . . that drunk before . . ." She said, then looked down and laughed. "How did you get your pants off while you were doing that?"

"I have many skills."

She reached down and pulled his shirt off, and as he stood, she moved up on the bed. He followed again, catching her, and she reached down to guide him inside her. She wrapped herself around him. He was solid, but dizzy with alcohol. He searched for a thought to escalate the pleasure, elevate him to a ledge he could throw himself from. It was like rummaging through a drawer in the dark, hand passing over images, memories, abstractions, trying to locate the exact right one by feel. He heard the echo from earlier: "You could do better." Something her friend, Betsy, had said to her one night after they got engaged. Jane asked what she meant, and Betsy said, "Someone whose parents didn't work at a takeout restaurant. Like, you really going to eat chow mein the rest of your life?" Or the guy Jane dated before John, who had called Jane and said, "You need a real man, not whatever egg roll he's got." Or her father, who had walked Jane down the aisle, who said to John when he asked for his blessing (although he and Jane had already agreed to get engaged), "I don't think you're right for her, son. It would be better, for both of you, if you stayed with your own people." But it was John over Jane in the dark now, and she was his to care for. His consciousness coalesced around their triumph and their power, and he was suddenly sober and she knew and pulled his head down to hers and kissed him. It was like a charge to a detonator. She clung to him until he lowered himself onto her. He could feel their skin sliding against each other as their breathing slowed.

"That was fun," she said.

John grunted his agreement.

"Our home," she said.

"Our home."

"Should we try soon?"

"Try what?"

"For a kid."

Blood rushed at the thought, and he moved inside her again. She laughed. "I don't mean tonight."

"Whenever you're ready. But I thought you were going to try to make partner first? I don't know that you'll be able to do that carrying a baby around."

Jane sighed. "You're probably right. But God, this felt good, didn't it? We should keep trying, even if we're rigging the game for now."

John chuckled, already leaden with sleep.

"No, no, you don't," Jane said, pushing against his chest. "Don't pass out on top of me."

John pushed with one hand and flopped onto his back. Jane sat up and walked to the bathroom. John heard her turning the lights out in the other room. When she returned, she stood in the doorway with a cigarette in one hand, ashtray in another.

"I love seeing you like that," she said.

"Like what?"

"Taken care of."

"I love seeing you like that," he said, turning onto his elbow so he could look at her.

"Naked?"

"Exactly."

She held the cigarette out to him, but he didn't take it. She crushed it into the ashtray, set it down on a stack of boxes, and crawled into the bed next to him. He turned his head toward her. She was on her side facing him, eyes closed. One of her hands lay upon his chest. His final thought before the alcohol and fatigue caught up with him was, *Please don't let me lose this moment.*

#

John lost the moment, and when he turned back to look for Harris to ask him if he remembered that night, if they had ever been that happy, Harris was gone, disappeared into the crowd on Broadway. He considered chasing after him, begging him to help him remember better, but stopped after half a block, moving out of the flow of foot traffic until he stood on a metal grate of a subway vent. Dank warm air wafted from below, carrying the odor particular to the New York subways—grime mixed with ozone. Why remind Harris of Chad, who had broken his heart three months after that night? Why remember that time better for himself? So that Jane would feel even more hollow whenever she got home? If that moment mattered, wouldn't John have remembered it—or the hundreds like it from those years?

John imagined that those moments would keep them afloat in tough times, but instead they were nails driven through the two of them, crippling and mangling them and any chance they could have saved themselves by swimming separately. It wasn't the first time John considered that Jane and the children would be better off without him. He wrestled with the thought when he was arrested, during the ride to be booked. *I shouldn't go home.*

But he had. *Because you're a coward.* Because where else would he have gone?

I shouldn't go home now.

And what? Sleep on the street? Nobody's doors were open to him. It was getting cold, too, this late in the year. Maybe he could use a token, ride the subway all night. *Until you run out of tokens.* He imagined himself, sore and disheveled, having to piss (Could he bring himself to piss off the platform? What about when he needed to shit?), somewhere maybe on the 6 train—John would avoid the lines that ran through the Upper West Side (What if the children saw him?)—and making eye contact with Geoff as he stepped onto the subway car (Geoff probably hadn't been on the subway in a decade, but John saw Geoff, clad in a tweed suit, custom shoes, and arrogance). Even standing on the street contemplating it, John lived the moment—the shame and disgrace worse than the cops shoving his head down to place him in the cruiser. At least then, John believed acquittal (not an exoneration) was possible and would be enough, but now that imaginary plastic seat would be the end for him. He'd rather be under that train than on it.

A rumble shook the metal grate John stood upon, shaking him from his reverie—a train, maybe that train, passing just beneath.

THIRTY-FOUR

Now

HUNTER SPRINTED UP THE SUBWAY STEPS TWO AT A TIME. Brennan, tapping away on her cell phone, breath fogging in the air, came into view as he crested the last set. Despite the chill, she wore only a light trench.

"Sorry," Hunter panted. "Train got stuck between 42nd and 34th."

"Typical."

"I said I'm—"

"I was talking about the subway."

Brennan strode off down Wall Street. Hunter followed but fell behind after weaving through a group of guys in suits. When he caught back up, he asked, "How do you move so fast in heels?"

"Practice."

They turned north off Wall Street and then left on Pine, which left them in front of a steakhouse. They beat most of the after-work crowd and grabbed a high-top table in the bar area.

"I didn't know you were going to call him again," Brennan said after Hunter came back to the table with their drinks. "I thought we were laying low for now."

"He called me."

"After you called him again."

Hunter shrugged. They'd stopped discussing their investigation since the rainy night in the bar a few weeks prior. Except for the hours they overlapped visiting their mother, Brennan essentially disappeared into work. Hunter broke his usual routine—wake, read, search for Nicki, visit his mother, meet Jenna—the week before to call Mark again. Mark heard Hunter out before hanging up on him, only to call him back yesterday to say that he'd meet them at the steakhouse.

Mark stepped through the entrance and glanced around the room. The pictures of him on the internet—headshots for banking conferences, a couple of him at fundraisers—were outdated. His hair was grayer, and his neck was starting to outgrow the collar of his shirt. Hunter waved, and Mark crossed the room. When he reached the table, the siblings stood and introduced themselves. Mark didn't take Brennan's hand when she offered it, so Hunter didn't extend his.

"Can I get you a drink?" Hunter offered.

"No." But he sat down in the stool across from the siblings.

"Thank you for coming."

"To be honest, I almost didn't show."

"Me either," Brennan said. "I didn't anticipate that this would be an easy meeting. But it's important."

"Fine. What do you want to know?"

Hunter took the lead. "Why don't you tell us what Jessica was like, when you met her?"

Mark looked down at the table as if the memory he wanted to locate was somewhere in the grain of the dark wood. "We met in a bar. We were both out with some friends. Jess was gorgeous. Perfect in that superficial way people are in their early twenties, you know what I mean? I ended up buying a round of drinks for her and her friends, and we started chatting. That's when I knew I was in trouble. You ever see someone like that? From across the room they're, I don't know, luminescent or something, and then you get close, and they got a million extra watts?"

Hunter nodded. He hadn't expected a Jersey investment banker/poet.

"She was like that. We started going out and, I don't know, things just moved really fast. You ever been skiing? Like you're on a slope and it doesn't seem like much, but then you get a dip, and next thing you know, you're going so fast you're gonna break your neck if you try to brake at all? It was like that. Except the slope was . . . I don't know . . . expectations. Then we got to the bottom, things leveled off, and she was different. Me, too, I guess."

"Different how?" Brennan asked.

Mark shook his head. "She realized she had nothing but flat ground in front of her. But she wanted that speed again. Her whole life, it was Connecticut, suburbs, good schools—it's like a factory. Except the product is girls who dabble in a career until they get married to a guy who could have been their dad and they stay home with the kids and drive a nice car to soccer practice before picking hubby up at the train station and they cry when the kids go to college and who the fuck knows at that point? Look, at my age, it seems like a nice life. But Jess, she saw that road and kept trying to get off it."

Hunter, who'd been off those roads since college, understood the metaphor.

"What I'm trying to say is that she was amazing. But for a long time, when we were married, I felt like I ruined it. Like I threw damp wood on her fire, and the smoke from that was choking us both."

"How did you, like you said, dampen, throw wet wood, whatever?" Hunter asked.

"I was a kid. I mean, I was a man, but I didn't know any better. I took her for granted. That she wanted to be a banker's wife, have my babies. That she'd be a subsidiary to me. All the things that made her the woman I fell in love with, I didn't take them seriously. I didn't want to deal with all the shit that frustrated us, so I started . . . you know, focusing elsewhere. Work, mainly."

Nothing about the conversation was going how Hunter expected, so he said nothing. Next to him, Brennan examined Mark's face like she was planning a surgery.

"You wanted kids?" Brennan asked.

"I did. She didn't. I thought it was a phase, like she'd grow out of it as we got older. But she didn't. Maybe she knew better than me that we wouldn't have worked out. Maybe she thought we were too broken to do it right. Maybe she just didn't want to be a mom. She just told me the timing was bad." Mark cleared his throat. "I think I will have a drink. Whatever you're having."

"I'll get it," Brennan said. "I need another, anyway."

Hunter glanced down and was surprised to see he'd finished his old-fashioned. Hunter stalled while Brennan was gone, asking Mark about where he was raised (Summit, New Jersey), college (Brown), and his career (mergers-and-acquisitions desks at various investment banks). When Brennan returned with the cocktails, Hunter turned the conversation back to Jessica.

"You were saying things got, uh, difficult with Jess. How did she handle it?"

Mark shrugged as he sipped his drink. He lowered the glass and his eyes to the table.

"Well, we all know she had an affair. That's why we're here, right? I was fucking pissed when I found out. At her. At Cathy. Your dad. Myself."

"When did you find out?" Brennan asked.

"For sure? After she died. I guess the night she died when Cathy explained why Jess was at her apartment. I suspected before, though. Like I said, I was distracted with my own shit. Never asked her."

"Sounds like the marriage was rocky," Brennan said. "You two ever fight? Hit each other?"

Mark's head snapped up. "Cathy tell you that?"

Neither sibling spoke. Mark sighed.

"Yeah, Jess and I fought. She had a temper and . . . I want to say I was a kid, that we both were and didn't know any better, but it's not an excuse. We would lose control. The two of us. But it wasn't like it is today. I never beat . . . No." He shook his head and exhaled before continuing. "I hit her sometimes. That's on me. Yes, thirty years ago, I was the kind of guy who'd smack his wife. I'm ashamed of that. I never laid hands on anyone since Jess. I worked hard to be better than what I was."

Mark blinked away some tears.

"You know," he said, "I felt guilty for so long. Like I drove her to that place. To your father. Then to that apartment. I spent a long time wrestling with that, asking myself what I could have done differently. The answer was everything and nothing, of course. I could've made a lot of different choices, but I didn't, and what's done is done, right?"

Hunter glanced over at Brennan. Mark didn't sound like a killer. He looked like a guy who needed a hug right now. But Brennan's thoughts lay behind a scaffold of clinical neutrality.

"How did you hear about her murder?" Hunter asked.

Mark's eyes fell to his glass. "I was home. Cathy called and said that I needed to come up to her place. I didn't know why Jess was there."

"So Cathy told you or the cops told you? About the affair?" Brennan asked.

"The cops didn't tell me. I think they tried to get me to admit that I knew about it, but I didn't. Like I said, I suspected, but I wasn't sure. Cathy told me, after the cops were done interviewing us that night. She needed someplace to stay, so I took her to the Plaza."

"Why the Plaza?" Brennan's voice was smooth and soft—like a newly made bed. Hunter saw the trap coming, but Mark had no idea.

"It was a nice place, and obviously she'd just been through a lot. We had an extra room at our place, and honestly, I didn't want to be alone, but the last thing either of us needed was for the two of us to go to my place the night my wife was killed. The optics would have been awful."

"You paid?"

"Yeah. Of course. She didn't have that kind of money."

"So she told you at the hotel? About the affair?"

Mark took a sip of his drink. "We argued about it, yes. I asked her why Jess had been at her place. The cops told me that they didn't know why she was there, but there had to be a reason for her to be there without Cathy. I didn't understand how Cathy didn't tell me before. We were close. I mean, I get it—she was best friends with Jess. But I thought it was the kind of thing she should have told me. We were friends, too, and spent time together, even without Jess."

Mark shook his head as if that could keep the pain of their betrayals away. Brennan leaned forward to rest her elbows on the table, and when the movement caught Mark's attention, she said, "Cathy told us that her boyfriend paid for her hotel."

Mark's face flushed dark red, like wine soaking into a tablecloth. Hunter expected him to head for the door, but Mark exhaled, shoulders falling as he sank against the back of the barstool.

"Yeah. Cathy and I were having an affair. Like I said, there is a lot I wish I could change."

He gulped the rest of his drink, the large square of ice clinking back to the bottom of the glass when he lowered it.

"You know what that starts to look like, right?" Brennan asked.

"Motive. I get it."

"For you and Cathy."

"Why? Jess and I were both cheating. Which Cathy knew. If I knew . . . Shit, if Jess knew, maybe we would have just ended things like we should have. I don't know. That's part of the reason I blamed Cathy. But she didn't want to hurt Jess. Or me. Besides, I know it wasn't Cathy."

"How?" Hunter asked.

"Because we were together that night. Cathy found Jess twenty minutes after leaving me."

"Why lie to the cops? At trial?"

Mark shrugged. "That night, we were worried. We knew it looked bad. So when she called me about Jess, we agreed not to tell the cops about the affair or the fighting. They figured it out, though—the affair, at least. When we were preparing for trial."

Brennan finally reacted, a look Hunter recognized well—an angry brow crease and tightening of her mouth. "What do you mean?"

"I mean something one of us said before the trial tipped them off, same way you got it now. My timeline sucked. I had like two or three hours to cover for when I was with Cathy. So I told them."

"Who?"

"The prosecutor and the short cop. What was his name? Bowman? Bauman?"

"What did they say?"

"They said . . . it was . . . they were pissed. But I told them they could confirm that we were together at the time she was killed. We booked a room at the Lexington Hotel that night. I paid in cash, but I used my own name. They confirmed it in the register. Then they told me and Cathy to stick to our original stories because it didn't matter. They said we didn't do it, and they didn't want to embarrass us or ruin our lives any further. They knew your father did it, and they didn't want to confuse the jury."

"They said all that?" Brennan said.

Mark nodded. He looked her in the eye. "It's the main reason I'm here. No offense, but I don't know either of you. I don't want to open a tub of shit and have it blow back at me." He took a breath and reached some quiet resolution. "Bauman and McCarthy told me that they knew your dad did it. I knew I didn't do it. I knew that Cathy didn't do it. I didn't think it was a big deal at the time. I thought that if we testified that we were having an affair, people might think we did it, even if we had an alibi. They'd think we hired someone or something. The way those two made it seem, they had airtight evidence your dad did it."

Brennan was furious. Hunter got ready to restrain her in case she attacked Mark.

Mark continued, "It didn't bother me at first. I was pissed. And what good would it do for me to admit the truth then? Maybe your dad did it. If he didn't, it wouldn't help catch the guy who did. So I didn't say anything. Who was I going to tell anyway? Over the years, though, the more I thought about what they did—what we did—it didn't sit right. But by then, it was too late. Everything was already fucked up, and what would be the point of telling anyone?"

Brennan turned her head from Mark, as if he were something too disgusting to look at. Hunter understood his rationalizations. It probably hadn't made a difference in the end, given the acquittal.

Hunter broke the silence by asking, "Did Cathy have other boyfriends? Someone who could have been at the apartment?"

"She says that she didn't. The cops leaned on her, too. I believed her. Who could she be covering for? We had been running around for about a year before Jess was murdered. We ended up together for a few years after until I couldn't face myself anymore. She never understood it. I did a lot of work after that. To make myself a better person. I didn't know what else to do."

Brennan shook her head without looking at Mark. Tears pooled in her eyes. If she'd looked at Mark, she'd have seen he was almost crying, too.

Mark said, "Look, I called you, I wanted to meet you, because I thought that . . . When you called me, Hunter, you said you wanted to apologize. And hell, even if your dad did it, you kids did nothing to me. You don't owe me an apology. What I'm saying is that when you called me, it made me think about all this shit again, and what if your dad didn't do it? I tried to put all of this behind me, but you kids hadn't. Couldn't. Because I lied and made your dad carry all of that shit alone. And you guys had to carry that, too. I figured I owed it to you to meet you and answer your questions. But also so I could tell you that I'm sorry for my part in that."

THIRTY-FIVE

Now

"I'M SORRY," HUNTER SAID TO JENNA WHEN HIS PHONE RANG on her nightstand. It was close to midnight. He swiped and said, "Hey."

"Sorry it's so late. Hope I'm not interrupting anything," Brennan said. "I'm just getting crushed at work. This is the first chance I've had to take a breath and call you back."

"I get it. It's fine. You headed home?"

"Still in the office."

"Bummer. Be careful going home, okay?"

"Of course. So you called me?"

Jenna rolled off the bed, and his T-shirt rode up her thigh until the curve of her ass peeked out from underneath.

"Hunter?" Brennan asked.

"Yeah, sorry. Lost track of my thoughts for a second." Jenna looked over her shoulder and winked at him as she walked to the bathroom. Hunter winked back and said to Brennan, "McCann called me back."

"What did he say?"

"He said that he didn't know about Mark's story. He wouldn't have done that. But it sounded like something Bauman might do. And McCarthy. McCann does not like that guy."

"So the only two guys who can confirm that the hotel had Mark in the register are dead or won't talk to us?"

"I went back through my scans of the police files. There's a note in there. It said, 'Lexington Hotel confirmed left at 11:00 p.m.' I didn't know what it meant when I first went through."

"Bottom of a page, right? I remember seeing that, too." Brennan sighed. Hunter raised his eyebrows. Her memory was uncanny. "So it wasn't Mark or Cathy."

"Which means," Hunter said, "it was Dad or whoever left the handprint."

"And we know Cathy was seeing Mark, so whoever left the print wasn't some boyfriend. Assuming we believe her."

"I think we can. She ended up with Mark. At least for a while."

"You think Cathy would know how to hire a hitman?" Brennan asked.

"No."

A sigh. "Anything on that waitress you were trying to track down?"

"No," Hunter said. "But I'll keep trying. Maybe it will get us something."

Silence. He imagined Brennan in her office, pacing.

"Bren?"

"Fuck." She exhaled deeply, then continued, "We've excluded two more suspects but not Dad. Which means it increases the likelihood it was him."

Hunter didn't say anything. He had been waiting his whole life for this moment, that he was the one who had been right, to validate the choices he'd made to change his name, to leave New York, to do something different than his father.

"I still don't think it was him," Brennan said.

"Okay." His relief surprised him.

"I gotta get back to work. I don't see much else we can do."

"Let's talk tomorrow."

"Yeah. Whatever. Good—" The line went dead as she hung up before she finished speaking.

Hunter set his phone on the nightstand. Jenna crawled back into the bed.

"Everything okay?"

Hunter shook his head. Jenna slung one leg over his, so she was straddling his lap.

"Anything I can do?"

"I don't think so. Thanks, though. I appreciate it."

Hunter stroked her bare thigh. It had been a long time since he'd had a regular girlfriend. They still avoided using any labels with each other, but that was what she was. They hadn't said they were exclusive, but he'd passed up opportunities since he'd met her. He thought about saying something. He inhaled. He would sound silly, telling her how he felt, and he was sure she'd make fun of him, but he trusted her to be kind.

"Hey, so I have news," she said, dropping her hand over his. "I got into a graduate program. Iowa."

"Hey! That's great!" He hated the relief he felt. "I didn't know you applied."

"I didn't want to say anything. In case I didn't get in."

He sat up so he could embrace her and consciously ignored how well she fit in his arms. He let her go and sank back against the headboard.

"I need to let them know soon. If I'm going to go."

"Of course you're going. It's like, what, the best writer's program in the country?"

Jenna shrugged. "It's two years. I really like New York pizza."

"Jenna."

"Yeah, I know. Still," she said as she fiddled with the hem of the T-shirt, "there are other variables."

Don't make her spell it out, he thought. He took her hands. "You should go."

She looked back up at him, her eyes dark in the shadows cast by her lamp.

"This is an incredible opportunity," he said. She blinked and tilted her head back to avoid giving her tears the mass they would need to spill. "You're smart. Hilarious. Beautiful. I've never met anyone who makes me feel the way you do. But you need to do this."

"You're not making this easy."

Hunter smiled. "Fine. Chances are I'll leave on assignment before the summer is over. I'll be overseas most of the time and preoccupied by work. Ask anyone who's ever dated me. When I come back, I'll be even worse because I don't want to be here dealing with my family's bullshit and the guilt that you may have turned down a life-changing program on the hope that I'm someone who can actually function in a relationship. You should avoid that at all costs."

The corner of her mouth curled into a wry smile. "Boy, you misread that."

"Further evidence that I'm unsuitable."

"Tell me that you might stay. That we can decide in August, or whenever I have to move, whether we can make New York to Iowa work for two years. Tell me you're open to that."

"If I tell you that, you'll send in the acceptance papers?"

Jenna nodded. "But you have to mean it." Her eyes didn't leave his face.

Hunter looked away at a wrinkle in the sheets. "I want to say yes. But I'm . . . We'll break each other's hearts. Better now than months of each of us assessing, judging, worrying about where things will end up."

"Even if none of this ever happened, we'd be doing that."

Hunter didn't respond.

"You're scared," she said. "That you'll get hurt."

"I'm already hurt."

"Then you're a coward."

"Better you know that now."

\#

Hunter couldn't sleep after he left Jenna's place. She was right. He was a coward. But knowing that didn't mean he could do anything about it.

He hated how empty his apartment was. Since finding the bullet at his place, he'd insisted that Jenna not come over. And although she didn't leave so much as a toothbrush there, next to how little he had, when she was around, the whole place felt like it had been waiting for her, her clothes on the floor, the sound of her moving around, the scent of her.

He sat up in the bed. Three a.m. Too late to try to find a bar, especially on a weeknight. He checked the latch on his door again. Then he popped his laptop open.

Over the past few weeks, he'd gone through all the databases he had access to through work, calling old phone lines for any Nicki Berger who was older than forty years old, which was too young, but then again, maybe she was a runaway all those years ago who lied about her age to get a job. There were all manner of reasons he couldn't find her. If she'd married or changed her name for some reason. A phone line or records in someone else's name. If she'd died. Moved to France.

Well, nothing to help him sleep like a brute force search on the internet. For what felt like the hundredth time, he typed out search terms using "Frontier" and variations of "Nichole" or "Nicki" and "New York" and scrolled through hits on search engines and social media. He knew he was probably covering ground he'd already covered, but he didn't feel like checking his notes or adding to them. He wanted to waste the time.

When he looked up, it was 5:00 a.m. He'd tried to shut his eyes once an hour before, laptop open on the bed next to him, but the moment the conversation with Jenna began to replay in his mind, he sat up and went back to scrolling.

He almost scrolled past it.

It was a photo on Facebook, buried among the multitude of posts about birthdays, date nights, and anniversaries, pictures of food, candlelit tables, and smiling faces. It was a scan of an old Kodak print, or maybe a digital photo of one—Hunter's eyes were too bleary to tell. In the snapshot, three servers stood in front of the small bar holding wineglasses and beers with a pretty blond woman in jeans and a sweater and an older man in a suit. Hunter wasn't a fashion historian, but the cut and fit of everyone's clothes felt at least two decades old. The text accompanying the photo read: "Nicki Klein Berger returns to visit her old stomping grounds and friends at Frontier after her honeymoon. RIP Ed." The post was nearly a decade old, but clicking on Nicki's name brought Hunter to her profile page. Her most recent post was a photo of Central Park taken the week before.

THIRTY-SIX

Then

JANE SURPRISED JOHN BECAUSE SHE WAS AWAKE WHEN HE came into the bedroom, sitting up in the bed reading a novel by the light of the lamp on her nightstand. She usually didn't outlast the kids by more than an hour, and they had been asleep for at least three. She took off her glasses and set her book—*Dinner at the Homesick Restaurant*—down on her lap.

"I was waiting up for you." They were the first words she'd spoken to him in four days.

Jane rarely spoke to him at all. When she and the kids left in the morning, she might send one of them in to give him the time she expected to be home. Occasionally, she'd call it out over her shoulder. They never discussed why this happened, but John understood. On nights when Jane's expected time was later than seven, John ate dinner with the children. On nights she was home early enough to eat, John went for a "long walk"—actually short walks to the bar around the corner. Jane's effort and concentration in maintaining the silence was impressive. John thought that there would be cracks eventually, a slow melting, but each time he thought that something she said might be it ("John, can you pick up cereal and eggs today?"), there would be another gap of days or a week before she spoke to him again, usually while passing through the room ("The kids and I are going to dinner with the Rameshes."). One afternoon, after four more days of Jane living her life alongside him as if he were invisible, John stood in the kitchen contemplating which food to throw in the trash so she would notice and ask him to buy some. Would she notice if eight eggs were suddenly gone? A half gallon of milk? Four apples? He missed the trial, when she would sometimes speak to Harris about him when they would debrief after each trial day: "You did a good job reminding the jury today that John is a real person." Ironic, because John didn't feel all that real at the time and certainly not after months of being treated like a ghost.

"What for?" he asked. He picked up the pajama bottoms he typically slept in.

"We need to talk about what you're going to do for work."

"I'm working on it."

"We only have a couple more months before we're through our savings."

"How is that possible?" They lived—even after each of them made partner—well within their means and saved aggressively.

She answered in a voice as flat and brittle as a pane of glass. "The kids' tuition. The nanny. We paid a ton to Harris. Insurance. We had to get the car fixed last month. The mortgage, food, electricity. We're bleeding—it's slow, but it's not stopping."

"But the stocks and investments—"

"Are for the kids' college tuitions!" she snapped. Then, calmer, "Our retirements."

"We can use it though, until I can get a fair payment from my firm."

Jane shook her head. She swung her legs out from beneath the covers so she could sit on the edge of the bed. Her gaze intensified. She was courtroom ready, despite the nightgown. John stood near the closet door, pajamas in hand.

"Jane, they owe me—"

"They are not going to pay you, John, and if you don't take the money soon, they'll end up giving you nothing."

"You don't know that."

"Walter called me."

"Fuck Walter."

"John, he's trying to help you. Same as me."

"I need time to think of something. They need me to leave quietly."

"Yes, they want you to leave quietly, and your only leverage is that you may end up making a spectacle of it. Their leverage is that you're not making any money until this is resolved. They can wait you out—which is why they've been doing that. It costs them nothing to starve you. But they have no reason to give you more than their offer, because the only action you can take defeats the point of you taking it."

"Their offer is bullshit."

"Yes. But Walter told me the number you gave them. You're not thinking right. They'll never give you that much. They're not going to give you half of that."

"It's what they owe me."

"You slept with an associate."

John's hands closed into fists. "They do, too!"

"Yours was murdered."

Jane looked to the bedroom door as if she could tell whether the kids were awake two rooms away. John's indignation drained from him in a violent flush, leaving a thick film of regret. Jane looked back, surprised that he hadn't started shouting. That was where these things usually ended.

"What if I got a job? To help float us until I can think of something?"

Jane bit on her lower lip—a habit she had when she was trying to restrain herself. When she spoke, the shape of her exasperation was apparent: "It would be a conflict."

"I know that. I mean something else—not a legal job. If I waited tables or something? Some places, waiters can make good money. It's all cash. It buys us some more time while I think of something."

"John, you've had months. You haven't thought of anything that will work. Neither have I, for that matter. Or Harris. You want to get into restaurants, fine, but get your payment from your firm first."

John shook his head but said, "Let me think about it some more."

"Fine. But stop dragging it out."

She sat back up into bed and picked up her glasses. John didn't move.

"But what then?" he asked.

"What?"

"About us, Jane. What do we do about us?"

"One thing at a time, John."

"Do you want me to stay?"

"I want to read my book and then go to sleep." She flipped the book back open.

"What are we doing, Jane?"

"I'm trying to end this conversation."

"Are you trying to end our marriage?"

John expected the goading to force her to bring her eyes back to his with another snappy comeback to put the discussion to rest, but instead she turned her book over onto her lap and stared at its cover.

"I don't know. Maybe."

Her equivocation was worse than her telling him that she did want to end things. Jane was decisive in every aspect of her life and personality. Despite months of being frozen out, the fact that she never asked him to leave gave him a reason to salvage something from the shredded shambles he brought them to. Jane must have had a plan, seen some solution worth keeping him around for. But maybe it was for the money—probably the last dollars he would make as a lawyer.

"Is that why you care about the money?"

She stared hard at him. "I care about you finishing the shit with your firm so you can start getting on with your life. As a lawyer? Not a lawyer?

With me? Without me? I don't know. But if you stay like this, you won't be anything, and it will be without me and without the children."

John tossed the pajamas he had been wringing in his hands into a corner of the room, pulled a pair of socks out of a drawer, and sat on the edge of the bed to put them on.

#

Jess had sat down on the edge of the bed facing away from him, as if she were looking out the window of the small hotel room, except the maroon curtains were drawn. Even if they'd been open, the only thing to see would be the dark windows of the building across the street. John, already mostly clothed, watched Jess slide her underwear on, then her skirt, and so on. It made him want to take it all off her again.

"Can you stay a little longer?"

"Nobody's looking for me."

"Not even your husband?"

"Especially not my husband."

"So why don't we stay awhile? The room's ours all night."

"You'll have to go home eventually," she said. The acid in her voice was pungent as vinegar. She grew still on the edge of the bed. Her eyes were cast down to where the dark blue carpet met the cream baseboard.

John swung his legs over so he could sit next to her. He wanted a drink.

"You look like you need a drink," he said. "Should we run downstairs and get one? Have room service bring one up?"

"I don't want a drink."

He slid his hand over to hers. She didn't pull her hand away, but it hummed underneath his like a trapped bird, heart racing.

"What's going on?" he asked.

"What are we doing?" she replied.

John walked around the bed to the small desk chair where his tie and jacket hung. He didn't want to have this discussion again. Over the past couple of months now, that question ran like a deep ocean current underneath every coffee or drink they shared, or when she carefully unknotted his tie, or he slid his fingers around to the back zipper of her skirt, or she kissed the side of his lips, or he buried his face in her neck, or she ran her thigh across his, or he entered her. Each time, regardless of who asked the question, there was no answer. It was a suspended chord, hanging, demanding resolution, leaving them in a dissatisfied silence.

"What are you doing?" she asked as he draped his tie around his neck to begin knotting it.

"Getting ready to leave."

She rolled her head back, eyes flicking toward the ceiling, the movement the frustrated doppelgänger of one she made ten minutes earlier as she came on top of him. In the earlier moment, John placed his hand gently on her neck in the way he discovered she liked, holding her down on him, moving deeper inside her even as her body tried to levitate off him. In this moment, he wanted to wrap his hand around her throat and press her into the bed so they could stop repeating this song.

"You just asked me to stay," she said.

John's fingers fumbled trying to pull the fat end of the tie through the loop. He knew it would be too short when he finished. He huffed and started pulling the knot apart.

"Are we going to fight about this? We just had a nice time. We both know this is all we can have."

She blinked her eyes and tilted her head back again, this time so he wouldn't see her cry.

"I'm going home to an empty house," she said. "Yeah, Mark's there. But we wave as we pass each other in the living room the same way I wave to Walter in the hall at work. How do I go there from here?"

"It's no different for me."

"Then why are we going back?"

"Because we have to. I have to. I have kids waiting for me. Maybe Jane isn't, but they are."

Jessica shook her head. He started back on his tie.

"We told each other that we wouldn't do this," he said, yanking the end of the tie around itself and his fingers, knowing that the silk weave wouldn't give if he knotted it right, if he pressed it up against his throat, under his trachea, and pulled on the short end as hard as he could until it was longer than the fat end, understanding he'd feel the pressure on his jugular veins first, before his throat closed. He'd panic eventually, but first he'd experience the savage glee of destroying something he hated. Didn't she know that he didn't want to go home either? That he didn't want to put his pants on and go sit in meetings where Geoff and his fucking minions expected him to be grateful that they had let his yellow face and slanted eyes into their club so he could sit in a corner quietly and only speak to congratulate them for being so smart? Yet, there he was, every morning at eight forty-five, at his desk like some dog who carried the paper in each day for its master.

John's fingers dug at the knot in the tie, but there was no give in it. The knot stopped sliding on itself, intractably stuck in a misshapen lump. He kept working the tip of a finger into a fold, but his nails were too short and his fingers too thick to find purchase.

"Do you need help?"

"No."

She walked over and reached for his tie.

"Don't," he said, "you'll make it worse."

She aimed for a wrinkle, her fingers passing his, obstructing him just as he felt a slight give in the fabric, a loosening. She wedged one of her nails into the knot. The tension she created pulled the knot tight again, and his fingers slipped back on the silk. John grunted in frustration and swiped her hand away, but her nail was stuck in the knot and it broke—something John felt in a vibration through the tie, his collar, translating into a tingle in his neck, running like electricity up through his scalp. Jess pulled her hand into her chest and sucked in a surprised gasp of pain.

She opened her fist to inspect the nail, shorn in a jagged edge close to the nail bed. Blood seeped from underneath it.

John reached out for her hand to inspect it, but she jerked it back, coiling tightly around it, only to uncoil and slap him with her uninjured left hand.

Heat flared in his cheek like a match lit too close to his face. His right fist flew up, demanding release. It was a biological imperative—the tension the same as in those moments before an orgasm when nothing could stop him from finishing. Jess didn't flinch. She wasn't yielding to the violence, she wanted it—rain for the fields of misery inside her.

The restraints in his mind frayed and broke, and John stepped back with his left leg, pivoting so when his fist started in motion, he spun and drove it an inch past Jessica's face and into the wall behind him. It was at the extreme range of his reach, which slowed his hand enough so that when his knuckles slammed into the wall with a hollow thud, he didn't break any bones—although it would be swollen and stiff for a week. As his fist rebounded off the wall, John allowed his momentum to carry him forward and around the corner of the bed away from Jess.

He stopped near the head, diagonal from Jess at the foot. Her hands balled into fists.

"What are we doing?" she repeated.

The sheets, still bunched into a careless pile during the sex they finished not even fifteen minutes earlier, lay between them like a tangled answer.

"We should stop doing it. Whatever it is," he said.

It started like an ambush. The first few tears and hitched breaths were upon him before he knew what was happening. Despite his brief, disorganized resistance, he choked off a sob. Jess took a step toward him, but John held up his hand, which he could barely open.

He backed away until he bumped against the nightstand next to the bed. He wiped the tears off his cheeks with his good hand. He felt the salt in them grinding into his skin. He wanted to smash his hand back into his face, to erase everything that was there, to pull at the flesh like it was a mask he could peel from his skull.

Jessica wiped a mascara-stained tear across her cheek, leaving a mark like a bruise.

"So this is it?" she asked. "If it is, say it. Don't make me say it."

He turned, like a coward, to the drawn curtains, and didn't look back as Jessica picked up her purse and her shoes, walked around the bed to the door, and left.

After the door clicked shut, John tore at the tie around his neck, now hopelessly tangled, before ripping it over his head like removing a noose.

#

John stepped into the bar followed by the cold night air. He passed at least three others closer to the apartment with too many people or too much light. A peek through the window of this particular shithole revealed that it was the Goldilocks of dead-end joints. The only other patrons were an old couple at the end of the bar farthest from the door, sitting shoulder to shoulder as they periodically raised bottles of Bud to their mouths. They didn't speak. John sat near the door and ordered whiskey. A double. And then another.

John didn't believe in fate or karma or some master plan. If there was a God in Heaven, His only plan was entropy. Any order in the universe was illusory—the whirlpool created by a blender. But John didn't subscribe to free will either. What were the choices of mosquitoes in a tornado?

Jane was right—he had no choice but to accept Geoff's pissant offer. He lived his whole life to avoid living like his father—an endless hustle to scrounge enough money to barely keep the electricity on, the rent paid, food on the table, and some clothes on their backs. He thought he rose above that struggle when all he had done was delay the day when he had to put an apron on and scrub dishes or fetch Geoff more butter for his toast. Taking the firm's money wouldn't make his marriage any happier than his parents', nor his children's lives better than his.

He slid off the barstool. His legs swayed. He didn't realize how unstable he was until he had to hold himself upright.

There was a pay phone in the back of the bar near the restrooms. He slid a couple of dimes into it and dialed Walter's home. The phone rang seven or eight times before Walter answered, slumber draped over his voice like a warm comforter. *Must be nice*, John thought.

"It's me."

"Fuck you, John. It's two in the morning."

"Tell Geoff I'll take the deal."

THIRTY-SEVEN

Now

"WHAT'S YOUR DEAL?" BRENNAN ASKED AS HUNTER DROPPED himself on the couch next to her in their mother's living room, disheveling the stack of documents she'd set next to her. He had let himself into the apartment moments earlier.

"Huh?"

"I told you that I was covering tonight. Don't you have somewhere to be? Weren't you going to something with Jenna?"

"We broke up."

"Oh." Her instinct was to ask him what he did wrong, but given her own history, the joke turned sour in her mouth before she uttered it. "I'm sorry."

He glanced at her surprise. He must have been expecting the quip. Then he gave a brief tilt of his head—as if he wanted to shrug but was too tired to lift his shoulder—and said, "Nothing lasts forever."

"Want to . . . um . . . talk about it?"

"Jesus, Bren, you don't have to sound so awkward about it," he said. "She got into grad school. She's leaving town at the end of the summer. It's fine."

She didn't think he looked fine.

"How's Mom?" he asked.

Brennan glanced at the closed bedroom door. "Hard to tell. Sleeping. She's sleeping a lot now."

Hunter nodded. Their mother had been waking less and for shorter periods over the past couple of weeks. Something to ask the doctor about the next time Brennan took her in.

"Hear back from Nicki yet?" Brennan asked.

"No."

"So you're just going to sit here while I work?"

"Just wanted some company, okay? I can work, too."

To answer him, Brennan turned back to the binder in her lap and continued with her highlighting. Hunter pulled his laptop from his backpack and began flipping through the files he'd scanned. She didn't ask him what he was doing. Neither of them spoke. It reminded her of the days they'd spent in Harris's office. More than that, with their mother in the next room, it felt like they were kids again. But better.

Before she could process why, there was a knock at the door.

"I'll get it," Brennan said. She wanted to stretch her legs. She'd been on the couch for a while before Hunter arrived.

She opened the door expecting to find the doorman with a package, or her mother's aide stopping to pick up something she left earlier in the day, or maybe a neighbor with extra cookies. But it was a tall man with graying hair so light, it looked white. She thought he looked familiar but couldn't place him.

"Brennan Lo," he said. He knew her. He flashed a badge. "NYPD. I have some questions. Let's step inside."

Despite years of legal experience, she nearly stood aside. "No. We can speak here."

He rolled his eyes and asked, "Did I hear someone call for help in there?" Then he stepped into the apartment, sweeping the door shut with his elbow as he did so. He moved so quickly and surprised Brennan so completely that she fell back a few steps so he wouldn't knock her over.

Hunter was already crossing the room, but stopped as the man flashed a badge at him.

"You have to leave," Brennan said. "I didn't invite you in."

The man laughed, a hollow bark devoid of amusement. "I'm here to discuss some stolen evidence with the two of you."

"We can discuss it at the station, with our lawyer," Brennan said.

"And then there will be paperwork and an investigation and arrests. I'll tell you right now, I'm not interested in all of that."

"Who are you?" Hunter asked.

"Detective Silas Bauman."

Brennan couldn't help it, she glanced at Hunter. When she looked back to Silas, Brennan recognized him. He'd sat at the table next to them at the diner in Larchmont before they visited Cathy. She'd thought him handsome. He'd been following them since the beginning.

"We're not going to answer any questions," Brennan said. "What you're doing is illegal."

"Uh huh," he said, nonchalantly. She knew how he thought. He had the badge and the gun. He decided what the law was.

"You two are fucking stubborn," Silas said. "But you're not idiots. Neither am I. I mean, I hoped you'd get the message by now, but you're not going to listen to anonymous threats. By their nature, you understand that something anonymous implies whoever is making them might be scared of getting caught, right? It's okay, you can say so."

Hunter nodded as Brennan said, "You need to leave now."

"Not yet," the man said. "You're not going to do anything. You're sitting on evidence you stole."

"If that were true, and if you could prove it, we'd be having this conversation in some interrogation room," Brennan said. "But if you did that, people would know what your father and McCarthy did."

"My father was a great detective," Silas said, pointing a finger at her.

Then he brought his hand to rest on his hip, incidentally brushing his jacket to the side and revealing the holstered pistol under his arm. "He was a good man who wanted to take murderers like your dad off the street."

"My father was innocent," Brennan said.

"He fucking did it," Silas said. "I know you want revenge against McCarthy and my father for trying to put him away. I am not going to let you ruin his name."

"We're not lying about your dad or anyone else," Hunter said.

"Don't say anything," Brennan said to Hunter, at the same time. She turned back to Silas. "Who told you we wanted revenge?"

Silas snorted. "I already told you I was smart, missy. You're not going to trick me. The two of you need to be smart, too. You know you can't go public with your lies about my father and McCarthy, right? You would have to admit that you stole police files."

"We didn't steal any files," Hunter said. Brennan threw him the *shut the fuck up* look she'd seen defense lawyers shoot at their clients.

Silas shook his head. "Copy. Steal. It's the same thing. You think I can't make those files disappear?"

"You'd let someone get away with a murder?" Brennan asked.

"Your dad already got away with the murder. My father had the right guy." Silas shifted his gaze between the two siblings. "I came here so you would understand two things. So you will be smart. First, I can act with impunity. At any time. Like now. Second, I am not anonymous, and I am fucking serious. You do anything that threatens my father, his reputation, his legacy, and I will know. And I will come for you."

Hunter raised a hand gently, as if he might reach out to pat Silas's shoulder. "Listen, you can calm down. We're at a dead end. We have no one left to talk to. It's over, okay? If we were in this to screw over your dad or McCarthy, we'd have done it already, right? This had nothing to do with them."

Silas's cold stare didn't waver. But he pulled a tissue from one pocket and used it to open the door. "Be smart. Otherwise, I'll see you around."

When the door shut, Brennan rushed to it and locked the deadbolt.

"That was bananas," Hunter said when she turned around.

"You okay?"

Hunter shrugged. "That was unnerving. He has issues. But I'm also a little pissed off. You alright?"

"He's as bad as his father. He needs to be off the force."

"But are you alright?"

"I'm actually relieved. It was a possibility that whoever was making the threats was the killer, but it's just that asshole. He's dangerous, but at least now we know his angle." She paused for a moment, compressing her anger into something focused. "I didn't want to give up before. I really don't want to now. Not while a guy like that is out there. We need a plan."

Hunter sat in one of the chairs facing the couch. "I guess I can call Vega. I don't know what he can do—and it'll probably get back to Bauman—but maybe there's something."

Brennan nodded. Her brain was already deconstructing the problem. Every option she considered led nowhere, but she felt better pinned down by those thoughts than confronting the fact that they were no closer to answers about Jessica.

THIRTY-EIGHT

Now

SEAN PINNED BRENNAN'S ARMS OVER HER HEAD AGAINST the wall. His breath was too hot in her ear, and when he bit at her earlobe, she twisted away from his mouth.

"Come on, *partner*," he whispered.

Brennan strained to pull her hands down, but Sean had better leverage. "Don't," she said. "Sean . . ."

He leaned in and ground himself against her hip, his erection a thrill despite the fact that she wasn't sure that she wanted to have sex with him. But if she didn't want sex, why did she go to his apartment? Because he called her to say he had good news for her? She needed some good news. It had been two days since Vega told them there was nothing he could do about Silas.

When she'd arrived, Sean led her into his home office, a small nook nestled between his bedroom and his kids' room. An email sat open on his laptop screen. It was from the chair of the firm to all the partners. The subject read "New Partners" and the text of the message indicated that the executive committee of the firm was supporting two new partners at the next partners' meeting. Her name was one of the two.

In her elation, she'd wrapped her arms around Sean. He kissed her and pushed her against the wall before lifting her arms over her head.

"You're going to be a partner," he said, dropping one hand to a breast.

"They still need to vote."

"It's a formality."

"Still," she said before managing to drag her hands down against his single arm.

Sean released her and stepped back, grinning like he was running for office. "I get it. I guess you could completely fuck something up and get disbarred in the next month or something."

Brennan shrugged. She knew bad things constantly happened, but maybe not to people like Sean. He probably had never even sold stock at a loss.

"You okay?" Sean asked.

"Yeah. Just a lot on my mind."

"I can help you get it off. Or just get you off." He thought he was so clever.

Brennan could acquiesce and find a few moments of release. She hated her indecision. If she went along, she wouldn't regret it. Much.

"Actually, can you get me a glass of water?" she asked, stalling.

Even as he turned away, she realized she'd decided to fuck him, but she needed his grin to be somewhere else. If she leaned over his desk, she wouldn't have to look at his face.

She faced his desk and dropped a hand between her legs to expedite matters. She knew the reaction he'd have when he returned to find her there, underwear around one ankle, skirt hiked up.

His laptop was still open, and she admitted to herself that the email excited her. The fact that he shared these secret things with her aroused her. Her gaze drifted aimlessly around his desk as she rubbed herself. Scrawled notes about some case on a legal pad. A credit card bill for $15,863.98. A pile of unopened junk mail. A page with Reliant Tires letterhead poking out from a manila folder. Something from their trial. She hadn't liked her client or their case, but she loved winning.

Brennan lifted the edge of the folder with the hand that wasn't occupied with herself. She didn't remember the document. It was a memorandum to the CEO. She stopped touching herself. The subject line read: "Tire redesign cost savings and risks." She pulled her underwear up as she read. She wanted to take a picture of it with her phone, but it was in her bag, two rooms away on his couch. Before she could do anything, Sean turned into the office with her glass of water. Brennan spun around, memo in her hand.

"What is this?"

Sean's smile disappeared like it had never been there. Then he blinked and the smile was back like it had never been gone.

"That's a memo," he said, holding the glass of water out to her.

"I never saw it before."

"You didn't need to. Why were you going through my things?"

"Why do you have this?"

"You going to take this water or not?" When she didn't move, he reached past her to place it at the edge of the desk.

"Sean." She sounded like she was about to cry. Her mother had taught her that she should keep her composure no matter what—it was the one thing she had control over. "Who else knew?" she demanded.

"Just pretend that you didn't see it. Okay? It's no big deal."

"I have to report this!"

"Do you?" Still smiling.

"I have ethical obligations. We have ethical obligations! How could you do this?"

Sean laughed at her. "This? This is where you're drawing the line? Bren, you're fucking a married man. Your boss. Because you wanted to make partner. And you're worried about a piece of paper?"

"We took an oath."

"Do you even remember it? Come on, this is . . . You never did anything like this? Bury a piece of inconvenient evidence? Decide something wasn't *Brady* because it wasn't 'material'?"

Brennan shook her head. Whatever her failings, she clung to her professional ethics. Society literally depended on people like her doing so, regardless of how fucked up their personal lives were. And hers was colossally fucked. She loved Sean because he had no redeeming qualities. She deserved someone as awful as him, but she couldn't sink to this level. Even as that thought crystallized, the rest of it played out in her mind. As he watched her think through the outcomes, Sean's smile brightened until it was unbearable in the small room.

"See? You understand. We were a team on that trial. You think people will believe you didn't know about this, too?"

"I didn't."

Sean shrugged. "What will I say, though? Don't make me do this, Bren. You report me, I'll say you were in on it, that you decided to report me because I wouldn't leave my wife for you. There's plenty of evidence that we were fucking."

"You wouldn't do that."

Sean's grin widened until it looked like the top of his head might slide off. "You're literally holding evidence that I would do exactly that. Anything to win, Bren. That case made me. Made us. You had everything riding on that case. They'll throw us both out of the firm."

Sometimes when Brennan read about a plane crash, she thought about the terror of plummeting thirty thousand feet knowing not only what the ground meant, but that it took *time* to fall that far. This was the closest she'd ever been to approximating that horror. All she had to do was agree to keep her mouth shut. She kept so many secrets for so many people. What was another one for herself?

"I can't let this slide, Sean."

His smile dimmed like a cloud passed in front of it. "It will ruin my life."

"I didn't do that."

"You're choosing to do it now!"

"It's not a choice."

"My kids, Bren. My family."

"Now you want me to think about them?"

"You weren't hurting them before."

Hadn't she been? She didn't know. It was irrelevant.

She started toward the door, but Sean was in her way. He reached out and placed a palm against her shoulder. The room was so small, even that movement backed her up against his desk. "I can't let you leave with that document."

"You're going to assault me?"

Sean didn't move. "You can't take that with you. I'll take it from you if I have to. Just put it on the desk. If it will make you feel better, you can pretend that I tore it out of your hands."

She wanted to believe that she could fight her way past him. Would she feel more helpless if he physically subdued her or if she surrendered without striking out? Had Jess made the same type of calculation thirty years ago?

"There were no good options, Bren. You should get right with that. The good news is that your best bad option is you get to become a partner. Go on with your career. Make your money."

He was right. Once he had the memo, he'd destroy it. Any accusation would be her word against his. She'd ruin both their careers at best. Worst case, she'd look like a crazy, jilted lover, and he'd skate. She knew how she'd advise someone else in her situation.

"How do I know you won't fuck me over at the partners' meeting?" she asked.

"I've been singing your praises for two years now. It might raise some eyebrows if I suddenly started saying you shouldn't be a partner. Like I said, it's a done deal."

She handed him the memo. "Why didn't you just shred it?"

Sean shrugged. "I don't know." His finger floated across her cheek light as a ghost, wiping a tear she hadn't felt run from her eye. "I guess I just liked having it."

#

Brennan avoided crying more during the cab ride back to her apartment. Her mother would have been ashamed that she cried at all. If her mother wasn't incapacitated, she would have raged at her about how she was to blame for putting herself in that room. She was like her father. Whatever Sean had done, Brennan wouldn't have been involved if she hadn't been fucking him.

She dropped her bags on her couch and went into her office. She sat at her father's desk—her desk. Maybe he would have known what to do. He would have understood, at least.

She couldn't ask any friends—she'd be exposing her attorney friends for the same reason she was hung out: There was an obligation to report ethical lapses, and the failure to do so was itself a violation. And if she told someone, she'd have to admit everything she'd been complicit in, at least the affair, and if she didn't report Sean's burying of evidence, that, too.

She stared at the empty surface of the desk. There were no answers there.

Frankly, the plaintiffs would likely recover something eventually—appeals and other suits were pending. There'd be a settlement. The attorneys would get paid cash, but the people who bought those tires would get a twenty-dollar coupon for new tires. Sean hiding that memo probably cost them another ten dollars on their coupons.

She opened the middle drawer in the right pedestal of the desk and pulled out a few sheets of stationery. She grabbed her father's good pen from the pencil drawer directly over her lap. As she shut the drawer, it clipped the edge of the pen, spinning it from her fingers. It fell and bounced off the top of her foot, skittering underneath her desk. She crawled underneath the desk to retrieve it. Maybe she would die down there. The pen was deep in the foot well, against the backboard. She shuffled forward on her hands and knees and grabbed the pen. She started to back out, but her blouse snagged on something.

She rolled her eyes—she couldn't even get in and out from underneath her desk—and twisted her head to see if she could see where the snag was. The side of the right pedestal caught her eye. Just behind the pencil drawer, there was a gap in the wood. Brennan looked left—there was no corresponding feature on the left pedestal.

She freed her blouse from the spur on the underside of the pencil drawer, then twisted onto her left elbow so she could get a better look at the pedestal. The gap was from a small piece of wood—a latch—that would slide into a space hidden by the pencil drawer's rails.

She realized she could have reached out underneath the desk with a little stretch and touched the latch if she had known it was there. But unless she was under the desk, with the pencil drawer open as it was now, and looking up, the feature would be invisible.

She ran her fingers over the wood. The latch slid with some pressure and revealed a fingerhold behind it. Brennan inserted her finger and gave a little tug. It was a secret drawer, a novelty designed to hide documents like a deed or a will. Brennan flipped over to her back so she could pull until it came loose into her hands. Paper shifted in the drawer in minute tremors as it stacked against the front end.

After she was out from under the desk, Brennan sat up on her floor with the drawer in her lap. It was lined with green felt and held sheets of heavyweight paper stacked about two inches deep. The topmost page was a handwritten letter in close block print in black ink. The letter was addressed *Dear J—*. The text ended halfway down the page. It was unsigned, but Brennan knew who wrote it.

She reached out like she was checking a body and touched the page just below the text. The paper felt fresh, which surprised her considering that it was at least thirty years old. She slid the page until a sliver of the sheet underneath showed. The top page and edges of the stack had yellowed almost imperceptibly compared with the white of the pages protected from the air. The drawer had protected the pages well.

She grazed the text with the tip of her finger like she was brushing an eyelash off a cheek. It was as close to touching her father as she had come in thirty years. This wasn't simply some object he owned like her desk—these were his thoughts, his labor in moving the pen across the paper. Other than her and her brother, these pages were the closest thing to him in the entire world. His fingerprints were probably still on the pages. His DNA.

Brennan pushed the drawer farther down her lap so her tears wouldn't drop onto the pages. Through blurred eyes, she read the top page.

> *Dear J—,*
> *I don't know how to find a way out of this. I can't sleep anymore. I don't see a future where we're together, and I can't bear it. It's empty, and no matter what I try to do to fill it with something that gives me hope, it comes to nothing. It's like I'm a contractor trying to build a house on sand from plans I can't see. Brennan . . .*

She stopped reading and sobbed until she was numb. She remembered the way her father said her name. Seeing it on the page in his writing was like hearing his voice in the room. She glanced at the page again. *Brennan.* She squeezed her eyes shut.

When she knew she wouldn't weep again, she wiped her hands on her skirt and quickly leafed through the pages by one corner without removing them from the drawer. She needed to preserve them and their order.

They all appeared to be letters, addressed to J—. Some were a few sentences on a page, others were multiple pages long. About a dozen of them were dated. Without reading the letters, she couldn't discern if there was any significance to the dated ones other than that they were in reverse chronological order—the dates went back in time as she flipped toward the bottom of the stack. Her father probably laid each new page on top of the prior one, but she couldn't be sure. Brennan estimated there were more than one hundred letters in the drawer. If there were a thousand, she would have wanted more.

At the bottom of the stack, separated from the others by a blank page, was a page without any writing. Colored pencil. She lifted the stack briefly to reveal a child's drawing. She didn't remember it, but recognized it as hers, a picture of her father.

She covered it with the letters as he had left it. She didn't cry again, not because she wasn't moved, but because she couldn't process everything she felt in the moment.

She left the papers in the drawer and slid it back into its place under the desk. Now that she knew it was there, she saw how easy it would be to slide it in and out while sitting at the desk.

She picked up her phone to call Hunter, but it was 3:00 a.m. She thought about calling him anyway, but decided against it and went to bed. She woke, face buried between her pillows against the morning light, her phone ringing on her nightstand. When she answered, her mother's home health aide told her she needed to come to the apartment, and quickly.

THIRTY-NINE

Then

ON HIS FIFTH DAY OF EARNEST SEARCHING, JOHN FOUND work. He spent two days calling former law school classmates, lawyers who worked deals with him, and former clients. The ones who had taken his call each said, "Sorry, I can't help you," in various formulations. Only two offered to ask around or to get back to him if they heard about an opportunity. At least three of them hung up the phone when they heard his name. On the third day, he showered, shaved, put on a pair of decent slacks—nothing too nice—and a collared shirt (again, nice, but not one of the tailored ones he owned), and took a train down to Greenwich Village. He considered Chinatown, but knew his Chinese wasn't good enough to serve "real" Chinese people. The tips would be too small anyway.

The first open restaurant he saw was a bright, airy place. He stood on the sidewalk for a few minutes, pretending to inspect the menu as he considered the likelihood that a former colleague would select this particular restaurant to dine in. He imagined their tip calculus as they sat at the end of a meal, finishing a glass of wine he had carefully poured for them, checking his math on the check, his impotent rage if they stiffed him, and his humiliating satisfaction if they tipped him well.

He walked into this first restaurant and asked a waiter if the manager was there. A middle-aged white guy with a salt-and-pepper beard came out from the back.

"Are you hiring?"

"Do you speak English?"

"I'm speaking English."

"You have experience?"

"Not recent."

"We're not hiring."

He repeated the process over two cold days, miles of streets, and more restaurants than he knew existed in Lower Manhattan. There were at least five that he had patronized in the years before his arrest. A few times, he got close—until they heard why he was switching careers. He couldn't bring himself to lie about it. Only one person recognized him—"Why do I know you?"—but couldn't recall why until John told him.

On the fifth day, John circled back through the West Village, covering ground he had tread the first day. The cold numbed his hands and burned his cheeks—it was at least ten degrees colder than the previous two days. On a street lined with row houses and skinny trees, he spotted a restaurant tucked into the ground level of a building just off Bleecker. Gold leaf script on the window introduced the place as FRONTIER. He peeked in. The floor was larger than he expected. The tables were spaced for cozy, but not crowded, seating. Staff in black clothing and aprons walked among them, setting plates, napkins, silverware, and glass tealight holders upon white tablecloths.

John tried the door, but it was locked. A waiter looked up at him through the glass of the door, pointed at his watch, and held up five fingers.

John called through the door, "I'm looking for work."

The waiter turned toward the back of the room and spoke to a skinny man hunched over a ledger at a short bar John hadn't noticed before. The skinny guy pulled a ring of keys from his hip pocket and opened the door.

"I'm Ed. The manager. Come in."

John followed Ed back toward the bar. Ed waved a hand at the stool. "You have a résumé?"

John nodded and opened his briefcase to pull one out. Ed didn't wait before continuing the interview.

"What are you looking for? Something in the kitchen?"

"Waitstaff."

"You legal?"

"Yeah. I was born here."

"You wait tables before?"

"Not in a long time. Not in a place like this. But I can pick it up pretty fast. I've been in a highly demanding service profession for more than fifteen years." John handed over the résumé.

Ed glanced down at it. "This is unconventional. You tired of a desk job?"

"It's a long story."

"I'm kidding," Ed said and looked up. "I know who you are."

John shrugged but didn't look away. "Not much I can do about that. Most people don't recognize me, if you're worried about that."

"I'm not worried about that. Nobody's here to pay attention to their waiter. Half of them will barely look at you. It's my staff."

"I don't think they recognize me."

"They'll find out who you are sooner or later. I'm worried whether they'll think they're safe. And whether they are, in fact, safe."

John looked down to his lap. He didn't need to explain himself to Ed or his staff. Part of him wanted them to fear him. Instead, he looked up and said, "I was acquitted."

Some long moments passed. Up close, Ed was older than he initially thought, probably ten years older than John. If the light were better, John was sure that he would see some gray in his hair. As the seconds passed, John wondered whether Ed was waiting for him to say something more. But John didn't speak merely to fill uncomfortable silences.

Finally, Ed handed the résumé back to John.

"You can trail tonight."

"I'm sorry?"

"We have a few big parties coming in tonight. I'm short-staffed. You'll trail one of my servers tonight. We'll see how you do."

"I just need to call home and let my family know."

Ed walked around the bar and passed a phone trailing a long cord from a shelf on the wall to John. Jane would still be in the office. He thought about dialing her there, but instead called the apartment.

"Hello?" Brennan answered after three rings.

"It's Daddy."

"Oh! Hi! When are you coming home?"

"Probably not until after you're asleep."

"I wanted you to read to me."

"I can't tonight."

"Oh."

"Tell your mom I may have found a job. I'll be late."

"Okay."

"I love you."

"I love you, too, Daddy."

"Let me talk to your brother."

He heard Brennan shout to Hunter, then the jostling as Brennan passed him the handset, and finally Hunter's voice saying hello.

"It's Dad. I'll be home late, so I wanted to say goodnight and I love you."

"Okay. Bye." The phone clicked dead.

John placed the handset back in the cradle and passed the phone to Ed.

Ed held out his hand again. "You can stash your briefcase behind the bar." John handed it over, then Ed shouted into the room, "Listen up! Staff meeting!"

There were three servers—two men and a woman—and a busboy. They gathered around the bar in a semicircle facing John and Ed.

"This is John. He's getting a tryout and will be trailing tonight. I don't want there to be any issues if you know who he is or find out who he is."

"Who is he?" a tall waiter asked.

"He's the guy who got accused of murdering that girl he worked with," the waitress said. She was in her late twenties, with bottle-blond hair and a South Brooklyn accent. The tall waiter still looked confused, but the others' eyes widened as they recognized him. John felt his face flush. The door was twenty feet away. He could slip out into the already-darkening afternoon without another word. But the moment was inevitable, and better to dispose of it up front.

Ed said, "He was accused. He was acquitted. This is the last we're going to talk about it."

The staff nodded.

When Ed was satisfied, he asked, "Who's he going to trail?"

The servers all looked at one another, each waiting for someone else to step forward. John glanced at Ed, guessing that he didn't want to force anyone to work with him, and wondered how he would resolve the impasse. Finally, the blond rolled her eyes.

"Fine. I'll do it, you fucking pussies." She looked at John. "Come with me."

She walked him over to the service station, which was tucked into a small vestibule between the dining room and kitchen, stocked with cutlery, glasses, linens, and the various implements of service.

"I'm Nicki. I hope you're a quick learner."

She taught him the table numbering, the opening procedures, the order of service, how to write the orders for the kitchen, how to order drinks from the bar, how food was to be expedited and run, which waiters were lazy, how to keep the kitchen staff from fucking up his orders, how to get the busboy to keep the water glasses full on the tables, how to bus the tables, how to drop the checks, how to turn the tables over between covers, and the closing process, mostly by performing these tasks in front of him while he scrambled about trying to stay close but out of her way, all the while running food or drinks to tables as she directed or busing them when she pointed at tables where the diners had finished their meal or prepping bread and butter in the back during the first rush of customers.

"Seems busy," John said at one point, passing Nicki with a stack of dirty plates as she totaled up a check.

"This is about average."

At the end of the night, Ed told Nicki to have John take one of the last tables they sat.

"That's my table," she said.

"You won't miss it." Ed walked back to the bar.

"Keep them moving," Nicki said. "We want to get out of here."

His table—a couple of guys on what looked like a first date—lingered for an hour. In between the closing tasks—wiping down empty tables, cleaning and restocking the service station, reconciling the credit card slips and tips with Ed—Nicki kept hissing instructions to him: "Don't hover! Don't ignore them! Chat a little! Stop talking to them! Wait for them to call for the check! Jesus, just drop the bill!" In the end, they tipped him twenty percent.

After, he found Nicki counting out her tips.

"What did they leave you?" she asked.

"Eight."

"We tip out the busboy at ten percent. Ed or whoever is covering the bar gets five."

"How much did we make?"

"We? I made two-fifty. You made eight. You have to pay your dues. We don't tip trailers."

Ed appeared next to him. "Come back tomorrow. Same time. You can trail again, take a few more tables, and we'll see about a spot."

John's fist clenched around the eight dollars. He'd worked solidly for seven hours. At his hourly rate, sitting at a desk, thinking, reading, talking on the phone, that time was worth thousands of dollars. He had a five and three singles in his hand, one of which he had to pass to the busboy. He could buy a beer or two, three if he went to the right bar and didn't tip. They wanted another day's work from him? Maybe he'd make forty or fifty dollars, depending on how many tables they let him take.

Nicki handed Ed his and the busboy's money while shoving her tips into her pocket.

"Come on," she said. "Let's go out. I'll buy you a drink. You worked hard."

"I have to grab my briefcase."

"Leave it. You can take it home tomorrow."

#

"Can I buy you a drink?"

John looked up from the stack of papers he'd been marking up. Jess stood in his doorway in a dark skirt and white blouse. Her hair was tousled. John knew she would swing it over a shoulder, close to her throat like a scarf, and absently run her hands through it as she concentrated. She kept herself from doing it during the day, but when she worked late or if she was out for drinks, she would indulge the habit.

John raised an eyebrow and flicked his eyes left and right.

"Floor's empty," she said, leaning against the doorframe.

John leaned back in his chair, pulling his tie back into place. They hadn't spoken since she stormed out of the hotel room nearly a month earlier.

"I need fifteen minutes," he said.

"I can do that," she said. "The Village work for you? There's that place on Barrow and Commerce?"

"The Grange Hall?" They had been once before.

"I'll see you there." She disappeared from the doorway.

Forty minutes later, he sat down next to her and her empty glass at the bar.

"I got a head start," she said. "I was getting worried that you were going to stand me up."

"Sorry. It took me longer than I thought to get through those last pages." Actually, they had gone fast. He'd barely touched the standard language in them. But he'd sat at his desk thinking about the times the past month when he'd not only written onto a blank page, but whispered into the empty air, "I miss you." He'd spent the weeks since they last spoke hoping she'd reappear. But each step he took to get to the bar was like walking to the edge of a quarry: the glance through the window to locate her, a peek over the edge at the topaz sheen below; and the final approach through the room, a freefall, the sheer face of the rocks blurring past until this moment—the smell of her perfume, the wry grin, and the cadence of her voice—a plunge into fathomless water. He couldn't swim.

"I forgive you," she said. "For now. If you buy me another."

She was drinking Glenmorangie. He ordered two, laid a twenty on the bar, and turned back to her.

"How've you been?" he asked.

"Fine," she said, nearly cutting him off. "What were you working on?"

"Some deal we're going to paper up and then it's going to fall apart. You?"

"Walter had me writing a brief on a motion to dismiss."

"You finish?"

"I wouldn't be here if I hadn't."

The bartender returned with their drinks. She raised her glass.

"To late nights."

"Late nights."

He met her glass with his, then took a sip.

"It's good to see you," she said.

"Yeah. You, too."

She pulled a pack of cigarettes from her purse. While she did so, she spoke without looking at him.

"The past month . . . it's been difficult, John. Trying to avoid you at the office."

"I know." He found excuses to visit the floor her office was on, hoping to run into her, but aside from a quick glimpse of her turning a corner or stepping into an elevator, he hadn't seen her. Afterward, he'd retreat to his office and shut the door, feverish with shame—embarrassed as if he'd been caught peeping through a neighbor's window—glad she hadn't caught him.

"Did you ever go looking for me?" she asked, offering him a cigarette.

He took one. "Once or twice."

The corners of her mouth twitched. "I shouldn't smile."

John shrugged.

"I was waiting for you," she said.

"I hoped you were. But I wanted you not to be."

"Me, too."

She struck a match and held it for him to light his cigarette. The tip ignited, the combustion's energy rippling down the length of the cigarette to tingle on his lips a moment before the smoke hit his throat. He turned to exhale as she used the same match to light her own.

When he looked back at her, she tilted her head to exhale through one side of her mouth but kept her eyes on him as she did.

They smoked, intermittently chasing a drag with a sip of their drinks. As time passed, it felt odd not to say anything, but if he spoke, he might say any of the things he had written on the sheets of paper he later shredded or burned or stashed in the hidden drawer in his desk at home, truths that would extinguish this moment, which he wanted to stretch like the last cigarette in a pack. He needed to pull a breath to keep it burning, but every inhalation brought him closer to the end, a span of time measured by the column of ash tenuously clinging to the last embers as he held his hand steady, pulling smoke through his lips, the heat searing his mouth, throat, lungs, for the brief quickening of his pulse and a moment of dizziness.

Jess didn't speak either. The month they spent apart had not given him any perspective for when she grew quiet like this. Was she thinking about ways to improve the brief she worked on earlier? Listening to the Billy Joel number that was blaring from the jukebox? Deciding what to tell her husband when she got home? Working up the courage to lay her thoughts open to him, to confess the unknowable and the unspeakable?

She crushed out the last of her cigarette and turned to face him directly. Her knee touched the side of his thigh, the pressure so slight he wasn't sure if it was there or his desire that it be there, and he couldn't look down because she wouldn't stop staring at him.

"If we could just do this," she said so quietly he almost didn't hear her over the music and chatter.

She didn't complete the thought, instead sliding her hips off the barstool so she stood in the space between his knees while she slung down the rest of her drink.

"Come on," she said. "Drink up and let's go before we start talking and ruin everything."

#

When he and Nicki reached the six-point corner of Bleecker and Seventh Avenue South, John asked, "Where are we going?" He hadn't asked earlier.

"Grange Hall. I know the bartender there."

FORTY

Then

THREE BEERS IN, JOHN TRIED TO KEEP PACE WITH NICKI, WHO gulped them down faster than anyone he'd ever seen.

"I hate warm beer," she said. "It has to be cold. Drink at your own pace if you're a wimp."

They were at the end of the bar, where it met the wall. The last time he'd been to Grange Hall, he and Jess sat in the middle of the bar. John avoided looking in that direction. Other than the wall, the only thing to look at was Nicki. She appeared no worse for wear despite slamming three beers in an hour. She changed out of her black shirt into a white blouse before they left Frontier. When he first met her, John thought her somewhat plain. But during the shift, she impressed him with her hustle and the charm she summoned for each table. As they drank, Nicki told John that she had been waiting tables at Frontier for two years.

"Before that?"

"I hopped around a lot. Sometimes places went under. Sometimes I got tired of the people or the money wasn't good enough."

"College?"

She rolled her eyes.

"Sorry," he said. If the beer hadn't already turned his cheeks and ears red, he knew they were flushed now.

"Why are you sorry? I would have gone if I wanted. Why do I need to pay all that money for someone to tell me to read some stupid books by guys I don't want to read? A waste of time. I saved tuition money. I got no debt."

"So you wanted to be a waitress?"

"I like restaurants. I like the cash. You can usually find someone to drink with after your shift, so you don't feel like an alcoholic. And when I walk out the door, I leave everything there, right? When I'm done, I'm done. I don't have to spend my time with my friends or at home stressing about work."

John must have looked skeptical, because Nicki said, "I feel like you're judging me."

"I'm not."

"Admit it. You're judging me a little bit. You think I'm some kind of party girl. Or stupid. Or unreliable."

"No!"

"Then what's with the face?"

"It's just," he thought for a moment, "different from people I know. Now, at least. I worked in a restaurant while I was in school. It was a means to an end. I never imagined it as . . . It wasn't something I wanted to do. And now I'm back."

"Why does it bother you? To be a waiter? Did you look down on us when you were a lawyer?"

"I'm still a lawyer," John said with a certitude as empty as the bottle in his hand. "And no. I didn't."

"So what's the big deal?"

"They'd look down on me."

"Who?"

"My former colleagues. My former clients. My friends. All of them."

"Didn't they always look down on you anyway?"

John was glad that the bartender showed up with two new beers. He took a long pull from his bottle and looked back to find Nicki offering him a cigarette.

"I didn't know you smoked," he said, pulling one from the pack.

"I do after three beers."

"What do you do after four?"

She laughed and smacked his shoulder lightly, then rubbed it as if she had hurt him, and said, "You'll have to stick around to find out."

Nicki put the cigarette in the corner of her mouth while she rooted in her purse for a lighter. Instead of remembering his last cigarette in the bar, John focused on Nicki's lips. When her hand emerged from the purse with a pink plastic lighter, John intercepted it and relieved her of the Bic. He lit her cigarette for her, and then his own.

"So are you really planning to work at the restaurant, or you just doing this until you can go back to being a lawyer?"

"You tired of working with me already?"

"Just curious."

"I don't know. We'll see how it goes. I need to pay the bills. And keep the boss happy."

"You know why Ed hired you, right?"

"He thought I was handsome?"

Nicki giggled again. "He's an ex-con. He's always looking to give someone a break or a second chance."

"I'm not a convict."

"I know," she said, raising her hands like he'd pointed a gun at her. Smoke rose from the back of one, the cigarette hidden like a plane crash behind a ridge. When she saw he wasn't leaving, she lowered them.

"Can I tell you something?"

"Yeah." John took a long drag on his cigarette. He readied himself for her to ask about Jess.

"I was surprised by how handsome you are."

He smiled before he could stop himself. "What?"

Nicki blushed. In her rush to confess, she exhausted her stockpile of courage and had nothing left. But she didn't avert her eyes. She took a quick sip from her beer.

"This is going to sound funny," she started, "but I saw your picture in the paper. And you're better looking than the pictures they used. I'm just saying."

John didn't respond. Which photo had she seen? The police walking him out of his building? His mug shot? One of him on the courthouse steps?

"I'm not hitting on you," she said. "I'm just saying that when I read about the case, I wondered why she was into you. You know?"

Yes, he knew.

"She was so pretty. And I thought—I mean, maybe I'm just not into Chinese guys—but I thought your photo was ehhhh. You looked like any other guy. I didn't see myself cheating on my husband with you."

"You have a husband?"

"No."

"So now you're here with three or four beers in you, and you're reconsidering your initial impression?"

"When you put it that way, you make me sound like a tramp."

"Nope. Just trying to figure out whether this is just the beer talking or whether I'm actually handsome."

"You're not as funny as you think."

John couldn't tell whether she was flirting with him or wanted him to think she might be interested. Did it matter? Hadn't he learned his lesson? Finish his beer, have another cigarette, head home, work again tomorrow. The last time he was here, shouldn't he have done the same?

#

Neither John nor Jess spoke until they got into the cab, and then only for Jess to give the cab driver Cathy's address.

"She went away for the weekend," Jess said before turning to look out the window. "Some conference for work."

John nodded. The cabbie chose a route—north on Hudson Street, kick over to Tenth Avenue, then crosstown at Ninety-Sixth Street and up Madison—that brought John within a few blocks of his home. He thought about telling the driver to stop so that he could get out. The next stoplight, he told himself, it would be close enough to walk home. They hit two before Ninety-Sixth Street crossed into Central Park. At the second, he brought his fingers to the door handle.

Jess slid across the black vinyl seat until she pressed against him. Her arm burrowed underneath his right arm so she could take his hand. John let go of the door handle. Jess dropped her head to his shoulder. Green light. The cab accelerated down Ninety-Sixth Street and beat the next light. Stone walls rose on either side of them as the street descended below the night-covered park.

#

"You're not going to return the compliment?" Nicki asked, turning in her stool to put her back to the wall and giving John full view of her shirt, unbuttoned down far enough that it required his concentration not to glance down at her chest.

"Compliment? You just said I wasn't funny."

"I said you were handsome."

"Fine," he said with a half smile. "You're very funny."

She laughed—nearly a bray. "You're an asshole."

John would have hated that bray if he heard it from a stranger. She was a stranger, but nobody laughed around him anymore, much less with him. Making her laugh was like slamming four more drinks. His stool felt wobbly. He reached out and grabbed the edge of the bar.

"You okay?" Nicki asked.

"Yeah. You got another smoke?"

She passed him a cigarette and took one for herself. This time, she lit his.

"Want to tell me about it?" she asked.

"Tell you about what?"

"Whatever's on your mind."

"You don't want to know what's on my mind."

"Sure I do."

"For one thing, your shirt."

"Don't be crude," Nicki said, sitting back and pulling the gap in her blouse closed. Then she smirked and leaned forward, the neckline of the shirt parted again. "Seriously, you can talk to me."

"I don't know you."

"You can know me."

The cigarette smoke coiled in the air between them. John tried to discern what Nicki was hoping to get out of him. John was drunk, not an idiot. She wanted something from him. Maybe a story about how she slept with him. Maybe his side of the story about what happened to Jess. Or perhaps she didn't care about what came before and simply thought he was good-looking.

"I don't want to talk here," he said.

"I live in Gramercy. We can talk there." Nicki crushed her cigarette out.

John took a final sip of his beer. Nothing felt right about the evening, but he hadn't had sex since before his arrest. The twenty months felt like twenty years, but each of those days was a day Jess hadn't seen. For a few minutes, John wanted to forget that.

"Let's get a cab."

#

They had walked to the door of Cathy's building through an empty street. Over the quiet, he could hear the hum of the cab's engine and the gritty peel of its tires on the asphalt as it drove off. John recalled a time when, like a vampire, he would have stood on the sidewalk until he received an express invitation to follow so he wouldn't appear presumptuous. Years before, the first time Jane invited him up to her apartment, they'd stood on the street for ten minutes after John walked her home from a date, chatting, then kissing, a stanza and refrain repeated. In the end, she'd simply taken his hand and led him to the door. Later, before they finally drifted off to sleep, Jane took his cock in her hand and said, "You need to take a hint. Don't ever make me work so hard for this again."

Jess held the door of the building open for him as he climbed the short stoop. He pushed the inner door open—the lock had been broken the whole time they'd been using Cathy's apartment. He followed her up the stairs, appreciating the fit of her skirt and the flex of her calves as she took each step on the toes of her high heels. Except for the percussion of their feet on the stairs and the jangle of her key ring as she searched for the apartment keys, the stairwell was silent.

He waited for her to undo the deadbolt on Cathy's door and considered leaving her there. Whatever pain the last month had brought, it simplified things for him. No more lies to his family, and no more stress someone in the office might discern a meaningful glance or discover an errant note. So why stay? Did he want a better coda for them than the catastrophe in the hotel room? Was he trying to throw them back on the runaway train so that they could finally derail properly? Or did he only want to fuck some of his sadness, anger, and regret back into her? And what was Jess looking for as she stepped into the apartment?

John closed and locked the apartment door. When he turned, Jess stood in the middle of the unlit room facing him, framed in a corona of ambient light from the windows. She began to unbutton her blouse. John crossed half the distance between them and stopped so that he could watch her undress. Nothing in the way she unhooked her bra, unzipped her skirt, or slid her underwear down her thighs revealed her reasons for doing so. It was like trying to divine the intention of a thunderstorm.

When she finished, he undressed. It was nothing as elegant as Jess, but she watched him without laughing.

She stepped into his arms, rested her head on his shoulder, and brought her arms around his back. John wrapped his around her waist above her hips. But for the fact that they were nude, it looked like they were dancing.

#

Nicki's apartment was a miniature version of Cathy's, except for the mottled black-and-white cat that padded off behind the couch when John walked in with Nicki.

"Ignore him," she said. "He's shy."

John hung his coat on the back of one of the two chairs at a small table near the door. Nicki tossed hers across an arm of the couch, about three feet away, then turned to the fridge. Everything in the apartment was two steps from all the other objects. The walls loomed close. A thick pipe ran up one corner of the apartment, throwing off so much heat that the paint on it bubbled in places. John wanted to open the single window for some air but guessed it would be stuck in its frame.

She handed him a bottle of New Amsterdam and presented the neck of her bottle to him. He tapped it with his. Nicki sat on the couch and patted the cushion next to her until he joined her. She stretched a leg out across his lap. The couch faced a small TV, rabbit ears rising from the back.

"New York is funny," Nicki said. "A few months ago, I'd see you on the news, and now you're in my apartment."

John placed his hand on her calf.

"Can you tell me about it?" she asked.

"The trial?"

"No. I read the papers. I want to know about you and her."

"There's not enough time."

"You in a rush?" She pushed her leg farther up his lap. "We can take our time."

John stared at the blank television screen.

"You had an affair with her," Nicki prodded.

"Yes." It felt like a lie, to reduce it to that.

"How did it start?"

"In the office. After our Christmas party."

"Why?"

John shrugged. "Why are we here right now?"

Nicki threw him a crooked smile. "I live here."

One corner of John's mouth rose in a half smile, then froze as Nicki raised one knee, bringing the heel of her foot to the inside of his thigh, and pressed. John flinched, but Nicki extended her leg slightly, pinning him into the corner of the small couch. The pressure was uncomfortable, but not unbearable, and when he stopped moving, she pivoted her foot so it brushed against his cock without releasing the discomfort caused by her heel.

"I can make this hurt," she said. "Or not. Depends on how you answer my questions."

"You tell me first," he said. "Why did you invite me over?"

Nicki shrugged. "Life's boring. I want to have a story. A secret. You can be both."

"Aren't you scared of me?"

"Ten people saw me leave that bar with you. You're not an idiot. You're not going to hurt me, right?"

"No," he said.

"Okay," she said. "I told you. Now you tell me."

"What do you want to know?"

"The stuff I didn't see in the papers. Like why."

"We were unhappy."

"Did she make you happy?"

"We did our best to make each other less unhappy. For a while at least. But I don't think either of us was capable of making the other happy."

"Did it end like they said?"
John shook his head.
"How did it end?"

#

"Is this the end?"

The question was a breath across his chest. Jess's head lay just above his heart. Her left arm, hip, and leg were draped over him in Cathy's bed.

John didn't answer. He tried to remember how they had made love, the sound of her, the smell of the crook of her neck. But he couldn't distinguish the presence of her from the memory he was saving for a time she might not be there.

"It feels like it, right?" she asked. Her chest pressed against his as she inhaled deeply.

John concentrated on the feel of her skin, the bare flesh of her stomach, the rough patch of her pubic hair against his hip, the pull of her leg. If he didn't confirm it for her, maybe she would think of a reason that this wasn't the bottom, that there were still depths to which they could fall.

"Why don't you say something?" Jess asked.

"I'm not going to lie to you. But I don't want to say it's over."

"I hate you," she said. "I hate you for not leaving her."

"What if I left her?" he asked, knowing he couldn't.

"I would hate you more."

She tilted her head up to his and pulled his face to hers. She kissed him, then rolled away to sit at the edge of the bed.

#

John remembered the curve of Jess's back, cast in blue from the dim light of the digital clock next to Cathy's bed, and her hair falling slightly past her shoulders.

"We broke up," he said. "I wouldn't leave my wife."

"Was that the night . . ."

"No."

Nicki drained the rest of her beer. She released the pressure in her foot, so that it simply rested in his lap. John imagined that it finally occurred to her that she was alone in her apartment with an accused murderer and approaching the point where if she kept asking questions, she would get to the one that she wanted the answer to but couldn't ask. Nicki broke the silence.

"You ever told anyone what happened that night?"

"No."

Nicki brought her feet off his lap, curling her legs underneath her, allowing her to lean toward John, but also making it easier for her to get to her feet faster than he could. It was a first step toward her straddling him or running. His relief at her removing her leg surprised him. He'd gone to Nicki's apartment to forget about everything that came before, not relive it with her.

"Do you want to tell me?" she asked.

John hesitated. It wasn't just the risk that the truth presented, but the shame, anger, and regret that were chained to the memory. But he was so weary, carrying the truth alone.

Nicki touched his shoulder. The warmth of her hand passed through his shirt. She said, "You can tell me. I promise I won't tell anyone."

"Promise me that you'll tell me you understand. Even if you don't."

She did, so he told her, and when he finished, she told him that she understood. He hoped he would leave the memory of that night with her, but it followed him home anyway.

FORTY-ONE

Now

WHEN HUNTER ENTERED THE ROOM, JANE SAID, "JOHN?"

"No, Mom," Brennan said, standing next to her bed. "It's Hunter."

She blinked. "Oh."

There was no recognition in her eyes.

"Hey, Mom," Hunter said, walking to the near side of the bed, across from Brennan.

"Are you a doctor?" Jane asked.

Hunter swiped at his eyes. "No. I'm your son."

She looked troubled. "I thought you were away."

"I'm right here." He took her hand, which was as hot and formless as sunbaked sand.

"That's good," Jane said. She turned to Brennan, who held her other hand. "Everything hurts."

"I know. We have medicine for you. It's going to make you sleep, so we wanted to make sure Hunter got here before we gave it to you. You remember? We talked about that when you woke up."

She nodded and looked around the room. "Am I home?"

"You're home. Me and Hunter are both here."

"Don't put me in the hospital."

"We won't, Mom. We're going to be here with you."

Hunter squeezed her hand. "We're right here."

Jane's fingers twitched in their hands as if she were trying to squeeze back. When she spoke, her words came slowly and gingerly, brow furrowed in concentration, as if she were searching through a deck of cards for the next word before carefully leaning it against the last one. "I wasn't an easy mother to have. I'm sorry for that. For everything you two had to go through. Don't be alone when I'm gone. Promise me. I love you too much to rest if you make the same mistakes I did."

"I promise," Hunter said.

"Me, too," Brennan whispered.

"I'll take that medicine now."

Brennan placed two pills in Jane's mouth. The glass of water was on his side of the bed, so Hunter held it to his mother's lips and helped her drink them down, trying to ignore the effort it took for her to swallow them. After, he wiped her mouth as she sank deeper into her pillow and closed her eyes.

"Stay with me?" she asked.

"Of course," Brennan said. "I love you, Mom."

Brennan looked at him like she was reminding him that he had a line. Hunter worried about her. She didn't seem to be in much better shape than their mother.

"We won't leave you, Mom," Hunter said. "I love you."

Their mother smiled weakly, eyes still closed. She said, "I love you both. I'll see you again."

They sat with her, mostly in silence, for the few hours until the end.

#

The next days were a blur. Hunter mostly felt numb—the cocktail of emotions coursing through him overloaded his receptors. The world developed a surreal patina. The merchants of the bereaved—the funeral home, the florist, the coroner—treated the siblings with a solicitous gentleness completely out of proportion to how they felt, the inverse of screaming in a library. It was the same with condolence calls from friends—the tentative "How are you?" like a mouse sniffing around a trap. Each one added a little more torque to the tight spring of his psyche. Every time someone said, "I'm sorry," like he might collapse brought him closer to the point of unraveling. Hunter found himself going for coffee, groceries, dinners just to interact with people who didn't know about his loss to remind himself what normal life sounded like.

He had no idea how Brennan was dealing with it even though they were camped out together in their mother's apartment making arrangements and sorting her effects. Hunter wanted to wait, but Brennan insisted on cleaning immediately. Bickering about it lifted his mood. That felt ordinary.

Brennan cleaned like a disheveled machine, filling trash bags, sorting clothing for donation, placing keepsakes aside for those who might want one, like a photo of their mom and Harris right after law school that hung in a small frame in the hallway. Hunter inferred how Brennan was grieving like an astronomer learning about the composition of distant planets by watching objects fall into them. Like when Brennan pulled an old silk scarf of her mother's from the drawer, brought it to her face and inhaled, then carefully folded it up and carried it out of the room to place it with her coat. Or when Brennan came in with the day's newspapers, flipping the pages of one with such agitation it looked like she was crumpling it, until she found what she was searching for.

"Look," she said.

"Jane Leigh, Co-Founder of Prominent Law Firm and Widow of Accused Murderer, Dies." A short obituary followed. Reading the words on the page was like seeing her body after she died—it was both his mother and nothing like her.

When Hunter looked up, Brennan was in their mother's office, pulling open drawers and arranging paper into stacks. He stood in the doorway.

"They couldn't just leave him out?" Brennan shuffled through a sheaf of paper without looking up.

"It was part of her life, right? Like ours."

Brennan didn't respond. She inspected all the drawers in her mother's desk to ensure they were empty, then tapped around them, before crawling underneath.

"What are you doing?" he asked.

"Checking for secret compartments."

"Bren, that desk is from Pottery Barn."

She withdrew her shoulders and sat cross-legged on the floor.

Hunter stepped into the room. "What's going on?"

#

Hunter stood over Brennan's desk, staring at a dead man's letters. He couldn't imagine his father writing anything so personal. Or with any emotion other than rage. Yet, the topmost page.

> *Brennan and Hunter can have a future. I tried, I did try, J—. I want to think that I fought for that future, to make them better than me, but if I'm here, all I can do is ruin them.*

Hunter stopped reading, pulse thundering in his temples. His father was wrong. He ruined their future. If he loved them, he would have stayed, tried to make it right, to show them how to overcome his stigma. Instead, the only example he gave them was how to run.

Hunter read the line again. He wanted to deny it, but the stack of letters proved it. After the accusation and the acquittal, his father had remained awhile before leaving. Hunter, on the other hand, fled the city the first day he was able to. How could he blame his father for the same mistake he made? Not to mention that Hunter made it with the benefit of hindsight. The pieces fell together for Hunter and kept falling, dragging down the beams and walls he built to hold himself together.

He sank to his knees, and his sister knelt beside him, took him into her arms, and held him as he sobbed against her shoulder.

"All my life, I wanted to be different than him," he said. "But I was the same."

#

Hunter went home to shower. They planned to meet at Jane's apartment in a few hours to clean. Brennan wanted the place ready to receive guests after the funeral. After Hunter left, Brennan placed the drawer with the letters back into its compartment. They agreed they would read the letters after they laid their mom to rest. Seeing them again, in order, reminded her that they'd never reordered the vouchers from Harris's files.

Having a task list—the calls to people who needed to be informed, planning the wake and funeral, cleaning—kept her mind from fixating on the stitching pain radiating from her heart. She added reordering the vouchers to the list. In some ways, the incredible pressure Brennan experienced felt like a cast on a broken limb—a healing agony. She thought about heading back to her mother's place early to keep cleaning.

On the other hand, the paper she'd taken out when she got home from Sean's a few days earlier still lay on her desk. She didn't know what she intended to write that night, only that writing or doodling might clarify what she should do. The page reminded her that she should draft a letter of resignation laying out the situation with Sean and walk away from the ensuing explosion.

Instead, she sat at her desk, took her father's pen from the drawer, and composed her mother's eulogy.

#

Harris and Andre left last after long embraces with the siblings. Brennan shut the door behind them. Hunter dropped onto the couch as he pulled his tie off. Brennan couldn't remember the last time she saw him in a suit.

"So that's that," he said.

Brennan sat in one of the wingback chairs opposite the couch, kicking her heels off her feet. The wake and funeral passed like a subway train—an unstoppable force blowing past her, glimpses of the occasional face as someone stopped to register their condolences. After, the siblings received mourners at their mother's apartment. It was mostly friends and former colleagues of her mother, but her friends and coworkers were represented, as were Hunter's. Even the waitress, Jenna, showed for a short while. Brennan's secretary, a middle-aged Indian woman, took both her hands with wet eyes, unable to find words for her sympathy. A few of her old friends showed, threw their arms around her, promised that they would find more time in the future. Paul stood awkwardly in the back of the room until she managed to break away and thank him for coming; he told her that he'd always looked at Jane like a second mother. They laughed when Brennan pointed out that Paul thought his own mother was insufferable. He left soon after.

"Your eulogy was really good," Hunter said.

"Thanks. Yours, too. She would have hated them."

"Yeah. These things really aren't for the departed, though, right?"

Brennan nodded. "I feel like I've been hit by a truck."

"We should eat," Hunter said, but the two of them sat there for a long time without moving until Hunter's phone rang.

"Hello," Hunter said, before his face brightened for the first time in days. "Yes, Nicki. Thank you for reaching out!"

Brennan listened to one side of the conversation, quickly gleaning that she was calling him so they could meet.

"Today?" Hunter asked, glancing at Brennan. She shrugged and nodded.

"Tell her to wear black," Brennan said, before he hung up. "In case Silas is watching the place, he'll think she's a mourner."

A few hours later, the doorbell chimed, and Hunter led a woman into the room. She wore simple black slacks and a black blouse. A long black coat was folded over her arm, obscuring the bag she carried. She was over fifty, Brennan guessed, but not by much. Her hair existed in the shade between blond and light brown, but Brennan saw glimpses of brunette and gray in the roots that were beginning to grow out.

"Hi," Nicki said. Her voice shook. "I saw the news about your mother. I'm sorry."

"Thank you," Brennan said, standing up. "Would you like to sit? Can we get you anything?"

"Yes, some water, thank you."

They gave her a glass of water and settled in the living room, the siblings on the couch and Nicki in one of the chairs. She pulled her folded coat off her lap, revealing a briefcase, which she set on the coffee table.

The memory of it slapped Brennan.

"I know you have some questions for me, but first, this was your father's. I wanted to give it back to you."

"I don't understand," Hunter said.

"This was your dad's. He left it with me." The more she spoke, the more her Brooklyn accent came out. "I went to his funeral, to talk to your mom about giving it back, but . . . but . . . you guys and your mom seemed so sad. I didn't . . . I'm sorry, I don't know what to say. I thought I'd wait awhile before I brought it to you."

Brennan smiled, sad, but kind. "It's okay. I think it's been a while now, right?"

Nicki failed to manage a return smile. "I lost track . . . I mean, I worried, after that, if I brought it back, I'd hurt your mom. Or you guys. You know, bringing him up again. And then as time went on, it was even more awkward, you know, showing up out of the blue. So it just sat in the back of my closet. I was so surprised to get Hunter's message. I'm sorry I kept it for so long."

Brennan stared at the briefcase. The leather had dried out, and some of the finish had frayed to reveal raw beige leather underneath. Otherwise, it was in decent condition.

"Thank you," Hunter said. "How long did you work with my dad?"

"Not long. Seems like it must have been only a couple of days."

Hearing that, Brennan wanted to send Nicki home. She was too exhausted to entertain a woman who barely knew their father.

Hunter asked, "After his trial, right?"

"Yeah," Nicki said. "Months later. He left it, the briefcase, at the restaurant."

"Oh," Hunter said. Brennan saw him coming to the same conclusion as her. They were too tired to deal with this.

"You two must be exhausted, from your mom," Nicki said before grabbing her glass of water and taking a sip with a trembling hand. "So let me . . . Did . . . did your dad ever tell you what happened that night?"

"He told you?" Brennan said.

Hunter leaned forward. "We were kids. Nobody ever told us."

The siblings exchanged a glance.

"Please, go on," Brennan said.

FORTY-TWO

That Night

WALTER SAT IN JOHN'S OFFICE AND CROSSED ONE LEG OVER the other. He was complaining about some associate who insisted on writing fifteen-page memos when five would do. John's finger still marked his location in the merger document he was reviewing when Walter had appeared in his doorway (the seventeenth sentence in the ninth subparagraph). John told him to go away; he still had at least three hours of work to do, but Walter ignored him and kept venting. The phone rang, and John lifted the receiver, cutting Walter off mid-sentence.

"John?" It was Jess. John hoped his face remained steady—his finger flinched off the document.

"Yeah," he answered.

"Can you come meet me? At Cathy's?" Her voice was a shattered window waiting to fall.

"Yes. Be there soon."

Before John finished placing the handset back in the cradle, Walter asked, "Who was it?"

"Huh?"

"I said, who was it? On the phone?"

John stood. His desk was covered with documents that needed his review before noon the next day. He decided better to return early the next morning than try to organize everything to take with him. Walter asked again who was on the phone.

"Nobody. Jane. I have to go."

"Everything alright?"

"Yes. Fine. Thank you, Walter, but I need to go."

"You want me to arrange for a car?"

"No. I'll grab a voucher on my way down."

He left Walter in his office. The trip to Cathy's was a dimly lit backdrop for the scenes he played out in his mind speculating what she would say when he arrived and how he might respond. Later, he wouldn't recall visiting the dispatcher's desk to arrange for the car and voucher or the elevator ride to the garage. Brooklyn, then Queens, blurred past as if he were drunk, a smear across the East River as the driver sped north on the FDR Drive. As he pressed the buzzer for Cathy's apartment, he realized he didn't remember walking from the corner where the driver left him. He didn't wait for Jess to buzz—the heavy wooden inner door was still broken. He pushed it aside and climbed the stairs to Cathy's apartment.

Jess waited for him at the apartment door as he crested the stairs, beer bottle in hand. Her eyes were puffy, the whites clouded pink, but her makeup was pristine. She still wore a skirt suit, but her feet were bare. She stepped aside and closed the door after he entered.

"I was worried you wouldn't actually come," Jess said, leaning against the door.

"I was worried. For you." John turned in front of the couch but made no move to sit.

"I'm late."

"For what?"

Jess glanced away, and he comprehended like a plane suddenly hitting a rough pocket of air and losing hundreds of feet of altitude in a few seconds. He reached out for the arm of the couch to steady himself, but it was too low, so when his fingers finally contacted the fabric he bent awkwardly at the waist, legs locked straight, as if he were bowing. Later, he would think that, if he had collapsed onto the couch, let gravity pull him deeper into the cushions, inertia hold him down, the weight of the air smother the impulses firing through his limbs, maybe everything that came after would have been different. But in the moment, John didn't want to show any more weakness—he was already ashamed of lurching to the arm of the couch—so he pushed himself upright and was immediately weightless with anger.

"How?" he asked. "I thought you were on the pill?"

"I was. Maybe . . . maybe it didn't work? It's not unheard of. Maybe I missed a day? A week? I don't know. Things were so fucked up, John. Between work and everything else going on between us. I was drinking a lot. I just . . . lost track. I figured I could get back on schedule."

"Are you only late? Or did you take a test?"

"I'm too scared."

"So you don't even know?" John's voice was steam erupting from a pressure-relief valve.

"I needed you with me." She looked down at her feet, shoulders slumped forward like she was trying to curl herself around her belly while standing. "I couldn't face it alone."

"You just need to piss! Jesus Christ! Stop being a little girl! You need me to hold your hand in the potty?"

"Fuck you, John." Jess's fists were clenched. Good.

"Why didn't you call your husband? Is it even mine? Are there more contenders out there?" He had spent so long throwing his truest ugliest thoughts into himself like bodies into a well, there was no more room for them. It was all poisoned. She wanted him? Let her have this part of him, too.

Jess covered the five steps between them quickly. She raised the hand with the beer bottle in it. John smiled. *Finally*, he thought.

She hesitated when she was within arm's length, and he tore the bottle from her hand and threw it behind him, where it smashed against a wall. Focused on the hand with the bottle, he didn't see the other as it landed across his cheek, whipping his face to one side. He heard the impact more than he felt it, but then the pain hit him like a dope rush. He grabbed her upper arms. He wanted to shake her, watch her head whip back and forth before throwing her to the couch or the floor, climb on top of her, and—what? Fuck her? Strangle her? Whatever it took to finally throw off the restraints that held all the pain inside of them.

As John hesitated, Jess thrashed until she tore her right arm free. She swung it at him again. John ducked and her hand glanced off the top of his head. He shoved her away, and she stumbled backward.

"I'm going to fucking ruin you," Jess said. "First, I'm going to report you to the firm. You think your partners are going to overlook you knocking up an associate? You're barely a partner. You're a mascot, an affirmative action project. Someone they can point to so they can pat themselves on the back and put off getting a Black partner for a few more years. They'll push you out. And after I've done that, I'm going to tell your wife. You think your marriage is terrible now? Wait until she hears how much more you liked to fuck me than her. I'm going to tell her in person so she can see your baby inside me. You think she'll let you visit your children after she leaves you? What about when they find out that you've been fucking around on Mommy?"

His gut lurched as fear knotted his viscera. "You don't mean it."

"I mean every fucking word. I'll take everything from you. You will be nothing."

The life she promised him was real for him in the same way that dream thoughts immediately manifested themselves in the logic of sleep. Sitting alone in some shitty office *(Harris's office.)* waiting for the phone to ring *(But who calls a solo tax lawyer to advise an international merger?)*, eating dinner alone at his desk because home is a one-bedroom apartment *(No, a studio.)* in Queens, when the phone rings and for a moment he's excited because maybe it's a client, but no, it's his divorce lawyer telling him that the judge has ruled that he only gets supervised visits with Brennan and Hunter and not joint custody because he can't provide a bedroom for them. But that life would come only following the shame of carrying his belongings out of his office as the secretaries gawked; the same routine in his building, doorman watching him carry two suitcases of clothes—packed while the kids visit Jane's parents—to the curb to hail a cab to stay in some shit hotel.

"I'll kill you." His voice was as quiet as when his lips were next to her ear, gasping for air, telling her that he only wanted to be inside her, that she was beautiful and perfect.

"What did you say? Fucking try it!"

She rushed at him again, both hands flailing at his head. He brought his hands up over his face like a boxer as she slapped and punched, most of the blows glancing off his hunched shoulders or landing on the sides of his arms.

"Do it, you fucking coward! I want you to!"

Her wild roundhouses exposed her face, throat, solar plexus, every vulnerable part of her. He could have her by the neck, squeeze, lever her down to the couch, pin her, knees on her chest, constrict until she lost consciousness, hold her until she lay still, until the blood stopped pumping to her brain, until no air passed to her lungs. Or he could punch her in the jaw, the belly, beat her until she lay too dazed to resist while he walked to the sink to find the kitchen knife that always lay in it (Jess told him once that Cathy used it to slice an orange each day) and return to her, turn her away from him so that when he drew it across her throat her blood would spray mostly away from him.

He was out of his body. It wouldn't even be him doing it. He would watch his body move—a boulder pushed down a slope. He shoved it, but the boulder was immovable. He dropped his hands—maybe if she got a good slap in, it would impel him to do what needed to be done. He took a right slap and a left from Jess. His arms twitched up for her throat, hands open. Jess faded backward, but not fast enough. His fingers came close enough to her throat for him to sense her pulse pounding through her carotids before they stopped and recoiled. His hands closed on nothing but air, and he brought his face forward, burying it in his closed fists, and screamed.

He shoved past her, turned at the door, and said, "No one will ever love you."

He could have been talking to himself.

John walked west until he reached Central Park. The verdant smell of trees and grass and soil invited him in, but it would be a mistake to walk across the park this far north at night. He was the coward she accused him of being. He wasn't brave enough to face the test with Jess or the ruin she promised. He was enough of a monster to betray his wife and children, but not enough of one to hit Jess—much less murder her. He lacked the resolve to complete their mutual destruction.

He turned south, down Fifth Avenue, the dark park to his right. He knew that he should get in front of the situation—go home and tell Jane about the affair, then go into the office in the morning and resign. Or maybe there was a path at the firm, if he could get a few key allies—Walt, for one—that would enable him to weather whatever Jess intended. He wasn't the first partner to sleep with an associate. Maybe they'd treat him as an equal for once and shrug at Jess, quietly counsel her to some other job elsewhere, and give him a stern lecture for form's sake and pat his back later at cocktails.

He reached Ninety-Seventh Street, where east-to-west traffic entered the park, sweating in the cool, muggy air. A few cabs passed, heading south on Fifth or west on Ninety-Seventh, but he didn't hail any. Jess had been emotional, scared. Maybe she wouldn't follow through on her threats if he was brave enough to return. What if he went home and confessed to Jane, and Jess turned out not to be pregnant? He turned back east, but second-guessed himself before he crossed the avenue. What if they argued again? What if she was pregnant? What if she wouldn't get an abortion? What if she demanded he leave his family? Had enough time passed for Jess to calm down—or had she grown more anxious since he left (he glanced at his watch) thirty minutes ago?

He reached Cathy's block fifteen minutes later, still damp with sweat and praying for a breeze. The street was still devoid of pedestrians. He hesitated before climbing the stoop to the building—so much had gone wrong, how could he possibly make it right? He considered ringing the buzzer to Cathy's apartment, but Jess didn't know he was going to return. Better to knock gently and say, "I'm sorry," through the door so that she could hear that he didn't want to fight. He shouldered the broken vestibule door open and mounted the stairs slowly, resolving with each step to remain calm, to do whatever needed to be done to placate Jess.

He stopped to listen at the door to Cathy's apartment but didn't hear anything from within. John knocked gently. The door moved in the frame slightly on the first knock and swung ajar on the second knock. A sliver of light escaped between the door and the jamb. The latch hadn't caught, which was odd because he had slammed it behind him when he left. Maybe Jess left and forgot to lock it behind her.

"Jess?" John barely heard his voice in the silent hall.

He pressed on the door with his knuckles. At first, John wondered if Jess had rampaged through her friend's apartment before leaving. The couch, typically perpendicular to the door, canted nearly parallel to it, exposing its back. The side-table lamp lay overturned, casting a parabolic light across the floor. The phone that used to sit next to it was missing. The chairs from the dinette were askew—one lay on its side. John stepped over the threshold.

He saw, past the top of the couch as he approached it, Jess's hand on the floor, palm down. John froze.

"Jess?"

No movement. John crept forward, forcing himself to take deep breaths, revealing more of Jess's body on the floor. She lay front down, head turned to her right as if searching for something underneath the couch, but her eyes were closed. Her right arm curled underneath her. Fresh abrasions marked her face, and now that he was closer, he saw that her cheek was swollen slightly. Bruises darkened her neck. Blood pooled underneath her from an unseen wound, dark against the worn carpet.

John stared at her back, looking for movement, but none came. Even if she weren't breathing, her heart might still be beating, carrying ever-lower levels of oxygen to her brain, pumping her blood onto the floor. He should try to staunch the wound. Even if her heart wasn't beating, he could perform CPR, blow air from his lungs into hers, compress her chest to move her blood through her body, mimic the functions of life long enough until help arrived. But what about the bleeding?

And how could he explain that he was there, that he hadn't hurt her, that he was merely trying to help? What if he left marks on her body or got blood on his shoes, and they blamed him for what had happened to her? It was his fault. He'd left her. As it was, nobody knew he was there or that he had even been there. If he left, nobody would ever discover he'd been in the room.

Check her pulse, he told himself. To what end, though? He would be leaving more evidence if he touched her. He'd be contaminating the crime scene. But if she'd survived to this point, if she were still breathing, she might live. If she was already dead, there was nothing more to be done. But each second he waffled, waiting for her chest to heave for air, increased the risk that Cathy would walk through the door or pass him on the way out and decreased the chances—if any—that she could be saved if he tried to help her.

Did he even want to save her?

If he didn't check her pulse, he wouldn't have to know whether he'd simply left a body or left her to die. Leaving her now, could he live with it?

He took a step to move around the couch, then froze. Someone clomped up the stairs. John fixed his eyes on the door as the footsteps reached the landing and approached. He could shout for help but couldn't find a sound louder than a whimper—like when he used to wake as a child with night terrors, sitting upright in his bed, mouth agape, silently screaming. He waited for the door to the apartment to open, but the unseen walker stomped past. The sound of ascending thuds carried from the hall as the person climbed to the third floor, then moved overhead as they curled to the next flight, and on and on again, until the stairwell was finally quiet.

She must be dead, John told himself. *You don't know*, immediately following. Better to not know than be blamed for her murder (or assault, she might be alive). He reached for the doorknob before stopping himself from touching it. There might be fingerprints on it (the killer's or his own). He used part of his jacket to grasp the knob as lightly as possible between his fingertips to turn it. He left the door open and prayed someone might pass who would help her (no, she was dead, he had to believe that, or he couldn't leave).

John hurried down the stairs to the street, using his jacket again on the inner and outer doors. He walked back across Central Park, head down, hoping no one would mark him, saying to himself, *You couldn't save her*. The words were never a comfort, only an accusation.

FORTY-THREE

Now

"DO YOU BELIEVE HER?" BRENNAN ASKED. THE BRIEFCASE rested on the coffee table between them. Brennan slouched in one of the wingback chairs now that Nicki had left.

Hunter shrugged. "She wasn't lying. Did he lie to her?"

"About fighting with Jessica? About wanting to kill her?"

Brennan buried her face in her hands. Her shoulders shook. Jessica waited for her father. To get there, to be there for her. She'd just needed him to help her. To love her.

Hunter came around the coffee table and knelt on the floor beside her. Brennan picked her head up.

"Why did she stay after he left?" she asked.

"I don't know."

Brennan knew. Jessica thought he'd come back. Brennan imagined her, watching the door, hoping he'd calm down once he had a moment outside the apartment, waiting for him to return, to make things right.

Hunter took her hand, but she couldn't look at his face. It was too much like her father's. "Bren, he didn't . . . it wasn't him."

He was right. Someone else had knocked on the door. Brennan

could see it—Jessica jumping up, elated he'd returned. Would it have felt any different for her if her father knocked on the door at that moment? Jessica opened the door, but it hadn't been her father.

Brennan knew she almost had it figured out, who it had been on the other side of the door, but she couldn't get past the defeat Jessica would have felt that her father hadn't come back.

How long had it taken, before she'd been stabbed? Had Jessica looked back to the door, hoping her father would walk in and save her? In the photos, her head was turned toward the couch, but it hadn't been the couch she'd been facing. Jessica would have been able to see the bottom of the door through the space beneath the couch. How long had she been able to see, waiting for the door to open, for her father to come back and save her?

"He left her there. Waiting."

"He came back."

Brennan shook her head. "He may as well have killed her."

Hunter said, "Based on the pathologist's report, Bren, she was already dead. Even if she wasn't, he couldn't have saved her anyway."

"Does it make a difference?" She finally faced Hunter. All of that waiting. For nothing. He was never coming back. "He didn't even try! You were right!"

"No," Hunter said. "We were both wrong."

FORTY-FOUR

Then

JOHN ARRIVED AT FRONTIER BEFORE ANY OF THE OTHER servers. Ed unlocked the door to let him in.

"You're going to have Section A," Ed said. "It's tables one through eight, over there. Oh, and your briefcase is still behind the bar."

"Sorry about that. I'll take it home tonight."

"No problem. You can start setting the room."

John set half the tables before Nicki arrived. They nodded at each other as she passed through on her way to the stairwell to the basement. John followed her down to the storage room where the staff hung their coats. She turned, apron and order book in one hand, as he opened the door.

"Hey," he said. "Do you know where I can find more napkins?"

Nicki pointed at a shelf opposite the coat hooks. John picked up a stack of cloth napkins, still bundled in nylon twine from the laundry, and walked to the door.

"You know," Nicki said, tying a waitress's apron around her hips, "the busboys will bring those up if you ask."

"I just wanted to say thank you for taking me out last night."

"Don't mention it. Seriously. We don't have to discuss it again."

It looked like Nicki wanted to say more, but before she could, John nodded and left. While he was setting the rest of the room, a young man with slicked-back black hair and a tailored suit opened the front door with his own set of keys and joined Ed and his ledgers at the bar. After a few minutes, Ed called John over.

"John, this is Claude. He and his dad own the place."

John shook Claude's hand, ignoring the mat of hair that covered the backs of his fingers and hand. Thick, heavy eyebrows perched above arrogant eyes.

"This is your second night?"

"Yes, my second night. I trailed last night."

"Your English is very good." Claude's French accent was out of a movie. Maybe something like the Vichy collaborator police chief's voice.

"I'm an American."

Claude turned to Ed. "Are you sure he's right for waiter? Maybe he's better in the kitchen?"

"He hustles. He's a good waiter."

"Of course, the Orientals all work hard. But is he rude like a Chinatown waiter?"

"I'm very polite," John said. Ed flicked him a glance as subtle as screaming *shut the fuck up* at him.

Claude regarded him for a moment, then said, "We will see. Carry on."

John returned to setting up the room for service, meticulously checking the table settings and double-checking that the server's station was properly stocked, all to ensure that he wouldn't be caught standing still. Ed and Claude remained at the bar, Claude drinking a glass of red wine. After they opened, tables filled quickly. John's section was half full within thirty minutes.

John was in the kitchen, placing loaves of bread in the warmer, when Nicki entered to drop an order ticket. She reached into the warmer for a loaf to slice.

"You okay?" she asked.

"I met Claude."

"Oh." She glanced around, then spoke quietly, "He's a dick. Whatever he did, don't let it get to you. He likes to give the staff a hard time."

When John returned to the dining room, Ed sat a couple in his section, near the window. The man's back was turned to John, but based on the graying hair and posture, John guessed he was at least two decades older than the woman—a young brunette in glasses. She looked vaguely familiar. The man picked up his menu with one hand and reached across to hold the woman's hand with the other.

John poured two glasses of water and brought them to the table. As he approached, the woman's eyes fixed on him, trying to place him, then widened in recognition as he reached the table. It wasn't until he set the first glass down that he caught a glimpse of the man's face looking up from the menu.

"John?"

John nearly dropped the second glass of water.

"Geoff." John placed the second glass of water on the table and resisted the urge to cover the waiter's apron tied around his hips.

"You . . . you work here?" Geoff turned to his companion. "Do you know who this is, Susan?"

"Yes. He was still at the firm when I was a summer associate."

Geoff looked back to John.

"John, are you our waiter?" Geoff asked again. The corners of his thin-lipped mouth quivered as he tried to restrain his mirth.

John's face bruised with humiliation. "Yes."

Geoff shook his head. "Jesus Christ, John. This is what you're doing now? I don't understand how you can show your face in public."

"We were partners, Geoff. You're no better than me."

"And yet, you'll be carrying my used plates from this table."

John turned to Susan, whose wide eyes flitted between the two men, and said, "You know, Susan, it was dinners like this that landed me here."

Geoff grabbed John's wrist. "Don't speak to her."

John kept his arm still. "Let go of me, Geoff."

Geoff dropped his hand, stood, and looked around the room. He saw Claude at the bar.

"Claude!" Geoff marched to the bar. John followed, weaving through tables, taking note that one table needed more bread and another a refill of their wine as he passed, even though he doubted he'd be in a position to bring them once Geoff spoke to Claude.

When Geoff reached Claude, he turned and pointed at John. "Do you know who he is?"

Several diners looked up from their tables. Their eyes followed Geoff's pointing finger to John. Claude's eyes narrowed at John like he was reading distant text, then he turned to Ed. Ed's face revealed nothing. Across the room, Nicki stopped walking to the kitchen to watch.

"He killed a woman. He was tried for murder."

John reached the bar. "I was acquitted."

"Is this the kind of person you hire?" Geoff's voice carried. Nearly every patron in the restaurant gawked at them. The clatter of plates in the kitchen became suddenly audible as all conversation ceased.

"Geoff," Claude said, nervously glancing around the room, "we did not know. It is only his second day."

Ed said nothing. John didn't blame him.

Claude turned his head to John. "Go."

"My coat is downstairs," John said. He left them standing at the bar to get his coat. He left the waiter's apron hanging on the hook in its place. When he crested the stairs back into the dining room, the hum of renewed conversations dropped, and heads turned to track him to the door. Ed stood with Nicki at the bar. He nodded at them as he passed. Claude stood at the table pouring wine for Geoff and Susan. Their eyes followed him across the room with most of the other customers.

On the street, wet, heavy snowflakes fell fast from a pigeon-gray sky. Halfway to the corner, Nicki called out for him.

"John! Your briefcase!"

He turned. She was in front of the restaurant, holding his briefcase out for him, squinting against the snow landing on her face.

"Keep it," John said. "I don't need it anymore."

FORTY-FIVE

Then

WHEN JOHN CAME UP FROM THE SUBWAY, THE SNOWFALL filled the air. It alighted on his coat in momentary puffs of white before it melted. It didn't stick on the ground either—it had been too warm the past few days. At best, the snow would survive as a charcoal slurry of slush, soot, dirt, and whatever particulates the flakes pulled from the air on their way to the street to be trampled by too many people and too much traffic. Only a couple of hours upstate, they projected two or more feet of accumulation, but some atmospheric effect blunted the storm's impact on Manhattan.

Wet grime covered his shoes by the time he reached his building. Snowmelt pasted his hair flat. The doorman, Calvin, stood underneath the awning by the door and ignored John as he entered the building. On the elevator to his floor, John wondered if he could get a job as a doorman. How long before people figured out who he was? *Good morning, Ms. Smith*, he would say. *Is it true?* Ms. Smith would ask. And that would be the end.

When John reached his apartment, he stopped, keys in hand. The kids' laughter pealed through the door, followed by Jane screaming, "I'm going to tickle you!" John touched the door lightly with his fingertips, like the apartment were a helium balloon that might float away. The laughter resonated through the door, buzzing through to his fingers. John was warm and light all at once, weightless as if he were in a hot bath. It was different from this side of the door. If he could burrow into the walls like a rodent, maybe he could live next to their light without dampening it, maybe it would be a way to carry on, stealing from their warmth and laughter, coming out at night to scavenge the crumbs of joy they left littered in the corners.

They were cavorting so loudly that they didn't hear him use his keys to unlatch the locks or open the door. Unadulterated by the plaster of the walls or the wood of the door, their laughter broke over him like a storm wave, an unstoppable mass shoving him off his feet, filling his eyes and lungs such that he couldn't see or breathe or find his feet to stand. None of this joy was his, and all of it was in spite of him. They couldn't see him standing in the small entrance hall from the living room. If he backed out of the doorway, retreated to the elevator, and never returned, the three of them could go on laughing like that forever.

But he stepped through, and an unthinking flick of his hand swung the door easily closed behind him. Jane and the kids looked up as he walked into the living room, laughter immediately dead on their lips. She was sprawled on the couch, Hunter and Brennan piled on top of her. John stopped for a moment. Jane put a hand on each of the children's shoulders.

"Daddy," Brennan said, pushing her hair out of her face, "we thought you were working."

"I was fired."

John left them there and walked through the room to his office, shutting the door behind him. He sat in his chair, coat still on. His desk was bare, except for the old brown leather blotter. He knew the surface of it better than the topography of his own hands, worn to a hard sheen in the center, scored with the ghosts of indentations from his writing, the edge stitching frayed on the border closest to him, and utterly purposeless. The desk, too. There was no job he would ever hold that would require him to have a blotter, desk, chair, or office.

Still, he stared at the blotter, reading the shallow trenches of old pen marks like a shaman casting bones, but there was no augury in them.

Jane entered the office, closing the door behind her, and then leaned against it—not unlike Jess that last time he'd seen her in Cathy's apartment. Whatever resolve she had when she slipped through the door softened as she regarded him like a sculpture. He saw himself through her eyes—wet with snow, disheveled hair, slouched down in his chair. Their eyes met, and he tried to articulate to her with his, *I'm sorry*. If she only understood that he couldn't put his remorse into words that might take days to recite and still not capture all of the things he didn't understand and didn't know but felt woven into every cell. Even if she understood the depth of his regret through some divine empathy, how did that heal her own pain, sadness, or anger, or assuage the hidden guilt she carried that she had failed him?

He couldn't make her happy, and not only that, his presence chained her to the burning wreck of their marriage. Their promises to each other, duties to their children, condemned them to sorrow—whether he found another job or not. He searched her eyes for some other truth, but there was none. His eyes began to burn as tears rose in them, so he looked away and saw the answer in the snow driving against the window.

Be brave, he told himself.

He turned back to Jane, resolved.

"I'm sorry," he said. "I just want you to be happy."

Jane shook her head. He'd said the wrong thing—if there was even a right thing to say. Maybe he should have said nothing—they could have stared at each other for a while longer.

"I should go," he said. "This isn't working."

"I'm not asking you to." She wasn't asking him to stay either.

"But it's what we need to do."

Jane wiped the back of her hand across her eyes. They were both good at avoiding tears.

"What are we going to tell the kids?" she asked.

"You'll figure out something later. For now, tell them I went to look for work."

"You're leaving now?"

"I don't think I should wait. I still have my coat on."

"Where will you go?"

"I'll figure something out. I may take the car."

She looked unsure. John needed to get moving. As he approached the door, Jane stood aside so he could open it. When he reached her, he paused briefly, then reached out and squeezed her hand. It was like he remembered. He imagined that she squeezed back before he let go.

Brennan and Hunter looked up when he came out of the office. They lay on the floor reading. John tried to smile at them and hoped it was convincing.

"I have to go out," he said.

"Okay," Hunter said.

John walked over and scooped him up into a hug. Hunter squirmed as John whispered to him, "I love you."

After John put him down, Hunter stomped to the couch and threw himself onto it to continue reading. John turned to Brennan. He knelt and kissed her on her forehead. She threw her arms around him. He pressed his cheek into her hair and said, "I love you, darling."

"I love you, too, Daddy."

"I'll see you again."

He turned to leave, Brennan already sinking to the floor to continue her book. The door to the office was still open, but Jane hadn't followed him out. She stood just inside, back to the living room, waiting for him to leave.

Silence shrouded the apartment as John pulled the door shut behind him.

FORTY-SIX

Then

THE SNOW WHIPPED PAST THE CAR WINDOW LIKE TELEVIsion static. It fell so fast that the highway was covered with an inch of filthy slush despite the traffic. Cars crept along as eighteen-wheelers blew past without regard. His car handled well in the snow, despite the slush. In front of John, the Thruway stretched away into the dark static while the frosted landscape blurred past at the edge of his headlights. In the distance, separated from the highway by a field and hazy snow, trees reached like black lighting from the ground to the sky.

Trees were critical to his plan. He didn't want to be in sight of the highway. A drift underneath some trees could hide a body for a long period. It would be quiet, restful maybe. The trees closed in on the road as the mountains swelled and receded around him. Not the peaks of the Rockies, but the Adirondacks or Catskills or whatever would have to serve. A low-gas warning lit on his dashboard. He drove another five miles, swerving once to avoid a compact that a passing truck nearly blew off the road.

The trees hugged the highway now. The snow still fell in light, airy flakes. The weather reports on the radio said that the snow would fall overnight and into the next day. Temperatures were not expected to rise above freezing for at least another week.

He figured that he had gone as far as he could go and pulled over, deep into the shoulder. Getting hit by a passing truck would be effective, but he didn't want to hang that guilt on some poor driver. He turned the car off, took a deep breath, and waited. With the weather and the darkness, the few cars on the highway in either direction drifted past in cones of spectral white light.

The snow and cold would preserve his body until it melted. He figured it would be in decent shape when discovered, but what did he know? The idea that it would freeze was oddly comforting to him. Imagining it as a piece of frozen steak helped him disassociate from it. When it was discovered, it probably wouldn't be badly decomposed, if at all. He might be recognizable. Finally, lying down in the snow felt more appropriate than abandoning himself to some river or leaving a bloody mess somewhere. Like he'd left Jessica.

He'd avoided thinking about that night the best he could, like a rancid smell he could ignore, but it hung on him, reasserting itself whenever a whiff of fresh air passed through. He'd never be free of it. It would cling to his family, too, if he didn't leave with it. Even though he knew, based on the autopsy, that she must have been dead when he returned to the apartment, that she couldn't have been saved even if he'd been standing there when she was stabbed, she wouldn't have been there but for him. He could have stopped their fall any number of times before that night, but he wanted it. Only she had hit the ground. He couldn't make up for that, but he could make it even.

He took a final look around. A pair of lights floated toward him, but they wouldn't see him this far over on the other side of the highway. He grabbed the bottle of scotch he'd purchased before leaving Manhattan from the passenger seat. The cold washed over him as he got out. The snow was five inches deep on the shoulder, cresting over the lip of his shoe and touching the cuff of his pants. He needed to commit before he could reconsider. He walked away from the road, peeling the wrapping from the top of the bottle as he went.

The snow was deeper in the trees. He hadn't anticipated that, but there had been snow the prior week. It melted on the road, but not here. With each step, he crunched through a crust of old snow beneath airy, fresh powder. He pulled the top from the bottle, enjoying the feel of the cork sliding free of the glass neck. He took a few quick sips from the bottle—enough to acclimate his throat to the burn and prepare it for the swigs he planned to take as he worked his way deeper into the trees.

He drank a quarter of the bottle before the melting snow soaked his socks and feet. He shivered but didn't feel too cold. When his resolve faltered, he told himself that it was fate. If he was meant to continue fighting, he'd see the lights of a house or stumble across a road as a car passed. If not, then he was simply completing the choice he'd made in his office standing at his window with Jessica.

Snow drifted down through the windless air. His breath blasted out two to three feet in front of him, strikingly visible. Snowflakes landed upon the icy rind on his jacket without melting. They crusted on his hair. He climbed a rise but could no longer see or hear the highway below and behind him through the trees. He stood for a moment, catching his breath and taking heavier pulls from the bottle.

Maybe Jane and the kids would find the letters he'd hidden. Three days ago, the thought would have terrified him. He'd considered burning them all over the past year, but instead kept adding pages. *More fuel*, he told himself. More of himself to turn into flame and ash when the time was right. Standing in the trees, though, shaking in the snow, he was relieved he'd left them. The truest parts of himself remained on those pages.

The world around him was naked and clean. The snow fell to his lips, and he loved the taste of it. Only the white noise of the flakes coming to rest in the woods reached his ears. He no longer shivered, but his feet were numb, and his fingers hurt. The slightest breeze touched the trees above him, shaking loose the accumulated snow, which fell to the earth with hollow thuds. He laughed but stopped immediately. The sound of his voice in the woods was unnerving.

A few minutes later, he crested the small rise, coming over into the wind. It blasted him as he came over a slight fold, tearing at his chapped skin. He considered returning to the pacific side of the ridge, but there was no going back, only forward. He swayed, slightly nauseated; the snow hurling past his face gave the impression of motion. He needed to finish the bottle to be sure, but he didn't want it anywhere near him when he stopped. He drank the final quarter of the bottle in one long pull, telling himself he could move out of the wind once he finished. He threw the bottle to one side. It clinked off a tree and impacted the ground with a hollow *whumpf* somewhere in the darkness.

Throwing the bottle pulled him to the side, and his legs shook as he regained his balance. He wouldn't make it much farther.

He started down the far side of the ridge. On this side, his legs plunged into the snow nearly up to his knees as he walked. The time between his steps stretched as it took greater effort to focus through the haze of scotch, fatigue, and numbness. He didn't know if he was ten feet or eighty yards from the top—he'd lost track of how many steps he'd taken.

He took two steps forward before stumbling on numb legs and sprawling forward into a deep drift. He'd fallen off a small hump hidden by the snow collecting against it, pooling, rising. When he regained his footing, he stood waist-deep in the drift. This was the place, and even if it wasn't, he couldn't go any farther.

He dug at the snow underneath him to make a comfortable space in the drift.

He'd imagined that, walking into the woods, he'd be at peace knowing that he'd freed his family from the specter of the man he'd become. But, as he reclined against the rise behind him, it felt like they were dying and that he would live forever with the grief he carried.

The small hollow brought him out of the wind, but it soon pushed snow up and over him. He lay for a long time, staring up at the trees and branches covered with snow and ice, fracturing the dark sky above him, his sorrow fading as he fought to cling to fleeting thoughts of Jane (her eyes, at their wedding, sharing all their secrets for once), Brennan (the squeak of her tiny voice trying to wake him in the morning), and Hunter (an infant, napping on his chest, tiny breaths fluttering across his neck).

FORTY-SEVEN

Now

HUNTER KNOCKED AND POKED HIS HEAD INTO BRENNAN'S apartment. After speaking to Nicki, they'd taken a cab back across town. He'd gone home to shower and change, but not before Brennan had handed him a key to her place.

"Bren?"

"In my office," she called.

He found her at her desk, laptop open, rearranging the scans of the vouchers from Harris's files, making notes on a pad next to her laptop. She was still in the black dress from their mother's funeral.

"I thought we were going to scan Dad's letters," he said.

"I just need to finish putting these back in order. We never did. Almost done."

"Did you open the briefcase yet?"

She shook her head. It was on the floor next to the desk. Hunter picked it up and sat in a chair next to window and popped the latches. The hinges were stiff, but they opened smoothly. The briefcase was mostly empty. Copies of his father's résumé, on paper slightly thicker than the stock he used to write the letters hidden in his desk, poked out of a pocket. Hunter ran his hands through the other pockets. They were empty except for one. He knew that they were photos before he pulled them out. One was of him and Brennan as kids, nearly babies, sitting back-to-back; the other was a black-and-white print of his mother—the kinds of photos his father may have kept on his desk at the firm, although Hunter didn't remember.

The last photo was a four-by-six snapshot. Judging from the background, it was a holiday party. His father, dressed in black tie, stood on one side of Jessica, who wore a red gown. Walter stood to her other side, thirty years younger, but already balding.

"Done," Brennan said, turning around from the desk. Hunter put the photos aside. Brennan pulled the drawer from underneath the desk. "Should we get started? We'll go in order, oldest to newest."

They set up Hunter's laptop and scanner on the desk in front of Brennan, and Hunter took the stack of letters and flipped them over so he would pull the oldest letters off the top. He left Brennan's childhood drawing in the drawer. He read each before passing them to Brennan, who read and scanned them before replacing them in the drawer.

The penmanship was neat, but the letters were difficult reading. Neither of them could fully process what they revealed about their father—that might take years. But reading them as a collection traced a period of his life from his affair through his death and confirmed Nicki's story about what their father had told her and more. They didn't speak as they read, but Hunter admitted to himself that he was relieved that Brennan was there to read with him.

"Who do you think he was writing these to?" Hunter asked when they took a quick break to eat some delivery.

Brennan shrugged. "Some read to me like they were definitely for Jess, some for Mom. But most I couldn't tell."

"Do you think she would have wanted to see them?"

"Mom?"

"I guess either of them."

"I don't know."

When they finished reading and scanning, they slid the drawer of letters back into the desk.

"Fuck, man," Hunter said. "That was rough."

"Yeah." Brennan reached over and squeezed his arm. "I'm glad you were here."

Before he could say anything in return, she stood up and stretched. "So what did we learn?"

Hunter, relieved at the change in direction, took her place at the desk and flipped through the scans of the letters before coming to one, probably written a few weeks before Jess's murder.

"This one," he said. "It talks about the first time he slept with Jessica. At the firm holiday party. Look at this photo."

He handed her the photo from the briefcase.

"Huh," Brennan said. "You have that recording from when we spoke to Cathy?"

Hunter pulled the file up, and they listened to the recording as they brewed coffee. Brennan was stirring sweetener and cream into her coffee when she shouted, "That's it!"

Hunter paused the replay. He'd zoned out for a moment. "What?"

"When we asked her when the affair started, she said Labor Day."

They listened again, then let the recording run further through when Cathy told them that the affair picked up again after Christmas.

"You rearranged the vouchers, right?" Hunter asked.

"A year of them. I bookmarked Jess's and Dad's."

"When were the earliest ones where they start going to the same place at the same time?"

Brennan and Hunter walked back to Brennan's office, and she checked her notes. "January, which is what Detective Bauman said at trial. I checked and didn't see anything different."

"So Jess slept with someone else before Dad?"

"Sounds like it."

"Didn't McCann tell us Walter told him about Jess and Dad? And the vouchers?" Hunter sat down and pulled up the notes he took after they spoke to McCann. "You remember that, right?"

"Yeah."

"He would have been her boss, right?"

"Yeah."

They looked at the photo of their father, Jess, and Walter laying on the desk.

Brennan said, "Pull up the vouchers."

She replaced Hunter at the desk and began flipping through the vouchers.

"Nothing from Jess from around Labor Day that year."

"What about Walter?"

"Hmmm. That Friday. He submitted it, but he didn't get picked up at the firm."

Brennan pointed at the screen. Hunter leaned over her shoulder to look at the address scrawled on the voucher. It was Cathy's building.

Brennan scrolled forward in time. "And look at this. Late January. A voucher from Jess. Then Dad. Then either the next voucher or the one after that, Walter. Again, here. Again here. Another one. But look. Half the time, he's just signing out the voucher, but not turning them back in."

"What does that mean?"

"He went down to get a voucher to see where they were going. But then he didn't use his voucher. Maybe because he knew they could be tracked."

She came to the last one in the pattern. The night Jessica was murdered.

#

Brennan and Hunter waited in the same conference room as the first time they met Walter. Hunter sat in a chair, while Brennan again stood at the window, this time in the indigo suit she used for closing arguments. It was the same color she remembered her father wearing. Beyond the window of the conference room, the setting sun shone through fractured clouds, bathing Manhattan in an angry red.

Walter opened the door and stopped at the head of the table, looking between the two. His cheeks sagged with extra weight, erasing his jawline and highlighting his pockmarked skin. It looked like he had two pieces of dough hanging from his face.

"I'm sorry," he said. "I heard about your mother. I couldn't make it to the funeral. I was out of town for work."

"I understand," Brennan said. "Some things can't be helped."

As Brennan moved around the table to sit next to her brother, Brennan said, "Do you mind grabbing us some water?"

Walter picked up three bottles from the sideboard next to the door and brought them to the table. Brennan glanced at her brother before taking hers by the cap and placing it in front of her. Hunter left his where Walter had placed it.

After he took a pull from his bottle, Walter said, "So, what's up?"

"Well, you know we were talking with folks who knew our dad," Brennan started, "and when our mom died, we were going through her things and thought you might want to see some of the stuff we found."

Brennan gave Hunter a nod. He pulled John's briefcase out from under the table and unlatched it. He swung it open and shuffled through some items before extracting a photo in a stiff plastic sleeve. He left the briefcase open on the table.

"We found a photo of you and our dad in our mother's things," Hunter said. He passed it over to Walter, who took it between his thumb and forefinger. In the photo, John and Walter leaned against John's desk, cocktails in the hands they didn't have around the other's shoulders.

"I remember this party. It was at your place. We were still associates," Walter said. "I think you, Hunter, were still a baby."

He held the photo up so he could see Hunter's face alongside John's.

"Amazing," he said. "You look exactly like him."

"Thanks," Hunter said. "We found this one, too. Tucked into his briefcase."

He slid the photo of the holiday party across the table. Walter looked down at it for a long time. John and him, with Jessica between them.

"I remember this, too," he said. "A firm Christmas party."

"That's Jessica DeSalvo?" Brennan asked.

"Yes."

"You were close with her?"

"I worked with her a lot. I was grooming her. For partnership. She was a good litigator."

"The first time we met, you told us you didn't know they were having an affair. My dad didn't tell you?"

Walter didn't lift his eyes from the photo. "Like I told you, I didn't know. And I don't know how or why things started between her and your dad. But I can understand why he did it. She was . . . something special. A beautiful lady and so brilliant. It would have been hard to resist her. I don't blame him for . . . succumbing to her, any of that stuff."

Hunter gestured for Walter to hand the photos back. Walter passed them back to Hunter, who took them by the edge, careful not to touch the spots where Walter had placed his fingers, and dropped them into a sealable plastic bag that Brennan produced from the briefcase. She sealed the bag. Walter cocked his head, confused.

"We also found some of my dad's old letters recently," Brennan said. "You told him that you knew about the affair."

"And this one," Hunter took a page from the briefcase and slid it across the table to Walter, "it talks about the first time he and Jessica slept together. The firm holiday party."

Walter scanned the letter.

"I don't get what this is about. What are you saying?" His eyes narrowed. "Your father killed her."

Hunter pulled a second plastic bag from the briefcase, and as

Brennan took her water bottle, again by the cap, to drop it into the bag, she said to Walter, "We'll come back to that. You used the vouchers to follow them, right?"

Walter gave a superior snort. "I don't know what this"—he gestured at the table and the evidence the siblings were collecting—"is all about, but I do know that I don't have to answer your questions."

They deposited Hunter's water bottle into a third plastic bag. The first two bags were already in her purse. Brennan left the last bag, bottle inside, on the table, then looked up and stared hard at Walter. He gripped the arms of the chair like it was about to fall through the floor.

"Nervous, Walter?"

He relaxed his hands. "About you two kids? No."

"Okay, you're not scared, so let's keep talking. You knew about the vouchers, right? You told the cops about them."

"The ones they used at the trial? No."

"Don't lie to me, Walter. The cops told us you did."

"The cops?" Genuine surprise undermined his attempt at bluster.

"The letter you're holding, it presents a timing issue. Did you know that Jessica told her friend that she slept with her 'boss' over Labor Day weekend? That's before Christmas. The vouchers, too. The earliest matching vouchers for our dad were from January."

Brennan crossed her arms, leaned back, and cocked her head as if she were working through a problem. "So who was Jessica's 'boss'? Jessica was a litigator, and my dad was a tax lawyer. She wouldn't have worked directly for him. Feels off that she'd call him her 'boss' as opposed to only 'a partner.' On the other hand, you supervised her directly, didn't you?"

"Is that what this is about? You think I slept with her?" Walter crumpled the paper. "I know we don't say these kinds of things anymore, but Jess was a slut. She probably fucked half the office before she even got to your dad."

Brennan remained calm as she kept the pressure on Walter. "You were in my dad's office the night she was killed. When Jess called him to come to Cathy's apartment. We know that, too."

"Yeah. So what?"

"Why didn't you tell the cops that? They didn't know what time he left until they checked the vouchers."

"Why would I mention it? We were friends. I was in his office a lot. That's how I knew they were having an affair."

"You, too, right? You slept with her?"

"No. Never."

Hunter reached into the briefcase and shoved another piece of paper across the table.

When Walter didn't move to take it, Brennan said, "Pick it up. You'll want to see it."

Walter dragged the page until it was in front of him.

"It's a voucher," she said. "From the Friday of Labor Day weekend. A car picked you up from her friend Cathy's place."

Walter gave a hard laugh, almost a bark. "Yeah, we fucked once. But Brennan, I don't know what else you got in that briefcase, but this circumstantial shit doesn't prove anything. You kids are angry. I don't know, maybe it's the grief, but it's beneath you to pull this shit."

Brennan ignored him and resumed her questioning in a voice honed to a dispassionate sharpness—a blade that would slice stone. She nodded at the voucher. "Did you forget that you submitted this when you tipped the cops to the vouchers? Or was that an oversight because you were so desperate to frame our father?"

Walter shook his head.

"It ate at you, didn't it?"

"I think we're done here." Walter rose.

"Are we?" Brennan asked. "Don't you want to know what else we have here? I think we can put you in Cathy's apartment that night, so . . ." Brennan shrugged. "Why not hear me out?"

Walter sat back down. His eyes fixed on the briefcase.

"It must've hurt," Brennan continued, as softly as a priest in a confessional. "To know that Jess chose him over you. This amazing, beautiful, talented woman who you were setting up to become partner. Maybe you were in love. Maybe you would've left your wife for her. You knew her marriage was on the rocks. You could've taken care of her, but instead she picked somebody like our dad."

"Yeah, I loved her. And it pissed me off, but it doesn't mean I killed her. If that's what you're getting at."

"You knew how to use the vouchers to find out where he was going that night when he left the office."

Walter shook his head and glared at them. Brennan and Hunter waited for him to say something.

"You followed him, didn't you? You were the next voucher that night after my dad, but you didn't use it. Just filled it out to see where he was going. Then you took a cab up?"

"Okay, we're done here." Walter strode to the door and paused. He turned to face them. "I'm sorry for your loss. I really am. Your mother was a class act. But you two need a different hobby. Coming in here, dragging up an old affair, and accusing me of murder? Get the fuck out of out of my office!"

"We deserve to know what happened," Hunter said.

Walter placed his hand on the door handle. "We don't always get what we deserve."

Hunter looked at Brennan, who nodded. Hunter closed the briefcase. "Okay. Thanks."

"Thanks?" Walter laughed. "For what?"

Brennan picked up the last bag with the water bottle inside and placed it in her purse.

"So you got my prints? What do those matter? They didn't find any other prints at the scene. No physical evidence, no case."

Brennan stared at him for a moment. Her father's self-satisfied smirk crept onto her face. "They found a handprint. On a chair near the door.

At the time, it wasn't in any of the databases, and because everybody was so eager to railroad my dad, they buried the print. But it's there, in the police files. I'm fairly confident it will match the prints we collected here."

"You fucking bitch."

Brennan shrugged. She'd been called worse. Hunter knew his sister didn't need defending.

Walter looked like he might try to physically restrain them as they pushed past him out of the conference room, but instead he said, "I'll call security. They'll stop you in the lobby. They'll confiscate your bags."

"Sure," Brennan said. "I'll insist the cops take them in as evidence."

Neither sibling looked back as they made their way to the elevators.

#

Once they were in a cab, Hunter reached across the seat and took Brennan's hand.

"You were amazing, Bren. I've never seen anything like that."

She squeezed his hand. Her breath came in ragged bursts she finally choked off.

"Did you get it?" she asked.

Hunter opened the briefcase. His digital recorder lay inside. He fiddled with it for a moment and then Walter's voice played, hollow inside the miniature speaker.

"Yeah, I loved her, and it pissed me off—"

Brennan raised her hand. Hunter slipped the recorder back into the briefcase.

"Do you think it's enough?" he asked.

"For a conviction? I don't know. But it's enough for me."

"Me, too." Then he spoke a thought that troubled him. "Mom didn't live long enough to know."

"Neither did Dad."

"Do you think, I mean, would it have brought either of them any peace?"

Brennan stared out the window at the indifferent world.

"No."

A few minutes later, the cab pulled up in front of a bar called The Badger. A short Latino man with salt-and-pepper hair stood in front. His jacket flapped in the breeze, flickering over a badge on his belt. Detective Silas Bauman paced next to him on the sidewalk. He glared as the siblings stepped out of the cab.

"Hey, Vega, you ever meet my sister?"

"Nope. I think I'd remember that."

Silas turned to Vega. "What's this about?"

Hunter smiled and said, "We got something for you."

"What?"

"A chance for you to correct your father's mistake."

FORTY-EIGHT

Now

JENNA CLIMBED ONTO THE BARSTOOL NEXT TO HUNTER AS the Mets blew a lead in the ninth. She'd cut her hair to shoulder length since the funeral.

"Can I buy you a drink?" he asked.

She smiled. "I don't think I've ever turned one down before."

Hunter called the order down to the bartender.

"They're blowing another one, huh?" Jenna asked.

"Yeah. We got that in common."

"Don't beat yourself up, kid. Some people are born losers."

"Okay, relax." He laughed. "Seriously, I wanted to thank you for coming to my mom's funeral. It meant a lot to me."

Jenna took the beer from the bartender's hand. "Yeah, of course. I know . . . I can't imagine. I care. I wanted you to know that."

Hunter nodded and took a sip of his beer.

"I got an assignment."

"Oh? Where?"

"Pakistan."

"That's far." She looked up at the game.

"Yeah." Hunter faced her until she turned back to him. "My sister and I, we found a bunch of letters my dad wrote. It's a long story, and I'll tell you later, but I've been reading them. Thinking about him. My mom. My life."

"Hunter—"

"Please, just listen? This won't take long. My whole life, I thought that I was doing something different from him. Not making the same mistakes he did. But I was running. Like him. I ran from my family, and we lost so much time. I ran from you."

Jenna sighed. "Look, if you're just telling me this so I'll understand, so I'll forgive you for not giving us a chance . . . I mean . . . I get it. I got it. We were done. You didn't need—"

"I didn't take the assignment."

Questions ran across Jenna's face, but she didn't ask them.

"I turned it down," Hunter explained. "I'm staying here. It's the first step, right? When you're lost? Stay where you are."

"What are you saying?"

"I'm saying I'll find another beat. Something here."

"Good for you. I'm still leaving."

"Yeah. I know. You should. I would never stop you. This opportunity is amazing. But I want to stop running from things that might hurt me. We still have a few months to figure this out, right? If you'll give me a chance. If you'll forgive me."

Jenna slid off her stool and wrapped her arms around him. She kissed his neck and then stood back.

"You know I might break your heart, right?"

Hunter nodded. "Maybe. But not like the Mets, right?"

#

The only woman on the executive committee of Brennan's firm was Denise Morgan. She was one of three Black partners, and the only woman among them. Denise practiced in the capital markets group, so Brennan never worked with her, although they had chatted at cocktail parties and firm lunches before. Denise was the final interview before Brennan was invited to join the firm out of the U.S. Attorney's Office. Still, Brennan half expected her not to recognize her when she knocked on her door.

"Brennan?" Denise waved her in. Brennan shut the door as she entered.

"I need a few minutes of your time. It's important."

Denise glanced at the envelope in Brennan's hand before waving a hand at one of her visitor's chairs. As Brennan sat, Denise pushed a pile of paper to the side so she could fold her hands on her desk.

"Denise—"

"Before you say anything, Brennan, you need to know we're going to elect you partner in two weeks. Do not, I repeat, do not tell me anything that's going to fuck that up. We don't have enough woman partners, much less women of color."

Brennan smirked.

"You're not going to like this, then."

#

"I can't believe that this is where you live," Brennan said, walking through Hunter's apartment. She stopped near an open window. A May breeze flowed through, hinting at summer and rustling her hair. "Your view sucks."

Hunter laughed from the other side of the island counter separating his kitchen from the living room. "The view from the bedroom is worse."

She turned and leaned against the wall. "We should eat at my place. At least we'd be able to sit down."

"Come on. Stop giving me shit. I'm trying to cook here."

"Looks like you're just throwing garlic around your kitchen."

Brennan turned to regard the picture of her and her mother on Hunter's wall. Her chest squeezed. The other photo from that day—the one their mother framed—now hung in Brennan's apartment. She reached out to straighten the frame on the wall. She grabbed Hunter's beer off his table and carried it to where he stood at the stove scraping garlic off a cutting board into a pan of oil. He jumped back as the garlic sizzled and popped off the pan.

"You're not inspiring me with confidence here. You should just give up."

"Jenna's coming over so you two can meet. I gotta finish this."

"Jesus Christ, Hunter. We could have done it at my place."

"I wasn't going to invite myself to have a dinner party at your place."

Hunter grabbed a bowl of cut chicken and added it to the pan.

"I'd stand back," he said.

Brennan took an exaggerated step away, and Hunter flicked the pan, tossing the chicken in the air. A couple of pieces missed the pan and fell to the stovetop.

"You got a couple of runners there," Brennan said.

"Fuck 'em. But speaking of runners, did you see McCarthy dropped out of the race?"

"I saw the headline." Walter's arrest by Vega and Bauman and the ensuing stories brought the buried handprint to light. McCarthy had tried for a week to bluster his way past it, but the donors abandoned him in droves after Bauman went public that McCarthy had "tried" to get him to intimidate the siblings. As they agreed when they handed the evidence over, the siblings said nothing to reporters who called except, "We hope Jessica, our father, and everyone else gets the justice they deserve."

As Hunter added some white pepper to the pan, he asked, "How'd it go today?"

"I made it. Denise pushed me through."

"What's going to happen to Sean?"

"He's been asked to resign."

"That's good, right?"

Brennan shrugged. "He'll land someplace else. They always do. It'd be different if they could have done something about that memo he hid. I get it. But still."

It ate at her. After Brennan reported the situation to Denise, there'd been a series of urgent meetings. Ultimately Denise came to her office to say that she would still be made partner and Sean would resign, but Denise didn't have the support to report Sean to the bar without evidence. Denise told her that she would support her decision to report him anyway, but left after saying, "I'm begging you. Don't throw your career away over this. You can do a lot of good here."

"I'm thinking it's time for me to get a new desk," Brennan said. "For my place."

"What about Dad's?"

"I don't know. Sell it, I guess? It makes me sad now. Looking at it. It's time I stopped . . . There's so much that I did, to be like him, try to prove he was a good guy. The father I wanted to remember. Maybe, one day, I'll get back there, despite who he really was. Or, better yet, for who he was. But first, I have to be someone more than his daughter."

Hunter scraped the chicken from the pan into a clean bowl and turned the burner off. He left the kitchen, pulling Brennan's hand so she'd follow. He led her through the living room to his bedroom, where his bed and a single nightstand seemed adrift on the otherwise-empty floor. Hunter pointed to a corner.

"You think it will fit?"

"You could fit a van in here. You really want it?"

"It's not only about him. If it were, I wouldn't want it. There's two parts to it. The part that's about him, having that desk here will remind me to reconcile how much I inherited from him, how I'm different. It'll remind me of the mistakes he made so I don't have to repeat them."

"What's the part that's not about him?"

"It was your desk, too. Longer than it was ever his."

Before she could get too sentimental about it, he grinned. "And, I mean, it has a secret drawer."

ACKNOWLEDGMENTS

My wife and love, Arminda Bepko, deserves more gratitude and adoration than I can express here—for being an inspiration to me, for carrying me through every dark time, for laughing with me in the light days, for our walks in the snow, and for living with the constant amusement and terror I've thrown her way.

For a book about family, thank you to mine for your patience, support, and love, particularly my sons, Bradford and Griffin; my brothers, Craig, Keith, and Derek; my late parents, to whom this book is dedicated; Dina, Marisa, and Christie; and Jean, Jerry, and JJ Bepko. I owe much, including my face and my lo mein recipe, to my grandfather, Siew Choong To, and my basic Teochew to him and my late grandmother, Sai Luan Tang. My late grandmother Dorothy, my aunts, uncles, and cousins, and my "adopted" family, Ann Thomas, Dan Rabinowitz, Sam and Caleb, will always have my gratitude.

This book would not be in your hands without Madelyn Burt, Ellen Scordato, and the Stonesong team. Thank you, Maddy, for believing in me, for your guidance and care, and for helping me achieve this dream, and to Ellen for carrying me forward. Similarly, I'm grateful for

ACKNOWLEDGMENTS

the wonderful team at Counterpoint Press, particularly my editor Dan López, for helping to tell this story with me, Dan Goff for the sharp eye, and Laura Berry, Yukiko Tominaga, Wah-Ming Chang, Megan Fishmann, Rachel Fershleiser, Robin Bilardello, Nicole Caputo, and Dan Smetanka.

Many friends assisted me as I shaped the drafts of this story and supported me in the writing process. For helping me write the best story I could tell, thank you to: Alyssa Jennette for cheering me on and lending an ear to my impromptu brainstorming; Amanda Daly, Valerie McCammon, Christopher Millay, and Christine Virnig for a decade of writing support, encouragement, and feedback; Janna Berke, Shoshana Bulow, Hane Kim, Ladan Stewart, Jennifer Vakiener, Charlotte Underwood, and Craig Zheng, all of whom volunteered their time, sharp eyes, and thoughtful insight on drafts (not to mention their invaluable friendships); Jennifer Vickery, Patrick Frisch, and Cheri and Vince Fandozzi for inviting me into their homes while I worked on the novel; and Ken Lee for his candid insights. I'm also incredibly appreciative of Lori Rader-Day for her encouragement and sage advice over the years.

For their inspiration, love, support, and camaraderie, thank you to Kaveh Haerian and Genevieve de Mahy; Kate Suvari and Chris Dysard; Cara Jackson; Mary McCann; Brian Markley; Caitlin Cline; Jon-Mychal and Adrienne Bowman; David Sajadi; Chris Shade; Maureen Nash; Harris Katz; Luke Nikas; and Lenni Benson. To those whom I know and love but did not have the space to name, thank you for enriching my life.

Finally, this novel uses snippets of the Teochew language—all food-related—that I learned from my grandparents and family. Teochew is the only spoken language I shared with my grandparents, and I speak it imperfectly. There are many Teochew, gaginang, as we would say, who live in a wide diaspora. Although I attempted to verify the romanization of the Teochew I used here, I hope that Teochew who read this novel will forgive any errors in my use of the dialect.

© Bradford Suthammanont

VICTOR SUTHAMMANONT is a lawyer and author. *Hollow Spaces* is his debut novel. He lives in New York City.